Murder at CINNAMON FALLS

Murder at CINNAMON FALLS

A Novel

R. L. KILLMORE

An Imprint of HarperCollins*Publishers*

Without limiting the exclusive rights of any author, contributor or the publisher of this publication, any unauthorized use of this publication to train generative artificial intelligence (AI) technologies is expressly prohibited. HarperCollins also exercise their rights under Article 4(3) of the Digital Single Market Directive 2019/790 and expressly reserve this publication from the text and data mining exception.

This is a work of fiction. Names, characters, places, and incidents are products of the author's imagination or are used fictitiously and are not to be construed as real. Any resemblance to actual events, locales, organizations, or persons, living or dead, is entirely coincidental.

MURDER AT CINNAMON FALLS. Copyright © 2025 by Necole Ryse. All rights reserved. No part of this book may be used or reproduced in any manner whatsoever without written permission except in the case of brief quotations embodied in critical articles and reviews. For information, address HarperCollins Publishers, 195 Broadway, New York, NY 10007. In Europe, HarperCollins Publishers, Macken House, 39/40 Mayor Street Upper, Dublin 1, D01 C9W8, Ireland.

HarperCollins books may be purchased for educational, business, or sales promotional use. For information, please email the Special Markets Department at SPsales@harpercollins.com.

Avon, Avon & logo, and Avon Books & logo are registered trademarks of HarperCollins Publishers in the United States of America and other countries.

hc.com

Originally published as *A Cinnamon Falls Mystery* in Great Britain in 2025 by Simon & Schuster UK Ltd.

FIRST AVON A PAPERBACK PUBLISHED APRIL 2026

Library of Congress Cataloging-in-Publication Data has been applied for.

ISBN 978-0-06-348244-9

Printed in the United States of America

26 27 28 29 30 LBC 5 4 3 2 1

for all the storytellers before me

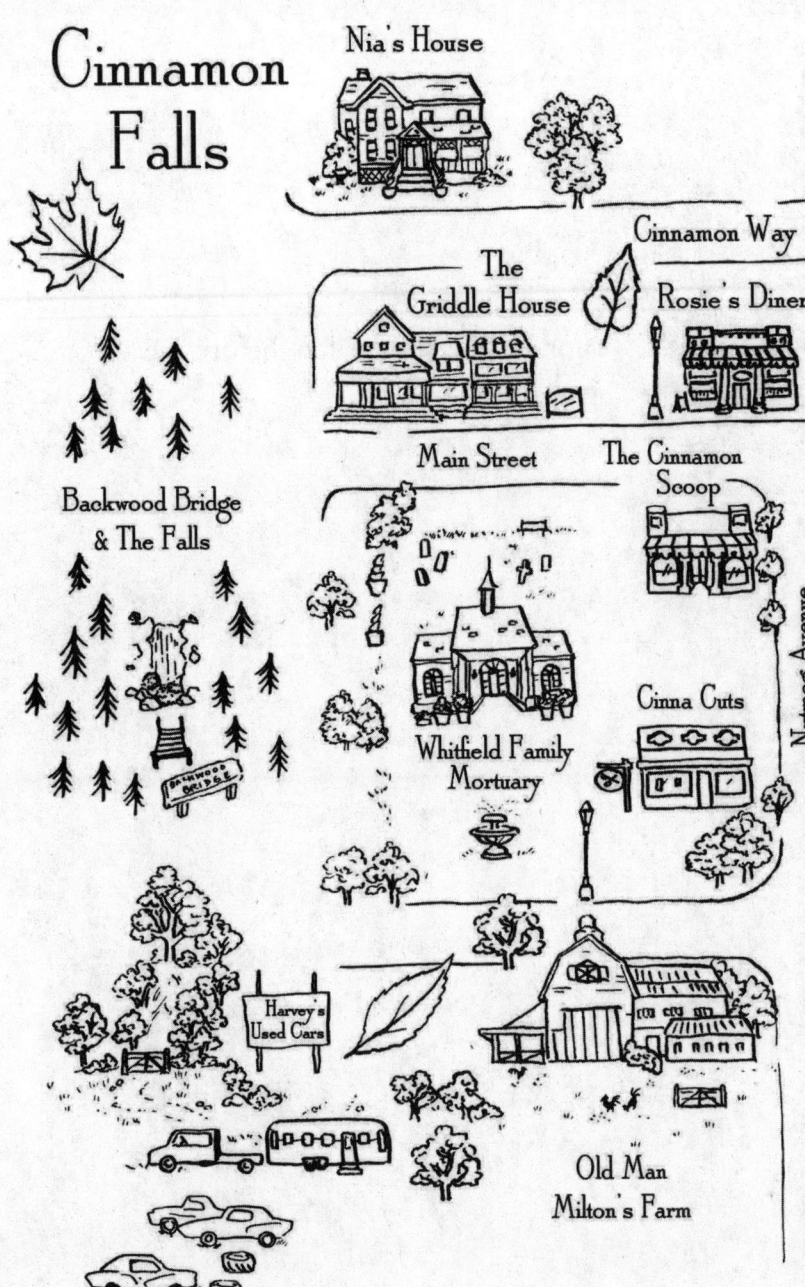

Chapter 1

Monday
Nia

There was, quite simply, a very reasonable explanation as to how Nia ended up back in Cinnamon Falls. She'd always imagined that she would return home in a flurry of triumph with a crowd of supporters chanting her name and throwing rose petals at her feet. Instead, she arrived with two suitcases full of regret, a wrap-around headache, and a serious need for a nap, or a large scoop of cinnamon swirl ice cream, whichever came first.

Let's start with the facts: Nia Janice Bennett has never been a homewrecker. So, when Miss All-Tits-and-No-Ass braved metro Atlanta's Monday morning traffic and showed up to Nia's three-story townhouse downtown at eight a.m., claiming Nia's man of two years was actually her husband of four, Nia could have contorted her body like one of those creepy circus performers and simply vanished into thin air.

Instead, she did the second fastest thing. She left.

In forty minutes and a maddening blur of tears, she stuffed every single item she'd ever owned, including her completely shattered pride and ego, into two rickety suitcases and an oversized purse that Bryant, her now married ex-boyfriend, had bought her last Christmas. She'd never even taken it out of the box before today. She didn't see a reason to carry a purse the size of a small Doberman. She could call that subtle foreshadowing.

Thousands of memories of their relationship flickered through her head like a highlight reel in the rideshare while she journeyed to the bus station – the moment they met in the copy room of her coveted internship at Gildman & Sons, Georgia's most powerful law firm, until now, the day she realized her entire relationship was a lie.

All she could think about on the commute was his smile. In the picture his wife all but shoved at her, Bryant's gorgeous brown face was pressed against hers, showing all thirty-two of his adult teeth. He was stuffed in a classic black tuxedo with a crisp white collar accentuating his expertly lined beard. His brown eyes were wide with an unbridled happiness, like someone had left him in a simmering pot on a hot stove. They both had their hands raised toward the camera, showcasing their matching rings, mocking Nia.

Ironically, he'd had the same expression with Nia

just a few days ago when they celebrated her graduation, minus the matching rings.

What had she missed, and most importantly, how could she have been so stupid?

That question was on a loop for Nia's entire trip back home to Cinnamon Falls. For the last two years, besides finishing grad school, her world had revolved around Bryant. If she was being completely honest with herself, everything felt a little emptier without him now.

Nia looked at her cell phone. Behind the screensaver of Bryant and her, it showed twenty-two missed calls from his number and another fourteen missed calls from an unknown number after she blocked him. She'd leave him to figure out his life in peace. He clearly had enough going on. There was no need for her to be in the equation anymore. Nia had never been the type of person to stir up drama but somehow it always, always found her.

Nia had managed to drag two uncooperative pieces of luggage across county lines, but this final leg of the journey would be the hardest – the bus ride into Cinnamon Falls. The cost of living in a small town was never having any business of your own. By the time she made it into Cinnamon Falls, at least one third of the town would know that Nia Bennett, the prodigal daughter, had returned.

Nia watched as the bus ambled toward her stop. Shawna Daniels, Ms. Pearline's great-niece, was all grown up now, and from the looks of it, worked full-time for her family's public transportation business.

'Nia Bennett?' Shawna eyed her with a knowing voice, giving her a focused once-over like Nia was an extraterrestrial sent down to destroy her homeland.

'Hey, Shawna,' Nia started, wrestling with the suitcases to make them stay upright.

'It's been a minute,' Shawna replied, stating the obvious.

It had been six years since Nia left Cinnamon Falls, but who was counting? The little girl with pigtails who used to sit at the steering wheel and marvel while her great-aunt maneuvered the big bus through the town's tight streets was the one doing the driving now. Their familiar lightning logo was proudly displayed across her polo shirt, the bright blue color matching the vehicle perfectly, like Ms. Pearline's always had. Nia was happy to know that at least some things had stayed the same since she'd been gone.

'How old are you now?' Nia wondered.

'Eighteen,' she replied. 'I graduated early 'cause Auntie Pearline wants me to get as much training as possible.'

An awkward silence drifted between them, until Shawna offered Nia a small smile. 'Let me help you with that.'

Nia slid a suitcase over to her while she loaded the rest of her bags onto the bus. Shawna stacked Nia's luggage neatly in the corral and slid into the driver's seat, buckling her seat belt and triple checking her mirrors. Nia noticed her nametag that read 'Trainee'.

'You in town to see Darius Lyons at the Fall Festival?'

'Darius Lyons?' Nia repeated, the name and all its glory coming back to her like the season's first snow, slowly and then all at once. She felt a pang in her chest and checked the date on her phone – October 6th.

Fall Festival always took place on the second weekend in October, which meant it was only a few days away. History said that the first settlers of Cinnamon Falls started the Annual Fall Festival as a way to bring the community together after the tough harvest season. Now, it was more of a tradition that shut down the entire town with parades, hayrides, eating contests, vendors, and the most coveted title for high school seniors, Cinnamon King and Queen.

'He's back in town to crown the new Cinnamon King,' Shawna said brightly.

Nia was sure the crown still fit his ego just fine after all these years. 'Isn't he playing for the Falcons now?' she asked. The last time Nia had thought about the town's golden boy, he was well into his football season. Just last year, his team won the championship, which probably made Mayor Lyons want to paint a mural of his son's face on the side of Town Hall. The mention of Darius being back in town didn't make Nia feel much of anything besides contempt.

'On a bye week,' Shawna said enthusiastically, pulling Nia from her thoughts of yesteryear. 'They let him come back special just for this. Can you believe it? Darius Lyons putting little ol' Cinnamon Falls on the map.'

Nia rolled her eyes. She had already had enough of yapping about Darius. It would take them forty-seven minutes to get from the bus station into town. She was looking forward to watching Georgia's four-lane traffic, badly paved streets, and morning smog give way to the lush green forests that crowded the quiet, one-lane highways. Despite the Darius chat, Nia was buzzing. She couldn't wait for the tantalizing aroma of cinnamon to pull her closer and closer like a warm hug from a loved one; something she desperately needed.

But instead of a quiet and nostalgic ride, she watched her seductive vision of a nap slip through her fingers. Shawna was nothing like her great-aunt. All those years of training at her aunt's helm proved to be useless.

By the time they'd gotten to the outskirts of town, Nia was sure she'd sustained the kinds of injuries that would qualify her for medical compensation. Shawna ground the bus to a stop so violently – sending all Nia's luggage catapulting to the front of the bus, then careening backward – that absolutely nothing could have prepared her for the look of satisfaction on Shawna's face when they arrived at the Bennett family ice cream shop, The Cinnamon Scoop.

The Cinnamon Scoop was the first established business in Cinnamon Falls, back when there was only a couple of hundred residents. Nia's great-grandmother, Ma-Clara, and her husband, Eugene Bennett, moved to Cinnamon Falls for work at the old spice mill. The mill processed cinnamon from the wild cinnamon trees that grew nearby and packaged it up to ship all over the country. Eugene would bring home some of the freshly ground spice, and Ma-Clara started making cinnamon swirl ice cream as a sweet treat. It wasn't long until word got around the town and Ma-Clara opened a humble ice cream parlor for the mill workers to enjoy.

The mill had burned down decades ago but the shop, and the Bennett legacy, remained.

'Here you are,' Shawna said with an accomplished smile. Even though The Cinnamon Scoop was the last place Nia wanted to go, since she hadn't necessarily left on the best terms with her family, she sprinted off the bus with the last bit of her life intact.

'Welcome back!' Shawna called before pulling off. The bus made a sickening crunch as she steered it into traffic on Main Street, back toward the bus station.

Nia stood on the sidewalk for a moment, catching her breath and observing the scene before her. Her father hadn't told her they'd given the shop an update.

She was so used to the cinnamon bun mascot with the googly eyes holding a silver spoon. In its place was a Neapolitan-colored awning that boasted the shop's name in a loopy script font. It looked too modern for a sleepy town like Cinnamon Falls.

Nia turned around, taking it all in. Maggie Shilling and the festival crew had already decorated Main Street in preparation for the weekend's festivities. A white banner as old as the place itself hung from the four-way traffic light that read, 'CINNAMON FALLS SINCE 1919'.

To be back in the thick of it all was humbling. Nia took in another deep breath, inhaling the faint smell of wild cinnamon from the forest. If it were quiet, she could have heard the rushing waterfall miles away.

Barkwood Bridge would be covered in bronze and ruby red leaves by now. Tons of tourists from all around Georgia come to snap a picture or two there. Eventually, they'd make their way into town to grab some apple cider at Rosie's or a magnet at the general store.

The Cinnamon Falls residents who lived here year-round loved it here. Everyone except for Nia.

She pulled on the door to the ice cream shop, figuring she would find it empty, especially before noon on a Monday. There was a fifty-fifty chance her father would be behind the counter, taking inventory or triple checking the temperature of the freezers.

Instead, Nia was met with the piercing screams of

joyful toddlers. Her father, Walter, was standing on top of the counter in his ridiculous cinnamon bun hat, with his arms splayed open and an animated smile on his face.

'And that's why I always say: the perfect scoop is the key to happiness!' he boomed, holding up an ice cream scoop like it was the holy grail. The children cheered as if he was delivering a fire and brimstone sermon. Nia wondered how much sugar these innocent children had been subjected to this early in the morning.

A hand belonging to an adorable little boy with glasses too big for his face shot in the air. 'So how does the cow make the ice cream?'

Her father's shoulders deflated, which meant he'd have to start his ice cream origins story from the beginning. But before he could, Marjorie, Nia's mother, emerged from the back of the shop with a tray full of individual bowls that held small dollops of pink strawberry ice cream. Nia's mouth watered at the sight. Chunks of bright strawberry, picked from the fertile soil on Old Man Milton's farm at peak season, were folded into the creamy strawberry base, Ma-Clara's signature recipe.

'Who's ready for strawberry?' Marjorie asked the group of waiting toddlers, who squealed in delight.

Her mother's hair had grayed at the temples since Nia had been gone. It was gathered into a neat ponytail, secured in a clamp. Her eyes were softer, and her smile lines more prominent, but she still looked the same.

Her father, on the other hand, hadn't aged a bit. He was clearly still jumping on top of Ma-Clara's good counters and making impatient children sit through a twenty-minute presentation on how ice cream was made before giving them a sample. It was the same speech he'd given when Nia's class came for Career Week all those years ago.

Her mother didn't look in her direction when she said, 'If you're gonna stand in the doorway, you might as well make yourself useful.'

Nia deserved that.

The last time they had seen each other, they'd had an exchange of words that was so blisteringly cruel that it still kept Nia up at night. She wasn't sure how her mother would react to her return. So far, this was much better than any of the scenarios she'd imagined on the bus ride over.

Nia stashed her luggage in an open booth near the door, grabbed a spare apron, pushed up her sleeves, and got to work. After washing her hands, she grabbed as much ice cream as she could carry and helped her mother dole out bowls to the squirming children, who had already begun questioning why some scoops were bigger than others. After the complaining died down, the only sound that could be heard were satisfied smacks of approval as the children worked on their ice cream.

'Well, well, well, if it isn't Nia "Never Coming Back" Bennett!' a familiar voice floated over to Nia as she wiped up a splotch of spilled cream from the service counter. 'Back like you never left! Did you miss scooping ice cream for the little people that much?'

Morgan Taylor hadn't changed at all since the last time Nia had seen her. The girl everyone thought was strange because she wore purple every day was still sporting her favorite color. This time, it made an appearance in her hair: a dramatic pixie cut with a flash of purple in the bang that swooped over her left eye. She wore a purple cardigan with a pair of ripped black jeans. Purple ribbon crisscrossed through the prominent holes.

'I actually did,' Nia laughed, remembering the slow nights in the shop when the two of them dreamt about getting out of this too small town. 'Nothin' like finger blisters and hand cramps that make you long for home. What about you? Herding crotch gremlins for a living treating you any good?' She nodded over to the kids who were enthralled in a story her mother was reading to them about an ice cream monster. Wide eyes watched Marjorie intensely with their tiny hands clamped over their open mouths, as her fingers curled in a sinister way.

'Livin' the dream,' Morgan said sarcastically, shrugging. They embraced for a long hug. Her voice dropped down to a whisper. 'The best part about it is, they believe anything I say.'

'That's how cults start,' Nia deadpanned.

'Next stop, world domination!' Morgan declared with her arms wide. The two women laughed together, before Morgan paused, assessing Nia in her entirety. 'So, you just passing through?' She gestured toward the stack of luggage that looked like Nia was staying for much longer than a quick getaway.

Nia opened her mouth to answer with a lie: *You know, just checking in on things*, but her brain decided against it. She'd experienced enough lies today to last a lifetime.

'I don't really know,' she answered.

Morgan nodded, her eyes searching Nia's, like the story of Nia's heartbreak was written all over her face. Thankfully, she changed the subject. 'So that means you're coming to the Fall Festival this Saturday?'

Before Nia could confirm, Morgan continued, 'I heard Darius Lyons is back. The whole town is like swooning over the fact that we have our very own celebrity now.'

Nia twisted her lips. 'Since when are you a Darius Lyons fan? If I recall correctly, you thought he was an idiot in high school.'

'Not just me,' Morgan corrected. 'Me, you, *and* Sienna thought he was a couple beers short of a six pack back then. Now, he's an idiot with access. You think he can put me on with Leon Crosby?'

'The actor?' Nia asked incredulously, holding back a laugh.

'Unfortunately for me, Darius is my only way in. Don't all the celebrities like, know each other?'

Nia hated to burst her bubble, but she was saved just in time. The sport watch on Morgan's arm beeped in a staccato fashion, flashing zeroes.

'Time's up!' she shouted to the group of kids. 'Lips zipped, hands on hips!' The children assembled in a straight line without fuss, placing one finger over their closed mouths and the other hand on their hips. Once they were all together in a perfect line she said, 'Let's dip!'

The children filed out of the ice cream parlor and lined up against the window, careful not to step out into the street. Morgan, satisfied with their performance, looked back at Nia just before heading out behind them.

'If you're not busy, stop by Rosie's tonight. I'm sure Jesse would love to see you.' She winked with a mischievous smile. If Nia wasn't in front of her parents, she would have thrown a tasting spoon at Morgan's head.

As Nia turned around, she saw her father furiously scrubbing the same squeaky-clean spot on the counter. Her mother had also busied herself, shuffling around the three meager children's books on the shelf.

'So, how much of that did you hear?' Nia asked, crossing her arms over her chest.

Walter turned to Marjorie and their eyes had a split-second argument over who would be the one to answer her first. If Nia were a betting woman, she'd expect it to be her father.

Her mother pointed her chin toward the stack of luggage at the door. 'So, what happened? Bryant left you?'

It was a good thing Nia wasn't a betting woman. 'He was married, actually,' Nia quipped, making sure to keep her head high. 'So, I left him.'

'Good girl.' Her father nodded his approval.

Nia watched as the satisfied smirk melted off her mother's face, replaced with an expression that looked as if it held its own memories of betrayal. She started across the room toward her daughter.

'Group hug?' Nia's little brother, Niles, asked as he appeared from behind the counter. He was much taller than she remembered.

For the first time that day, Nia laughed. She laughed so hard that she cried.

Chapter 2

Jesse

Old Man Milton had three roosters that could wake the dead. Jesse could be six feet under the dirt, and he would still be able to hear Shadrach, Meshach, and Abednego in the afterlife. But, if it weren't for their daily wake-up calls, he'd miss the sunrise over Cinnamon Falls each morning.

Jesse had woken up in different cities all over the world, but nothing compared to home. From the vantage point of his balcony, he could see the sun rise above the waterfall through a small break in the forest of wild cinnamon trees. The honey golden sun spread its magic over all living beings, persistent, dripping between the tiniest crevices of the earth to extend its light. Jesse was thankful it saw fit to adorn his home; thankful that, for at least another day, life existed there.

Jesse began his day the same way he did every morning, thanks to military training, with a sun salutation and some deep stretches to get the blood flowing. He followed that up with his high intensity interval training routine of ten non-stop rounds of push-ups, air squats, burpees, sit-ups, lunges, and the finisher, mountain climbers, until sweat was dripping from every pore and his muscles screamed for him to stop, and even then, he kept going to feel the breath in his lungs.

It was close to six-thirty a.m., which meant his father would be up and dressed soon, ready for his morning coffee and newspaper. His mother, on the other hand, was a night owl and would sleep through an earthquake if they let her. She'd only wake this early if it was absolutely necessary; and seeing that it was a quiet Monday morning, it wasn't.

Jesse showered, slung a robe over his damp body, and headed downstairs in time to see Lil' Charlie hop out of the cargo bed of his father's pick-up truck with today's news folded under his arm. Mini Charlie, his younger brother, watched excitedly, swinging his feet over the edge of the truck.

Charlie Kent and his sons ran *The Cinnamon Chronicle* from Old Man Milton's farm all the way to Main Street in record time each morning. The Kent Boys took turns delivering the paper and today Lil' Charlie gave Jesse a cocky smirk before launching it up his driveway. It zipped through the air like a missile and Jesse snatched it down before it had a chance to slap him squarely in the face. That boy had an arm on him. It was no wonder he was the rising star on the Timberwolves at Cinnamon Falls High.

'You still got it, Unc!' Lil' Charlie called out. Jesse chuckled, giving the family a polite wave from the doorstep, even though he wanted to flip the kid a bird.

Unc, short for Uncle, made him feel like he was a fifty-five-year-old man with orthopedic shoes. Jesse wanted to tell Lil' Charlie that he'd been playing football longer than Lil' Charlie had been alive, but then he'd be proving him right.

Jesse glanced down at his watch. He was about to be late for breakfast duty. He scrambled inside just as the coffee pot he'd set out last night began to bubble.

'Bacon and toast?' Jesse asked as his father climbed into his usual seat at the head of the kitchen table, slow and steady. He made sure not to turn his head as he watched his father out of the corner of his eye. Robert Shaw hated it when Jesse analyzed his every move. He said it felt like he was in a fishbowl. But, at his age, Jesse couldn't trust that his father would tell him if his hip was acting up again or if his shoulder felt funny this morning. He wasn't the kind of man who asked for help. It had only taken one slip and fall for Jesse to move his parents in with him two years ago.

Robert and Evelyn put up a fuss, but in the end, Jesse won. It was a privilege to care for his parents, one he cherished dearly, especially since he was dreading the day when he wouldn't have them anymore. If it were up to Jesse, he'd put the two of them in a glass box and keep them forever.

Robert gave a low grunt in approval of today's breakfast menu. Jesse set the newspaper down next to Robert's cup of piping hot black coffee – he didn't take it any other way, claiming the key to a long life was staying away from sugar, but Jesse knew where he kept his stash of caramel candies. He wasn't fooling Jesse for a second.

Although his parents were nearing their mid-seventies, the two were still whip sharp, even if their bodies had started to retire. It was hard work raising two moody, elderly teenagers, and since Jesse was their only son, all of it fell to him.

Robert slipped his reading glasses onto the bridge of his nose. He carefully separated the comics, the Arts section, and today's crossword puzzle, leaving it for his wife. In a couple of hours, when she woke up for lunch, they'd work on it together. When Jesse got home later, another completed puzzle would be attached to the fridge. The bottom of the page would display their initials together, R+E, surrounded by a heart. Teenagers.

'Let's see what Cinnamon Falls got goin' on,' Robert mumbled.

An hour later, Jesse was dressed and ready for the day. Pops was still at the table reading, grunting and mumbling in a language only he understood.

'I'm gone, Pop,' Jesse told him, grabbing a protein shake out of the fridge. He'd grab some lunch at Rosie's later. 'I'll be back late, sometime after dinner. Want me to bring you anything back?'

'Your mother wants some bananas.' He looked over his shoulder and whispered, 'It's our anniversary tomorrow – bring home some roses, will you?' He reached to fish his wallet out of his pants pocket.

'Anniversary?' Jesse questioned. 'You and Mom got married in May, Pop.'

'I asked her to be my lady on October seventh.' He pointed to the date on the paper. 'I'm old, but I can read. That's tomorrow, ain't it?'

Jesse nodded. 'Roses it is.'

Jesse took the back roads into town so he could smell the wild cinnamon trees. There weren't that many anymore, but growing up, he could smell the cinnamon all the way down at the school house. The distinctive, spicy-sweet bite and earthy undertone always made him think of Rosie's sweet apple cider. It wouldn't be long until she'd be selling it by the bucket load at the Fall Festival on Saturday.

On the second weekend of October each year, the

entire town transformed into something out of a children's storybook, where every cobblestone street, every red-bricked storefront, and every tree lining Main Street glowed with autumn's golden touch.

In town, the shops on Main Street became a display of fall magic; dressed for the season, their windows painted with cheerful scarecrows and swirling leaves. Pumpkins of all sizes, large, small, perfectly round, and lopsided, sat in clusters on every step and storefront, some intricately carved with grinning faces, others glowing softly from within.

Above, twinkling fairy lights were woven through the bare tree branches, their soft golden glow enveloping the town in a cozy, nostalgic warmth. The historic columns of the old buildings, painted in shades of ivory, were wrapped in garlands of dried corn stalks and cinnamon sticks, filling the air with a comforting, familiar spice.

When Jesse was a child, the Fall Festival had been the best time of the year, the beating heart of Cinnamon Falls. It had been nothing short of a dream, a seasonal wonderland that made his hometown feel like the kind of place where time slowed down, where magic existed in the glow of the festival lights.

Now, as law enforcement, the Fall Festival was a pain in the ass. Between the drunk and disorderly, and the petty vandalism, it was the busiest time of the year for the Cinnamon Falls Police Department.

Once Jesse arrived at the station, he finished reading

the reports he'd left on his desk the week before and drank a few sips of bitter coffee in the name of camaraderie. He had only been on the force for a little over a year, which meant he was on designated patrol duty. The senior ranking officers thought of it as grunt work; and Jesse let them think he hated it too.

The truth was, he enjoyed patrolling. Interacting with the people who had a hand in raising him kept him humble and reminded him of his priorities.

While other people might dislike small-town life, no place in the world made him happier than Cinnamon Falls. Some would call it predictable, or boring. But there was a safety in the predictability that he cherished. He had never been good with change and had always hated surprises. This town was an anchor, not in a way that dragged him down, but in a way that kept him steady. He needed that in his life.

Jesse journeyed down Main Street, ambling past Harvest Square, where all the festivities took place. Maggie Shilling, once again, had sprinkled her fall magic along the sidewalks like a cinnamon fairy godmother.

Orange and gold garlands were draped from lamp posts. Hay bales lined the walkways with rustic wooden signs that would direct the crowd toward cider stations, pie tastings, and the pumpkin carving tent.

Storefronts boasted fresh coats of paint, and many had added a few festive touches: a smiling scarecrow in a flannel shirt here, a bucket of candy corn there. Jesse imagined Maggie, clipboard in hand, marching across the square like a general preparing for battle. Her battle being fall perfection, of course. Cinnamon Falls was starting to transform. In just a few days, this street would be swamped with residents celebrating fall.

Jesse stopped at the corner when he saw Mrs. Guy with her hands on her hips. Her tight-lipped expression and furrowed brows told him something was wrong.

Mrs. Guy had been married to Mr. Guy, the owner of Guy's Grocery, one of the two grocery stores in Cinnamon Falls. Guy's Grocery always had fresh fruit and fair prices. Since Mr. Guy passed two years ago, Mrs. Guy was doing her best to keep her husband's business afloat singlehandedly. Most people who had lived in town for a while still shopped at Guy's. The transplants who moved in from Atlanta and needed a 'change of pace' preferred the all-natural, gluten-free kinds of products to be found two blocks over at Cinnamon Grove. Jesse shopped at both places. A little wheatgrass never hurt anybody.

'Mornin', Mrs. Guy.' Jesse joined her on the sidewalk, staring down at the splintered pieces of wood by her feet and observing the instructions for a display stand in her hands. 'Need help with that thing?'

'Officer Shaw, just the man I needed to see!' Mrs. Guy clapped her hands together in a satisfied fashion. She thrust the paper at him. 'Sly James sold me this display stand two weeks ago and it's broken already.'

Even though Mrs. Guy claimed to be a grieving widow, she didn't let that stop her from flirting with Jesse every chance she got. If he wasn't changing light bulbs that were too high for her to reach or lifting boxes of goods, he was fixing a shelving unit, or, like today, a display case. She paid for his services in food, so he wasn't complaining. Her pork chops and pan-fried apples were better than his mother's, even though he'd never tell Evelyn that to her face.

It wasn't lost on him that Mrs. Guy was as much of a smoke show now as she was back in the day, at least according to the men in the barbershop next door. Bones' Barbershop was unusually busy for a Monday morning and Jesse didn't have to question why.

Jesse focused his attention on the four-tiered stand. It appeared to be solid pinewood with a rustic weatherwood frame, sturdy with four angled bins that he was sure she would use to display fresh produce.

'Do you have a drill?' he asked, taking another long look at the mess in front of him.

She disappeared inside the store and returned with the power tool. She handed it to him like a bomb.

'I can make it stand for ya,' he said, and her cheeks flushed a deep red. *Oh no.* 'I mean, I can fix it.' Panic crowded his voice. 'But you should call Mr. Sylvester once the store opens in an hour or so. You'll need another piece of wood to hold the weight of the baskets.' All the words came out in one clump.

'I'll do that,' she said breathily.

Jesse quickly got to work repairing the display stand. Ten minutes later, after some elbow grease and a few new screws, Mrs. Guy had a functional stand. Jesse returned her drill and she gave him a slow and uncomfortable once-over. 'If you ever get tired of the uniform, you'd make a fine handyman, Officer Shaw.'

Jesse didn't know what to say so he changed the subject with a tight-lipped smile. 'Call Mr. Sylvester if you need anything else. I'm sure he'll take care of you.'

She clutched the drill to her chest. 'Thank you, Officer Shaw. Can I bring you some lunch past the station a little later?'

'I'd appreciate that, and some bananas if you have them?' Jesse recalled his father's request.

'Sure thing,' she responded. Sometimes, policing paid off.

Jesse was about to jump back in the car and continue the patrol up Main Street when he noticed Harold Bones outside Bones' Barbershop, pretending not to listen to his interaction with Mrs. Guy. He feverishly swept the doorstep to his shop as Jesse crossed the street in quick strides.

'I should arrest your ass for jaywalking,' Mr. Harold commented jokingly.

'You can't arrest the police,' Jesse said, making sure

to block Mr. Harold's view of Mrs. Guy. He wanted to see how long it'd take Harold to push Jesse out of the way. It was common knowledge that Mr. Harold had been crushing on Mrs. Guy since they were in grade school, and even though it'd been two years since her husband passed, ol' Bones was dragging his feet on asking her out.

Each time he stepped around Jesse to see Mrs. Guy, Jesse followed. Harold kissed his teeth out of frustration. 'I'm about to assault the police if you don't get out of my way,' he threatened with his broom.

'You better move, Jay. You know how he feels about Ms. Guy,' William Reed, Mr. Bones' newest barber, warned from inside the shop. He was a transplant from the city. He claimed he was from Macon, Georgia, but any place outside of Cinnamon Falls was a big city, which made him a local celebrity.

Jesse walked inside and with a fist bump greeted Will, who was cleaning tools in a blue solution.

'What's up, you getting a cut today?' Will asked.

'Nah,' Jesse answered. 'On the clock. You know, cop life.' He gestured around himself.

'Fighting crime one basket at a time.' Will laughed, nodding toward Mrs. Guy who was filling her now functional display stand with meticulously arranged tiny pumpkins. 'I know you gotta miss combat, man. You went from being John Wick to Barney Fife.'

It was clear to Jesse that Will's only military references were Hollywood productions. He was probably one of the guys who played Call of Duty and swore they could shoot a sniper rifle. In reality, it was a whole lot worse than what it seemed in pixels.

Jesse shrugged, pushing down the memories that kept him up at night. 'I prefer this,' he said coolly, keeping his response brief.

Will nodded, catching the hint that any discussion of the past would be off-limits. The two were cool, but they weren't *that* cool.

'I gotta run,' Jesse continued, tapping the face of his watch like he had somewhere to be. He said his goodbyes to Mr. Harold, who still couldn't get that suspicious patch of dirt from around his front door, and hopped back in his patrol car.

Jesse slowed to a stop at the yellow light on Nutmeg Avenue and Main Street when he spotted Morgan Taylor crossing the street with a gaggle of kindergartners. They were assembled in a painfully straight line that made him wonder how she got sixteen small children to behave. They were coming out of The Cinnamon Scoop, the spot with the best root beer floats in town. It must be Career Week, a time when the elementary kids get to go around to all the local businesses. Soon, Morgan and her crew would venture to the police station.

The light turned green and Jesse pulled alongside her at the curb.

'Good morning, Ms. Taylor,' he called through the passenger side window.

Morgan smiled back at him, before turning to the gaggle of children and instructing them to stay on the sidewalk. She took a few steps toward the car and stooped down next to the window.

'Officer Shaw,' she responded in a sing-song voice. 'What a coincidence, just the man I needed to see.'

Jesse eyed her suspiciously. 'That's my second time hearing that today.'

Morgan's mouth held a playful smirk. 'I have some news for you.'

'Are you waiting for me to read your mind or something?' he asked, growing annoyed.

'Guess who's back in town?' Her eyes danced with excitement.

'I know all about Darius Lyons.' Jesse waved her away, underwhelmed. 'It's been damn near front page news for months—'

She rolled her eyes. 'Nia Bennett.'

Jesse could have sworn he was breathing. When he pulled over to talk to Morgan, he was sure that he'd been alive, but hearing Nia's name stole the air from his body. His heart did a fragmented beat and the butterflies he hadn't felt since he was in active duty came rushing back to him. Shooting pain danced in his fingers from gripping the steering wheel and he felt hot all over.

Instinctively, he looked to his left at the ice cream shop that he'd found he could barely drive past since she left six years ago. The windows were tinted in a way that customers couldn't see inside, which was a good thing for him and his aching heart.

Nia Bennett back in Cinnamon Falls? Memories unfurled in his brain, one after the other, of the last time he held her in his arms; and how empty his life felt after she'd gone.

'Damn, it's . . . been a while,' he heard himself say. He didn't know how he was forming words.

'Yeah, she seemed happy to be back. I invited her to Rosie's tonight,' Morgan said nonchalantly. 'You still comin', right?'

Jesse nodded. 'I'll be there.'

'See ya tonight then!' she said brightly, rapping her knuckles on the door. 'And work on your poker face, Jay. You look like you've seen a ghost.'

As Morgan walked away, Jesse put the car in park and leaned back against the headrest, expelling the breath he'd been holding. He hadn't seen Nia since she left Cinnamon Falls with his shattered heart in her hands. He was going to see her tonight, in just a few hours.

Everything was changing.

Chapter 3

Nia

What does a girl wear to see her ex-boyfriend for the first time in six years? A formal gown? A pair of ripped jeans? Thigh-high boots and a miniskirt? Nia tried on every outfit she'd managed to squeeze into her suitcases and nothing felt like 'it'. A breakup and a reunion in one day were too much for her to handle.

'Just put something on, you're going to make me late for the game,' Niles whined. He was a senior at Cinnamon Falls High and – unfairly – able to drive anywhere he wanted, including a late basketball game at the school. When Nia was his age, Dad still had to drop her off places. By her sisterly calculations, that meant Niles had to chauffeur her to Rosie's tonight to make it even. Niles crossed his arms over his chest impatiently and leaned against the doorjamb of her childhood bedroom.

'It's a basketball game. What can you possibly miss in the first five minutes?' Nia asked.

'It's just dinner at Rosie's,' Niles mocked. 'What does it matter what you wear?'

'It matters,' she answered, 'because I haven't seen Jesse since I left. I want to look . . . nice.'

Nice, she repeated to herself. No, she wanted to look like a bombshell, but that wouldn't happen tonight. She realized when she stormed out of Bryant's home that she'd left all her toiletries behind, including her hair and makeup products. She'd have to run to the mall in Asheville, the next town over, if she wanted to look decent for the rest of her time here. *And how much time am I spending here, anyway?* she asked herself, but she didn't have an answer to that question yet. Time would tell.

'You look okay to me.' Niles shrugged. 'Here.' He tossed a fitted gray sweater to her from her open suitcase. The collar folded down, exposing her shoulders. 'Wear these with it,' he instructed, picking up a pair of light wash jeans from the pile of clothes on the floor. 'And those.' He pointed to a pair of black, pointed-toe, ankle boots. 'Do that curly puff thing with your hair and let's go, Ni-Ni,' he said, before stomping off down the hall. 'You've got five minutes before I leave you!'

Just a few years ago, Nia was tasked with dragging Niles around when she went out with her friends, who treated him like a living baby doll. Now he was the one rushing her. Times had changed.

She'd had this silly notion that time would stop

when she'd left Cinnamon Falls, and that upon her eventual return she'd come back home to her immortal parents and annoying baby brother, who would still have mysterious cheese dust on his fingers and be glued to his iPad.

But no, he was grown now and apparently had some fashion sense. Nia slipped out of her leggings and put on the clothes he'd suggested, giving herself a once-over in the mirror. The outfit was cute, but she would never tell him that. She smoothed out the wrinkles in the sweater and snapped on a pair of silver earrings, accessorizing with a thin silver necklace and a set of silver bangles. This would have to do.

Nia went to her mother's room in search of a bristle brush and some styling cream to tackle her natural hair. Pulling her hair up into a bun, her fingers coiled the ends to do the 'curly puff thing' like Niles suggested. While there, she rifled through her mother's perfume collection and chose something sweet with vanilla top notes and a friendly, but not overpowering, floral undertone.

Now for her face. She lightly patted some concealer under her swollen eyes to give the appearance that she hadn't been crying half the day, and swiped on some mascara to accentuate her brown, almond-shaped eyes.

It wasn't the bombshell look she was going for, but at least she looked presentable.

Taking the stairs two at a time, Nia walked past her parents, who were cuddled up on the couch watching an action movie. Rounds of gunfire popped on the screen and her mother covered her eyes with buttered fingers from the popcorn resting in her lap.

'Have a good time, Ni-Ni.' Walter reached up for a hug. He pulled her in close and whispered, 'Good to have you back, sweetie,' planting a sloppy kiss on her temple.

Midnight, the family's defiant Bombay cat, growled threateningly. She'd been giving Nia the silent treatment since she'd arrived home earlier that day. Nia couldn't blame her – she had been gone for six years without an explanation. Nia reached to scratch between Midnight's ears and the cat showed Nia her teeth. She would come around when she felt like it.

'Leave my girl alone,' her father said, slapping Nia's hand away. Midnight snuggled deeper into his lap. Nia swore he loved that cat more than anyone else in the house.

'Is that my good perfume?' Marjorie questioned, eyeing her.

Nia pivoted quickly. 'Let's talk about how Niles gets to drive now? You wouldn't even let me go to the store by myself!'

'He's a growing boy,' Marjorie said, with a softness in her voice that made Nia physically sick. 'He needs his independence.'

'Independence? He's seventeen!' Nia looked to her

dad for backup, but he shrugged, staying out of it. She opened her mouth to argue some more when the sound of a blaring horn cut her off.

'You better get in that car before he leaves you,' her mother chuckled, and Nia ran out of the house before Niles could back out of the driveway.

The car ride over to Rosie's was excruciating. It was the second time today that Nia had been unsatisfied with the transportation in this town. Niles might have good fashion sense now, but he had terrible taste in music. The gibberish he forced her to listen to should be illegal in at least ten countries. But not even his trash music could distract her from reliving the last time she'd seen Jesse.

She and Jesse got together during summer of eighth grade and were practically inseparable up until the day she'd left. He'd never once tried to call or text after they had broken up. It didn't even matter to block him on social media as he never used it. Nia knew that he only had the same old photos on his Instagram from years ago, because she shamelessly checked his page on the odd occasion.

Okay, fine, it was often, but he didn't need to know that.

'Can your boyfriend drop you home?' Niles asked, as he pulled into a parking space outside Rosie's

Diner. Inside, Nia could make out Rosie behind the counter, her head thrown back, laughing with one of her last customers as they were leaving the bar. Her shoulder-length, black hair had a streak of gray in it, as if she couldn't get any cooler. From this angle, Rosie glowed like someone had been taking real good care of her, yet she was still robust and no-nonsense as ever. Sienna would have loved to see this version of her mother.

The thought of Sienna Rose brought a pang to her heart. She should still be here.

'Boyfr— what? Are you *that* busy you can't pick me up in a few hours?' Nia questioned. She wasn't falling for Niles' attempt to distract her.

'A few of us are going to Barkwood Bridge after the game, that's all,' he admitted. 'I won't be back until late.'

Barkwood Bridge had a parking lot that overlooked the waterfall. When Nia was in high school, she and her friends would spend hours up there away from the prying eyes of parents, finally able to let loose after all the tourists had left for the season. She guessed it was time for a new generation to discover the joys of unsupervised fun, but it still gave her pause.

'Late?' Nia repeated. 'What's late?'

He shrugged. 'I dunno, like, midnight?'

'It's a school night, Niles! Mom lets you stay out with the car until *midnight*?' This was egregious. A true travesty of justice. She couldn't believe her mother had gone soft on her brother like this. Marjorie would never have let this fly with her.

Niles rolled his eyes. 'Can he take you or what?'

Nia took the time to be nosy since clearly no one else in the house was concerned about Niles' whereabouts. Cinnamon Falls was a small town and more than likely he wouldn't get hurt, but ever since Sienna, she couldn't take the chance. 'Who's a few of us?'

'Come on, Ni-Ni.' A smile played on his lips, which told her he was meeting with a girl.

'What's her name?' Nia tickled his ribs and he swatted her hands away.

'You remember Shawna Daniels? You might not. She was in my grade,' he started.

Nia almost jumped out of her skin. 'Please tell me you don't let her drive this car!'

'I drive,' he assured her. 'We're just . . . hanging out, you know?' He shrugged in that non-committal way guys often did when they were hiding their feelings.

'Don't be makin' no babies, Niles. I mean it.' Nia tried to use her parental voice and added in a wagging finger to make sure he knew she meant business.

He laughed, embarrassed. 'Nah, nothing like that. We just talk. Well, she talks . . . I just listen mostly.'

Yeah, she and Jesse were just talking and listening once, too. She still couldn't believe her baby brother, whose room once mysteriously smelled like eggs, was old enough to like girls. She leaned across her seat, pulling him in for a hug. He was too tall to put in a headlock now, so she scrubbed her hands over his waves instead.

'Chill, Ni-Ni!' he laughed, smoothing his hair back into place. He flipped the overhead mirror down, checking himself out again. 'Get your man to drop you home, aight? I'll see you in the morning.'

Nia hopped out, but before he could pull away, she added, 'I need you to run me to the mall in Asheville tomorrow.'

'I've got a game tomorrow so I can take you after school around seven, is that cool?'

'Cool,' she answered. 'Be safe, I'll see you tomorrow.' She watched Niles pull away and drive down the road until his taillights disappeared around the corner. It felt like a little piece of her heart went with him. When the street was clear, Nia finally built up enough courage to step inside the diner.

'Are you kidding me?' Rosie shrieked when she locked eyes with Nia. She jetted from behind the counter and Nia braced herself for impact. Rosie was not a small woman. She always reminded Nia of Miss Trunchbull from *Matilda*, in size but not attitude. She had a triple-watt smile that made Nia feel like she was the light of her world, and she was always as sweet as her scrumptious apple cider.

Nia had spent countless hours in Rosie's Diner with Sienna growing up. Her mom would watch her from the door of the ice cream parlor until she made it safely down the street to Rosie's when she was tired of slinging soft serve to customers.

Unbelievably, Rosie's Diner was still the same. The comforting smells of cinnamon and butter cloaked her like a warm winter coat. During operating hours, conversation crowded every corner of the fifties-style bar. The setup boasted red leather booths that looked to have been reupholstered in the last six years, and a high-top bar ran the length of the room and was always packed with customers enjoying Rosie's famous cinnamon desserts on display under glass holders. In the center of the room hung a vintage neon sign in the shape of a rose, her signature.

The residents of Cinnamon Falls didn't play when it came to Rosie. There was a deep, mutual respect for the woman who catered their most precious memories. Between graduations, birthday parties, weddings, baby showers, christenings, and funerals, Rosie supported everyone from the cradle to the grave.

Before Nia could protest Rosie enveloped her, nearly lifting her off her feet. After a moment, Rosie released her and took a step back to get a good look at Nia. Rosie's eyes were an intense, warm brown and her gaze had a way of making Nia feel both seen and held accountable. As a child, she hated that Sienna's mother could know everything she'd been thinking. Now, she couldn't wait to tell her all the things that were on her mind.

'Nia,' Rosie said with glistening eyes. 'Where have you been, my girl?'

Nia glanced around and spotted Morgan sitting against the far wall in the largest booth, laughing next to some people she couldn't make out from her angle.

'I moved to Atlanta, just finished grad school,' Nia reported, dutifully showing Rosie the pictures on her phone, being careful to skip over the ones with Bryant in them.

'Congratulations! You look gorgeous in that cap and gown! How long are you in town for?'

Nia wanted to tell her the truth, but right now wasn't the time. They'd need a shot of something strong and no prying ears.

'I'll come by this week so we can talk about it?' Nia offered.

'Of course.' Rosie smiled. 'Morgan and company are over there.' Nia followed her gaze to the rowdiest booth. Laughter erupted from that side of the room. Morgan caught eyes with Nia and waved her over.

'Let me know if you need anything.' Rosie patted Nia's hand, even though Nia still knew her way around the diner's kitchen.

'A cinnamon bun, please.' Nia had been craving one since she got back in town. The fluffy gooeyness of Rosie's cinnamon buns was unmatched. The cinnamon spice paired with the bold crunch of the toasted pecans always made her feel like Rosie had made each one specially for her.

'I'm trying out a new pumpkin spice recipe this year for the Fall Festival. You gotta let me know what you think.' Rosie spun on her heels excitedly, disappearing behind the counter and into the kitchen in a flourish. Nia took a deep breath. It was time to face her fears and journey over to Morgan's table.

Darius Lyons spotted her first. The scrawny kid she, Sienna, and Morgan used to despise was long gone. Scrawny and Darius didn't belong in the same sentence anymore; he was all broad shoulders, thick arms, and a chest that filled out his designer jacket like it was sewn on. His deep brown skin and disarming smile made it easy to see how he'd become Cinnamon Falls' golden boy. Diamond earrings the size of dimes glittered in his ears. He looked like he belonged on a billboard for athletic wear, not casually dining with friends like it was just another day in his life. Nia wondered how Sienna would feel if she had known that six years after high school she'd be hanging out with their arch nemesis.

'Not Miss Big City back in town!' It was obvious he'd already had too much to drink from the slur in his words. Dark shades shielded his eyes. It was only nine p.m. Nia wished she'd thought to pack her sunglasses so that Darius couldn't see her rolling her eyes at him.

Across from him sat Jesse, who glanced up at Nia, mid-conversation with a woman seated next to Morgan. Nia didn't recognize her at first, but as she got closer, she realized it was Victoria Nathan, Darius' girlfriend. She was almost unrecognizable behind all the makeup. Nia couldn't believe they were still together. She thought for sure he would have left her the second he made it big. Even sitting down, she was a head taller than Darius. Her statuesque frame made her impossible to ignore. Her glowing brown skin boasted that she lived in a world where stress and worry simply didn't exist. Her plump cheekbones drew out her sharp eyes that could cut stone. But she still wore that annoying expression, an ever-present smirk, like she was smarter than everyone in the room.

Jesse's eyes fixed on Nia's and they both managed a polite smile. She wanted to melt through the floor. He looked amazing; his caramel-colored skin was unblemished, and in the time they had spent apart he'd grown into his father's rugged, square-jawed looks. His red flannel shirt boasted his muscular chest and athletic build. He looked casual and comfortable, like he hadn't spent the last hour of his life rifling through his closet in preparation to see her.

'That's you,' Nia responded to Darius, tearing her eyes from Jesse's. 'Mr. World Champ.'

Darius wore his team ring on his pinky finger since the other fingers were occupied with rows of flashy diamond bands.

'Something slight, you know,' Darius said as Victoria reached over and brushed invisible lint off his shoulder, her glittering engagement ring making a grand entrance. It matched the studs hanging off her ears.

Jesse scooted inward, making room for Nia on the booth's end. She sat down beside him and noticed there was no ring on his finger. On the other side of him sat a large bouquet of red roses. Were those for her?

'I didn't expect a reunion tonight,' Nia said, attempting to break the tension.

'News travels fast in Cinnamon Falls,' Jesse replied. 'Welcome back.'

'Thank you, Jesse.' Nia couldn't bring herself to make eye contact with him just then, but she could feel the heat coming off him in waves. She looked across the table at Morgan, who busied herself with the condiment packets on the table.

Rosie chose that moment to arrive at their table, carrying a large plate stacked with cinnamon buns.

'You're a saint, Rosie,' Jesse said first, piling up the used dishes on the table to make way for the new ones. 'Though I can't eat another thing,' he claimed.

'Nonsense,' Rosie protested. 'Eat up!'

Rosie diligently pushed the plate of six sticky buns into the middle of the table. The warm aroma of cinnamon and butter made Nia's mouth water at the sight. The buns had an orange swirl in the center and cascading heavy cream on top, sprinkled with toasted nuts. Nia wasted no time grabbing one from the plate.

'I'll bring you all back some cider?' Rosie asked the table.

'Yes, please,' Nia mumbled around a mouthful of a cinnamon lover's delight.

'None for me, thank you,' Victoria spoke up. She scooted back from the dessert plate as if it was going to become conscious and eat her. Nia noticed her corner of the table had been clear; only a perspiring glass of water before her.

'You're buggin',' Darius commented, grabbing a sticky bun for himself and ripping into it. 'People wait all year for these.' He turned to Rosie. 'Catering for the festival again this year?'

'As always,' Rosie answered. 'I'm meeting with Maggie tonight to go over the menu. We're trying out something new this year. Speaking of, I'm surprised to see you back in this neck of the woods.' Rosie's eyes took inventory of the dishes and began to clear the table. 'In town to crown the new Cinnamon King?'

Darius swallowed the chunk of food in his mouth. Nia couldn't see his eyes because of the obnoxious sunglasses but she could guess he wasn't looking Rosie in the face.

'For a coupla days,' he responded coolly.

'Celebrating, I see.' Rosie removed the numerous

shot glasses that were stacked together next to Darius.

'Two reunions in the same day calls for some libations,' Morgan said, dancing a jig in her seat.

Rosie glanced at Victoria, noticing her lack of enthusiasm for the food in front of her.

'Is there something I can get you instead?' Rosie's voice, though comforting, had a sharp edge to it. 'I could whip up anything you'd like.'

'Could I just have a simple garden salad?' Victoria asked, a pinched smile on her face.

'A . . . salad,' Rosie repeated, like she'd never heard of it before.

'Yeah,' Victoria scoffed. 'Lettuce, tomato, a little cucumber. A salad.'

Rosie narrowed her eyes. 'Coming right up.'

'Just chill, babe,' Darius said to her as Rosie walked off, the clinking of dirty dishes fading away.

'Can't even get a decent salad in this place, I hate it. I'm starving. Everything is deep fried and slathered in butter.'

'It's just a few more days.' Darius tried to comfort her by planting a sloppy kiss on her cheek. She pushed his face away, making a show of wiping the kiss off with her hand.

'Hate is a strong word,' Jesse commented. He sliced into his cinnamon bun methodically. 'What's wrong with Cinnamon Falls?'

'Please don't get her started,' Morgan jumped in, attempting to change the subject.

Nia squirmed in her seat. Jesse loved his hometown and Victoria sounded a lot like Nia had in their senior year of high school. It was the main reason she and Jesse broke up: she had been desperate to leave, and he wanted to stay.

'Enlighten me,' Jesse prodded.

Victoria rolled her eyes, not giving in. 'I'm ready to go,' she told Darius, who had a forkful of cinnamon bun on its way to his waiting lips.

He hesitated, then placed the fork down on the plate and wiped his mouth. He reached over and dapped up Jesse and said his goodbyes to Nia and Morgan without fuss. He slid out of the booth and allowed Victoria to walk ahead of him just as Rosie was approaching with the salad she'd requested. Darius dug in his jeans pocket and peeled off a blue bill from a big stack of others and tossed it on the table.

'We're heading out,' he muttered, keeping his head low.

'And who's driving?' Rosie inquired. 'The last thing I need is for your father to have my head over you.'

'We'll be fine,' Darius assured her. 'A quick twenty-minute drive, nothin' major.'

Rosie placed a hand on her hip, raising one skeptical eyebrow. 'Be careful 'round those Falls. It gets dark at night,' she called to them as they exited.

Victoria grabbed her man by the hand and led him out of the door. The group in the booth watched as the pair left the diner and jumped into a souped-up

F-150. A hip-hop song blared through the speakers as Darius skidded out of the parking lot.

Rosie ran her fingers through her hair and stomped away without looking back.

'What was that about?' Morgan asked.

Jesse shook his head like he had more to say but wouldn't. Even though the place had gone back to regular operations, Nia couldn't help but notice how tense Jesse was.

'We should go,' he said. 'You need a ride home?'

'I'll take her,' Morgan volunteered.

They made their way to the exit. Nia stopped at the counter and spotted Rosie in the back with a phone glued to her ear; its cord snaked around her pointer finger.

Nia waved, letting her know they were leaving.

'Come by tomorrow,' Rosie mouthed and Nia nodded before blowing her a kiss. Rosie pretended to catch it in the air and placed it over her heart.

Then, the three of them stepped out into the night.

Chapter 4

Tuesday
Jesse

Jesse first heard the rattling in his dreams. The vibrating phone clattered on his dresser and shook him out of his slumber. Through cracked eyes he found the bedside clock staring back at him. It was one-thirty in the morning. Jesse fumbled to answer the phone, but before he could get it to his ear, he knew something was wrong.

'Jesse, I need you down here at Rosie's, son,' Chief Vernon Prescott said in a controlled voice. Since Jesse and Chief Prescott had been working together, Prescott had never addressed him with a term of endearment. His clipped tone made Jesse sit upright in his bed.

Jesse stumbled toward his closet, clawing for appropriate clothing with the haste of a chronically late man on his third strike at work. 'I can be there in fifteen minutes,' he responded, the phone hooked between his neck and ear as he jumped into his pants. He fastened the belt and moved on to pulling on a sweatshirt.

'Make it ten,' Chief Prescott said curtly. 'No sirens,' he added, before hanging up.

No sirens? Jesse's mind flew into overdrive. *What could possibly have the Chief out of bed at one in the morning? And why would it be happening at Rosie's Diner?* Jesse questioned as he moved expertly through the dark house toward the garage. He stopped in the kitchen to scribble a note for his father, who would be expecting breakfast in a few hours. Before he left, Jesse filled up a vase with water and tossed the roses he'd promised his father inside. He wished he had the time to make a nice arrangement, but even his parents' anniversary would have to wait.

Then, with his overheads flashing, and sleep still in the corners of his eyes, he sped through town toward Rosie's Diner.

Jesse pulled up, exactly ten minutes later, to find Main Street eerily still, aside from the police presence outside Rosie's. As Jesse got out of the car, he was met with the guttural wails of a woman's cry. With his heart pounding in his chest, he took a quick inventory of the scene: Bud Wade and Terrance Chambers, Cinnamon Falls' detectives, were consoling a sobbing Maggie Shilling. Chambers was doing his best to keep her upright, but the hyperventilating woman was proving to be too much for the lanky detective. He was starting to lose his grip on her.

There was no Rosie to be seen.

Jesse noticed Grace Whitfield's old-school Chevy Caprice – which he had always been jealous of – was parked in Rosie's lot. If the coroner had beat him to the diner, things were bad.

'Sit her down,' Chief Prescott ordered, and the officers gently guided Maggie to the curb. Prescott looked like he'd gotten even less sleep than Jesse. His usual gruff demeanor and nonchalant attitude were nowhere to be found. He looked heartbroken and, even worse, horrified.

Chief Prescott approached Jesse before he got too close to the diner, his heavy footfalls deliberate and commanding. The man was built like a bulldog – thick-necked and barrel-chested, with a round belly that strained his uniform shirt. The blue and red lights flashed against the sweat-slicked skin of his ruddy face, highlighting the deep lines carved into his forehead and around his mouth. His steel-gray eyes, sharp and unyielding, locked onto Jesse with a quiet intensity that rooted him to the spot.

Despite the late hour, Prescott's uniform remained immaculate, crisp blues stretched over his solid frame, his polished badge gleaming under the streetlights. The black leather belt cinched tightly around his wide waist creaked slightly as he moved, weighed down by a holstered gun that Jesse had never seen him draw. His boots, spit-shined to perfection, reflected the swirling police lights like mirrors. As he came to a stop in front of Jesse, he inhaled deeply, with a slow, measured breath.

'What do we got?' Jesse reluctantly asked, even though he could infer the answer. He took in deep breaths like he'd been trained to do when he needed his mind to slow down. The Chief's somber expression only deepened his suspicions. From Jesse's angle, he could tell Prescott was swallowing down a sob. Internally, Jesse braced himself for the news.

Prescott paused before answering. 'It's Rosie,' he said finally. 'She's . . .' The Chief shook his head as if he couldn't bring himself to say the words.

No.

Jesse had taken bad news before. He'd been trained to compartmentalize; to push down his emotions and to heighten his logic at a time like this. It was second nature to codify a bleeding wound and deal with it later. And one day, much later, he'd have to deal with the pain that he was feeling: hot knives plunging into his belly. He wanted to double over and scream like he'd seen Maggie doing.

A black rage he hadn't felt in years coursed through his veins and he wanted to rip up the pavement with his bare hands. He was afraid that if he opened his mouth an animalistic sob would claw its way out.

He leaned back against his car, placing his palms to the cool metal to ground himself.

Jesse managed to eke out, 'How?'

The Chief shrugged, his eyes meeting the ground like the facts were too hard to bear.

Chambers and Wade had finally maneuvered Maggie into the back of the cruiser. When Wade closed the door, Maggie leaned her head against the window and pulled her knees to her chest like a toddler scared for her mother. Chambers swaggered over to where Jesse stood with the Chief, Wade tight on his heels.

'Maggie called the switchboard a little after midnight,' Chambers reported, glancing over his shoulder at the woman whose cries had simmered to whimpers. The gangling detective laced his long fingers behind his neck. Jesse couldn't help but notice his gleaming wedding band. Chambers took a deep breath and shuttered his eyes closed.

Terrance Chambers was one of the implants from the city. He was only a few years senior than Jesse and had clinched the open detective position with ease. With ten years in cop work at Atlanta PD under his belt, Chambers thought he'd 'take it slow' in Cinnamon Falls, where, according to him, 'crime doesn't happen'.

Despite his boasted track record, Jesse wasn't sure if Chambers had what it took. It was obvious he'd jumped out of bed and chosen the first thing he could find – pajama pants with his wife's face printed on them. *He couldn't find a decent pair of jeans?* A sliver of Jesse's faith in the detective wilted away.

'From what we could get out of her, she was meeting with Rosie at midnight to go over the food for the festival this weekend,' Chambers continued.

'At midnight?' Chief Prescott cut in.

'Why were they meeting so late?' Jesse asked.

'Alexis is part of the Festival Committee with Maggie,' Chambers stated, referring to his wife. 'They have been meeting non-stop to coordinate all the hoopla.' He threw his hands up in frustration. 'Sometimes she doesn't get home until eleven o'clock at night. It's a huge thing.' He shook his head.

'So it makes sense for Maggie to be meeting with Rosie at that time of the night,' Prescott confirmed.

'Sir, Maggie said she walked in and just found her like that,' Wade contributed, his eyes meeting the road.

Bud Wade, a stout and serious man, had been a cop in the Cinnamon Falls Police Department since before Jesse was born. He was just shy of retirement and made sure everyone knew about it. He had a round torso that stretched the seams of his uniform and a neck that had long since disappeared into his square, stoic shoulders. Wade didn't speak unless he had something worth saying, and when he did, people listened. Jesse wondered if he was just as rocked by the news.

'She's all broke up 'bout it. I believe her, Chief.'

'Found her like what?' Jesse was afraid to ask, but he had to know. Did she slip and fall? Had she hurt herself? He attempted to make his way around the men when Prescott placed a hand to his chest, stopping him from going any further.

'Jesse . . . Rosie was killed,' the Chief revealed, moving his hand up to Jesse's shoulder and searching his face.

The words hit Jesse like a boot to the stomach. He was just wrapping his brain around the notion that the woman who'd practically raised him was somehow gone from this world. His rage sprouted another venomous head knowing someone had brutally ripped her away with intention.

'Angie called me from reception, and I called Grace to meet me down here. She's thinking that the time of death is between ten p.m. and midnight.'

Jesse wanted to collapse but he braced himself by putting his hands on his knees. When he'd left Rosie's Diner with Morgan and Nia, it was nearing nine-thirty. Just an hour later, she was gone. If only he had stayed. Just one hour more, and Rosie might still be alive.

'What's the cause of death?' Jesse asked weakly.

'Blunt force trauma to the head.'

Someone let out a sound that Jesse could only compare to a wounded animal. It took him several long seconds to realize that it had been him. It took both Chief Prescott and Bud Wade to get Jesse upright again. He sucked down deep breaths of air. The cinnamon smell that would usually bring him comfort and memories featuring Rosie's smiling face was making his stomach churn.

His world spun off its axis.

'Someone murdered Rosie?' The words felt unreal leaving Jesse's lips like he was starring in a film, and somebody, somewhere was seconds away from yelling, 'CUT!'

'Not only that,' Chambers added. 'They left a note: "Who Will Be Next?"' he read aloud. Chambers' face was ghostly white as he spun his cell phone around to the men, revealing a picture. Jesse immediately recognized the rose embossed pattern on the tabletops in Rosie's Diner. A ripped piece of paper stood out on the table reading 'Who Will Be Next?' in erratic and rushed handwriting.

'You know what this means, right?' Chambers put his phone away and crossed his arms over his chest.

The men exchanged quick and desperate glances. Wade asked breathlessly, 'There's a serial killer in Cinnamon Falls?'

It took Jesse a while to pull himself together before he could build up enough courage to cross the street to Rosie's Diner. He remembered that when he was a kid growing up, his mother and Nia's mother would watch them from the door of The Cinnamon Scoop while they walked the few steps down to Rosie's. Main Street seemed so big back then. He knew, deep down, that nothing bad would happen to them in the minutes it took to get from the ice cream parlor to Rosie's. In fact, Rosie would be right there, hanging out of the door and waving to their mothers that they'd been received safely.

It was unnatural to see the place now, roped off with crime scene tape and surrounded by officers. The Chief had called other patrolmen to block off Main Street before the rest of the town woke up for regular business, and even Mayor Asad Lyons had come down to the scene. Dressed in a suit that looked like it could fund Jesse's yearly salary, he and Chief Prescott stood to the side, conferring.

Jesse spotted Grace Whitfield, the town's coroner, standing in the doorway. Grace and her brother, Gage, ran the Whitfield Family Mortuary. Grace's father, Genesis, had served the residents of Cinnamon Falls for generations, and after medical school Grace had returned to continue her family's legacy. She was deeply loyal to her family and always approached her work with compassion and respect. Her mother had picked the perfect name for her. Jesse had always admired her dedication to the families she served. Death was hard for anyone to deal with, but Rosie's would hit the town hard.

Grace looked exhausted. Her thick hair was pulled to the top of her head in a hasty bun, accentuating her soft features. The professional smile she usually had was gone. Her lips were twisted with worry. She pushed a pair of her clear-framed glasses back up on her nose with the wrist of her gloved hand. She clutched a camera in the other.

She was looking for someone. Her serious eyes scanned the crowd of officers outside the diner. For a split second, she moved past Jesse's face, but returned to catch his gaze like she'd been looking for him all along. Her face softened at the sight of him.

On noodle legs, Jesse crossed the street toward her. They embraced, short and sweet, an offer of condolences he knew, before she delivered the tragic news.

'She fought like hell.' Grace steeled her jaw. She gestured toward the camera, wordlessly asking if he wanted to take a look.

Jesse shook his head. He didn't *want* to know anything more, only wishing to remember Rosie as the ball of light she was. But he had to know every single detail if he wanted to sleep another night. He had to see it for himself.

He stepped around Grace and walked inside Rosie's Diner before the strength left him. Her body had been removed, thanks to Gage who'd come by with the hearse. When he stepped inside it felt as though he'd entered another time zone. The usually loud diner that trapped the melodic laughter of the townsfolk was strangely silent besides the mumbled orders on police radios.

Jesse took in everything around him in disbelief – the diner had been wrecked. Glass crunched beneath his feet as he picked his way through the ransacked restaurant. He traced it to the display case that looked as if one of the overturned barstools had been smashed against it. Cases of Rosie's custom ceramic mugs reserved for cider were smashed and scattered on the floor. The neon sign above their heads sputtered on and off like someone had taken a weapon to that too.

'She was here,' Grace said. Her calming tone cut through the raging in Jesse's head. Jesse followed where her finger pointed to the first booth by the door. 'Slumped over.'

Jesse recreated the scene in his mind while Grace continued.

'She was waiting on someone. There was a cup of cider here.' She indicated the side of the booth where Rosie had been sitting. 'It was still warm when I got here.' Grace let him see the picture she'd snapped on her camera. It was a bird's eye point of view allowing him to see the entire scene.

If it weren't for the blood pooling under Rosie's body, she looked like she'd simply fallen asleep from exhaustion. Next to her manicured hand was the ripped note. Grace flipped through the pictures she'd taken, skipping over the ones that were too much for Jesse.

She pointed to the close-ups she'd snapped of Rosie's hands and arms. 'See those marks?'

'Defensive wounds?' Jesse asked.

Grace nodded. 'Rosie was a big woman. It would take more than a little teacup or two to take her down.' She gestured to the mess on the floor. 'They hit her with something large. Something heavy.'

Jesse started to scan the room to see if anything else felt out of place or was missing, but his eyes clouded with tears. He batted them away just in time to hear Chief Prescott yell for him.

'Shaw, get out here!'

Before he could turn to leave, Grace offered Jesse a hug. 'Thank you,' Jesse whispered, holding her close for a moment.

Back outside, Jesse met with the Chief, along with the rest of the team of officers. Chief Prescott wasted no time in doling out duties to the men: contacting Rosie's next of kin and her employees. Mayor Lyons carved out detours with a few officers to accommodate Main Street's shutdown, while Chief Prescott wanted to get the facts straight before everyone woke up and rumors started flying, if they hadn't already. It was only a matter of time before Elaine Matthias was down here in her news van demanding answers.

'Shaw, you know these streets better than anyone. I want you to work with Chambers to figure out the last twelve hours of Rosie's life. We backtrack her movements. I want to know about every car that came up and down this street since this time yesterday. I want to know every single person who sat in that diner, you understand?'

Jesse nodded, pleased to receive his marching orders. He wanted to get started immediately. Jesse also noticed the disappointed expression on Chambers' face but put it out of his mind. This was about getting justice for Rosie, not their personal feelings.

Chief Prescott pressed on. 'Wade, you take Ms. Shilling back to the station. Get her some coffee – the good stuff out of my office, not that piss you all drink – and get her statement. As far as we know, she was the last person to see Rosie alive.'

Wade interjected, 'You couldn't think that Maggie w—'

'I don't know what to think right now,' Prescott fired back.

'Chief's right,' Chambers spoke up. 'At this point, everyone's a suspect until me and the rookie check out their alibis. You find something, you bring it to us. That note is telling me that this person isn't done yet.'

'Rookie?' Jesse questioned, taking a step toward Chambers. He knew Chambers was trying to press his buttons and he'd just landed on the right one.

Chambers sported a slick smile and shrugged. 'It's just a figure of speech.'

'Not now!' Prescott boomed. 'We have a responsibility to a town full of people who are going to wake up terrified and expecting answers from us. I need everyone to do their damn jobs, you got it? And fast! You hear anything, you call me first.'

'Yes, sir,' Jesse responded through tight lips.

'Beat each other up on your own time.' Chief Prescott pushed through the crowd of men and walked toward his cruiser. 'I want answers, gentlemen!' he called before peeling away from the scene.

Jesse could feel Chambers' eyes on him while the other officers dispersed to follow their orders.

'Well?' Chambers asked. 'Where do you want to start first?'

Jesse took a look at his cell phone. It was nearly three a.m. They had another hour or so before Rosie's bakers would come in to start the day's batches of signature desserts. It'd be a few more hours before the rest of Main Street's shops would spring to life. It was going to be a sad day in Cinnamon Falls.

'First, you're going to go home and change those pants,' Jesse said without looking over at his temporary partner. 'Then, you're going to meet me at the station in an hour.'

Chambers kissed his teeth and crossed his arms over his chest. 'And what are you going to be doing?'

'Taking care of my people,' Jesse answered. He separated himself from Chambers and ducked back inside Rosie's Diner, leaving Chambers and his wife's cheesy expression in the parking lot.

Chapter 5

Nia

Nia was suffocating. She sputtered out a cough, pushing the hefty obstruction off her face. She slapped on the bedside lamp to reveal Midnight's yellow eyes looking back at her, outraged. She must have decided that Nia's face was the perfect spot for a good night's sleep, even if it meant Nia's death.

'Dad, your cat is trying to kill me again!' Nia groaned.

Midnight stared back at her, indignant.

'Night-y,' Nia's father sang from downstairs in that voice parents use when they're trying to bribe their behaviorally challenged child. 'Come get some breakfast, mama. Your sissy is so cranky in the mornings.'

Midnight sauntered off Nia's bed with the attitude of a fourteen-year-old girl, flicking her tail for good measure at her nemesis. Nia had shut her door last night, but the sneaky little cat always found a way around it. Midnight would attempt murder again,

Nia was sure of it. She owed Midnight an apology for her absence over the past six years and Midnight was ensuring that she'd receive it, in this life or the afterlife.

She would have to get in line, Nia thought. There were a handful of people Nia owed an apology to and today she was going to start with the person closest to her. Her mother.

Nia's father had always said that Nia and Marjorie were just alike, which was why they bumped heads so frequently. But Nia couldn't see the correlation between the two. If anything, she felt she got her laid-back personality and sense of humor from her father. The most she inherited from her mother were her soft but serious eyes, and her buttery caramel complexion. Everything else, even down to the size ten shoe, she attributed to her father.

Nia ventured downstairs to find her home in full hustle mode at seven a.m. She spotted her father exiting out of the back door to enjoy a morning coffee on the deck. Midnight followed him excitedly, ready to chase the adventurous birds who dared to swoop down onto her lawn to grab an innocent insect for breakfast. In the kitchen, her mother was standing at the island making an enormous sandwich.

'Are you seriously still making Niles lunch?' Nia asked, disgusted at her mother's antics.

'Good morning to you too,' Marjorie replied, never breaking her concentration while she chopped the crust off the sandwich and expertly folded it in aluminium foil. 'He's got a game today and your father and I are meeting with Maggie Shilling tonight to talk numbers for the festival, so we'll miss it.'

'This is sickening, you know that, right?' Nia pulled a glass out of the cabinet and filled it with orange juice.

Her mother shrugged at the comment. 'At least he still needs me. You were always so independent. You never needed help with anything. Niles still lets me be his mom. So, I'm going to be for as long as I can.' Marjorie had moved on to plucking grapes from the stem one by one and placing them in a plastic bag.

The words hung between them for a moment, before Nia decided to break the silence. 'I do need you, Mom,' she said, taking a seat at the bar across from her at the kitchen island. 'More than ever right now.'

Of course she needed her mother. Before she'd decided to leave town, she felt smothered. Cinnamon Falls had felt like she was constantly under a microscope, especially after Sienna passed. At the time, she didn't think leaving would change anything for anyone but her, but now, she had started to see just how much had changed.

Only two nights ago she had been lying beside a man she thought was the love of her life watching reality television. She was indescribably happy. Her tragic life back in Cinnamon Falls was the last thing on her mind. She had gone from having everything she could have ever asked for – a well-paying job at a high-powered law firm, a handsome and hilarious boyfriend, a closet full of shoes and bags (more than she could ever wear in this lifetime) – to living out of a suitcase and sleeping on a twin-sized bed back in her bubblegum-pink childhood bedroom.

Marjorie looked at her daughter. 'Talk to me. What happened with Bryant?'

Nia shook her head, remembering that she was planning to have this exact conversation with Rosie later that day. She wished Rosie were here now, so she didn't have to cut her heart open twice, but maybe it would be good to talk it out instead of holding it all in. It'd been a while since she'd gotten her heart broken. Six years to be exact, but the pain of heartbreak was never unfamiliar.

'I don't even know.' Nia sighed, still finding herself trapped in that moment of emotional whiplash. Her heartbeat quickened in her ears as she remembered how startled she was to hear a knock at her front door that morning.

'I thought that Bryant had forgotten something, which he almost never did, or maybe he'd ordered breakfast for me. I pranced to the door, expecting a surprise from my thoughtful boyfriend. But instead, I found myself face to face with a woman who looked like she hadn't slept in days. She told me that the apartment was their family rental for when Bryant stayed late at the office and couldn't make the drive home to Augusta. He had an entire life without me, hours away. Everything he'd told me was a lie.'

'And what did Bryant say?' Marjorie asked, her hands on her hips, eyebrows pinched together.

'I haven't spoken to him,' Nia admitted. 'I didn't know what to do. I panicked. You know, after Jesse, I just thought I would make a new life as a single woman. I didn't expect to meet Bryant and I damn sure wouldn't have fallen in love with him if I knew he was married! I can't believe everything was a lie. Mom, everything felt *so* good. Am I an idiot for missing him right now? For wanting the lie back?'

'You're a woman,' her mother replied. 'Regardless of what transpired before yesterday, you loved Bryant, but love costs, honey.'

'Grief,' Nia mumbled.

'It's the price we all pay. But you can't measure your worth on the mistakes of a man.'

'I'm just so mad at him.' Nia pounded her fist on the kitchen island, making her glass clatter on the marble countertop. 'And mostly, I'm mad at myself. I keep combing through our memories, our messages, our pictures, to see what I'd missed. How didn't I know? How was he able to keep a whole life hidden for years?'

'He's a liar,' Nia's mother deadpanned. 'That's what liars do. They get you to believe in their twisted fantasy.' Her words felt like Nia had been slapped across the face with the hand of reality. 'You had pure intentions. You went into that relationship open and honest.'

Nia shook her head, wishing she'd guarded her heart more. 'The good thing about love is,' her mother continued, 'that it never dies. The love and devotion that you showed that man is going to make its way back to you tenfold.'

Nia wanted to believe her mother. But all she felt was rage. Rage and sorrow. She couldn't see how love could penetrate the brick wall she'd been building over her heart since Bryant's wife showed up at her door.

'I think I'm done with love for a little while,' Nia muttered, downing her cup of juice. She rinsed the cup and placed it in the dishwasher. 'I just need some time to get myself together.'

'You're home now, take as much time as you need.'

'Mom?' Nia asked before she headed upstairs.

Marjorie turned to look at her. 'Yes, honey?'

'Can you make me a sandwich before you go too?'

Nia realized how much their smiles matched when her mother replied, 'Of course, Ni-Ni.'

Nia returned to her room, eyeing her phone that was charging on the bedside table. Had Bryant called or texted? *Why do you care?* one side of her brain admonished her. Her ego wanted him to beg for forgiveness and grovel at her feet. But her heart wanted to simply move on. She wanted to forget that he even existed in her life. He'd turned her life upside down in a matter of minutes and everything still felt like it was crashing down around her.

Nia was going to have to quit her job. She muffled a sob. She'd worked so hard to score the internship at Gildman & Sons, and when Mr. Gildman offered her, out of ten other interns, a coveted research assistant position, she felt like things were finally starting to level out for her outside of Cinnamon Falls. She was forging her own path beyond her family's. Now what did she have to show for her hard work? Nia was starting to regret ever leaving home in the first place.

She tapped the phone screen and it glowed with notifications from an unfamiliar number. She didn't have to open the messages to know it was Bryant. As she suspected, he was begging to explain himself in person.

Pick up the phone, one message read.

Talk to me Nia, please, another asked.

She didn't have to read the other messages to know they all had the same sentiment. She hadn't seen an apology yet.

Niles skidded past her room on his way to the kitchen with Midnight nestled in his arms. She must have grown bored with her morning Olympics.

'You still need me to take you to Asheville later?' Niles asked.

Nia nodded, keeping her eyes on the cat, who was

keeping her eyes right back on Nia. 'If you don't mind,' she replied.

'How was last night?' he asked, stroking Midnight down her back. She nuzzled her nose into the crook of his arm.

'Weird,' Nia admitted. 'It was cool to see Jesse. I wanted to catch up, but Rosie got upset so it was kind of awkward toward the end of the night.'

'Upset with who? Everyone knows not to mess with Rosie when Jay is around. They'll end up in handcuffs.'

'Jesse's an officer now?' Nia was pleasantly surprised. With his father's military background and his love for his hometown, Nia knew he'd do anything to protect it. It was the perfect job for him.

'He didn't tell you?'

'We didn't get a chance to talk like that, really. Everything happened so fast and then we left.'

'I drove past on the way home and the light was still on. I figured you two were in there, catching up or whatever.'

'How was your night?' Nia asked, lowering her voice so their parents couldn't hear. Niles crept further into her room, looking over his shoulder. He placed one hand over Midnight's ears for good measure.

'It was cool.' The way Niles' cheeks flushed, Nia knew the night was more than cool.

'Just cool?' Nia questioned.

'Real cool,' he repeated with a mischievous smile,

and Nia knew she wasn't going to get anything else out of her little brother. He lifted his hands from the cat's ears.

'I gotta run to school, so make sure you feed Midnight since we'll be out of the house today. She likes the tuna crisps, not the salmon ones Mom likes to give her.' Midnight's ears perked at the mention of her favorite meal.

Nia rolled her eyes. 'This cat gets better treatment than me.'

'She's cuter than you.' Niles shrugged matter-of-factly, dropping Midnight on Nia's bed.

'I appreciate that,' Nia responded sarcastically.

'See ya later, ugly!' Niles called before turning and heading downstairs.

'I guess it's just us gals today,' Nia said to the cat. Uninterested in bonding, Midnight hopped off Nia's bed and followed Niles down the steps. 'Apparently not,' Nia muttered.

'Ni-Ni, your sandwich is in the fridge,' her mother shouted from downstairs. 'We won't be home 'til late. Dinner is in the oven for you and your brother.'

'Thanks, Mom!' Nia responded.

Since the house was empty of people, and Midnight's threats of imminent death were neutralized for the time being, Nia figured she'd catch up on the sleep that had been rudely interrupted.

She'd been dreaming that she was sitting at the service counter in Rosie's Diner, laughing until tears with Sienna like they did when they were little girls. Behind the partition, Rosie was cooking everything she had in her kitchen to appease their requests. Nia and Sienna were surrounded by a comically enormous amount of cinnamon buns they could never eat in a million lifetimes.

Just when Nia could feel sleep welcoming her back into its cozy arms, she heard her phone vibrate. Her heart jumped in her throat. *What if it's Bryant again?* Nia couldn't imagine having a productive conversation with him right now. She'd only scream until her voice disappeared. So, she let it ring, never looking over, until it eventually stopped.

She rolled on her back and stared up at the ceiling. What was she going to do?

The phone rang again. Nia didn't answer.

It rang again.

She finally decided that she couldn't run from her decisions anymore. She'd have to tell Bryant to leave her alone and enjoy his married life.

Get a grip, she told herself. *Put your big girl panties on!* She took a deep breath and answered the phone without looking at the caller.

'Listen, Bryant—' Nia started, ready to lay down the law. She was tired of running from her grief. Today was going to be the beginning of her healing journey and it started with cutting Bryant off for good. It was over between them, and he never had to worry about seeing her ever again.

Her mother's frantic voice cut her off mid-sentence. 'Nia, it's Rosie! Main Street is blocked off!'

Nia sat up ramrod straight in bed. Her heart stomped around in her chest. 'Mom, slow down. What's happening?'

'Main Street, it's all blocked off! I don't know if we can get to the shop! They're saying . . . Oh, God,' she moaned, deep and guttural. Nia heard her mother dry heave and spit. In the background she could hear her father attempting to soothe his wife, telling her to take deep breaths in through her nose and out of her mouth. Nia could hear sobbing between the rustling of the phone.

'Talk to me!' Nia begged. 'Hello?' She was growing frantic.

Her father must have taken the phone from her mother because his voice was the next she heard. 'It's Rosie, Ni-Ni. She's gone.'

Chapter 6

Jesse

Jesse had spent the last hour sobbing in Barkwood Bridge's car park. When Chambers left him at Rosie's, he waited until the detective's car was out of sight and then drove to the waterfall. At that time, it wasn't yet sunrise; the night sky had been the perfect cloak for him.

He'd held his hurt in for as long as he could, and now he was finally alone. Barkwood Bridge had always been the place he came to when life became too overwhelming. The solitude coupled with the roaring waterfall made it the ideal place to confess one's sins or lay down one's burdens. Jesse was there to do the latter.

He was thankful for the support of the reinforced rope bridge when he unleashed another body-quaking cry from his belly. Jesse allowed the waterfall to take his grief with it on its journey away from Cinnamon Falls, dumping itself into a larger body of water miles away. He liked to imagine his grief was following that same path.

When he had no more tears left to cry, he made his way back toward the station to meet Chambers. A new feeling had settled over his heart now the initial shock of Rosie's death had worn off. Jesse wasn't sad anymore; he was furious. Someone had the audacity to take Rosie, of all people, away from him. Away from Cinnamon Falls.

He imagined the person sleeping peacefully, thrilled that they'd gotten away with it. It would be their last night of sound sleep. He hoped that the hairs on the back of their neck were standing upright and that they could feel him hunting, inching closer and closer, even in their dreams.

By six a.m., the station was buzzing. The morning crew wouldn't normally show up for another couple of hours, but the Chief had called the entire force out of their beds.

Jesse kept his head down most of the morning, dodging the pitiful stares and awkward conversations where Rosie was referred to in the past tense. He had to stay focused. Jesse fished around in his desk for an empty notepad and wrote down every detail he could remember about last night.

First, he drew a rough sketch of Rosie's Diner from a bird's eye view, outlining each table and chair. Then, he mapped out every customer who was simultaneously dining with him the night before. Jesse approximated that there were about seven people, including the five people from his party. He wrote a list of the names as a starting point.

He immediately scratched his own name out, then Nia's and then Morgan's. An elderly couple, Mr. and Mrs. Blackwell, were seated at the counter when he first arrived. There was no way either of them could have physically killed Rosie. He scratched their names out. He couldn't imagine Victoria or Darius bringing harm to Rosie either. She was Cinnamon Falls royalty. No one in their right mind would touch her. Who could have done this? He scratched out their names too, leaving him with no potential suspects, and just as confused as when he started. He folded both pieces of paper and tucked them into his pants pocket.

By the time he'd finished, Chambers had arrived decked out in a three-piece black and white pinstriped suit. He completed the look with a pair of patent leather, hard-bottomed shoes that click-clacked on the station's tile floor. All he needed was green hair and Jesse would be terrified to say his name three times out loud.

He strode over to Jesse's desk, a trail of sarcastic wolf whistles and belly laughs following behind him from the other officers. Chambers upturned Jesse's trash can with the toe of his shoes and rested one foot on the top. His pants leg rose above his ankle exposing his socks: his wife Alexis smiled back at Jesse.

'This better for you, rookie?' Chambers teased, too

close to Jesse for his liking. He could make out the patch of hair on Chambers' face that he'd missed shaving and the bulging vein in his neck. Chambers had been waiting on this moment and Jesse wasn't going to give him the satisfaction of being bothered.

To be fair, Jesse could have wrapped his fist in Chambers' tie and brought his chin down on the side of his desk before the detective knew what was happening to him. His teeth would make an acquaintance with his fat lip and, if Jesse was lucky, he would have shattered a few. He imagined Chambers doubled over in pain. It'd wipe the cocky smirk off his face in an instant.

Instead, he turned to the detective and said, 'About time. I'm driving.'

With Main Street reserved for police vehicles only, it took Jesse mere minutes to make it to the mortuary across town. It was so quick that he and Chambers didn't even have time for a conversation, much to Jesse's pleasure. The two men made it painfully obvious that they didn't like each other. Everything aside from Rosie felt like a distraction to Jesse, but as soon as he'd slapped handcuffs on someone, he was getting Chambers back.

The Whitfield Family Mortuary sat on top of a grassy hill on the outskirts of town. The two-story traditional white brick structure was outlined in stately columns and the manicured bushes and elaborate concrete bird bath seemed too romantic for a place that housed the dead. The first floor held the funeral home, where Gage was based. In the basement mortuary, Grace presided.

As the second oldest business in Cinnamon Falls, the Whitfields had treated the departed residents of the town since its inception. Yet it was Jesse's first time making the trip on official police business.

He maneuvered the cruiser down the cobblestone driveway and parked next to Grace's Caprice. Chambers let out a low whistle when he got out of the car, eyeing the old-school beauty and its midnight-black candy paint. Classic cars were a staple in Cinnamon Falls. As soon as Jesse got his finances in order, he was going to get his own candy-painted Caprice.

'The funeral chick drives that?' Chambers questioned.

Jesse ignored Chambers and started toward the back door of the funeral home. Motion sensor floodlights popped on, following the men until they reached a set of wooden double doors. Jesse knocked softly, knowing Gage would be expecting them.

Chambers kissed his teeth while they waited. 'Listen, rookie. I don't want there to be no bad blood between us.'

Jesse shook his head and said, 'There's that rookie word again.'

'You're still wet behind the ears.' Chambers shrugged. 'I bet this is your first homicide.' Jesse was about to rebut when Chambers barreled on. 'I'm willing to bet this is the first time someone's even died unnaturally in this place.'

Jesse clenched his jaw so hard, sharp pain shot through his gums. 'What's your point?'

'You all have no idea what you're doing, do you?' The way Chambers was eyeing him, like he had a fortune teller's magic eight ball, Jesse wanted to put his head through the wall. 'Chief was so adamant about including you, but I think you're way too close to this. You couldn't even go inside the diner without collapsing. You expect me to believe you can handle seeing her on a metal slab? They told me you were some kind of war hero—'

Before Jesse knew what was happening, he had Chambers pinned against the wall. The detective's shirt and tie were crumpled between Jesse's iron fists and Chambers was inches away from his face. The bug-eyed terrified expression on his face was enough to satisfy Jesse for the next several weeks.

Gage Whitfield pulled open the door and took in the sight of the two men: Chambers inches off the ground with his back pressed against the wall and Jesse with fire in his eyes.

'Grace,' he called for his sister. He turned, unfazed, leaving the officers in the doorway. 'It's the police.'

Jesse released Chambers and took a step back while

the man smoothed out the wrinkles in his suit. He spotted Grace making her way toward them.

'Do your job and I'll do mine,' Jesse said after a long pause.

Focus, he told himself.

'Copy,' Chambers mumbled in response.

The mortuary was freezing. The sickly-sweet smell of death hung in the air. Jesse steeled himself. He wasn't going to give Chambers the satisfaction of seeing him break his character again. Jesse hated how easily he got under his skin.

Focus, he repeated, bringing himself to the present moment.

'I've known Jesse since we were kids,' Grace told Chambers as she meticulously organized her tools on a metal table. Dozens of what looked to be file cabinets ran from the floor to the ceiling.

'Has he always been this uptight?' Chambers asked as if Jesse wasn't in the room with them.

Grace looked up at Jesse sheepishly. 'Jesse's all business all the time,' she replied. The two shared a quick chuckle at his expense.

'Speaking of, let's get to it,' Jesse said.

'See?' they both said at the same time.

Jesse shook his head. He'd walked right into the trap. He joined in on their laughter and felt the tension release in his shoulders. Uncrossing his arms, he shook out the tightness that had built in his bones. When was the last time he'd laughed? It felt like he'd lived a million lifetimes since he left the diner last night.

'Are you sure you can handle this?' Grace asked. Under normal circumstances, he would have truthfully told her no. He was already having a hard time breathing and his stomach felt like it wanted to expel the dinner he'd had the night before.

Jesse nodded, refusing to meet eyes with Chambers who, Jesse knew, had a smirk on his face. Grace snapped on a pair of gloves and brought goggles down over her eyes. She handed the officers a mask and gloves each.

With great effort Grace pulled out one of the cabinet drawers and Jesse expected to see rows and rows of file folders. Instead, he was met face to face with Rosie's lifeless body. The woman who Jesse thought was invincible had her eyes shut tight. Her one-of-a-kind gray streak of hair was matted to her forehead with blood.

After a brief pause, Grace spoke in a sterile voice. 'Rosslyn Sienna Rose, age fifty-six, died of blunt force trauma to the head between the hours of ten and twelve p.m. last night.'

Rosslyn. Jesse realized he never knew her real name in all these years. She'd always been Rosie to him. Somehow, it humanized her; like learning that Superman was merely Clark Kent, after all.

'What are you thinking for the murder weapon?' Chambers asked, leaning in and inspecting Rosie's wounds. His face was just inches away from her body and his beady eyes roamed her like she was a buffet with too many options. Jesse tamed the lion roaring in his chest.

Grace shrugged.

'Your best guess?' Chambers prodded.

'Something heavy; maybe a skillet or one of her rolling pins. I'll know more when I can complete a full autopsy.'

Chambers pointed to the bruises that dotted Rosie's forearms. With a gloved hand he gently lifted her arm, exposing a semicircular bruise on her forearm. He lifted the other arm and discovered the bruise had a twin. He brought her hands over her face like she was playing peek-a-boo, revealing a circle-shaped print.

'She fought her attacker,' Chambers said, mimicking the action of hitting her. 'But they must have bested the woman, bashing her in the head for the final blow.'

'That could be true,' Grace offered. 'One more thing.' Grace ran her thumb over a black-blue circular bruise on Rosie's bicep. 'This bruise looks older than these.' She pointed to Rosie's arms, showing them the difference in color.

'Did Rosie have a spouse?' Chambers asked the room.

'I heard she was messing 'round with Harvey Briggs,' Grace volunteered.

Chambers looked to Jesse for confirmation, but Grace's information was merely speculation. Jesse had also heard that Rosie had been messing around with Mr. Briggs, but he had no idea if it was true or not. He wasn't privy to her personal business, and Harvey Briggs wasn't exactly the kind of man to take a woman out on the town to show her off.

'Who's that?' Chambers asked with a light in his eyes. He looked like a dog who'd just gotten a bone. He flipped out a pad and scribbled the name down.

Grace answered, 'He owns the junkyard and the used car lot on the edge of town, out past Ol' Man Milton's farm.'

Chambers scribbled on. 'And do you think he was in town last night? He could have come to the diner, they got in an argument and boom, over the head.' He imitated hitting someone. 'Dead Rosie.'

Jesse shook his head. Mr. Briggs was a recluse and a man of very few words, but was he a murderer? Jesse didn't recall seeing him in the diner. His crew were the only ones left at closing.

'When will you know more?' Jesse asked, consulting his watch.

Grace shifted her weight and placed one hand on her hip. 'Rosie isn't the only dead person in Cinnamon Falls, you know.'

'Make this one a priority,' Chambers advised before

Jesse could ask her nicely. 'Chief needs this one solved fast.'

'I don't take orders from you or Vernon. I'll do the best I can,' she compromised.

'Thank you, Grace,' Jesse said. 'Anything you can do to help us out, we'd appreciate it.'

He and Chambers turned to go when he added, 'If you find anything else, call me.'

She saluted sarcastically before the officers closed the door on her, leaving her as the only living being in the chilly room.

Chapter 7

Nia

The police had Main Street blocked off from Rosie's Diner all the way down to Bones' Barbershop; no one could get in or out. For businesses that sat between Rosie's and Bones' place, that meant there would be no traffic that day. The businesses on the outside of the barrier were slammed with confused, scared customers and angry owners alike. Even though Nia's parents were grieving there was still money to be made, which meant there was coffee to be prepared and ice cream to be served.

This time of the morning, their bestseller was the Cinnamon Queen: one hefty scoop of Ma-Clara's original cinnamon swirl ice cream floating over piping hot espresso and crowned with whipped cream and caramel drizzle. Nia could make them with her eyes closed at this point.

Even Midnight, a notorious homebody and all-round human hater, did her part in lifting the mood.

She moseyed between the shop's tables, bringing squeals of joy to customers who she allowed to scratch between her ears. Nia guessed she could feel the weight in the atmosphere too.

As much as Nia wanted to help, she couldn't concentrate on anyone but Rosie. After she spilled her second tray of Cinnamon Queens, her parents kindly suggested that she get some fresh air. She didn't want to be alone with her wandering thoughts; but the shop, filled with customers speculating about Rosie's quality of life, was starting to make her feel like she was drowning.

It immediately brought her back to high school before Sienna was found. Everyone had to share their personal story about *her* best friend before they knew she'd died. It was maddening how quickly people became vultures to death's leftovers.

Midnight hopped in the window, eyeballing Nia's every move as she stepped outside at her parents' suggestion. From Nia's vantage point, she would normally be able to see Rosie's bright red glowing logo and know the diner was open for business. Today it was off and even the street looked sad about it.

Police officers swarmed around the barriers that lined the road. News vans were parked at the perimeter, their cameras craned to see above the chaos and give the at-home viewers an exclusive view of the tragedy.

Nia was still in disbelief. Her mother said that Rosie was gone. Gone where?

Rosie would never leave Cinnamon Falls or her diner behind, and she definitely wouldn't leave Sienna. And if her mother didn't mean it literally, that meant . . . Nia couldn't even finish her thought. Someone like Rosie didn't just die. She was way too cool for something so trivial as death.

Nia knew that if she could see Rosie's Diner herself, she might be able to wrap her mind around what had happened.

Outside, Nia crossed the street and watched the police reroute commuters and buses from Main Street and Nutmeg Avenue to Cinnamon Way, one street over. The streets intersected a few blocks up from Rosie's. All she had to do was walk up Cinnamon Way and double back once the barriers stopped. It was a roundabout way to get back to Main Street and would take her nearly twenty minutes, but it would be worth it.

If she was stopped, she could blame it on Niles. Cinnamon Falls High sat at the end of Cinnamon Way. She'd pretend that she was picking him up from school and walking him back to the parlor. It was believable enough, and thankfully, her father's last name still held a lot of weight in town. If she had to, she could pull the Bennett Family card and talk her way out of anything. Or as her last resort, she could call Jesse.

She hadn't been able to stop thinking about him since they left Rosie's Diner the night before. She had so many unanswered questions that were floating around in the back of her mind. How long had he been an officer? Why didn't he mention it? Had he brought those roses for her? Most importantly, did he miss her? Why didn't he call? Her number hadn't changed, and neither had her Instagram handle. Did he ever think about her? Or had he moved on with his life completely? Had he found someone else to love? Nia couldn't blame him if he had. They hadn't left on good terms. In fact, Nia hadn't left on good terms with anyone.

Nia knew that her mother thought she had fled from Cinnamon Falls in an attempt to escape her grief surrounding Sienna's death. At the time, Jesse couldn't understand why going to Barkwood Bridge, a place that used to be so romantic for them, made her physically ill. Nia hadn't the words to explain how she was feeling and thought it would be easier if she dealt with her feelings on her own, instead of lashing out at everyone around her.

She wanted to go to a place where no one knew her name, or her family, and wouldn't look at her with sympathetic eyes and placating statements, knowing that her best friend had taken her own life. No one understood how a place with fewer than eight thousand people made Nia feel so claustrophobic.

Atlanta had been different. It was the fresh start she desperately needed. The life she curated away from Cinnamon Falls was perfect. Or had felt perfect.

How did everything she'd worked so hard for disappear so suddenly? And as if the universe couldn't get any more ironic, six years later Nia ran right back to the place she'd been dying to get away from.

The thought stopped her in her tracks: she was a runner. When home became too overwhelming, she ran to Atlanta. When her dream life exploded before her eyes, she packed the same bags she left in and ran back home. Now with Rosie gone – Nia realized she had nowhere left to run.

A wave of emotions crashed over her. Every time she got something good in her life, it was snatched from under her. First Sienna, then Bryant, and now Rosie? Her chest felt tight, and she had to sit down on the cold concrete to center herself. Her nose stung with incoming tears. Nia couldn't swat them away fast enough as they started to stream out of her eyes. Her body shook under the weight of the overwhelming sorrow that wracked her heart.

Everything was falling apart, and she couldn't do anything to stop it.

After the sobs subsided, Nia realized how crazy she must have looked. This was surely rock bottom. What would Sienna think of her right now? She'd be livid, Nia was certain. Her mother was rumored to be dead, and Nia was crying on the curb about it? Sure, Nia's life had gone to shit in a matter of days, but there were more pressing issues at hand.

Nia collected herself and continued walking,

concentrating on the rhythm of putting one foot in front of the other. She reached the intersection where Cinnamon Way and Main Street met, and just as she predicted, the barriers stopped.

Patrolmen were busy directing traffic and weren't paying her any attention. Before she could be seen, Nia ducked behind Guy's Grocery. A thin alley connected all the businesses on Main Street; and if Nia was being honest, labeling it as an alley was too generous. It was more like an extended slab of concrete where most owners kept their trash or leftover storage. Here, Nia was going to put her expensive Pilates classes to the test if she was going to make it to Rosie's Diner without being seen.

After three intense close calls, where Nia had to press her back against the buildings and clap her hand over her mouth not to be seen or heard, she finally made it to Rosie's back door. She thought that the police would be surrounding the place on all sides and that she'd be arrested without question, making the climbing and scratches all for naught, but there was no one guarding the door. She felt the handle, hoping her lucky streak continued, but it was locked.

Nia hoped that Rosie had remained the same woman and hadn't moved the spare key she'd hidden for Sienna. She counted the bricks that rounded the back door's frame and lifted the fourth one, finding the weathered key underneath. She slipped it into the lock and turned the doorknob quietly, hoping there wasn't a team of officers on the other side with their guns drawn ready to take her head off. Instead, she found Rosie's kitchen to be ghostly empty, save for the appliances waiting to be used. A bare sink, a cold stove, and empty prep station stared back at her.

Memories of happier times, when she and Sienna would go to Rosie's after classes, felt like a lifetime ago. Now, there was no soft clinking of dishes by satisfied customers, or the mouthwatering smell of freshly baked cinnamon buns. There was no hum of chatter from the regulars who always greeted the workers by name. Rosie's kitchen staff weren't shouting out orders or laughing at each other's antics. And worst of all, there was no Rosie, with the megawatt smile or hugs that bordered on smothering.

Nia could make out a low rumble of voices on the main floor; police, she assumed. She removed her sneakers so that the rubber soles didn't squeak against the floor and alert them to her presence. She made sure to keep herself low to the ground as she crawled through the kitchen toward Rosie's office. It was the last place she'd seen her alive. Nia remembered how striking Rosie looked, like she'd have decades to go before she was on death's radar.

'What happened to you?' Nia whispered to the empty room. She softly closed the door behind her. She thought the place would be ransacked, but it seemed like the police hadn't made it this far yet.

Rosie's office was a mess and a half. Unopened

boxes of supplies crowded the floor. File cabinets were stuffed to the brim, drawers spilled over with pages of what looked like unsuccessful recipes, inventory logs, and bank statements.

Framed photos of Sienna hugged the office walls. Little Sienna missing her two front teeth smiled widely for a school picture, another showed a slightly younger version of her gripping an oversized stuffed animal happily. Tree-printed wrapping paper was crumpled at her feet. It must have been Christmas. The last photo was a cutting of the front page of *The Cinnamon Chronicle*; the night Sienna won Cinnamon Queen. She looked timeless; her hair piled on top of her head in pinned juicy curls, clutching an enormous bouquet of red roses to her chest, waving to the crowd, sitting on top of a green 1970 Mercury Cougar.

Nia's eyes brought her to the landline mounted on the wall. When she was leaving the diner last night, Rosie was on the phone. Who did she call? Nia looked through the history on the Caller ID next to the phone. Nia and Sienna always made fun of Rosie for having a landline, but today it worked out in her favor. Nia used her phone to snap pictures of all the numbers from the last few days. If she asked nicely, maybe Jesse could tell her who they belonged to.

She moved on to Rosie's desk. It was covered in papers and receipts with Rosie's loopy signature. There were paint swatches of a kaleidoscope of pastel colors. Did Rosie plan on redecorating? Nia flipped through everything, careful to keep it all in its place and in order. Underneath the papers, she discovered a desk calendar. It was open to October 2019 – the exact month and year Sienna died, like time had simply stopped.

Nia ran her fingers across the Saturday of her last Fall Festival – when Sienna was found at the bottom of the Falls. Rosie had never recovered from that night, and if Nia was being totally honest with herself, she hadn't either. In the column circled in red marker were the words 'MEET A. L.' Nia snapped a picture of it.

She moved on to the double desk drawers. She pulled open the top drawer, finding the normal contents: pens, Post-it notes, paper clips, and an array of rose-printed office supplies. The bottom drawer held an accordion file of pink rose folders. Nia fingered the tabs at the top naming the folders' contents: tax documents and sensitive paperwork for employees. Nia pulled the files toward her to see deeper into the drawer. She found a finger-sized hole in the metal underneath. A false bottom.

With one hand she found the flashlight on her cell phone and, with the other, she pulled up the metal frame. Inside she found a manila folder that looked different from the others. This one was stuffed with clippings, papers, receipts, and other documents Nia couldn't make out.

Carefully, Nia pulled the thick file out and placed it on the desk. A piece of paper escaped, floating across Rosie's desk, and Nia came face to face with her best friend, pixelated and preserved in black and white. Nia recognized the picture from their senior yearbook photos. She remembered how they practised their makeup on each other so there would be no flashback. After all, Sienna said, these pictures would live on forever. Even on paper and all these years later, Nia could feel the intensity in Sienna's eyes.

The picture was from an article in *The Cinnamon Chronicle* detailing Sienna's death. Nia flipped open the folder and read the headline:

TRAGEDY AT THE FALLS: LOCAL TEEN FOUND DEAD IN APPARENT SUICIDE

By: Elaine Matthias

Cinnamon Falls, October 7 – The peaceful town of Cinnamon Falls was shaken yesterday evening when the body of 18-year-old Sienna Rose was discovered at the base of the town's iconic waterfall. Authorities have preliminarily ruled the death as an apparent suicide.

Sienna, a beloved member of the community and recent graduate of Cinnamon Falls High School, had been crowned Cinnamon Queen just hours earlier during the town's annual Fall Festival. The weekend-long celebration turned somber as news of Sienna's death spread.

Nia couldn't read anymore. She had the article practically memorized anyway, having read it over and over many times before, wishing she could find the answers as to why Sienna would take her own life. The unanswered questions still haunted Nia to this day. She hadn't been to Barkwood Bridge since.

Why hadn't Sienna talked to her? Nia hadn't wanted to believe that Sienna was suffering in silence, and neither had Rosie. They had both learned to live with the fact that they may not have known her as well as they thought. Nia flipped past the article and felt her breath catch in her throat.

Official-looking documents with letterheads and signatures stared back at Nia. She grazed over words like *skull fracture* and *lacerations*, *contusion*, and *trauma*. She flicked through the rest of the papers and spotted red question marks circled in the columns or arrows pointing to chunks of information. It was Sienna's autopsy report.

Nia was about to start on the rest of the file when soft footfalls sounded just outside the closed door. She clutched the folder to her chest and ducked under the desk, squeezing herself into a ball for the umpteenth time that day and held her breath.

The office door flew open. 'Tell the guys to get this too, will you?' someone said. Nia couldn't make out who the voice belonged to, but she knew it wasn't Jesse; and if the officer took two more steps he would find her under the desk. Nia pulled herself impossibly tighter and clinched her eyes shut for good measure.

'Tragic,' the other officer mumbled. 'First her daughter jumps off Barkwood and now Rosie gets whacked a few years later. Never seen anything like it.'

Nia's eyes popped open. Rosie was *murdered*? Nia bit her arm to keep herself from sobbing out loud. Who would have killed Rosie? And why?

'It's a shame. I loved Rosie,' another voice added. 'I hope whoever did this gets the needle, man.'

'Rosie didn't deserve this.'

The voices faded away and Nia took that as her cue to unfold herself from her hiding space and get the hell out of there. It was only a matter of time before they discovered her shoes at the back door. Nia searched around quickly and spotted a plastic bag. She dumped the folder and all its contents inside. She tied it tight, slipping the handle around her wrist, and made a mad dash for the door.

In one swoop she grabbed her shoes and slipped out of the back door the way she came. Before she headed back up the alley she replaced the spare key under the fourth brick above the door. Then, without looking back, she did what she did best: she ran.

It took much convincing; Nia even had to pull the Bennett Family card, before she was allowed behind the service desk at the police station. Even though she and Angie had gone to school together their whole lives, she still was hesitant about granting Nia permission to go past the counter. The force was on high alert, rightfully so. But this was an emergency.

'Through the hallway to the right,' Angie directed Nia while she answered the non-stop ringing phone on her desk.

'Thank you, Ang.' Nia smiled, but Angie was already on to the next pressing matter, hooking the phone to her ear, her hands flying across the keyboard.

Nia had never seen the inner workings of a police station other than on scripted television shows. Pictures of officers, some she recognized, others she'd only heard about through word of mouth, lined the walls. The acrid smell of burnt coffee made her wince.

She found Jesse at his desk, alone, with one hand cradling his head; the other was gripping a pen so hard his knuckles were white. He was concentrating on a list of some sort; several lines of text had been scratched through from what Nia could see.

'What is it?' he barked, without looking up.

Nia's heart was in her throat when she asked, 'Can we talk?'

Jesse shot upward, knocking his head against the lamp that dangled overhead. He straightened his clothes, brushing what looked like a bunch of crumbs to the floor. Nia never knew Jesse to be a snacker unless he was stressed, and judging from the open bags of potato chips, he hadn't been eating well.

'Nia! I wasn't expecting it to be you, I'm sorry, I just—'

She searched her former lover's eyes, red-rimmed and puffy. She could tell he'd been crying. Her eyes probably looked the same.

'Is it true?' Nia asked on wobbly legs. She'd sprinted all the way to the police station – the only things powering her were determination and sheer adrenaline. By the time she reached the station she'd run out of both.

'Sit down.' Jesse moved quickly, offering her his chair. Nia sank into the cracked leather seat. Her legs felt like static. Jesse found a bottle of water and unscrewed the cap, handing it to her. She drank the whole thing down in four large gulps.

'Deep breaths,' Jesse coached her, taking her hands in his. 'Come on, Ni. Breathe in and hold for four seconds. Breathe out and count to four.' Nia nodded, following his orders. Jesse breathed with her, his face just inches from hers. She was so nervous that the breathing technique was starting to be counterproductive.

'You okay?' he asked. 'You must have heard about Rosie?'

Nia nodded, keeping her eyes on the floor. If she looked up at him, she was bound to liquefy. He hooked one finger under her chin, tilting it toward him.

'I'm going to find out who did this.' His voice was different; a deeper baritone that had the finality of a Shaw promise.

'I just don't understand. I heard she was killed.' Nia could barely get the words out; they were too horrific to repeat. 'Why?' she pleaded. Tears spilled out of her eyes before she could stop them.

'Please, Ni.' Jesse pulled her into his arms and cradled her, pressing her into his body. 'I won't stop until I figure this out, I promise you. I loved Rosie too—'

The mention of Rosie's name made Nia remember why she'd come to the station in the first place. Reluctantly, she peeled herself from the hypnotizing heat of his body. 'I need you to take a look at something.'

'I'm swamped, Ni,' he started, gesturing around to the busy station. 'Cap is on my head and Angie will probably get her ass chewed off for even letting you back here.'

'I just need five minutes.' Nia shook the plastic bag at him and proceeded to empty the contents onto his desk, fanning everything out.

Jesse's eagle eyes searched the pages. He fingered Sienna's autopsy report. 'Where'd you find this? Is this stuff all about Sienna's death?'

'I think so,' Nia responded, cautiously dancing

around questions she knew he didn't need to know the answer to. He was still the police, after all, and she was sure stealing from a crime scene was some kind of arrestable offense.

Nia chewed her bottom lip as she watched Jesse carefully examine each page. Finally, he shrugged. 'Rosie's daughter died tragically. It looks like she was just trying to make sense of it all.' He was quiet for a beat, then added in a knowing voice, 'I think we all were at the time.'

He crossed his hands over his chest and Nia knew that the minuscule magical moment in time where he was Jesse, her ex, was over. The wall was back up. Sienna's death had been a sensitive time in their relationship, and it was clear there was still unfinished business between them, things they both needed to say. But for now, he was back to being a hard-nosed officer with a pressing deadline.

'What if this has something to do with Rosie's murder?'

'Where did you even get this, Nia? Tell me you didn't go to the diner?'

He couldn't have expected her to tell the truth. 'I—'

'Actually, I don't want to know.' Jesse placed his hands over his ears and shook his head. 'I need you to go home and get some rest. Let me and the guys here figure this out.' Her hands were in his again, and he was using that articulated voice parents use for unruly toddlers. 'We have enough on our plates here as it is. Every single resident is clogging the tip line with rumors they heard second and third hand. Please just let us handle this.'

'At least let me help,' Nia pleaded. She was convinced she'd found that folder for a reason. 'This can't be a coincidence, Jesse.'

A tall, slim officer leaned over the cubicle wall between his desk and Jesse's. 'Sorry to break up this lover's quarrel, but we gotta go.'

Jesse groaned and snatched his jacket off the back of his chair.

'This time, I'm driving.' The other officer ran ahead while Jesse hung back. He stooped a few inches down, making sure he was face to face with his former lover.

'Promise me you'll stay out of this investigation, Nia. I can't have anything happening to you, or your family.'

Nia agreed wordlessly. Jesse squeezed her tiny frame against his and followed his partner out of the door. As she watched him jog away from her, Nia realized that she may have left Cinnamon Falls physically, but her heart had stayed.

Chapter 8
Jesse

Jesse suffered through twenty-seven agonizing minutes of questioning about his love life by the time the pair of officers made it to the outskirts of town. They hadn't even managed to leave the parking lot before Chambers asked a question about Nia. Jesse thought he'd made it clear that their personal lives were off-limits. They were coworkers, not friends.

'All I'm saying is she's cute. You should give her a chance.' Chambers shrugged. That was the fourth time he'd called Nia cute. Nia wasn't *cute*. Household pets were cute. Bows on newborn babies were cute. Otters were cute.

Nia, on the other hand, was otherworldly; a kind of beauty that grown men rode into battle for. Her brown skin, like polished amber, glowed warm and rich in every hue. Her hair was its own masterpiece, sometimes pressed long and silky, cascading past her shoulders, other times a crown of soft curls that framed her face. She wasn't tall, but she carried herself with quiet confidence, like someone who didn't need a stage to command attention. Those big brown eyes could stop him mid-sentence, wide and observant, always calculating, always seeing more than she let on. Her button nose crinkled when she laughed. Nia moved through the world like someone who took life seriously, because she did, but there was an elusive softness in her too, especially for the people she loved.

Jesse hadn't thought he'd have such a visceral reaction to seeing her again after all these years. When Morgan said Nia was back in town and that she would be joining them for dinner, he was nervous, sure. Seeing his ex-girlfriend after such a long time apart was nerve-wracking, and made Jesse wish for the days when he was still taking orders in the military. That was easier than sitting for an hour beside the woman who'd owned his heart since he was twelve.

Seeing her last night snatched the breath from his body. He wanted to maintain his cool, calm nature but his brain sounded like TV static when Nia came around. He could live in the echoes of her laughter. He still remembered the unbelievable softness of her skin, and the way her body molded into his when they would cuddle together on her parents' couch. Those memories had carried him through the toughest times of his life when he was away from his family in foreign lands, not knowing if he'd make it back home in one piece.

When he saw Nia at the station with red-rimmed eyes, he would have fought the gods for making her cry. Even though she'd caused him the worst heartache he could imagine, he had to admit he'd never fallen out of love with her. She'd left him, that was the truth of the matter. But Nia left everyone. As much as he wanted to hate her, he couldn't.

He didn't know how he'd react if his best friend, who he spent every waking moment with, suddenly took their own life. Her partner in crime was here one day and gone the next in the blink of an eye. Jesse knew Nia had been struggling after Sienna died, and he thought he was doing everything he could to be there for her. But it wasn't enough. Nothing could bring Sienna back and that was all Nia wanted.

She could have stuck a knife through Jesse's chest the day she told him that she was leaving Cinnamon Falls for good. She broke up with him so matter-of-factly that he had to question if the love they shared had really occurred. Or had their relationship been a figment of his wildest imagination? In many ways she had been his anchor; he saw his entire future in her eyes. He was content with spending the rest of his life as her partner.

Once they broke up, she left the following day, and Jesse was in shock that first year without her; floating through life like an escaped birthday balloon.

After the pain settled in, the second, third, and fourth years were a blur. Without giving it a second thought, he joined the military. That time in his life had been spent between the bottom of a bottle and the helm of a rifle. He'd been so wild, so reckless; years were spent buried under the need to feel anything other than hurt. His state-appointed therapist told him he had to *feel* his feelings in order to heal from the things that hurt him.

What haunted him the most was regret. Why didn't he go after her? He'd heard in passing conversation that she'd moved to Atlanta, just a few hours away. He could have gotten in his car and gone after his girl years ago. How much of his life would have been different if he hadn't let her walk out on him? Why hadn't he fought for her?

'This the place?' Chambers asked, yanking Jesse from his runaway thoughts. Chambers leaned over the steering wheel and got a good look at his surroundings.

Jesse hadn't been out to Briggs' place in years. He remembered dragging his father to Briggs' lot when he had saved enough money to purchase his first car. It used to be filled with rows of cars so shiny, he could see them gleaming from the road.

Briggs had everything: from beaters to new models and some in between. Jesse vividly recalled Grace buying her Chevy Caprice from Briggs. He'd been envious ever since. It was tradition for seniors to show off their classic cars and drive down Main Street during the Fall Festival. Then, at the very end, the Cinnamon King and Queen were revealed, usually in the best ride of them all. Most kids borrowed them from family or friends, but if you bought one, you bought it from Briggs.

Jesse hadn't been a student in high school in quite a while and maybe times had changed, he considered. Still, Jesse wondered what had gone wrong because Briggs' property looked like it'd been completely abandoned. A few corroded cars sat in the overgrown lot; determined grass pushed through the concrete and sprang up around the wheels. The whole place looked like it should have been bulldozed years ago.

Jesse nodded reluctantly and could see a cloud of negative thoughts forming in Chambers' mind. He slowed the car to a stop next to a rusted gate that was guarding a winding dirt road up to Briggs' trailer. A weathered sign hung on a nail that read, 'KEEP OUT'. Next to it was another smaller sign that read, 'HARVEY'S USED CARS'.

'Not exactly the best businessman,' Chambers mumbled. He hopped out of the car and tried the gate's latch, and to Jesse's surprise, it popped open with ease.

Chambers guided his car up the small hill and Jesse studied the ghosts of the good cars they passed on the way in, rusted over and crumbling. Harvey's trailer sat at the far end of the lot and even from the car Jesse could see that its front door was ajar.

Chambers got out and removed his service weapon

from its holster. His beady eyes did a continuous sweep of the vast property while they approached the dilapidated home.

If Briggs wanted to shoot us, he would have already, Jesse wanted to say.

'Mr. Briggs?' Jesse called before ascending the steps. Silence answered him. A curious wind swept dirt around their shoes while they waited for Briggs to answer. The inside of the trailer remained dark.

Jesse got louder. 'Mr. Briggs? It's Jesse, Robert Shaw's son.'

'That's how you identify yourself?' Chambers muttered, stepping around Jesse. 'Harvey Briggs, this is the Cinnamon Falls PD, come to the door!' he demanded, raising his weapon toward the door. He inched his finger toward the trigger.

Jesse pushed the nose of the gun down. 'This is a friendly visit,' he reminded Chambers.

A recluse like Harvey Briggs wouldn't take kindly to police at his front door, especially ones with weapons drawn. Behind the trailer was a thick line of trees – the end of Old Man Milton's farm. He could have seen them coming and ran. Jesse wondered if he was standing just feet away, watching them.

'Friendly, my ass. This is our number one suspect, start acting like it.'

Not to me, Jesse thought. He started up the wooden stairs, hoping the sagging slats would hold under his weight. The screen door was barely hanging on by a crumbling pair of hinge screws and a prayer. Another kick of wind made the door swing open and Jesse took that opportunity to peek inside.

An astonishingly neat trailer with a tidy kitchen stared back at him. Two plates and two cups had been stacked carefully in the dish drainer. The white electric stove was spotless as if it hadn't been cooked on, ever. To his right, under the window, sat a small circular table covered in a light blue and white checkered tablecloth. Two wooden chairs had been upholstered to match.

Further into the trailer, a tan plaid couch that had seen better days sagged against the far wall. The patchy carpet had fresh vacuum lines and a television almost the size of the trailer wall itself was perched on a three-legged coffee table directly in front of the couch. Past the living room were three open doors. Jesse could make out the corner of a bed and a nightstand in the room at the end of the hall: Harvey's bedroom.

Jesse trod lightly, unsure of what he'd find if he went in any further.

'Mr. Briggs?' Jesse called again and there was no answer. 'Anybody home?'

Chambers shouldered past him and into the trailer. His gun traced the length of the room and he continued down the hall, dragging in dirt. Jesse watched as Chambers checked every room, weapon at the ready. His footprints tracked this way and that.

If Jesse were Harvey Briggs, he'd be sending the police station a bill.

'He's not here,' Chambers said, stating the obvious. 'He must have skipped town.'

'Maybe he's on vacation,' Jesse offered, however implausible.

Chambers scoffed. 'Vacation, my ass. Look at this place.' He plucked a white flower from a vase on the kitchen table. 'He's got real flowers in this dump, are you kidding me?'

'Let's go,' Jesse said.

Chambers nodded and turned to go. 'When we get back to the station, I'm putting an APB out on this Harvey Briggs guy. Y'all told me he's this big time car salesman and this man is one doorframe away from being unhoused; he's mysteriously missing, and you want me to believe he *didn't* hurt Rosie?' Chambers listed each reason on his fingers.

'I don't know what to believe, alright?' Jesse fired back. 'I'm just as confused as you are—' he fussed, following Chambers down the steps and into the car.

'Oh, I'm not confused, rookie.' Chambers wagged his finger at him like he knew something that Jesse didn't. 'Despite what you see on TV, murder ain't always some big mystery to be solved.' He slid inside the sedan and snapped his seat belt into place. 'In real life, it's pretty obvious.' Chambers threw his car in reverse and skidded out of Harvey's lot. 'This is our guy, mark my words.'

'We have no evidence of that,' Jesse reminded him. 'You're just speculating.'

Chambers kissed his teeth. 'This makes the most sense and you know it. You're so caught up in your feelings for this place that you can't see how it's clouding your judgment.'

Jesse scoffed. 'Nice to meet you, kettle. They call me the pot. *You're* talking to me about clouded judgment? Hanging this on Briggs is jumping the gun, man, and you know it.'

Chambers grumbled, 'And they told me you were MP. What were you doing in the military police, ordering supplies or something? Chief said he wanted this solved asap—'

Jesse's pocket vibrated just as he was about to respond. He dug his phone out and placed one finger in his ear to drown out Chambers' ranting and answered.

'Right up here on the left,' Jesse instructed. Chambers pulled into the driveway of Jesse's home and put the car in park.

'Nice digs,' he commented.

Jesse always wondered how a stranger would view his home. When he bought the modest, two-story, brown brick family home a couple of years ago he thought he'd have a family of his own to fill it. In some way, that was still his reality. He didn't have a wife, the picket fence or the dog, but he had a lifetime of love waiting just beyond the front door.

'Thanks, um, you don't have to get out if you don't want to. This won't take long.' It physically pained him to realize that Chambers could possibly be his first guest.

'It's all good,' Chambers said coolly and unsnapped his seat belt.

'My parents live with me,' Jesse admitted. 'Fair warning, my mother will offer you food.'

'Good, 'cause I'm starving.' Chambers rubbed his hands together in excitement.

'I warned you,' Jesse mumbled, and stepped inside.

Evelyn was glued to the television when he walked in the door. On the screen, a blonde woman cried dramatically and then it faded to black. His mother was relaxing in the oversized recliner chair in the living room. Her feet were propped up on two pillows like Jesse always did for her before bed. *Her ankles must be swollen again*, Jesse figured. On the TV tray next to her was an empty teacup and cereal bowl. The bouquet of roses he'd brought home were placed in the bay window on her other side, getting lots of natural sunlight. They looked stunning between the hanging jade plants.

Jesse stepped into the room; his mother's warm scent of vanilla and shea butter greeted him first. He leaned over the back of the recliner and planted a kiss on the top of her head.

She turned to look up at him. A smile of surprise lit up her face. Jesse would never get tired of seeing it. Back when he was playing high school sports, he'd always look for his mother in the stands. It made him play a little harder and run a little faster to hear her cheering him on.

'JJ, what're you doing home so early? Did Rob call you?'

He was grateful that the news about Rosie hadn't reached his house yet. It was just another normal day for his parents.

'Yeah, Dad called just a few minutes ago.'

'He's around here somewhere. Look at what he got me!' She motioned to her flowers with a smile that spread from ear to ear. 'It's our anniversary.'

'They're gorgeous,' he responded.

She noticed Chambers standing in the doorway, looming over his shoulder.

'Vernon finally gave you a partner? I'm Evelyn, Jesse's mother.' She extended her bejeweled hand.

Jesse's mother was a lover of fine things, and jewelry was no exception. A true fashionista to her core, his mother always looked her best even when she didn't feel it. Why she needed rings on every finger when she spent most of her time in the house, Jesse didn't know. But that was how his mother had always been, and aging wasn't slowing her down one bit.

Chambers stepped into the room, took Jesse's mother's manicured hand, and brought it to his lips.

'A pleasure to meet you, Mrs. Shaw. You've got a lovely home.'

Jesse wanted to put him in a chokehold until he begged for mercy.

She smirked, flattered. 'My son gets his interior design skills from me,' she bragged.

'Of course he does. It looks like a magazine centerfold in here.' Chambers was laying it on thick, and the way his mother was blushing, she was eating it up. The truth was his mother had hated the chestnut-brown leather couches. She said it looked like frat boys lived upstairs. But the oversized recliner had grown on her and it was now her favorite spot in the house.

Jesse rolled his eyes and left the two of them conversing to find his father. Jesse had barely put one toe in the kitchen before he heard him fussing. 'Pop, what's going on?'

'I'm going to make us sandwiches for lunch.' Jesse took a look at the ingredients his father had displayed on the counter: lettuce, tomato, onion, and thick sliced bacon. 'But this ain't the cheese we like.'

Robert tossed the grass-fed aged cheddar to Jesse, who examined the package, realizing his grave mistake. Last week when his father added sliced cheese to the grocery list, he'd forgotten that they liked a particular brand from Guy's Grocery. The offending cheese was from Cinnamon Grove. It was the same kind of cheese, just in different packaging, and better for him more than likely; but the old man was particular. Jesse should have known better.

'It comes in a blue package.'

'You called me off work about cheese?' Jesse folded his arms. 'It's the same thing, Pop.'

'It ain't the same thing. I took one look at it and knew. It doesn't even smell right.'

'I'll bring some home tonight, okay?' Jesse offered. 'For now you'll have to eat your sandwich without cheese.'

'Who eats a sandwich without cheese?'

'Plenty of people!' Jesse fussed back. 'You don't need all that cholesterol anyway.'

'You ain't no doctor,' his father grumbled.

'I am the police, though,' Jesse countered.

His father beckoned him closer and lowered his voice. 'What happened this morning? You ran out of here in the middle of the night . . . Ain't been back since. Your mother was worried.'

Jesse knew that was code. His father was actually the one who was worried and didn't want to admit it. Jesse shook his head. 'Not good, Pop,' he relayed.

His father harrumphed. 'They finally got you workin' something?'

Jesse nodded. He grabbed two bottles of water out of the fridge for the road.

'That your partner in there?' His father pointed toward the other room.

'You could call him that,' Jesse responded, taking

a look over his shoulder. Bits of Chambers' conversation floated over to the kitchen. Then, a raucous laugh exploded from the living room.

'He from the city?' his father questioned.

Jesse nodded. 'Atlanta PD.'

His father frowned disapprovingly. 'Tell him to back up off my woman.'

Jesse sputtered out a laugh, but his father's expression didn't change. 'He's married, Pop.'

'Did I stutter?'

'We're leaving now,' Jesse said, shaking his head. 'I'll bring some cheese from Guy's when I get back home, okay?'

'Thank you,' Robert replied. He arranged his bagel on a plate and spread both sides with a generous amount of creamed cheese. Jesse watched as his father carried his lunch to the other room and introduced himself to his guest.

Chambers and his mother were standing at the mantel above the fireplace that held childhood photos, mementos, and long-forgotten memories of victories won while Jesse matriculated through school. They gestured to a photo of Jesse at prom; his arms were wrapped around his then girlfriend, Nia. Her eyes were hidden behind her cheeks, exposing her glistening white teeth. Jesse, on the other hand, was looking at Nia with a goofy smile and an expression that so clearly read that he was a teenager madly in love.

Jesse could still picture that night in his head. Nia had worn a sparkling sequin, midnight-blue gown that moved like liquid when she danced. Her natural curly hair had been pressed straight and styled in long juicy curls that framed her face. After all the years, Jesse still kept the memory bottled up in his mind. He tapped into it when he needed to escape.

'Lookin' sharp,' Chambers teased, flipping the picture around to him. He raised one eyebrow in curiosity. Jesse squared his shoulders. He wasn't providing any further explanation.

'He shoulda been nominated for Cinnamon King, he looked so good,' Evelyn gushed, wiping a film of dust from the glass and putting it back in its place.

She'd just gotten her hands on Jesse's baby pictures when his phone vibrated. It was a text from the Chief asking him to report back to the station. Moments later, Chambers patted his pocket, clearly having received the same message.

'We gotta go,' Jesse announced.

'Already?' Evelyn asked. 'I was just about to show him your—'

'Now,' Jesse demanded, pushing Chambers out of the room.

'Come on,' Chambers begged. 'We were just starting to have fun!'

On the way back to the station, Chambers broke the silence in the car. 'When you said your parents lived with you, I thought you were lying.'

'Why would I lie about that?' Jesse questioned.

'It's just . . .' Chambers paused for a moment, pressing his lips together like there were things he wanted to say, but couldn't. 'I respect that, man, that's all. Caring for your parents can't be easy. My hat's off to you, for sure.'

Jesse watched the detective while he fought back his emotions and kept his eyes on the road. Chambers brought a fist to his mouth. His lips trembled.

'You lost someone?' Jesse asked on a hunch. Only a few things made a grown man tear up, and losing a parent was high up on the list.

Chambers nodded and cleared his throat. 'It's been a while. My parents passed when I was in high school. I wish I would have gotten the chance to take care of them like . . .' He gestured to Jesse. 'She reminded me of my mom, that's all.'

'My condolences to you, man,' Jesse said. He couldn't think of anything else to say to bring him comfort. Besides, he was sure that he'd heard it all in the years between now and then. It was the thing Jesse feared the most: losing his parents. Chambers was a grown man with a family of his own now and still couldn't talk about his parents without crying. Jesse was dreading the day he'd have to face that hurdle. He wasn't sure if he'd ever be strong enough to keep going without them.

'Appreciate that,' Chambers replied. He choked down some water and the unlikely pair continued the journey in silence.

Back at the station, Jesse and Chambers were pulled into an emergency briefing. It was nearly time for the daily news. Chief Prescott knew he couldn't get away with shutting down Main Street any longer without an explanation. The mayor's office had already begun getting calls, and it had barely reached noon.

Jesse felt like he'd been up for two days straight. It'd been a long time since he'd operated at full capacity with little sleep. But he knew it'd be a long while before he returned to his bed again.

The Chief, Mayor Lyons, and Sergeant Raines faced the officers as they filed into the meeting room. Jesse and Chambers took a seat in the front row. Jesse found some relief in knowing that no one looked like they were operating at one hundred percent. Raines, especially so. Today was supposed to be her first day back from maternity leave. The station had planned to have a party for her return, but Jesse guessed all of that was placed on hold for more pressing matters.

After everyone had filed in, Chief Prescott barked, 'Catch us up to speed. Raines is back and walking into the situation blind so let's start from the top.'

Chambers took that as his cue to go first. He stood pressing out the wrinkles in his suit by flattening his hands against his shirt and pants.

'First of all, good to have you back, Sarge,'

Chambers started. 'Hope you had an easy delivery and a healthy baby.'

The room let out a round of applause. Sergeant Noelle Raines was a woman of few words. She was efficient and liked to keep small talk to a minimum. Her mouth was chronically pressed together in a straight line, mostly in disapproval, Jesse assumed. She was the first woman officer in the Cinnamon Falls Police Department – a transplant from another county in Georgia – and had been serious since Jesse met her. Her piercing brown eyes seemed to read people like a book. Most people folded under the pressure of her stare.

They landed on Chambers in a way that made Jesse sit up a little straighter. She tucked her chin-length bob behind her ears and crossed her hands behind her back. She dipped her chin, silently thanking him and the other officers for the warm welcome. Jesse noticed that she still didn't smile.

'I'm going to step out,' Mayor Lyons said with a sigh. 'You've got ten minutes to think of what you're going to say to this community. I'll stand beside you all and do my part, but you've got to come up with something. The Fall Festival is in four days—'

'Are you still really having that thing?' Chambers asked in disbelief.

'It's tradition. It's always the second weekend in October, rain or shine. No exceptions,' the mayor stated.

Chambers scoffed. 'Not even murder?'

Mayor Lyons spun on his heel and walked out of the room. Before closing the door behind him, he stuck his head in and said, 'Ten minutes, Prescott. I don't care what you tell these people, but it better be something good.'

'Here's what we got. Rosslyn Rose was found deceased a little after midnight in her diner, with a handwritten note next to her. It reads, "Who Will Be Next?"' A collective grumble bloomed around the room. 'Maggie Shilling called the emergency line—'

'Who's Maggie Shilling?' Raines asked. She pushed her tortoiseshell glasses up on her nose.

'Head of the hospitality committee,' Chief Prescott jumped in. 'She does all the decorations, coordinates all the vendors and stuff for the festival.'

'Hyper blonde lady that puts the pumpkins down Main Street every year?' Raines clarified.

'That's the one,' Bud Wade confirmed.

Chambers continued. 'Angie got the call through dispatch after midnight. Wade, Chief, and I were the first ones on scene. The coroner arrived shortly after and photographed the scene.'

A projector screen descended from the ceiling showing enlarged photos that Grace had taken. Sergeant Raines took a step back.

'What are we thinking?' Her eyes swung over to the Chief. 'I've got Matthias calling my line every two minutes for a statement about this.'

'Murder,' Jesse blurted out.

She crossed her arms over her chest. 'That's obvious.'

'Well,' Chambers cut in, 'blunt force trauma is the cause of death. But the coroner saw some defensive wounds and some bruising. We thought it could be her significant other, like a domestic type of situation. The rookie—' Jesse cut his eyes at Chambers. 'Shaw and I went to the boyfriend's place but he wasn't there.'

'And?'

'That's it,' Chambers admitted.

Sergeant Raines faced the room. 'So, we've got absolutely nothing.'

Jesse fought internally whether to keep his idea to himself. It would be a bad look to bring up the mayor's son, but he hadn't checked their alibis yet.

'I, uh, have a question,' Jesse spoke up. He felt everyone shift in his direction.

Raines unbuttoned her suit jacket revealing a matching vest underneath. She was the queen of tailored suits and rocked a deep woodsy green today. Jesse noticed her glasses matched the buttons on her vest. He appreciated the small details. She took a seat on the edge of the desk and pulled off her glasses. 'Let's hear it, Shaw.'

'I'm still working on verifying alibis, but I was at the diner last night with a few friends. Darius Lyons, his girlfriend, Mr. and Mrs. Blackwell were there and I—'

'I'm glad you brought that up, Shaw,' Chief Prescott jumped in. 'I spoke with Darius myself this morning while I met with Mayor Lyons. He and Victoria were at the diner last night and left around nine-thirty. He said when he left Rosie was her usual self.'

'So, like I said, absolutely nothing,' Raines deadpanned.

'Can I suggest something?' Bud asked from the corner of the room. Jesse had almost forgotten that he was there. 'I think we need to be concentrating on the note the killer left us.' He pointed a remote at the screen and a photo of the note slid into view.

'"Who Will Be Next?"' Raines read aloud. 'What is this, some kind of threat?'

'Maybe that's what they want us to think,' Bud countered. 'We haven't had a murder in this town since I been alive. Now all of a sudden, we've got someone runnin' around bashing folks over the head? It's unnatural. I, for one, think it's an out-of-towner.'

Raines nodded, following her former partner's lead. 'Could be. But what's the story on our victim? Why Rosie? What's she been up to? Who's she been dealing with?'

The room of men fell silent.

'That's where we start, then,' Raines said, looking at the Chief for confirmation, who gave her a nod of approval.

Chief Prescott was unnaturally quiet, but alert. If Jesse's mind was in overdrive, steam should have been coming out of Prescott's ears. 'Raines,' he said at last, 'I know it's your first day back, but I want you to take the lead on this.'

Jesse's heart dropped through his stomach. If Raines was taking the lead, that meant he was officially off the case. Chambers and Wade would be Raines' second in command, and Jesse would be back to patrolling.

'Shaw, Chambers, catch her up on anything pertinent. When you're done, Raines, meet me in my office.' Chief Prescott exited the room and Jesse watched his detective dreams follow behind him.

Chambers slithered over and clapped him on the back. 'Don't let it get to you, rook. Let the professionals take care of it.'

Jesse left the room before anyone had the chance to stop him and returned to his desk. Maybe Chambers was right all along, and he had been too close.

Jesse knew Sergeant Raines was a competent and fair detective. He wasn't familiar with her homicide skills, partially because violent crime wasn't a thing in Cinnamon Falls. A little vandalism and underaged drinking were the most action he'd gotten since he left the military.

Jesse could stand guard all night and shoot five miles downrange. He could disassemble and reassemble any rifle in a matter of seconds. He wasn't scared to take a bullet or put one in someone to protect the people he loved. But, murder? That kind of raw hatred was something totally out of his league.

Focus, he told himself, cradling his head in his hands. Just then, his desktop computer notified him that he'd received a new email.

It was from Chambers: *Break Room Now*, it read.

Jesse sped to the break room to catch Chief Prescott, Mayor Lyons, and Sergeant Raines standing together side by side on the television screen. The angle was from the back of the Great Hall in Town Hall, where the mayor usually made announcements. A thin aisle divided the room between dozens of rows of folding chairs on each side. Concerned citizens filled the seats and had begun crowding around the stage. Chief Prescott stepped up to the podium, adjusted the microphone, and surveyed the crowd.

With a solemn expression, he cleared his throat and began, 'Good morning, citizens of Cinnamon Falls. It is with a heavy heart I stand before you today to address the tragic loss of one of our own, Rosslyn Rose, affectionately known to all of us as Rosie.' Gasps flittered throughout the crowd.

'Rosie was the cornerstone of this town, and her sudden passing has shaken us all. I want to assure you that we are doing everything in our power to find the person responsible. Our investigation is ongoing. Sergeant Raines and our officers are following up on all leads, speaking with witnesses, and reviewing evidence to bring swift justice to Rosie and her family.'

Sergeant Raines stepped into the spotlight next to

Chief Prescott while he continued. 'I want to be clear: the safety of Cinnamon Falls is our highest priority, and we will not rest until we have answers. I know there will be questions and concerns. I will answer a few at the end of this statement. For now, if anyone saw anything unusual near Rosie's Diner last night, please call our tip line. The number should be showing on the screen now. Your information could be vital in helping us solve this case quickly. I urge you all to remain calm. Cinnamon Falls is a place full of strong and resilient people. Our officers will work tirelessly to ensure the safety of every resident.'

The Chief leaned in closer to the microphone and focused on the camera. His stare was so intense, it felt like he was talking directly to Jesse. 'And to the person who did this, we will find you, and you will be held responsible.'

He righted himself. 'Questions, please.'

Hands flew in the air and a wave of words cascaded all at once. Chief Prescott pointed to someone out of frame who asked, 'What is CFPD's plan for the Fall Festival this Saturday?'

Jesse wanted to throw up. A woman was dead and all they cared about was whether they would get to bob for apples this weekend?

The Chief gripped the sides of the podium and answered, 'I understand how important the Fall Festival is to this town. Right now, the Cinnamon Falls Police Department's sole focus is solving this case and ensuring the safety of every resident. As of now, no final decision has been made.' Chief Prescott stepped to the side so the mayor could be seen. 'I am working closely with the mayor's office and event organizers to evaluate all possible options. We will provide an update as soon as we can.'

More hands flew in the air. The Chief pointed to another and a male voice asked, 'Are there any suspects, Chief?'

Prescott inhaled sharply. 'At this time, we are investigating multiple leads and evaluating all evidence. Sergeant Raines here is an excellent detective and I know she and her men will get to the bottom of this. I want to emphasize this is an ongoing investigation. We are not naming any suspects at this time.'

Raines leaned in and said, 'If anyone has any credible information, please share it with the tip line.'

'One more question and then we need to get back to work,' the Chief told the room while he chose the next person. 'Elaine, yes?' he asked.

Elaine Matthias was the Editor-in-Chief of *The Cinnamon Chronicle* and had been a no-nonsense kind of woman since Jesse took her journalism class in twelfth grade. Her deep-set brown eyes missed absolutely nothing when it came to details. Chief Prescott and Elaine had had a rocky relationship over the years. She held onto stories like a dog with a bone. She once sent the whole town into a frenzy when she wrote a six-week series on rabid raccoons that she alleged were government experiments. Jesse couldn't lie, he'd almost believed her. The evidence was overwhelming.

'Is it true that there's a serial killer in Cinnamon Falls and that Rosie was the first victim?'

Gasps flooded the room, and then the crescendo of conversation began. Dozens of people began talking all at once, demanding answers. The cameraman zoomed in on Chief Prescott and Jesse could see the bones working in his jaw. His fingers gripped the podium impossibly tighter.

'Ms. Matthias, let me be very clear: we have no evidence to suggest that Cinnamon Falls is dealing with a serial killer.'

Elaine didn't let the Chief take a breath before she followed up with, 'Was there not a note found at the scene saying that someone here would be next?'

The masses erupted. Hands flew in the air and screams of both concern and horror collided.

Chief Prescott looked over his shoulder at Raines with fire in his eyes. They conferred silently and he shouted, 'While a note was found at the scene, we are still determining its significance!' The crowd simmered to hear the rest of his statement. 'What I can say with certainty is that the CFPD is treating this case with the utmost seriousness, and we will get to the bottom of this. We will provide updates as we have them.'

Across the room, Chambers locked eyes with Jesse.

How did Elaine Matthias find out about the note? The only people who knew about it other than Chambers and Wade were staring back at Jesse on the screen.

The realization slammed into him like a steel-toed boot: someone was feeding Elaine information. There was a mole in his department.

Chapter 9

Nia

After the afternoon rush finally subsided, Nia and her parents returned home. Several officers went business to business to inform them that Main Street would be blocked for the rest of the day.

While Marjorie prepared their dinner, Nia found herself back upstairs in her bedroom, poring over every document she'd stuffed in the plastic bag she'd found at Rosie's. Most of it laid out the details of Sienna's death. Nia had learned more about how her friend died in the last few hours than she had known for the past six years.

She was told that Sienna leapt off Barkwood Bridge late at night after the Fall Festival. She was found the next day, washed ashore, broken and lifeless, and Nia's life hadn't been the same since. She had always wondered why her best friend, who was deathly afraid of water, chose Barkwood Bridge to end it all. The police assured her that Sienna took her own life, and according to the autopsy report, they were right. No further explanations were ever given.

So why was Rosie saving these papers? Why keep them hidden away in a false-bottom drawer? Was she afraid that someone would get a hold of them? Who would care that much about Sienna's death besides the two of them? What had Rosie been up to before she died? Did this have anything to do with why she'd been killed?

The questions spinning around in Nia's head prompted her to remember that she still had to find out who Rosie was on the phone with when she'd left the diner last night. So, she asked the only other available specimen in the house who could help her, and keep it a secret: Midnight.

Midnight was fast asleep, curled in a tight ball at the foot of Nia's bed. She'd spent most of her day around people and needed to take some time to herself to regulate her emotions; at least that was what her father said. Nia didn't mind, as long as she didn't try to stop her from breathing in the middle of the night again.

'Midnight,' Nia whispered. 'You asleep?'

Midnight's black tail flicked at the mention of her name. Her ears perked and she cracked one yellow eye at Nia.

'Go get Niles. I need his help with something.' Her brother should have been at school, but the students were sent home after the news about Rosie was broadcast.

Midnight buried her head and ignored her request. 'I'll give you salmon crisps,' Nia bribed.

Midnight didn't move.

'Tuna crisps, I mean. Lots of them – all you can eat.'

The black cat lifted her head that time, analyzing Nia and her offer. She sprung off the bed and disappeared. Moments later, Nia heard Niles' footsteps pad down the hall toward her bedroom. Midnight sauntered in first. Her little brother brought up the rear with a confused and annoyed look on his face.

'What's going on?' Niles asked, pulling his headphones off his head and roping them around his neck. 'Nighty came in and just plopped on my keyboard. She wouldn't let me type until I got up and followed her. We're losing, so this better be good.'

'Can you pause the game for a sec?' Nia asked. 'I need a favor.'

'No, I can't just pause the game. It's not *Mario Kart*—'

At the door, Midnight meowed impatiently.

'What did you promise her?' Niles asked, panicked.

'Tuna crisps,' Nia admitted.

'She's going to haunt you for the rest of your life,' Niles said. His eyes widened like he was genuinely afraid. 'How much?'

'. . . All she could eat?' Nia said reluctantly.

'Dad, code red!' Niles screamed over the banister. 'Nia promised Nighty unlimited tuna crisps!'

Nia's father screamed like he was an extra in a scary movie. 'Nooooo!'

Midnight howled over the commotion.

'You better get her those treats, and soon, if you want to live,' Niles warned.

'I am not about to let a twenty-pound feline boss me around.'

'Twenty pounds? Are you crazy?' Niles swooped up Midnight and cradled the cat in his arms. 'She doesn't mean that. You're not fat, don't even think that.' Midnight mewed. 'Don't think about it for one second. You're an icon, a legend.'

'This is y'all's problem now. She thinks she's a human!' Nia pointed out indignantly.

'She's a member of this family, Nia!' her father defended from downstairs. How could he even hear what they were talking about?

'She's a cat!' Nia screamed back.

'How dare you.' Niles shook his head in disgust. Midnight leapt out of his arms and sprinted downstairs when she heard the distant and melodic sound of a snack bag crinkling. Nia hoped her father was doling out the tuna crisps generously as she'd promised. She wanted to wake up tomorrow without her own death being the first thing on her mind.

'I need your help with something,' Nia said, straightening the papers on her bed and clearing a spot for Niles to sit. She pulled her phone off the charger and flipped to the pictures she'd taken of

Rosie's Caller ID. 'Can you tell me who these numbers belong to?'

Niles took the phone and studied the pictures. He flicked forward and backward. 'Don't recognize them,' he said nonchalantly. 'I'm about to get back on the game.'

'Wait, can't you like, reverse search them or something?'

Niles scoffed. 'Do I look like Steve Jobs to you? Why can't you ask your boyfriend? I'm sure cops have all kinds of ways to trace numbers.'

'Come on, it's about Rosie,' Nia begged.

'Even more of a reason to get the cops involved.'

'Please?' Nia asked, all out of other options.

Niles was quiet for a moment and then he said, 'Give me a second. I'll see what I can find.'

Nia fell back on her bed and watched her ceiling fan make its rounds. Today felt like it'd never end. Between the phone call she'd gotten this morning from her mother and now, Nia felt like she'd been up for a week straight.

Jesse's last words to her resounded in her mind. *Promise me you'll stay out of this investigation.* At the time, she really meant that she would. She wanted to keep her word to him, but after watching the press conference, she couldn't sit idly by and wait for the police to rely solely on tips to solve Rosie's murder, especially considering there could be a serial killer on the loose.

A cold shiver slid down Nia's spine. Was there really someone out there, lurking in the shadows, planning to kill more residents of Cinnamon Falls? Even worse, could Rosie's killer be hiding in plain sight? Could she have served them this morning at The Cinnamon Scoop? *Easily*, she thought. Dozens of people had filed in and out of the shop that morning. Had she made small talk with Rosie's killer and didn't know it?

Chief Prescott had urged for people to remain calm, but there was nothing reassuring about having no idea who killed Rosie. It was frightening to think that anyone could be next, and the police, the people sworn to protect them, had no idea where to look first.

Nia refused to wait for the police to give a damn about the people she loved. When Sienna died she ran, leaving Rosie here to deal with the aftermath. Now that Rosie was gone, Nia could feel something inside of her – a nagging, prickling feeling – that told her that she had to figure this out. She couldn't run from her problems anymore. She was going to face her life head on, and that meant figuring out who'd killed her best friend's mother and putting them behind bars where they belonged. She didn't have the opportunity to do it for Sienna, but now that she was back, she vowed to bring Rosie's killer to justice.

Niles returned just a few minutes later with a pad of lime-green Post-it notes in his hand. 'The first number is for Harvey's Used Cars.' He peeled one off and flicked it toward her. 'I had to pay a dollar to see whose number the second one was. It's registered to someone named Edwina Rutherford.'

'Who the hell is that?' Nia mumbled.

Niles shrugged. 'I don't know, but you owe me a dollar.' He threw down the pad on her bed. 'Can I go now, Sherlock?'

Nia shooed her brother away. She sat at her childhood desk and fumbled through the drawers until she found a notebook. She ripped out the pages that had been written on: lecture notes, recipes, and journal entries, until she reached a clean sheet of paper. She wrote Rosie's name at the top and began to list out everything she could remember. Then, she searched the internet for Harvey's Used Cars.

A picture of Harvey Briggs standing in front of a lot of shiny cars came up first. What was Rosie doing calling Mr. Briggs last night? Nia circled his name in her notebook. Then, she searched for Edwina Rutherford. It linked her to an article on the Cinnamon Falls Public Library's website. Mrs. Rutherford used to be the head librarian some forty years ago. Another article linked to an obituary. Mrs. Rutherford had passed just the year before. *How could Rosie be calling a dead woman?* Nia wondered.

She continued to read, discovering that Edwina Rutherford was survived by one son, Edward Rutherford Jr. Nia searched that name and found a picture of him. She couldn't stop the gasp from slipping out of her mouth when she saw a picture of him standing next to Rosie.

Edward Rutherford was almost as tall as Rosie was, towering beside her in the photo, a wide, toothy grin stretched across his face. He was holding a rolling pin like it was a prized possession, flour dusted across the dark ink of the tattoos that snaked up both forearms and disappeared beneath the sleeves of his black T-shirt. His long, dark hair was pulled into a low bun at the nape of his neck, with a few loose strands falling around his temples, giving him the look of a rockstar-turned-pastry-chef.

Rosie gripped his shoulder proudly like he was her own. The warmth between them radiated even through the screen. The picture linked to a two-year-old article in *The Cinnamon Chronicle* about Rosie's award-winning cinnamon buns.

Edward Rutherford was Rosie's head baker, and Nia needed to talk to him now. If she was back in Atlanta, she'd take Bryant's car and head straight to his house. But now she had to be more strategic about her moves. She had to find a way to talk to both Harvey Briggs and Edward Rutherford, and she knew the perfect person for the job.

Chapter 10

Wednesday
Jesse

When Jesse returned home Tuesday night, he was half the man he used to be. All he could think about was Rosie. He made dinner absentmindedly, tossing together a salad and making his mother's favorite recipe, lasagna. His parents, normally talkative, were somber and quiet too, despite their anniversary. It was like a hush had fallen over Cinnamon Falls; everyone grieving the loss of Rosie. When he embraced his parents before bed he made sure to hug them a little tighter.

The next morning, Jesse reluctantly added a new name to his list of suspects: Harvey Briggs. He did so locked in the bathroom stall at the station, the only place he knew for sure he wouldn't be watched. The question in his mind was: How did Elaine Matthias know about the note? Jesse didn't want to believe that anyone on the force would talk to Elaine Matthias about anything.

The only person who made sense on his list of suspects outright was Harvey Briggs. If the rumors were true of their relationship, and now Briggs was in the wind . . . Jesse hated to agree with Chambers, but it was looking like the detective was correct.

Still, Jesse couldn't imagine a quiet and easy-going man like Briggs would hurt the woman he loved. Jesse wasn't familiar with the details of their relationship, but he knew Rosie was happy in the days before she passed. What changed?

Jesse returned to his desk to find Sergeant Raines waiting on him. The petite woman spun around in his chair when he approached.

'My office,' she said to him in a stern voice, and Jesse had no choice but to follow. He could feel the eyes glued to his back from the other officers. He knew what was coming and braced himself for the bad news.

Jesse closed the door behind him and Raines sat down at her large, polished desk. The wood gleamed like it was made out of glass. The feminine, soft lavender walls always gave him pause considering Raines was a woman with a hardened stare and an even tougher personality. He wondered if she was the same drill sergeant at home with her children.

'You need to speak with me, Sarge?' Jesse asked, taking a seat in a chair opposite her desk.

'Chief wants me to take you off the case,' she said plainly. Even though Jesse thought he'd braced himself in the hallway, he still had to hold onto the chair's handrests to ground himself. He knew more about Rosie than anyone on the force combined. He should have been the one leading the case.

'Understood,' Jesse replied simply.

Raines cocked her head like he spoke a different language. 'You were close with the victim.'

'Is that a question or a statement?' Jesse asked.

'Both,' Raines said. Her eyes narrowed like she was trying to read the thoughts that were forming in his mind.

Jesse nodded. 'I was very close with Rosslyn Rose, yes.'

'Describe the nature of your relationship.'

'She was like my second mother,' Jesse admitted. 'Practically raised me and my friends.'

'Hmm,' Raines said. She pushed her glasses to the top of her head and laced her fingers together. 'Who do you think did this?'

Jesse realized the purpose of the meeting was to pick his brain. Raines and Chambers were both out-of-towners. They had no idea what Rosie meant to Cinnamon Falls. He wondered if Raines had pulled Wade into her office too.

'I wish I knew,' Jesse answered. The list of names he'd curated and crossed out was burning a hole in his pocket.

A moment of silence filtered between them while she studied his face. Jesse had served four years in the military. He knew how to keep his emotions intact in front of a superior officer. He could do the staring game all night. He was fuming inside, but on the outside, he was a statue.

'Go home,' Raines ordered. 'Take the day to mourn for your loved one.'

'Yes, ma'am,' Jesse answered. He stood to go, ready to remove himself from her presence. He needed some time to think and get his mind together. Going home was the perfect opportunity to regroup.

'First thing tomorrow morning, I need a report in my hands of everything that you and Chambers collected.'

'Yes, ma'am,' Jesse repeated.

'You're free to go,' she said. She dismissed him with a wave of her hand, and then busied herself with the paperwork on her desk.

Fallen leaves crunched under Jesse's boots as he made his way to the parking lot. He had two stops to make before he went home. He had promised his father cheese yesterday from Guy's but it was easier to snag something quick and healthier for dinner over at Cinnamon Grove.

The doors at Cinnamon Grove slid open automatically at his arrival, revealing a bright white interior that looked more like a science lab than a grocery store. Greens were being spritzed by an automatic water filter against the far wall. Dozens of bins of polished produce were eager to be picked. Aisles of colorful packages were displayed ahead of him from all over the country. His stomach growled in anticipation.

Normally, he would take his time to peruse each aisle, discovering a new dish to try out. But today he didn't have the time. For once, he was going to follow orders and go home.

Raines and Chambers were as close to finding Rosie's killer as he was. Just because he'd been pulled off the case, didn't mean he had to stop investigating on his own. He knew that he could find the killer quicker than Chambers ever could. The detective was too brash for the people of Cinnamon Falls. They'd never open up to him like they would to Jesse.

Jesse was so lost in his thoughts that he didn't realize he wasn't alone in the aisle. He turned to find Victoria Nathan studying the nutrition label on a bag of mixed nuts. He didn't recognize her with the tan trench coat knotted at her waist. A cap with Darius' team logo was pulled over her hair, shielding most of her face. This was the perfect opportunity to find out where she was when Rosie died.

'Essential nutrients,' Jesse started, hoping not to startle her.

'What?' Victoria frowned, looking just as annoyed

as she had at Rosie's. He wondered if that was her default personality.

Jesse pointed to the bag she was holding. 'Protein, fiber, healthy fats . . . They're good for you.'

She rolled her eyes. 'Darius is allergic to peanuts. I need to make sure there's none in the bag, nosy,' Victoria replied.

'Well, not everyone with a peanut allergy is allergic to tree nuts. See, peanuts are legumes—'

'Thank you, Encyclopedia Brown,' Victoria cut him off and tossed the nuts into her hand basket and maneuvered around Jesse like he had the plague.

Jesse pointed to the items in her basket: a bushel of greens, a few tomatoes, and a cucumber. 'Decided to make your own salad?' Jesse joked, hoping she would pick up on the hint.

'A girl's gotta get her greens in.' She studied the food in Jesse's basket: grass-fed beef, a few power shots of ginger, turmeric and lemon, some fresh produce, and cheese.

'Burgers tonight?' she asked.

'Spaghetti,' Jesse corrected, wishing he had an angle to segue into her whereabouts Monday night. He had to bite the bullet and get it over with before the conversation grew stale. 'I'm sure you've, um, heard about Rosie by now?'

Victoria sighed. 'That's why you're talking to me, isn't it? Here I thought you were actually worried about my man's health, but you're trying to get information out of me. Did someone tell you I was here? This town is too damn small,' she fussed. 'Can't even shop in peace.'

'I'm actually here to get some things to make dinner tonight,' Jesse clarified. He shook the basket at her for good measure. 'You just so happened to be standing here.'

She sighed. 'What do you want, Jesse?'

'Where'd you go after you left Rosie's?'

'Mr. Lyons was throwing Darius a surprise Welcome Home party at the house. I had to keep him occupied until everything was ready, and when Morgan invited us to Rosie's, it was the perfect opportunity. All of our friends and family were at the party. Hell, half the town saw us there. Ask anyone!' She gestured widely as if they were surrounded by an audience.

'All night?' Jesse pressed.

'If you must know, my man made love to me until the sun came up. So, we were both a little busy . . . All night,' she said with a smirk.

Jesse resisted the urge to vomit.

Victoria's phone let out a high shrill. 'Now, excuse me, Mr. Officer. That's my man calling and I think he wants another round.' Victoria winked at Jesse and waited until he moved out of her way. He watched her saunter out of the aisle with the phone pressed to her ear.

'Hey, baby . . .' Her voice floated away until

she was too far for Jesse to hear the rest of the conversation.

If there was a party at Mayor Lyons' house Monday night, someone he knew had to have been there. All he had to do was find someone who was cool enough to get invited to the mayor's house. As much as Jesse wanted to obey Sergeant Raines' orders to go home, he had another mission under his belt.

Bones' Barbershop was quiet on a Wednesday afternoon. Jesse arrived to find William Reed watching old episodes of a courtroom TV show with a hard-nosed judge.

'Hardest working man in law enforcement.' Will greeted him with a dap and spun an empty service chair around to him. Jesse sat beside him and watched the show for a minute, enthralled at people's ridiculous antics in a court of law.

'Gettin' a cut?' Will asked. His eyes went to the grown-out taper on Jesse's head. Jesse had planned on getting his normal Friday afternoon cut later this week as it had been their routine for a few months now. But today was different.

Jesse was glad he'd turned into a regular so that he didn't have to use Will's complicated online reservation system anymore. Will carved out Fridays at three p.m. for Jesse specifically, and their routine appointments had turned into a budding friendship. Jesse was relying on their bond to navigate this complicated conversation.

'For sure,' Jesse said, making sure to keep his voice at an even tone.

'Heard your boo was back in town,' Will joked. 'I knew it was only a matter of time before you came to get lined up.' He laughed and tossed the cape around Jesse's uniform, clasping it behind his neck.

Jesse fisted a laugh. 'Hold on, you see yours all the time and haven't said one word to her.'

A zip of pain flashed through Jesse's ear as the clipper nicked his helix. 'Oops.' Will laughed while Jesse cradled his ear.

Pulling out his phone, Jesse pretended to write a review. 'Zero stars. Will retaliate if love of his life is mentioned. Will go to war behind Morgan Taylor.'

The men's roaring laughter filled the shop's walls. Before long, Bones joined the conversation to see what they were laughing about.

'I gotta slow walk it, man,' Will said. Jesse watched his reflection in the mirror while his barber tried to explain why he hadn't asked Morgan out yet.

'Is this the Heartbreak Hotel or a barbershop?' Jesse questioned, pointing to Mr. Harold. 'You're scared to talk to Mrs. Guy, who you've been eyeing since you were a teenager.' Tears spilled out of Mr. Harold's eyes as he tried to catch his breath.

'And you,' he continued, eyeing Will, 'can't even muster up a "hello" to the most eccentric woman in the world! She wears purple every day! It's an easy lay-up!' Jesse mimicked dribbling a basketball and making a shot. 'Y'all are pathetic!'

'What's even worse,' Bones added in, 'he sees her every time he picks up Angel from school!'

'Ha-ha.' Will rolled his eyes. He tried to hide his smile, but Jesse caught his expression in the mirror. Just the mention of her name had the man blushing. 'She's my daughter's teacher, it's a delicate relationship.'

'Angel will only be in Kindergarten once,' Jesse said. 'Next fall, she'll have a different teacher. That's how school works.'

'Yeah, a whole year from now,' Will reminded him. 'I'm just trying to keep it PG for now, you know? Angel loves her, though. Won't stop talking about her. *Ms. Morgan* this, *Ms. Morgan* that,' Will said, mocking his daughter's tiny voice.

'You wish that was you, huh?' Jesse cut in, and the room exploded into laughter once again.

'Back to you.' Will changed the subject. 'What's the occasion? I expect you on Fridays, my guy.'

'I just came from Cinnamon Grove and decided to get a cut while I had some time.'

'Riiiiight,' Will replied in a tone that meant he didn't believe Jesse. 'You come every Friday at three since you started getting cuts by me. Now you here on a random Wednesday afternoon. What's the deal, bro?'

Will clearly knew that Jesse was the kind of man who found solace in a solid routine. Maybe Will knew him better than he thought.

'Am I the cop or you?' Jesse joked, hoping that keeping the conversation light would get the job done.

'It ain't like you, is all I'm saying,' Will replied. 'I mean this whole week has been weird, though. I'm still in shock that Rosie died.' Will pointed over his shoulder in the general direction of Rosie's Diner. 'Me and Angel look forward to those big cinnamon rolls every year at the Fall Festival.'

Bones commented, 'Yeah, what's up with that, Jay? They sayin' anything about Rosie's killer?'

'Now you know he can't talk about it,' Will said.

'I'm just sayin'.' Bones shrugged. 'People 'round here saying there's some kinda serial killer. They naming ol' Harvey Briggs for it too.'

Jesse took a short breath before talking. It always amazed him how fast gossip spread.

'Like Will said, I really can't say, Bones. I'm, uh, off the case,' Jesse admitted. The words tumbled out of his mouth and as much as he wanted to push them back inside, he couldn't. Funnily enough, his chest felt lighter, like he could breathe again.

'They had you *on* the case?' Will punched the air in celebration. 'I thought they gave the detective spot to the other guy? They put you on the case? That's major!'

Jesse couldn't help but smile at Will's enthusiasm. His perspective was one way of looking at it. He was happy that he at least got to do something different than patrolling. It did break up the monotony of his day, but he was the most tired he'd ever been. His mind was exhausted. All he wanted was to curl up into bed and start this week over, but this time, with Rosie alive.

'Thanks,' Jesse replied, 'but I was promptly removed.'

'That's why you're here on a Wednesday.' Will had finally connected the dots. 'You got fired.'

'What? No! I'm just off the case, that's all. Listen, I need to ask you about last night, though.' Will spun Jesse around in the chair to face him so that he could cut his hairline straight.

'What's up?' Will asked.

'Did you go to Mayor Lyons' party?'

Will nodded and a playful smile formed on his lips. 'Hell yeah. It was packed! I thought that I was getting there early, you know? I had a plan. I dropped Angel off with my sister-in-law, came home, got fresh, and headed up there around seven-thirty, you know.'

Jesse loved when Will told stories. It was ninety percent of the reason why he started getting his hair cut by him. One day, Harold had been double booked and Will was the only barber available. Barbershop rules were to never trust the new guy, but Will was on point. Plus, the stories he told about his life before Cinnamon Falls were equal parts hilarious and concerning. It didn't matter that Jesse was technically law enforcement and could lock him up for it; everything was confidential within the four walls of the shop.

'I heard the mayor got a thing for cars, so I pulled out the '59 Eldorado on 'em. I get up there, and there's nowhere to park. You know I'm not parking it on the street. So, I go up to the gate and they valet me right next to a '70 Caprice. You know how long I've been looking for one of those?'

Jesse only knew one person in Cinnamon Falls with a Caprice. What was Grace doing at Darius Lyons' Welcome Home party? Jesse put a pin in that thought.

Will continued. 'Anyway, I get to the party and it's cool. Good food and good drinks. The music sucked, but I met some cool people. I finally met the short lady that was putting out pumpkins and decorating for two weeks straight.'

'Maggie Shilling,' Bones chimed in.

'That's her! I met Darius Lyons too. I got close enough to him that I think them diamonds is real.'

'Ain't no way!' Bones exclaimed.

'Got a picture wit' 'em.' Will found his phone on the table next to him and scrolled to find the picture. He handed his phone to Bones.

'Man, it's all blurry, you can't even tell!' Bones pulled the phone to his face and Will snatched it away.

Bones said, 'All you can really see is the chain on his neck.'

'That's the point! I'm telling you, the kid's got money. Those diamonds are real,' Will replied.

Jesse reached for the phone to look at the picture. It was a blurry Darius Lyons alright. Jesse flipped the phone over and Will's camera was streaked with fingerprints and grease marks. That would explain the blurry photo. Jesse tapped the photo to get the timestamp: 10:37 p.m.

'Did you see his girl there?' Jesse asked.

'Which one? It was some fine honeys in there. I mean ticket on the dash kinda fine.'

Jesse pulled away from Will's clippers and found his phone. He opened Instagram and typed in Victoria's name in his friends list. He showed her page to Will. 'Her.'

Will let out a low whistle. He snapped his fingers. 'She's gorgeous. That's Darius' girl?' he questioned.

'Let me see.' Bones reached for the phone. 'Victoria Nathan,' he read. 'Why does that name sound familiar? Is her momma Tammy Nathan?'

'How would I know that?' Will asked, annoyed.

'Her momma so fine they could be sisters.' Bones scrolled on Jesse's phone and showed the two men Victoria's post. It was a photo of her and her mother, and Bones was right.

'Damn,' Jesse and Will said at the same time.

Victoria and Tammy Nathan could have been

identical save for Tammy's smile lines and slight wrinkles under her neck. Their unblemished hazelnut skin and bright smiles were almost hypnotizing. In real life, Victoria never gave off irresistible vibes. The internet was a scary place.

'So she was there?' Jesse asked. He didn't want to press too hard, but he needed to check them off his list. 'When Victoria and Darius left Rosie's they were at each other's throats.' He hoped Will would take the bait.

'That's why he looked pissed when he came in! We waited there all night for him. I guess it was some kind of surprise party. It was nearing ten-something when I was about to call it a night. I'm an old man now.'

Jesse was teeming with anticipation. 'What time did he get there?'

'I took that picture as soon as he came in the door and then I left. I think that was like, ten-thirty.'

'You left a party before eleven o'clock? You the youngest old man in the world.' Bones shook his head.

'That was the only reason I went! I'd already spoken to the mayor and showed him the Eldorado. We supposed to be getting together to compare our car collections.' Will had a satisfied smile on his face.

Jesse, Morgan, and Nia left Rosie's after Darius and Victoria around nine-thirty. He distinctly remembered getting home just as his mother was getting settled in for the late show she liked to watch at ten. If Darius got to his party at around ten-thirty, that meant Jesse was back to square one.

Will whipped out a hand mirror for Jesse to view his haircut up close. He checked himself out in the reflection and loved the results. At least it wasn't a totally wasted visit.

Chapter 11

Nia

Nia woke to the soft patter of leaves brushing against her bedroom window. The house smelled faintly of maple syrup and her dad's fresh waffle batter, but the weight of Rosie's death still hung heavy in the air. After breakfast and a shower, she needed to clear her head. She pulled out her flat iron and began straightening her curls; the familiar hiss and tug of the tool was a small comfort against the chaos. A little moment of calm, of warmth, of routine, was what she needed most.

Morgan arrived at Nia's house promptly at three p.m. Even though Nia and Sienna had become friends first, adding Morgan to their circle was like adding the sprinkles on top of a cool, creamy vanilla cone. Her eccentric ways and sense of humor complemented their friendship perfectly. Where Nia was sarcastic and serious, Morgan and Sienna were playful and whimsical. Nia knew that Morgan would be down to help her, and the drive to Asheville would be the perfect opportunity for Nia to make amends.

The weather was ideal. The sun occasionally dipped behind the clouds giving the atmosphere a bite of brisk air that prompted a little more than a T-shirt and a little less than a sweater. Nia settled on her old navy blue Cinnamon Falls sweatshirt. She'd worn it in her senior photos and hadn't since. It was a little more snug than she remembered, but still fit well.

She'd been feeling nostalgic since last night. Combing through Rosie's documents had forced Nia to think about a time in her life that she had all but willed herself to forget. But the pain only waited for her return.

As Nia watched Morgan pull up outside the house, Midnight appeared in the foyer, studying her. Nia sighed and paid her toll of tuna crisps before Midnight allowed her out the house. The cat had the memory of an elephant and, apparently, bribing her with unlimited treats was an egregious act severely frowned upon in the Bennett household.

'Since you promised her unlimited treats, make sure you grab some while you're out,' her father reminded her. 'I'm not trying to be the next person to wake up dead in Cinnamon Falls.'

Midnight paced menacingly behind her father's feet.

'I won't forget,' Nia promised and jetted out of the house.

Nia slid into the passenger seat of Morgan's indigo truck. 'You look adorable!' Morgan squealed. She leaned over and gave Nia a tight hug. Today, Morgan sported her favorite color in a high ponytail that cascaded over her shoulder and finished in a curl near her belt loops. She carefully backed out of the driveway and onto the road.

'It's giving Nia Janice Bennett, class of 2018,' Morgan laughed. 'It's been ages since I've seen your hair straightened.'

'I had to do something to take my mind off Rosie,' she admitted.

'The news about Rosie gutted me. I didn't know what to say to the kids yesterday morning before they dismissed us.'

'What did you say?' Nia asked. She couldn't imagine how scared and confused the children must have felt. Her heart ached for them.

Morgan knocked away the tears that spilled down her cheeks. 'I had them write letters to heaven.' She forced a smile. 'It was so precious, Ni, but also the hardest day I've had since I started.'

Nia found a napkin in Morgan's glove compartment and handed it to her, taking a few for herself. On the drive over, the two of them reminisced about high school; the days that seemed so long turned into years that flew by with lightning speed. The good times she thought would last forever disappeared just as quickly as they'd come.

Time didn't stop when Sienna died. It kept on marching, dragging Nia along with it. She got to keep living while Sienna and now Rosie wouldn't live to see another day. The guilt of simply surviving was eating away at her.

At the mall in Asheville, after stocking up on some hygiene essentials, Nia and Morgan decided to shop for outfits for Rosie's inevitable memorial ceremony. It was only right to wear something as bold as Rosie had in life. Besides, shopping cured a lot of things, including heartbreak.

'What do you think Sienna would be doing right now?' Nia asked.

Morgan placed a plain black A-line dress back on the rack. 'I . . . don't know,' she answered. 'She'd be pissed, mostly, I think.'

Morgan was right. While Nia was rigid, and Morgan was playful, Sienna was fiery. If she were here, Nia knew that she'd be sleeping at the police station, making sure that every person was doing their job in finding her mother's killer.

'Furious,' Nia commented, aimlessly searching through the racks of clothing. 'I've been sorting through it all in my head,' she started. 'And I found some things at Rosie's that I want to check out.'

'You . . . what?' Morgan froze. 'You went to Rosie's?'

Nia crept closer to her and lowered her voice. They were the only two women in that section of the department store, but she couldn't risk anyone overhearing what she was going to say.

'I found some papers in her office and—'

'They had Main Street blocked off all day yesterday. How in the hell did you get inside? Don't tell me Jay let you in.'

'That doesn't matter,' Nia answered. She didn't need to get into the frivolous details of her felonious ways.

'So, you stole evidence from a crime scene, is what you're telling me?'

'Well—'

'And then you got in *my* car and asked me to take you across county lines?'

'I—'

'Have you lost your mind?' Morgan asked a little too loud for Nia's liking. Across the way, a salesperson inched closer toward them.

'Listen,' Nia implored. 'Let me explain.'

Nia started at the beginning. She explained how her married ex-boyfriend had completely blown up her life and sent her packing back to Cinnamon Falls. Then, when she finally got comfortable with the idea of being back home, she finds out one of the only people she'd been hoping to see, after all these years, had been murdered. She wasn't going to let another person get snatched out of her life without fighting back. She had to see this through, no matter what it took.

'I get all that, but when you called, you didn't mention potential jail time, Nia.'

'But—'

'And I'm missing the part where you apologize for pretending like you *actually* wanted to hang out.' Morgan dumped all the clothes she had in her hands on the nearest rack and bolted out of the store. Nia tossed the dresses she was holding and followed after her.

'Morgan, wait!' Nia begged, chasing after her friend. Morgan was fast, and was already down the hall by the time Nia reached the doorway. She slowed behind an elderly couple getting on the escalator and it gave Nia a window of opportunity to catch up to her.

'Morgan, please, I'm sorry!' Nia stepped onto the escalator behind her and the two descended together. Morgan had nowhere to go and Nia used it to her advantage. 'When Sienna died I just couldn't take it, alright? It was like I died too.'

'How do you think *I* felt?' Morgan shot back and crossed her arms over her chest. 'I didn't have a lot of friends when I first moved here. People weren't exactly friendly to me, but you and Sienna were different. I was finally happy. And when she died . . .' Morgan choked back tears. Her full lips trembled with all the things she wanted to say but couldn't. She didn't have to speak, Nia understood how it felt to have feelings more complex than words could describe. 'And then you just left with no explanation!'

'I had to—' Nia started.

'Part of me wonders if it were me that night at Barkwood Bridge, would you have left then?' The escalator ended, dropping them at the ground floor, and Nia was stunned to silence. 'I know you left for yourself, Nia. But I want you to realize how much it hurt to lose you too.'

Nia launched herself into Morgan's arms and the two of them sobbed in the middle of the mall, other shoppers giving them a wide berth. Nia mourned for Sienna and the friendship they'd lost as a trio. She cried for that version of Morgan who had been broken in her absence; the girl who learned to keep living after losing so much, and lastly, they cried for Rosie.

'When do you plan on telling your boyfriend that you're playing Sherlock Holmes behind his back?' Morgan asked while she twirled a paper straw between her fingers.

Nia and Morgan had decided to stop for a bite to eat at a no-name restaurant in the mall before they headed back to Cinnamon Falls. In circumstances like these, they would normally go to Rosie's after a day of shopping. It was the perfect happy hour spot. Now, she realized, they'd have to find someplace else.

Nia rolled her eyes. Boyfriend was pushing it.

'I don't,' she admitted. She hadn't planned on

sharing anything with Jesse, unless she desperately needed his help. At the station, he wasn't interested in Rosie's folder. She decided to let the police handle it their way, and she would handle it hers. 'I kind of promised not to interfere with the investigation.'

'And he believed you?' Morgan twisted her lips.

'I need to talk to Harvey Briggs,' Nia said. 'He was the last person Rosie called before she died.'

Morgan shrugged and took a sip of her red wine. 'That's not surprising. She's been seeing Harvey for about a year now.'

'She . . . What?' Nia could have been knocked over by a feather. A year? That was a substantial amount of time. Had Rosie been in love? Did Jesse know this?

Morgan shook her head. 'It wasn't like she broadcasted it all around town, but people knew he and Rosie had been getting closer.' Morgan smirked. 'Apparently he came to the diner one evening and they sparked up a conversation.'

'Just like that?' Nia asked.

She nodded. 'From what I know, she was pretty happy. She probably called him before she closed up like normal.'

'That makes sense,' Nia mumbled, connecting the pieces in her head to make a timeline of Rosie's events. 'What about Edward Rutherford?'

'Who?'

Nia produced the picture she found while doing

her search last night. 'Rosie called him too, about an hour before she called Harvey.'

Morgan took the phone and brought it closer to her face. 'That looks like Eddie with long hair.'

'It's an old picture,' Nia said.

'Well, then, yeah, that's Eddie, the shift manager. He usually worked the early morning shifts at the diner.'

'And, what about him?' Nia waited for Morgan to elaborate.

'And he always got my order wrong, I know that much. I wish The Cinnamon Scoop was open early so I could get a decent combination of caffeine and a sugar rush,' Morgan fussed.

Nia snapped her fingers in front of Morgan's face. 'Focus!'

'She fired him,' Morgan stated. 'As a matter of fact, she let him go just a few days before you came home. Crazy if you ask me, being so close to the Fall Fest.'

'You know why?' Nia asked.

'Do I look like human resources? One day he was behind the counter making terrible lattes at six a.m., and the next he wasn't. For one thing, my coffee order has been right ever since.'

Edward Rutherford just shot to the top of Nia's list. 'Where do you think I could find him?'

Morgan jeered, 'Are you seriously trying to play detective?'

Nia grew stoic. 'I'm not playing, Morgan. I'm going to find out what happened to Rosie.'

Morgan sighed and threw down the shredded straw. 'Then you're going to need some backup.'

After finishing their meal, Nia and Morgan found themselves sitting in the parking lot of a convenience store. Morgan read aloud from the morning's edition of *The Cinnamon Chronicle*. Elaine Matthias had already covered Rosie's passing. Meanwhile, Nia was watching the door for Eddie Rutherford to make an appearance.

Morgan called around and found out where Eddie had gone after he left Rosie's. Cinnamon Falls was a small place and the only other place to find work after you'd been fired would be one town over, in Asheville.

'"Cinnamon Falls woke up to devastating news on Tuesday morning",' Morgan read aloud. '"To the tragic and untimely death of beloved local business owner Rosslyn Rose. Known as the heart and soul of Rosie's Diner, a staple of Main Street for over three decades, Rosie was found deceased inside her restaurant early yesterday morning. Law enforcement has officially ruled her death a homicide, marking the first murder in Cinnamon Falls."'

Nia watched as people filed in and out of the

convenience store. Eddie would have to take a break sometime. 'Come on,' she whispered.

Morgan continued. '"According to initial reports, Maggie Shilling, Director of Hospitality, discovered Rosie's body, and dialed 911. Law enforcement has yet to confirm if she is considered a witness or a person of interest in the case."'

A jolt of electricity shot through Nia's body. She turned to Morgan, who was reading intensely. 'Rosie said she was meeting with Maggie on Monday night, remember?'

Together, they said, 'Maggie was the last person to see her alive.'

Seconds later, Eddie Rutherford strolled out of the convenience store. Tattoos matrixed across both his arms; a puzzle of colors and designs. A limp cigarette hung from his lips. He walked toward the side of the building and took his first puff, throwing his head back like he'd been waiting all day for that moment in particular.

Nia was about to ruin it.

'There he is,' Nia announced. She threw her shoulder against the car door and hopped out before she lost her nerve.

'Wait!' Morgan trailed behind her.

Eddie paced around while he puffed on his cigarette and kicked the loose gravel at his feet. By the time he looked up, Nia and Morgan had him cornered. Eddie threw his hands up. Terror flashed in his eyes as if the women, weaponless in broad daylight, were planning to rob him. His half-smoked cigarette hit the ground and rolled away.

'You Eddie Rutherford?' Nia asked. Her voice had a hard edge to it. She'd never heard herself sound like that before. She hoped she wouldn't break character.

'Who wants to know?' They had Eddie spooked. His eyes darted between her and Morgan. He concentrated harder on Morgan, and Nia could tell he was searching their faces to see if he knew them from somewhere. 'What's this about?'

'Your terrible coffee,' Morgan mumbled under her breath.

'Rosie,' Nia said. She stepped closer to him to capture his full attention. 'Why did she call you the other night?'

Eddie shook his head and gathered himself. Nia could tell by the confused look on his face that he wasn't expecting a talk like this to be about his former boss.

'What are y'all—'

'Answer the question!' Morgan demanded.

'Uh, she fired me for no reason,' Eddie admitted. His hands, still in the air, were trembling. 'She owes me for the hours I worked. I called so I could work out a time to come pick up my check.' His hands dropped down to his sides. 'What are you two here for, to shake me down about who she calls?'

'She's dead.' Nia finally said it out loud. Her nose

twinged, signaling that tears were on their way, and she pushed the feeling down.

Not here. Not now, she told her body. She could cry another day. Right now, she had to handle business.

'Whoaaaa.' Eddie backed up so far that he collided with the side of the brick building. 'Rosie? She's dead?' Color drained from his face and the smug look he had moments before was gone.

'It's been all over the news.' Morgan shook her newspaper at him. He turned his head sideways to read the headline. A picture of Rosie was plastered on the front page. Nia couldn't bear to look at her pixelated smile, frozen in time.

'You know anything about it?' Nia didn't know what mob boss had taken over her body, but she was going with it.

Eddie dropped down to his knees, cradled his head in his hands and began to sob. Morgan looked at Nia, frantic. This was not how they'd planned on the confrontation going. Someone was bound to call the cops. Nia had to get answers, fast.

'Are you serious right now?' Eddie asked between sobs. 'Rosie's dead?'

'That makes you one of the last people she talked to.' Nia squatted so that she was at eye level with Eddie. 'I know this is hard for you. Take a few deep breaths,' she coached, just like Jesse had done with her. Eddie followed her lead and his hiccups waned.

'We just need to know if Rosie sounded different on Monday night.'

'What do you mean?' he asked.

'Did she sound . . . I don't know, not herself? Did she mention anything out of the ordinary?'

Eddie shook his head. 'She was pissed that I came in late again and that she had to do the Fall Fest orders by herself this year. It's a lot of work, even for two people, and I offered to come back to at least help her, but she wouldn't listen. She wouldn't even let me get a word in. Said she gave me too many chances.'

'Was that true?'

Eddie sucked his teeth. 'Yeah, but I was a damn good baker, alright? I was a little late here and there, but Sam and Arianna can't bake half as good as I can.' Eddie paused, his breath catching in his throat. 'I slaved night and day in that place, and she fires *me*?'

'You were upset with her?' Nia asked.

'I was mad as hell.' His fist collided with his head. 'I was so stupid!'

'Whoa, whoa, whoa!' Morgan stepped in front of him. 'Chill on the abuse. We're just asking a few questions, trying to figure out what happened to our friend. What did you say to her?'

Eddie looked up at them both. Tears cascaded out of his crystal-blue eyes. 'I told her I hated her . . . that I wished . . .' He hiccupped again. 'I wished . . . she was dead.'

Chapter 12

Nia

Nia had always thought that Rosie was unique; a one-of-a-kind person who existed all on her own. From her style, to her laugh, to her kindness, Rosie was like royalty. But, when Nia arrived at her candlelight vigil that evening in front of the diner, she learned that Rosie was in fact one of four. She was younger than her other three siblings, and according to them, she was the glue that kept the family together.

Rupert was the oldest and didn't say much to the people who shared their condolences with him. He was a gruff man who kept his hands in his pockets and his eyes on the sidewalk. His creased dress pants, practical golf jacket, and frequent consultation of his watch told Nia that he looked like he had a million other places he would rather be than at his sister's memorial.

Rosie's twin sisters, Rubina and Rebecca, were more talkative, but only just. All of Rosie's siblings were as freakishly tall as she had been, and sported enamel rose pins that were clipped to their clothing. They stood around awkwardly, shocked, at the outpouring of love their sister had received from the Cinnamon Falls community.

As soon as the news broke Tuesday morning, Rosie's Diner was flooded with gifts of roses, candles, teddy bears, and pictures of Rosie as the town mourned their loss.

Eddie, Sam and Arianna, Rosie's bakers, agreed to work in the kitchen for the sake of Rosie's vigil. It hadn't taken much convincing from Nia and Morgan for Eddie to join his old crew. He was more than happy to get his job back, even if just for the time being. Chief Prescott agreed that they could serve hot chocolate and cinnamon buns out of the diner's back door until they ran out, as long as no one came inside and disturbed the crime scene. It was what Rosie would have wanted – to keep her people fed even in her absence.

People packed Main Street like sardines to pay their respects. Even though it was a somber occasion, it felt like a rainbow after the storm in Nia's heart. She'd been vacillating between emotions of sorrow and hope; existential dread and acceptance; but this proved that Cinnamon Falls had loved Rosie just as much as she had loved the town. Candles flickered in the twilight like fireflies, casting a warm glow over teary-eyed faces and handwritten notes tucked between bouquets of sunflowers and roses. Someone played a soft hymn on guitar, and the crowd joined in with reverent, broken voices.

Someone handed Rubina a microphone. After a brief moment of ear-splitting feedback, she addressed the crowd that had gathered in the streets.

'I want to say thank you, on behalf of my sister. We all chose to move away from Cinnamon Falls after our parents split up. I'm sure most of you didn't know Rosslyn had siblings. I, for one, haven't been back since Sienna . . .'

The crowd grew still. Rupert stood beside his sister and placed one hand on her back, and Rebecca grabbed her hand. Rubina cleared the frog in her throat and started again. 'We haven't been back since Sienna's funeral.'

Morgan placed her hand in Nia's at the mention of their friend's name. Nia was so glad that Morgan was there to support her. She didn't know how she could have possibly made it through the rest of the day without her. Before they left Eddie Rutherford blubbering on the curb, they'd invited him to the candlelight vigil and hightailed it back to Cinnamon Falls. Nia was thankful they'd decided to come to the vigil early because it felt like almost every resident had come to mourn Rosie's life.

Nia and Morgan managed to stand on the family's side, facing the masses. From this vantage point, Nia could see the entire crowd. She scanned the sea of people on high alert. As much as she wanted to be present, and mourn with the rest of the town, her grief had sprouted into anger, and she couldn't help but think that one of these people had killed Rosie. The nagging feeling was back in her gut and even though it had bad timing, it hadn't lied.

'We are so incredibly grateful for the calls, the texts, and the cards—'

'The flowers and all the food,' Rebecca added in.

'It is amazing to see our sister so well loved. We appreciate all of you more than you'll ever know. Rosslyn loved this place. When we all decided to leave, she fought us tooth and nail to stay. It's nice to see the love she had for this town be reciprocated. I know she's somewhere looking down on us, happy.'

Mayor Lyons approached the family. Nia almost choked on his musk-scented cologne as he passed by. Rubina handed the microphone to him like it stunk. The mayor cleared his throat, gripping the microphone a little too tightly.

'You know, Rosie and I didn't always see eye to eye. In fact, I think she enjoyed bossing me around more than most people in this town.'

A few chuckles bubbled up. He smiled, eyes scanning the crowd. 'I'll never forget Fall Fest, oh, what was it, eight years ago? Rosie insisted we try something new and host a pie-eating contest outside her diner. Sounded simple enough, until we forgot to label which pies were for the contest and which ones were for sale.'

He paused as a ripple of amusement stirred in the crowd.

'So there I am, chest deep in a sweet potato pie, competing with twelve other folks, when Rosie comes barreling out of the diner with her apron flying and shouts, "'Y'all are eating my lunch orders!"'

The crowd erupted in laughter.

'We were mortified. And of course, instead of canceling the contest, she just rolled up her sleeves, went back in the kitchen, and whipped up a whole new batch. Only Rosie could chew someone out and still send them home with a slice of pie and a smile.'

He chuckled, eyes twinkling. 'She was fire, sugar, and steel all in one. Cinnamon Falls will never taste quite the same without her.'

The mayor passed the microphone out to the crowd so everyone could have a chance to talk about their relationship with Rosie. As time passed, Nia got to hear how much Rosie had a hand in. She didn't just cater the Fall Festival, she also handled petty matters between residents, serving as a mediator and a therapist. Ethel Lawson, who ran Cinna Cutz, the all-women hair salon, claimed Rosie saved her marriage. There were dozens of stories just like that of Rosie saving the day. Nia wondered how someone so loved could become a victim of such violence. It was clear that everyone loved Rosie.

Everyone except for one person. Nia kept her eyes on the crowd, scanning for anything out of the norm.

She spotted one of Rosie's sisters out of the corner of her eye approaching her.

'This is going to be so embarrassing if I get this wrong, but aren't you one of Sienna's friends? Your family owns that cute little ice cream shop on the corner?' Rosie's sister Rubina asked. 'What happened to the old logo with the googly eyes?'

'Nia Bennett.' Nia stuck her hand out to Rubina, who shook it enthusiastically. 'And this is Morgan Taylor.' Nia stepped back so that Rubina could see Morgan standing beside her. After the talk at the mall, Nia never wanted Morgan to feel left out again. She wasn't the third in their friend group. She had been friends with both of them and Nia was going to treat her like that. 'We were all close.'

'Purple hair! Yes, I remember you from the funeral.' A knowing smile didn't reach Rubina's eyes when she reached over to shake Morgan's hand. Nia wondered how long it would take for a genuine smile to return to her face. She thought about Niles, and if it were her sibling, she didn't know if she'd ever manage to smile again.

'Thank you all so much for being there for Rosslyn. After the funeral, we had our own lives to get back to, but it was tough leaving her here all alone.'

'Then why did you?' Morgan asked flat out. She was as subtle as a gun. 'You didn't miss her?'

Rubina sighed deeply. 'We tried to get her to come with us to Atlanta, but she wanted to stay. This place was full of bad memories for us. It tore our family apart, and then our only niece . . . Well, you know.'

They knew all too well.

'I think it broke Rosslyn. She wasn't the same after that.'

None of us were, Nia thought.

'She didn't believe it for one second, you know,' Rubina added. 'She couldn't accept that her baby girl died in that horrific way.'

Morgan clutched Nia's hand so hard that her nails dug into Nia's skin.

'She didn't believe Sienna jumped?' Nia asked. Her insides were quaking and even though she was outside in the crisp October air, heat crept up her back and neck. She pulled the sweatshirt off her neck, but it didn't help.

'Of course not,' Rubina scoffed. 'Sienna hated the water, that much I remember. I worked so hard to get a pool in my backyard so my niece and nephews could come swim in the summertime. It was my goal to be the cool Auntie but Sienna never got in, ever.' Rubina sighed. 'I told Rosslyn this place was haunted years ago. Nothing good comes from small towns like Cinnamon Falls.'

Nia and Morgan met eyes. Another puzzle piece snapped together in Nia's mind. She knew there had to be a reason that Rosie had saved all of Sienna's paperwork other than being a grieving mother.

Rubina's twin sister Rebecca walked over to join them.

'You okay, Bean?' Rebecca removed the Styrofoam cup from Rubina's hand and sat it down on the curb. Her eyes darted between Nia and Morgan, sizing them up in seconds.

'Just chatting with Sienna's friends,' Rubina replied. 'You remember, um—'

'The lawyer's here,' Rebecca interrupted. 'We have to go figure out what to do about this place.'

'It wasn't like she had a will, Bec. Let them keep it,' Rubina whined. 'Do *you* want to run a freakin' diner?'

'Let's go, Bean,' her sister said, firmer than the time before. 'You're talkin' crazy.' Her hand was resting on her sister's waist, turning her away from Nia and Morgan.

'Rubina, now!' Rupert ordered, standing just a few steps away.

'I miss when Rosie was the youngest,' Rubina grumbled. She wrestled out of Rebecca's grip. 'I can walk by myself!'

Rebecca let her go and joined her brother with matching looks of disapproval. Rubina made sure to grab her cup before following after them. Their sudden departure left Nia reeling.

'Rosie didn't have a will?' Morgan whispered. 'That seems hard to believe.'

Nia turned to look up at the empty restaurant, her

mind whirring. The sign was still dark above it. What had Rosie been thinking in her last moments? Was she afraid? Did she know the person who killed her?

'Sienna is gone, who would take it over?' Nia wondered out loud.

Morgan slapped Nia's shoulder hard. She spun around to her friend, ready to reciprocate the blow that would be sure to bruise by morning.

'Ow! What the hell is wrong with you?'

Nia followed Morgan's trembling finger as she pointed through the crowd. On the outskirts of the throngs of people stood a hooded man. He tried to mask his face, pulling his hood down to cover most of his facial features, but after analyzing his pictures, Nia could tell who it was.

Morgan whispered, 'Let's go.'

Nia and Morgan pushed through the crowd to get to him.

Chapter 13

Jesse

Before Jesse left the barber shop that afternoon, Bones had mentioned that the Main Street businesses were organizing a candlelight vigil for Rosie. Jesse thought that it would just be close family and friends, but when he had to park at the station and walk down to the diner, he knew that the word had spread far and wide.

Rosie's Diner was blocked off. The front door was sealed shut and her neon logo that usually cast the entire street in a sultry red glow wasn't shining. But the light from each person's candle basked the block in gold.

Rosie's family made an appearance. Jesse didn't have to wonder which were her siblings. Her twin sisters and brother towered over most of the residents. Jesse found it humorous to watch them bend down to hug everyone who shared their individual condolences about their sister. Rubina did most of the talking, while Rebecca looked on with misty eyes. Rupert, on the other hand, hadn't looked up once. He kept his head lowered like he was deep in prayer. Jesse couldn't imagine what the man was feeling. If it were anything like he'd felt this morning, he knew Rupert was counting the seconds until he could get out of the public eye.

Jesse surveyed the rest of the crowd and spotted Sergeant Raines and Detective Chambers. He guessed they were doing the same things he was: watching for anything or anyone out of the ordinary.

Jesse knew the only way he could see the crowd in its entirety was to keep moving. He journeyed through throngs of mourners as the microphone passed through the crowd while they shared stories about Rosie. He made it to the outer edge where the crowd tapered out and ran into Maggie Shilling, hanging back like she didn't want to be seen.

'Jesse!' she exclaimed, pulling him in for a hug. 'I can't believe it.'

Ms. Maggie was so petite, it felt like he was cradling a rag doll. He thought back to yesterday morning when Chambers couldn't keep a grip on her because she'd been so upset. He couldn't imagine how shaken up she felt and the drama that she'd been through since then.

'I'm so sorry,' he said. 'Are you just leaving the station?'

'They kept me in there like some kind of criminal!

Someone told me there was an article and they're calling me a person of interest!' Maggie's eyes were big as saucers. 'All I did was call the police, Jesse, I swear.'

'I believe you, Maggie,' Jesse assured her. 'Did you talk to Sergeant Raines?'

Maggie's expression soured. 'Of course I told her. None of them believed me. I kept asking for Wade or for you, but no one would listen. They kept saying that I . . . that I had something to do with this.'

Jesse searched the crowd for Raines and Chambers with fire in his belly, but his eyes landed on Nia and Morgan instead. The glow from the crowd's candlelight washed Nia's face in an angelic golden dust. It didn't matter if it had been ten minutes or ten hours since he'd seen her, his heart still did a double step in his chest. It was like time slowed as he watched her.

He took her in from head to toe. Her normally curly hair was straightened with the ends bumped under, held out of her face by a headband. She wore the signature navy blue and gold Cinnamon Falls sweatshirt over a white collared blouse. He hadn't seen that on her since they were in high school. Straight-legged jeans were cuffed over a pair of leather loafers. She looked like she went to Asheville Prep. The girls were pushing through the crowd, Morgan tight on Nia's heels, and were headed his way.

'There's no way, Jesse. I would have never done

this. You know what this town means to me. I would never.' Maggie cried in his chest and Jesse did his best not to break down with her. There were so many pieces of the puzzle missing, and for Raines and Chambers to accuse Maggie of murder was too far. Jesse knew they were spitballing, trying to make anything stick, but they'd crossed a line now.

'I know it's tough, but can you tell me what happened that night, Maggie?' Jesse asked.

Her chest heaved with a heavy sigh. 'I got to Rosie's around midnight like we agreed. I'd been running errands all day and the diner was my last stop of the night. The front door was locked, which I thought was weird since Rosie was expecting me, but it was late at night . . .' Maggie trailed off.

'How did you get inside?' Jesse brought her back to the present.

'The back door,' Maggie said. 'Rosie showed me where she kept her spare key in case I ever had to get in if she wasn't around during one of the Fall Festivals a few years back. I walked through the kitchen and she wasn't there, or in her office. I went on to the service floor and I could see her in the first booth. I called to her and she wouldn't answer. She was slumped over and I thought maybe she'd fallen asleep or something, and when I tried to shake her awake, that's when I saw the blood.' Maggie clapped her hand over her mouth, holding back tears.

'I didn't know if she'd hurt herself or if something

worse had happened. I was panicking, Jay. I called the emergency line and the next thing I know they were dragging me out of the diner. They put me in that cold room all night and didn't let me go until this morning!' Maggie fisted her hands in her hair.

Jesse hated making her relive the night that would haunt her for years to come, but he had more questions. 'Did you see anything else, Ms. Maggie? Anything at all? Even the smallest thing could help—'

She glanced around nervously, biting down on her lip. She took a step closer to Jesse and he did the same. She looked up at him like her eyes held the secrets she couldn't bring herself to say. She sighed, exasperated. 'I—'

She stepped back suddenly and shook her head. 'I told them everything, Jesse, I swear. I just can't believe this is happening. Have you heard anything about the festival? All our hard work will be for nothing!' she cried.

'I'll take care of everything, I promise,' Jesse said. He placed both hands on her shoulders. 'Go home and get some rest. I'll figure it out.'

Maggie gave him a sad smile and Jesse felt like he was eight years old again, scared and crying because he'd lost sight of his parents at the Fall Festival. Ms. Maggie had spotted him, grabbed his hand and walked him up and down Main Street until he'd found them. After all these years, he still hadn't forgotten her kindness that day.

'Your momma raised a good boy.' She was too short to pat him on the top of the head as she would have back then. Instead, she wrapped her arms around his torso.

'If you think of anything, anything at all, you call me, okay?' Jesse said. Maggie nodded before she turned and disappeared within the crowd, just in time for Nia and Morgan to barrel past him like runaway bulls.

He reached for Morgan's arm as she brought up the rear. 'Whoa, whoa, whoa, where are you two headed?'

Morgan grabbed a hold of Nia's shirt and they both skidded to a stop.

'Jay!' Morgan exclaimed with wide eyes. 'What're you doing here? I mean, I know why you're here . . . Why we're all here.' She turned to Nia. 'Nia, look, it's Jay!'

Nia looked shocked at his presence. Did his haircut look *that* bad?

'What's up?' Jesse asked. Nia glanced over her shoulder at whatever they'd been chasing. 'Expecting someone?' he tried again, when he didn't receive an answer.

'I thought I saw Niles,' Nia blurted out unconvincingly.

'Right,' Jesse said, examining the two women closely. They were nervous about something, but what? His thoughts backtracked to yesterday when he saw Nia at the station. Did it have something to do with Rosie? Jesse narrowed his eyes.

'What are y'all up to?'

'Mourning, like everyone else,' Morgan snapped. 'What are you up to? You're out of uniform. Is this official police business?' She pointed her chin toward Chambers and Raines who were still standing around, scanning the crowd like their eyes were made of lasers.

'I'm here as a civilian,' Jesse responded coolly. 'Payin' my respects.'

'What's going on, Jesse? People are scared,' Nia whispered. Her eyes searched his. 'Can you tell us anything?'

'You know I can't,' Jesse said. He stuffed one hand in his pocket. The other scrubbed the back of his neck. 'Besides, I'm not working it anymore.'

Nia frowned. 'But yesterday you said . . . They took you off the case?'

'Who do they think is going to figure this out then? Because I don't trust top flight security for one second,' Morgan commented, nodding toward Raines and Chambers.

'It's for the best,' Jesse lied. 'I'm better with the people anyway.'

Nia rolled her eyes and stepped closer to him; so close, he could smell her perfume. It was different from the one she wore last night. It was a playful and bouncy citrus fragrance that made him think of the summers they'd spent together. He wanted to grab the back of her neck and kiss her.

She looked up at him. Her innocent expression made his knees wobble. He could barely breathe when she said, 'There's no one I would trust to get the job done more than you, Jay.'

Chapter 14

Nia

'You got that man wrapped around your finger!' Morgan exclaimed as she carefully maneuvered her truck out of Rosie's parking lot. The crowd parted to clear the way for her vehicle. Through the passenger window, Nia kept her eyes on Jesse, and he did the same, holding her gaze with an intensity that sent a shiver down her spine.

When she left six years ago, Jesse had been handsome in a charming and easy-going way. But now, his once-lean frame had hardened into broad shoulders and a muscular build, the kind that came from years of training, and not just genetics.

The maroon Henley he wore stretched across his chest. His jaw was sharper underneath his close-cropped beard. His features were more defined, and the boyish softness she once knew was now replaced by a quiet strength that made it impossible to look away. Pterodactyl-sized butterflies flapped wildly in her stomach, a reminder that she wasn't as unaffected as she wanted to be. It wasn't until Jesse was out of her line of sight that she finally exhaled.

Morgan slapped Nia's arm playfully. 'I saw those puppy dog eyes you gave him. He was ready to get on one knee!'

Nia couldn't recall a time she'd ever felt like this with Bryant. Where Bryant was comfortable and cozy, Jesse felt irresistible and mysterious. Who was this new version of Jesse? Who had he grown to become in the years they'd spent apart? Nia was curious, that was certain, but she knew she'd make no progress on that front without an apology. He deserved that.

Nia hoped that they would have some alone time so that she could finally make amends. She didn't know how long she would stay in Cinnamon Falls, but she didn't want another day to go by without him knowing how she felt.

Nia tried to hide her blush behind her hands but Morgan had already caught her expression. 'It's just complicated right now,' she said.

Being around Jesse made her feel *things* and she wasn't sure if her heart was ready to take another plunge. Technically, she was lying to him. She promised that she wouldn't interfere with the investigation, and she was doing everything but keeping her promise. If Jesse ever found out, he'd probably flip. For now, she had to keep everything between her and Morgan until she had something substantial;

something that would make him believe that there was more to Rosie's death.

Besides, she still had unfinished business with Bryant and her life back in Atlanta. It was only a matter of time before someone from Gildman & Sons called to ask where she was. She planned on quitting, but then Rosie died, and all her plans had been derailed. As much as she wanted to sort out that part of her life, she had more pressing matters on the home front.

If they hadn't run into Jesse, Nia and Morgan would have had the opportunity to talk to Harvey Briggs and hear his side of the story. One second he was there at the memorial, and the next he was gone. But Nia wasn't worried. She knew where he lived.

Morgan didn't need to be convinced to make the drive out to Harvey's Used Cars. She had already shaken down a suspect outside of his workplace. What was making a house call?

'What's complicated about getting your man back?' Morgan asked. 'I don't even think Jesse has even looked at another woman since you left. Well, except that one thing with Grace,' she mumbled.

Nia's mouth dropped open. 'Grace Whitfield?' The nerve of her. Her father was practically the richest man in all of Cinnamon Falls and she goes after Nia's leftovers? Had she always liked Jesse?

'Calm down,' Morgan advised. 'It was only a couple of dates, I think. Nothing serious.'

'You *think*?' Nia asked, incredulous.

'I'm pretty sure Jay let her down easy. The man has always been in love with you.'

Nia tried to shake the jealous thoughts out of her head. Jesse deserved someone to love. After all, she was the one who'd ended things. She should be happy that he'd found someone else. In reality, Nia was trying to calculate how long a detour to the Whitfield Family Mortuary would take.

'So, what's the plan when we get out there?' Morgan switched on her bright lights to illuminate the road ahead. The sun had set long ago, casting jagged shadows of the trees that stretched over the quiet, one-lane highway to Harvey's. Nia hadn't been to the outskirts of town in ages. She felt a nauseating mix of determination and unease at the same time.

'Are we good-cop-bad-cop-ing this thing, or what? I personally call dibs on the bad-cop role because you're too nice, just saying.'

'I kind of want you to stay in the car,' Nia admitted sheepishly.

Morgan hit the brakes and Nia narrowly avoided slamming her front teeth on the dashboard. 'Are you kidding me? Leave me in the car like I'm some misbehaved puppy? What if something happens to you? What if you go missing? You want me to tell your momma how I dropped you off in the middle of the woods and stayed in the car? I don't think so!'

'Fine,' Nia relented, secretly appreciating the

backup. She didn't want to face Harvey alone. She'd had few interactions with him growing up, and didn't know much about him. While all of her classmates went out to Harvey's to get old-school cars to one-up each other, she had to get rides to school in her father's ancient Subaru station wagon from the eighties. But, if Rosie had cared for him in the way that Morgan described, he couldn't have been all bad.

Morgan accelerated again and the two carved out a game plan for the conversation with Harvey. Nia needed to know about Rosie's final moments. Had Rosie said anything to him that would help Nia find out who'd done this to her? What if she was walking directly into the lion's mouth?

Harvey's Used Cars looked like it had seen better days. Between the overgrown weeds and the rusting cars, business had to have been in the pits for him for a while. Morgan unlatched the gate and traveled up the winding dirt path slowly until they came to a run-down trailer. Inside, a light flickered.

Morgan parked her truck and both women hopped out. Nia wished she had a weapon, or something other than her two hands, as she knocked on the screen door. She heard movement inside. Nia felt around in her purse until she found a set of keys. She slipped her finger inside the loop, the metal key cool between her fingers. If she had to fight, at least she could do a little damage to her attacker.

'Who is it?' Harvey demanded.

'Um, Nia Bennett, Mr. Briggs,' Nia replied in a soft tone, hoping to imply that she meant no harm.

'The girl uses her real name.' Morgan shook her head, mumbling. 'And she wanted me to stay in the car.'

'Shut up!' Nia whispered.

The interior door banged open, slamming against the opposite wall, loud as a gunshot. Both Nia and Morgan gasped as a disheveled Harvey Briggs stepped into the screen door. His colossal stature alone could easily prompt intimidation from the most secure man. His skin was wrinkled and weathered, like he'd spent many days outside in the sun. His hands were tough and blistered, and his oil-stained overalls gave him the look of a tired mechanic.

Mr. Briggs kept a tidy home compared to his exterior. The smell of old coffee and cigarettes permeated the air. The rugged man offered Nia a seat on the worn couch, and although she didn't want to go in any further, she also didn't want to be rude. His living room was only illuminated by the light of the TV and Nia examined every inch of the place that she could see, especially if these were to be her last moments.

Very quickly, Nia determined that Mr. Briggs was a man in love. Small feminine touches stood out among the abundantly masculine design of his place, like the quaint walnut coffee table with scalloped edges that housed a TV so wide that Niles would have surely committed a crime for it. Another dining table set for two was pushed against the far wall. A flower hung limply out of a little white vase. Either Briggs had been preparing for someone's arrival, or he frequently kept the company of a woman. If Nia were a gambler, she would guarantee that there were two toothbrushes in his bathroom.

'Whatever you're lookin' for, I ain't got it. I just got back in town. I haven't even unpacked my damn bag. You'll have to come back after the weekend.'

Morgan was still standing next to the door and Nia looked at her to confirm if what he'd said was true. From her vantage point, she had the perfect line of sight of the entire trailer.

'Suitcase,' Morgan mouthed, gesturing down Mr. Briggs' hallway.

Briggs' yellowed eyes swung over to Morgan. 'Who are y'all, anyway?' he asked, giving her a suspicious once-over, then concentrating back on Nia.

Morgan grinned and hooked her thumbs in her belt loops, too deep into her bad-cop act. 'Your worst nightmare: women with questions.'

His brow furrowed. 'What—

'Rosie's dead,' Nia blurted out. Her heart shook against its cage, as she braced herself for his response.

Harvey froze, tilting his head to one side, and stared at her like she spoke a foreign language. 'No, no, no, no,' he cried. 'Rosie can't be dead.'

'You were just at her memorial service,' Morgan said with her hand on her hips. 'Don't act like you didn't know.'

'I got home ten minutes ago!' Spittle flew out of Briggs' mouth when he screamed. He fisted his hands in his hair. 'Rosie, baby, no!' His face crumpled into tears and suddenly the tough, grizzled man collapsed into sobs. He dropped to his knees and the trailer shook under his weight. The tiny white vase teetered and crashed to the floor, sending ceramic shards everywhere.

'God, forgive me,' he cried, burying his face in his hands. He pulled himself into the fetal position, rocking back and forth on the ground, muttering, 'God, forgive me. God, please forgive me.'

Morgan looked at Nia, panic in her eyes. Did he just confess?

'What do you mean?' Nia asked. She scooted to the edge of the couch. She wanted to reach out to him, to console him.

'Tell us what happened, Harvey. Why do you need forgiveness?' Morgan demanded.

Before he could answer, flashing red and blue lights swarmed the living room. The crunch of boots on gravel raced closer and closer. Morgan leapt out of the way seconds before the front door to Harvey's trailer was kicked off its hinges, exploding into the trailer.

'CFPD!' someone yelled out.

Morgan screamed and Nia dropped to the floor instinctively, covering her head. Harvey struggled to stand. He turned to run and was instantly brought down by two burly officers who tackled him to the floor. The living room table collapsed under the weight of three men. The TV popped and fizzled out until the room was plunged into darkness – save for the red and blue lights chasing each other across the walls.

A petite woman stepped inside the trailer, her gun aimed at Harvey's head. 'Harvey Briggs, you're under arrest.'

The two officers who restrained Harvey made way for a tall, lanky man. Nia recognized him from the station yesterday with Jesse. He snapped a pair of handcuffs on Briggs' thick wrists. Still crying, Harvey didn't resist while they hoisted him to his feet and dragged him out of his own home.

Nia blinked up at the tall officer from the ground. 'I can explain,' she said, offering him a smile.

The short woman joined his side, looking down at Nia in disapproval.

'Oh, I can't wait to hear this.' The male officer crossed his arms.

Morgan, flat on the floor beside Nia, whispered, 'This is the most exciting thing that's ever happened to me.'

'On your feet!' the short woman demanded.

Nia and Morgan scrambled to stand. Someone flicked the light on at the panel near the door. The trailer was trashed.

Harvey's front door had a boot print-sized dent in it and its impact had ruined his kitchen. Pots and pans were everywhere. The sink must have gotten hit in the chaos because the faucet was wildly spraying ice cold water all over the group. Nia's teeth chattered. What were the odds that the day she straightened her hair, she'd get it wet?

'Start talking,' the short officer demanded. From her voice alone, Nia could tell she meant business. She was going to have to use both her Big Joker cards if she wanted to get out of this.

'This is Nia Bennett,' the taller officer said in a knowing voice. His badge read, 'T. Chambers'.

'So, Jesse does talk about me,' Nia said, throwing out her first card, The Jesse Name Drop.

The woman's eyes narrowed at Nia. 'Bring her in,' she announced to the crew of officers who were standing in the doorway, and then stomped out of the trailer.

Nia blanched. 'Wait! I didn't do anything!'

'Mmmm, technically trespassing, interfering with an investigation,' Morgan said, listing on her fingers.

'You're not helping!' Nia said with a glare.

Chambers spun her around and forcefully married her wrists together. Nia winced as the metal cuffs tightened, pinching her skin. Morgan held out her arms to the other officers standing nearby.

'I've always wanted to know what this feels like,' she said giddily.

'Ma'am, you're not under arrest—'

'Cuff me, coward!' Morgan demanded.

He sighed and obliged, slapping a pair of cuffs on her too.

Nia had never been in the back of a police cruiser before. In fact, she had never been in trouble with the law before in any capacity. Her mind was on overdrive, coming up with plans to get out of the cuffs and stop her parents from finding out. She could already see the disappointment on her mother's face. Niles would be snapping pictures of her heading into the cell, and keeping them as leverage for years to come.

'I cannot believe this,' Nia grumbled. She rested her head against the window.

'I can,' Morgan said. From the tone in her voice Nia could tell that she was smiling. 'This is exactly the kind of bird-brained activity that you'd come up with.'

Nia was not in the mood for jokes.

'No, but seriously. Do you think they'll let us share a cell? You think it's an *Orange Is The New Black* kind of situation?' Morgan chirped.

Nia groaned, wishing she wasn't handcuffed so she could smother Morgan.

'What? I'm just saying. If we have to spend the night, I want the top bunk, no take backs.'

Nia forced her eyes shut as the cruiser drifted over the gravel leading out of Harvey's place. What had she gotten herself into? She came here to look for answers about Rosie and she'd gotten herself arrested instead. Her mind flashed back to the moments before the cops arrived. Had Harvey been confessing? What did he need forgiveness for? Why did he pretend he hadn't heard about her murder?

Nia was drowning in more questions than answers. She should have listened to Jesse and stayed out of it. Beside her, Morgan began chuckling.

'What is it?' Nia asked, annoyed. If Morgan cracked another joke, Nia was going to bite her way out of the cruiser.

Morgan cackled, threw her head back and said, 'Jesse is going to be *so* pissed.'

Chapter 15

Thursday
Jesse

For the second night that week, Jesse was woken up by a phone call from work. He hadn't slept much, just a few hours, when his phone vibrated on the table. Jesse reluctantly cracked his eyes and the clock on the opposite wall read 5:32 a.m. He'd been put off the case, what could anyone at the precinct want with him at this time of the morning? Jesse groaned and brought the phone to his ear.

'Shaw,' he grumbled, wiping the sleep out of his eyes. He had been in another dreamless sleep – something he rarely experienced. For a long time he'd been haunted by the ghosts of battle: the rat-a-tat-tat of gunfire and harrowing explosions. Other times, like tonight, he got lucky.

Until he wasn't.

Angie sounded stressed when she responded. 'Uh, you might want to get up here as soon as possible, Jay.'

He sat up straight in bed. 'What's going on?'

Why didn't the Chief call, or Raines, if it were something that important?

Angie sighed. 'Nia Bennett was arrested tonight. I've got her and Morgan Taylor booked together in a holding cell. I was going to call her emergency contact . . . a Bryant Green, but she insisted I call you—'

Jesse didn't have to hear the rest. He was already out of bed and getting dressed. He fumbled around in the pre-dawn light, pulling on a pair of jeans and sliding on the first shirt he got his hands on. He stuffed his feet in a pair of shoes and hustled down the stairs. He was halfway through the door when he realized it'd be the second time that he wouldn't be preparing breakfast for his father. This job was changing his routine, and that was giving him anxiety. He did things in order for a reason. He needed stability.

Jesse scrawled a note for his father and used a magnet to tack it to the refrigerator. There was plenty of food, but Jesse enjoyed making his parents' meals. It kept him grounded. Now his mind was running at top speed, and he desperately needed time to slow down so that he could catch his breath and regroup.

He made it to the station in record time. The usual bustling station was silent at this hour of the morning. Angie was stationed at the front desk, manning dispatch and the tip line simultaneously. The woman needed a raise.

Overhead, the humming fluorescent lights kept him company while he waited for Nia and Morgan to emerge. Deep within the station he heard the holding cell door buzz.

He saw her legs first. Nia's hips swayed toward him in a hypnotizing motion. Her jeans had been ripped at the knee and Jesse knew for a fact her jeans hadn't been ripped at the memorial. Had she fallen? A hot rage rushed through him at the thought of someone hurting her. The crisp white blouse she had on earlier was wrinkled and stained. When she fully came into view he realized that she was soaking wet. Her curls had returned and whatever makeup she'd been wearing was smeared down her face and sweater. She cradled her arms to her body, rubbing her wrists where handcuffs would have gone.

Jesse vowed to take the arresting officer apart limb by limb.

Nia looked up at him, finally. She pressed her lips together and Jesse couldn't tell if she was embarrassed or if she was about to laugh. He wanted to take her in his arms and kiss her all over her body and make this hellish night of her life go away. He also wanted to know why he had been woken up at five-thirty a.m., and he hoped Nia had a good explanation.

'Getting arrested on your third day back has got to be a new record.'

Nia opened her mouth to respond when the door buzzed again. Morgan pranced out of the holding cell. She was sporting a smile like she'd just come from an amusement park. Jesse noticed that she looked significantly less disheveled than Nia.

'What should we get arrested for next – tax evasion? Money laundering?' Morgan asked Nia. She rambled on, suggesting all different kinds of arrestable offenses. Nia, on the other hand, was silent. She was blank behind the eyes like numbered sheep were hopping through her brain.

Jesse signed the paperwork for their release, and Angie handed him two bags of the women's belongings. Morgan counted every coin in her wallet before she trusted that her purse was the one she came into the station with.

Outside, the sun was beginning to rise. Jesse took in a deep breath of the crisp autumn air. He needed to clear his head. He cruised down Main Street before taking the highway to Morgan's place. The town looked like the aftermath of a horror movie. Without Maggie Shilling's diligent pruning, the decorations that normally brought joy looked unkempt and somber in the morning light.

The ride across town was surprisingly silent. Jesse

thought that Morgan had gotten the hint that he wasn't in the mood for jokes, but she had fallen fast asleep in the backseat.

Nia shook her friend awake.

'Call me later,' Morgan told Nia, bleary-eyed. As she got out she quietly added, 'Take it easy on her, Jay.'

'Goodnight, Morgan.' Jesse gripped the steering wheel. He hated that he was so predictable. He'd rehearsed what he wanted to say the entire drive over. Mostly, he needed to know if Nia was okay. Once Morgan had reached her front door and got inside safely, Jesse pulled away from the curb.

'Go ahead,' Nia relented.

'What happened?' Jesse asked, keeping his voice even.

Nia showed him her raw wrists. 'I was arrested,' she said sarcastically.

Jesse pulled the car over. He couldn't have a conversation with her without looking at her. He needed her to see that he was serious. It wasn't time for fun and games. His job and his livelihood were on the line. She needed to start talking, and fast.

'Be more specific,' Jesse requested.

'I went to Harvey Briggs' house.' She paused and added, 'I also talked to Rosie's head baker, Eddie Rutherford.'

Nia said it so quickly, Jesse shook his head to make sure he heard her right. 'What were you thinking?'

Nia sighed and picked at her fingers. 'I was thinking they might have some answers.' Jesse started to interject but Nia cut him off. 'They were the last people Rosie called. I looked it up.' She flashed a picture on her phone of what looked like a Caller ID. 'I just thought one of them could tell me something . . . Anything about Rosie's last moments.'

Jesse scrubbed his hands down his face. 'What did you find out?' he asked through gritted teeth.

'Nothing.' Still, Nia wouldn't look at him. 'Eddie knew nothing and Briggs cried when I told him that Rosie was dead. He looked shocked. He kept asking for God's forgiveness. It was the saddest thing I've ever witnessed. The sounds that came out of him . . .' Nia covered her ears like she could still hear the horrors in her mind. Jesse knew that feeling all too well.

'Nia, you're done with this. Do you understand?'

Nia scoffed. 'You can't tell me what to do.'

Jesse faced her full on. He hooked a finger under her chin, forcing her to look at him. 'I am not going to watch you put yourself in danger.' He lowered his voice, taming his anger. 'You need to let us work this case.'

Guilt flickered across her face. 'You can't expect me to sit back and do nothing, Jay. Someone murdered Rosie, *our* Rosie! Don't you get that?' Nia wailed.

'Of course I do. You could get yourself into some serious trouble, Nia!'

'She'd do the same thing for me!' Nia screamed. Tears crowded her eyes and the pain in her voice made Jesse feel like his heart was in a vice grip.

Jesse realized that he could warn her about the consequences of her actions all he wanted, but Nia wasn't going to stop looking until she got answers. And neither was he.

He sighed and placed his hand palm up on the console between them. It was something they did in high school after a bad fight; a truce to put the past behind them and move forward. Jesse didn't know if she would remember, but his heart hoped for the best.

Nia's hand slid on top of his, palm down. They intertwined their fingers. The deal was done.

'You owe me breakfast for dragging me into your bad decisions.' Jesse pulled onto the road.

Nia giggled and his heart did a little dance at the sound. 'Fine, but I get to pick the place.'

After Rosie's Diner, The Toasted Pecan had the best all-day breakfast in Cinnamon Falls. What used to be a quaint family-owned bakery had been expanded to a full-service cafe in the early nineties after families complained that the pecan sticky buns should be available year-round. Jesse had been craving a home-cooked meal and Clarissa Hargrove's pecan waffles with slow-churned cinnamon butter were going to do the trick.

Nia and Jesse were the first customers of the morning. Mrs. Hargrove had just lit the fireplace when the two walked in. The exposed brick walls and wooden beams gave the place a timeless and rustic feel that made Jesse feel right at home. They settled into a booth near the fireplace. Nia stripped off her damp sweater and laced it on the back of a nearby chair so the heat could dry it out. Jesse immediately offered her his sweater without a second thought. He was thankful he'd thought to grab his jacket before leaving the house.

Nia disappeared to the bathroom and returned quickly, swimming in his sweater. The black crew neck sweatshirt that was proving to be too tight across his pecs, stopped at her thighs. Deep down, he knew he wouldn't be getting it back.

She looked like she had pajamas on. They shared a look, both clearly thinking the same thing, and shared a laugh so deep it made his belly ache.

It was moments like this that made Jesse miss Nia the most. He hadn't found a woman who could make him laugh as easily as she could, and if he were being truthful, he wasn't looking. There had been others; a date or two, or three, but nothing as substantial as the friendship they had found together. Physical aside, he longed for connection more than anything. Looks faded and bodies changed; it was

Nia's kindness that drew him to her. As serious and strait-laced as she was, she was also spontaneous and fun. She was magnetic and Jesse longed to be close to her. The six years they'd been apart were unbearable.

Nia warmed her hands at the fire.

'Figured you two needed some liquid electricity at this hour.' Mrs. Hargrove delicately sat two steaming coffee mugs on the table. 'I'll be back in a minute to take your order.'

Nia ripped the top off three sugar packets stacked in a line and poured them into her hot coffee.

'Still ruining a perfectly good cup of coffee, huh?' Jesse joked. He was like his father in many ways; meaning he liked his coffee black. Adding creamer or sugar was a rare occasion when he needed a sweet pick-me-up. Being across the table from Nia was all the sweetness he needed.

'Still judging me for it?' she responded with a playful light in her eyes. 'I grew up on ice cream for breakfast, lunch and dinner, okay? I need a little sugar with everything.'

There was a beat of silence between them while they enjoyed their warm beverages together. Jesse had no idea what she was thinking, but he was content in the silence. He'd been craving her presence since she'd walked out of his life six years ago. He wasn't going to ruin the moment with words. He'd let her take all the time she needed.

'I'm sorry for leaving,' Nia said after a long while.

Jesse sat back in his seat, taking in the words that punched him in the chest.

'You didn't just leave, Nia. You disappeared.'

Nia swallowed, hard. 'And if I had stayed, I never would have left home.'

Jesse blinked, caught off guard. 'What do you mean? You had your mind pretty made up. There was nothing I could have said or done to stop you. Trust me, I tried.'

'I loved you, Jesse.' His chest tightened. Somehow, the airy cabin became claustrophobic. 'And I knew if I didn't go, I'd hurt you.'

'Too late for that,' Jesse mumbled.

'You're not hearing me,' Nia emphasized. 'I was lost after Sienna died. I didn't know how to process those feelings. You tried your best to love me through the pain and I'll always remember how you were there for me; how kind you were to me in my lowest moments. But I needed to get away. I was so fixated on starting over and forgetting about this place.'

'All you talked about was leaving me. We fought constantly,' Jesse reminded her. 'You didn't even seem like yourself anymore.'

'I wasn't,' Nia shot back. 'I'm not the same anymore, Jesse. Everything is different now.'

Jesse decided to stay quiet and give her the chance to explain.

'It was never about you. Leaving didn't make me

forget you. It didn't make me stop missing you. I never stopped loving you.'

Jesse exhaled and shook his head. 'I needed to hear that six years ago,' he responded.

Nia offered her hand, palm up. There was something softer between them now. A cushiony feeling that made Jesse feel lighter by the second. He reached across the table, his fingers brushing hers until their palms connected.

He interlocked his fingers with hers. 'You're back now, and whether you plan on staying or not, I'm not letting you disappear again.'

Hours later, when Jesse returned to the station for his shift, he made a beeline for Chambers' desk. On the paperwork he'd signed to get Nia and Morgan out of the holding cell, Jesse read that Chambers was the arresting officer. He was the one who'd caused Nia to massage her wrists all morning from where he'd locked the cuffs too tight. Jesse had already warned Chambers once about messing with the people he loved; he had no problem reminding him.

Jesse found Chambers' desk empty and it took the wind out of his sails. He was looking forward to seeing the look on Chambers' face when Jesse towered over him.

'Where's Beetlejuice?' Jesse tossed the question to the officers roaming around in the bullpen.

Bud Wade answered, 'Press conference.' He flipped his wrist over. 'Should be coming on soon.' He nodded toward the break room where a bunch of officers were already gathering. Jesse joined them, taking a seat near the back door.

On the screen, the cream and brown Cinnamon Falls flag was on display along with the Georgia state flag, flanking the empty podium on both sides. Town Hall was crowded. Jesse heard the hushed rumble of conversation. The mayor arrived on screen first, the camera pushed in tight on his smiling face. Chief Prescott filed in behind him, followed by Sergeant Raines, and finally Detective Chambers. Jesse booed him in his head. Sergeant Raines, as surly as ever, showed no emotion. Chambers took her lead and kept his expression blank too.

Chief Prescott approached the microphone. Jesse hadn't seen the man smile in forty-eight hours, and now he couldn't stop showing his teeth. Something was up.

'First of all, I want to say thank you to the incredible hard-working officers of Cinnamon Falls.' A smattering of applause broke out in the room. The Chief turned and applauded the officers behind him. Chambers had the nerve to wave to the crowd. 'We are pleased to announce that we have Rosslyn Rose's killer in custody.'

Had Harvey Briggs confessed between last night and this morning? Jesse wondered. He thought back to Nia's conversation just a few hours ago: *He kept asking for God's forgiveness.* That was hardly a confession. They must have had some solid evidence to make the Chief call a press conference. It had only been two days since Rosie was murdered. Were Raines and Chambers *that* good? What had he missed?

Hands shot in the air from concerned citizens, and Jesse already knew what they were going to ask.

Prescott continued. 'This was a tragic loss for our community, but we are dedicated to upholding peace, and ensuring swift justice is served. Our officers are the best of the best. Thanks to them, Cinnamon Falls is safe tonight.'

Mayor Lyons stepped up to the microphone, pulling it down to his height so that he could be heard clearly. 'With the case officially closed, we are happy to announce that the Fall Festival will proceed as planned!'

The crowd erupted, cheering, and Jesse began to question his reality. He knew the people of Cinnamon Falls would cling to whatever the mayor said to bring a sense of peace and normalcy to their homes. Truth was out the window. All they wanted was an arrest so they could sleep undisturbed at night, and it didn't matter what or who it cost.

Chapter 16

Nia

Surprisingly, Nia slept peacefully once Jesse dropped her home after breakfast. She thought she'd have nightmares about spending the night on cold concrete for weeks to come.

Harvey's confession.

The ear-splitting *bang* when his front door was kicked in.

A gun pushed in her face.

The screaming.

But when she woke, all the memories of yesterday's adventures were waiting to remind her. Her hips and back were sore from where she'd thrown herself on the ground. Her wrists throbbed where the handcuffs had rubbed against her skin and her shoulders had a dull pinch of pain every time she moved.

The misty autumn afternoon didn't help either. All she wanted to do was return to her subconscious dreamland. But she had unfinished business. After watching the abysmal press conference, Nia knew the police had arrested the wrong person.

She had been in the man's presence for less than an hour, but she could feel in her core that Harvey Briggs was innocent. He was in love with Rosie, Nia could tell it in his eyes. He wasn't just shocked at the news of her death, he was afraid. Of what? Nia didn't know.

There was more to the story, and somehow, she'd been looking at this all wrong. She needed to start from the beginning, and she could feel it in her gut that the beginning started with Harvey Briggs.

Nia rolled over to find Midnight snoring next to her in bed. Nia looked over her shoulder, and sure enough, her bedroom door was cracked. How Midnight could enter a locked door, she didn't know. The cat was a certified ninja. And maybe, just maybe, Nia was becoming her favorite person in the house.

As soon as the thought crossed Nia's mind, Midnight stirred awake and stretched. She stuck both paws into Nia's side and craned backward, shaking out her polished black coat. She pounced on top of Nia and purred, pushing her head under Nia's hand, forcing a few scratches behind her ear. Nia happily accepted the offer of affection.

'You're kinda nice sometimes,' she said. Then she realized the reason why Midnight was being so suspiciously adorable.

'Tuna crisps,' Nia grumbled, remembering the

blood oath she'd mistakenly made. She scooped Midnight up in her arms and took her downstairs to the pantry and then realized another grave error she'd made. In all the melee, she'd forgotten to go to the grocery store to get more snacks like her father asked.

Nia sat Midnight down on the floor and she immediately began to pace at her feet.

'Here's the thing,' Nia explained to the bloodthirsty animal. 'I went to jail, right? And—'

'You went to jail?!'

Nia's heart leapt into her throat, and she slammed the pantry door shut to reveal Niles standing behind it. He was carrying two plastic bags full of tuna crisps. She silently thanked whatever gods were listening that it was only Niles and not her parents.

'Shhh!' Nia warned, snatching the snacks from him. She ripped open a packet and tossed a few down to Midnight, who pushed them away with her paws.

'What do you think, she's some common peasant who eats off the floor?' Niles asked bewildered, taking the bags back from his sister. 'Put it in her bowl, you weirdo. Do you eat off the floor?'

Midnight followed dutifully behind him. Nia heard the distinct ping of crispy snacks hitting Midnight's bowl, followed by soft crunches of satisfaction immediately after.

'That's my girl,' Niles said to the cat in a baby voice.

Nia rolled her eyes, but figured she would be helpful since Niles had saved her from facing her own mortality.

'You know she's bullying all of you, right?' she asked, as she restocked Midnight's side of the pantry.

Niles reminded her, 'You were just explaining to a cat why you were in jail and I, for one, would love to hear it.'

'Keep your voice down,' Nia warned. The last thing she needed was her mother to hear that she'd spent the night at the station. Or worse, her father. He was normally an easy-going guy who was rarely ever mad. Nia was quite sure that getting arrested for trespassing would be cause for her never seeing the light of day again.

'It's five-thirty p.m. on a Thursday.' Niles gestured to the clock on the microwave beside him. 'Mom and Dad are at the shop.'

'Then why aren't you at practice or something?' Nia questioned.

Niles stepped back to reveal his clothing: a white collared shirt and black slacks. 'I had work study today.'

Nia loved her work study days when she was in high school. She'd worked as a researcher at a law office in Asheville. Twice a week she would leave school early and catch the bus to the next town over, and spend her afternoons poring over old files at the lawyers' request.

It was quiet and meaningful work, and gave her the experience to score her position as a research assistant at Gildman & Sons. That reminded her, it'd been four days since she'd left Atlanta and she hadn't reported to work. Even if she didn't go back to the city, she didn't want to burn a bridge with the biggest law firm in the state. She still had her future to think about, however undetermined it was.

'What do I do? Oh, thanks for asking.' Niles stepped around her and finished filling Midnight's part of the pantry, while Nia snapped out of her thoughts.

He clipped off his badge and tossed it on the kitchen counter. It slid over to Nia and she beamed at his very first work ID.

'I'm the digitizer at the County Clerk's office. Well, most of the time I help all the old people with their computers, so I'm basically a glorified help desk; it's always their passwords. Just write it down, I tell them. This one lady, Miss Eloise, I have to reset her password almost every day. It's sad to see them struggle with technology. The digital divide is real and we need to do something about it—'

'I'm so proud of you.' Nia hated being sentimental around her brother but the pride she felt was overwhelming. Above everyone, she felt the worst for leaving Niles, and missing his years of maturation. When she'd left, he was still shorter than her, way more annoying, and had no concept of personal space. Now, he had his own job and could drive all by himself. She'd missed so much in so little time.

'Please don't start that.' Niles backed away from her. 'You were gone, now you're back. I get it. We don't have to cry about it.'

'But we do,' Nia responded. She opened her arms for a hug and, reluctantly, Niles took a few steps toward her. His shoulders slumped and he poked his bottom lip out.

'You were gone forever, Ni-Ni,' he whispered.

As soon as Nia heard his voice wobble, she pulled him into her arms. The little boy she'd left was growing into a man, and they most certainly did have to cry about it.

Niles drummed his fingers along the steering wheel nervously. 'You're seriously going back in there after what happened last night?'

They were parked on the opposite side of the road from Harvey's Used Cars. The misty rain was quickly turning into a downpour, making his dirt road a muddy mess. If Niles didn't go in now, her father's sedan was sure to get stuck at the bottom of the hill.

'I need my car,' Morgan added from the backseat. She knocked her purple bangs out of her face. 'I had to take the bus this morning to school. That girl almost killed me. I—'

Nia reached behind the seat and pinched Morgan's

leg, cutting off her rant. 'I just have a feeling there's more to this place,' she said.

She hopped out and ran across the street to open the gate while Niles maneuvered the car inside. Slowly, they made it up the hill and, sure enough, Morgan's truck was exactly where they'd left it yesterday.

'Glad to know my car isn't worth impounding,' Morgan mumbled.

Nia and Morgan both thanked Niles for the ride and got out of the car. Morgan climbed into the driver's seat of her truck and Nia slid into the passenger seat.

Niles aligned his car alongside Nia's window. 'Don't get arrested again, Ni. I'm serious. I'll be forced to tell the parentals . . . Or Midnight.'

Morgan leaned over. 'Come on, nothing bad ever happens in broad daylight,' she reasoned.

Niles gave them a serious but unconvinced look, shook his head, and drove away. Nia's phone buzzed with a text: it was a video of Midnight fighting with an innocent bird in their backyard. The bird was losing. Another text buzzed in that read, *This could be you*.

'Let's get out of here.' Morgan started her truck and made a wide circle to turn back toward the entrance. Nia looked back at Briggs' trailer; the interior door was crushed, hanging out of the entryway. She was sure rain was getting inside. She imagined it pooling under his carpet, waterlogging the place entirely.

The angle of the truck gave Nia a chance to see

behind Briggs' trailer – there was a small patch of trees that weren't as high as the others that stretched toward the sky. Through the patch she noticed what looked to be an outhouse.

'Morgan, stop the truck,' Nia demanded. She gestured toward the trees. 'Pull around back.'

'Tell me again why we're snooping around an accused murderer's home?' Morgan asked, while she navigated the truck behind the house. They arrived at the clearing of trees, and up close, Nia could tell it was a shed. A very big shed.

'Because something about this doesn't add up. Harvey knows something about what happened to Rosie. You saw him blubbering like a baby; that wasn't remorse, that was fear.'

Nia zipped her jacket up to her chin and tied her hood tight around her head.

'This is where I draw the line,' Morgan said, crossing her arms over her chest. 'I refuse to do the rain.' She pointed to her new hairstyle: a slicked-back ponytail with blunt cut bangs with purple highlights.

'Fine.' Nia rolled her eyes. It was quicker for her to go alone anyway.

She stepped out of the truck and crunched through damp leaves and twigs toward the structure. The shed was old – weathered, thick wooden planks, painted a deep forest green to match its surroundings. Nia wouldn't have seen it at all had it not been for the clearing in the trees.

The single window, too high for her to see through, was thick with condensation. A rusty padlock hung from the door's handle. Nia tried her luck, but the lock did not budge when she tugged on it. Rain slipped inside her hood, sending a shiver down her back. She wished she'd worn her boots instead of her sneakers. Her shoes were going to be soaked through.

'You know what people keep in locked sheds?' Morgan shouted from the truck. Her voice echoed across the field. 'Illegal things! And probably snakes!'

Nia vowed to come back to the shed when it wasn't raining. She'd be more prepared and wouldn't have any comments from the peanut gallery. She turned to head back toward Morgan's truck when she noticed a black pick-up truck parked behind Harvey's trailer.

The faded logo on the side boasted a silhouette of a buff male, who she assumed to be Harvey, showing off his giant biceps. Underneath were the words 'HARVEY'S USED CARS' with a contact phone number.

Before she knew it, she was headed toward his back door. She didn't think about the squish in her socks or the chattering of her teeth. She powered forward with tunnel vision, that nagging feeling getting stronger within her.

The sliding door unlatched with ease and she stepped directly into Harvey's bedroom. A small section of tile was reserved at the door, while the rest of the room was carpeted in a lush burgundy shade that took Nia by surprise. Shoe tracks crisscrossed this way and that like someone had already ransacked the place. His mattress had been tossed, one side barely hanging onto the bed frame while the other sagged against the carpet.

A red light flashed in Nia's peripheral vision. It flashed again, then once more on a rhythm. Nia crouched down where she stood to look underneath Briggs' bed. It was a cordless telephone.

Nia stepped carefully, making sure to align her steps with the ones that had come before her as she crossed the room. She retrieved the phone: it flashed with one new voicemail. Nia's heart pounded in her chest when she pressed the play icon.

Rosie's voice crackled through the speaker. 'Harvey, it's me.' There was a pause as if she were gathering her thoughts. Then, she heard her tiny whisper, '*Come by tomorrow.*'

Nia would never forget that those were the last words Rosie ever said to her. In her mind's eye, Nia watched herself walk out of Rosie's Diner and blow Rosie a kiss. She wished she would've known that was the last time she would ever see her.

The message continued.

'I hate how we ended things.' Rosie exhaled sharply. 'I don't want to fight anymore, okay? I made a fool of myself just now and I realized you were right. I was too focused on the past. I should have been looking at what's right in front of me . . . You. I just want to make things right. I—' There was a beat of silence. 'I'll stop sticking my nose where it doesn't belong.'

To play this voicemail again press one. To save it, press seven. Nia pressed one, pulled out her cell phone, and recorded the message. Nia thought about putting Harvey's phone back under the bed, but pocketed it instead.

She turned and ran faster than she ever had before. Rain slapped her in the face as she dashed down the steps and charged across the field.

Morgan scrambled to unlock the truck's door and Nia leapt inside.

'Go, go!' she shouted, drumming her hands on the dashboard.

Morgan peeled away from Harvey's home.

Chapter 17

Jesse

For the first time in days, Jesse felt more like himself again. The dreary afternoon gave way to a thin misty rain, the kind that clung to the skin and made everything smell like damp earth and nostalgia.

After everything that had happened, the murder, the investigation, the sleepless nights, it felt good to be back on his usual patrol. Part of him was relieved that the case had been solved. He could focus on moving forward, maybe even talking things out with Nia now that the Fall Festival was officially going ahead. He wasn't naïve enough to think they were back together, but maybe, just maybe, he could take her out to Barkwood Bridge like they used to in high school. Maybe it'd give her some closure. Maybe they could start over, different this time.

But those thoughts evaporated the second he reached the intersection at Main Street and Nutmeg Avenue. Jesse ambled past Rosie's Diner; the inside was dark. In all the years he'd lived in Cinnamon Falls he'd never seen her diner empty or closed. He wondered what the family would do with the restaurant. Would they liquidate it and the town would make way for something new? What could possibly fit there other than Rosie's? Cinnamon Falls without Rosie didn't feel right at all.

Hence the rain, he thought. Even the universe was mourning.

Harvest Square sat in the middle of it all, home of the Fall Festival. Trees did their best to shield the festival crew from the rain as the workers moved quickly under their plastic ponchos, setting up booths and tents; their bright yellow rain jackets sticking out against the drab backdrop.

Jesse imagined Maggie Shilling doling out orders and shouting commands in rain-soaked clothing. His eyes scanned the crowd, searching for Maggie. He owed her a check-in after yesterday. She must be ecstatic now that the festival was officially underway. He wanted to make sure she was okay.

He drove around Harvest Square, his gaze flicking toward the workers hauling heavy bags from trucks, assembling what would soon be the heart of the festival. Some unzipped bags of long pieces of metal that looked to be the bones of an enormous tent. They folded and hoisted until finally the one side of it had been secured in the ground.

Two women dragged another bag to the tent, this

one much heavier than the other. Jesse parked his car and fished for his jacket on the backseat. He couldn't sit idly by while a bunch of drenched festival workers struggled.

He zipped up his jacket and then came the scream.

A blood-curdling, gut-wrenching sound that cut through the gray drizzle like a blade. Jesse froze for a millisecond – just long enough for his pulse to spike.

Without another thought, Jesse sprinted toward the direction of the sound. One handed, he vaulted over the park's wooden bench, barely registering the sharp sting in his knees as he hit the ground running, and then bolted toward the field. A woman collapsed on all fours, clawing at her hair. Her piercing screams rent the air like sirens. Jesse recognized her immediately: Alexis Chambers.

Alexis scrambled backward, her eyes wild with terror, her hands shaking as she pointed toward the unzipped duffel bag beside her. 'Someone help! She's in there!'

The festival workers stood frozen, their faces pale, covering their mouths in horror. Jesse crept toward the bag, his heart in his throat, his stomach in knots.

All the screaming around him was drowned out as Jesse focused only on his heartbeat resounding in his ears. He forced his legs to work and unholstered his service weapon, keeping it trained on the unmoving duffel bag.

He took one careful step.

Then another.

Then another, until he was standing over it.

Maggie Shilling stared up at him with dead eyes.

His knees buckled beneath him. He hadn't realized he'd fallen until he felt his pants soak through from the damp ground. His breath came in ragged gasps.

The woman he'd consoled yesterday was gone, replaced by a ghostly pale body. Her lips were tinged a sickly shade of blue, and her once-vibrant eyes were now glassy and vacant. She had been stuffed inside the bag like garbage. Jesse felt like his insides were caving in. His hands trembled as he unzipped the bag further, revealing a crumpled piece of paper pinned to her soaked jacket.

Who Will Be Next?

Jesse pressed his fingers to his nose, trying to stop the burn in his throat. The cold drizzle had turned into a steady rain, each drop drumming against his skin as the reality settled in.

They'd arrested the wrong man.

And now Maggie was dead.

He spun around to sit rather than kneel. Dozens of horrified workers faced him, rain dripping from their hoods.

'Stay back,' Jesse said weakly.

He forced himself to move, gritting his teeth through the devastation as he grabbed his phone.

'Dispatch, this is Shaw.' He swallowed down the bile in his throat. 'I need immediate backup at Harvest Square. We have a homicide.'

Sergeant Raines and Chambers arrived minutes later, barking orders to clear the scene and lock down the town square. Chambers rushed to his petrified wife, cradling her in his arms. They shared a heartfelt kiss before she was escorted away in a police vehicle. Jesse, however, stayed next to Maggie, the rain soaking through his uniform. He was too furious to find the strength to leave her.

They'd gotten it wrong. Raines had arrested Harvey for Rosie's murder, and now there was another victim; someone else he cared about, someone else he loved. Prescott stood in front of the entire town, telling them they were safe. Telling them his detectives had caught the killer. Now Maggie was dead because of their blind confidence.

Jesse's hands clenched into tight fists against the damp grass. His teeth ground together, his rage boiling over.

'Shaw.' Raines approached him first.

'You said you got the guy,' Jesse growled and shot to his feet. 'You two.' He pointed to Chambers, who had hung back. 'You stood in front of these people and told them they were safe!'

Jesse didn't care that he was shouting at a superior officer or that everyone who was within two feet of them could hear him. He was enraged, and more than that, he was broken. Another citizen of Cinnamon Falls had died because of their negligence and their ridiculous superiority complex.

Raines exhaled; her expression carefully controlled. 'Shaw, take a breath.'

Jesse let out a bitter laugh. 'A breath?' His voice rose. 'A *breath*?'

He jabbed a finger toward Maggie's body, rain dripping from his fingertips. 'Maggie Shilling is dead because you were too damn arrogant to listen!'

Chambers put his hands on his hips. 'Hold on. We couldn't have known—'

'That you got the wrong guy?' Jesse interjected, his voice low and lethal. 'I told you that from the start!'

'This doesn't mean that Briggs didn't do this,' Raines replied in a calm and measured voice. 'He could've moved the body before—'

'Quit arguing! We need to clear this scene before Elaine gets the jump on this,' Chambers whispered to both of them. 'People are starting to panic.'

Jesse stepped next to Raines, his jaw so tight he felt like it would snap. He got close to her ear so that none of the onlookers could hear.

'Do whatever you think you have to do to justify this in your head. I'm going to stop this. Now.'

Raines' nostrils flared and she whipped around as Jesse stomped away. 'Shaw, get back here!'

Jesse didn't stop.

'That's an order, rookie!' Chambers yelled after him.

Jesse tramped toward his car, his pulse pounding in his ears. Maggie deserved justice. And he was going to make damn sure she got it.

Minutes later, Jesse stormed into the Cinnamon Falls Police Department. Angie fought for his attention, but he headed straight for the locker room. His jacket, jeans, shoes, and briefs had been soaked through. He peeled off each item of clothing, replacing it with the spare set of clothes he left hanging in his locker. He didn't feel like talking with anyone. He had enough in his mind that he needed to sort out.

He dug around in his soiled pants pocket until he found his list. The ink had smeared from the rain, but he remembered each name on it. He found a pen and scratched out Harvey Briggs' name. There was no one left.

There was something he'd been missing, and he was tired of being on the defense, watching the people he loved get picked off one by one. He started with the basics, what he knew about the victims. Someone chose them for a reason. Who would have a grudge against Ms. Maggie *and* Rosie? Someone from the festival crew? What would they stand to gain by killing either of them?

Rosie's restaurant was her pride and joy. Maggie loved coordinating the Fall Fest and ran it all on a tight ship. Neither woman had pockets deep enough to drive someone to murder.

When he reached his desk, Angie was there with a worried look on her face. 'Chief is pissed,' she said. 'He wants you in his office. Now.'

'Thank you, Ang,' Jesse replied. She gave his forearm a friendly squeeze. A thought dropped into his mind like a coin in a wishing well. Before Angie got too far away he asked, 'Can you compile all the tips you've gotten on Rosie's murder?'

'All of them?' Angie's eyes bugged out. The tip line had been ringing non-stop since Rosie's murder was announced. He couldn't imagine the types of foolish things Angie had to weed through to find legitimate tips and not annoying small-town gossip.

'The most credible ones,' Jesse clarified. 'The ones you think we should've followed up on.'

'Of course,' she replied. 'Give me about an hour?'

'Take your time,' Jesse responded. Angie was doing him a solid even though he knew she was aware that he was off the case.

Jesse expected to be fired soon. He'd disobeyed a direct order from a superior officer and, quite frankly, given everyone at the crime scene his ass to kiss. The citizens of Cinnamon Falls deserved competent and thorough police, and if Chief Prescott couldn't understand where he was coming from, it was best that they parted ways anyway. He was prepared to defend his actions and lose his job, but he had to get his facts straight first. It was clear that Chambers and Raines had no idea how to solve a murder any more than he did. They might have had the experience, but Jesse had the home team advantage.

So, he started over from the beginning.

At his desk, Jesse pulled up the police department's internal record system. It housed the criminal past, and present, of every single resident in Cinnamon Falls who'd crossed through the station doors. Jesse typed in Harvey Briggs' name and read the arrest report. Briggs was brought in on suspicion of murder, but the corresponding file was empty. In the after action log, Raines noted that Briggs had confessed. It didn't mention anything about Maggie Shilling.

Jesse began to pull up Briggs' previous records that had been collected throughout the years. Harvey Briggs, sixty-one, had lived a quite interesting life. He'd bounced from one foster care home to the next for the formative years of his life in Atlanta. He'd racked up extensive charges as a juvenile: robbery, petty theft, and even some grand larceny.

The crime didn't stop in his adolescence. Over two decades ago, Jesse discovered Harvey had been arrested on two felony charges: one for theft, and one for fraud.

Since then, however, it looked like he was on the straight and narrow. His criminal record ended in the early two thousands when Harvey moved to Cinnamon Falls. Jesse learned that Harvey's Used Cars first opened for business in 1999. It looked like Harvey had found a solid business venture and changed his life around for the good.

Harvey Briggs already had two charges against him. Going away for double homicide would mean he wouldn't see sunshine for a long time – maybe ever again. What kind of man who knew first-hand how cruel jail could be would jeopardize his freedom by murdering his supposed significant other?

To Jesse, it didn't make any sense. Unless, of course, there was something he was missing. He needed to look into Briggs' financial records. It hadn't taken Jesse long to find out about Briggs' criminal past. What if someone else knew about it too? Gossip spread faster than truth in Cinnamon Falls. What if Briggs was covering for someone? He filed that thought away and got up from his desk.

Jesse's feet felt like cinder blocks as he walked to the Chief's office. He remembered how proud his father was of him when he secured the position on the force. *Would he still be proud of me now?* he wondered.

Chief Prescott looked like an angry bull sitting

behind his messy desk. Papers hung sloppily out of manila folders stacked on top of each other. If Jesse breathed wrong, he was sure one of the towers of papers would collapse.

'What is this I'm hearing about you pulling Nia Bennett out of holding in the middle of the night?' Prescott asked.

Jesse took a seat across from him. He guessed Prescott hadn't been informed about the news of his actions at the crime scene yet.

Jesse kissed his teeth. 'I wasn't letting her sit in a cell until Raines decided what she wanted to do with her.'

'She was caught trespassing at our primary suspect's residence at the time of his arrest,' Prescott said, as if Jesse didn't know the details of the situation. 'You didn't think to check in with me or—'

Raines busted in the door unannounced. 'I gave you a direct order, rookie!' She stomped inside the Chief's office and stood next to his chair. He looked between her and Jesse, confused and bewildered.

'You got another person killed,' Jesse fired back. 'I've been telling Chambers all along that Briggs wasn't the guy!'

Prescott glared at Jesse. 'You had no business pulling Bennett out of lockup without our permission.'

'And you had no business leaving the crime scene like a petulant toddler!' Raines chimed in.

This was going nowhere. Jesse wasn't a child to be scolded. He understood the consequences of his actions, but that didn't mean he would apologize for them. Jesse had never felt as strongly about anything as he did about Briggs' innocence, especially after seeing Maggie's cold body. He crossed his arms coolly, hoping to bring the emotions down.

He spoke in an even tone. 'Chief, I didn't think Nia should have to sit in holding all night long for a mere coincidence.'

'Coincidence?' Raines scoffed.

'It was more than a coincidence, Shaw. She was caught interfering with an investigation,' Chief Prescott added.

'Do you really think Nia Bennett had something to do with Rosie's death?' Jesse asked, baffled.

Prescott cast his eyes down toward his desk.

'I think it's pretty coincidental that as soon as she waltzed back into town two people are dead,' Raines said.

Hot rage zipped through Jesse's body. He clenched his fists to keep from flipping the furniture. 'Nia didn't kill Rosie, and she damn sure didn't kill Maggie Shilling! Can't you see how you're wasting your time chasing the wrong people?'

'Or maybe she's not as innocent as you assume,' Raines said with a smirk.

'What are you even talking about?'

'We looked into your girlfriend after we found her

at Briggs' house. She didn't tell you about her love affair back in Atlanta?' Raines asked. She leaned forward and tossed him the file that was on the Chief's desk. It flapped open to a picture of Nia's mugshot from the night before. 'Bryant something or other . . . turns out he's married?'

Jesse's pulse pounded in his ears like a drum cadence.

'What's this gotta do with the case?' he asked, on the brink of internal combustion.

'Just sayin', Shaw, maybe you don't know her as well as you think.'

Chapter 18

Nia

Morgan pressed the pedal of her truck to the floor until they reached The Red Fern Tavern, a rustic dive bar nestled directly between the town of Cinnamon Falls and Asheville. It had a laid-back atmosphere and was the perfect place to talk without being noticed by regulars and eavesdroppers.

It felt like Nia and Morgan had held their breath for the entire drive over. Together, they slid into two open stools at the bar. The patched leather seats on wobbly legs let Nia know this place had seen its fair share of drunken nights. The stale smell of fried food, whiskey, and cheap cologne permeated the air. As the front door opened and closed, cigarette smoke wafted in from the group of chain smokers outside. Before them sat a few cloudy bottles of liquor that were displayed on the glass shelves, thick with furry dust.

Behind the bar, a slim girl with diamond studs tacked in her dimples walked over. Her smoky eye shadow, winged eyeliner, and voluminous eyelashes made her look mysterious and exotic. Her Red Fern Tavern T-shirt had been jaggedly cut above her waist, exposing another stud in her belly button. Her name tag hung from the split in her shirt, showing off her hot pink push-up bra. Amber was her name.

'Can I get you ladies something?' Amber asked, placing down two cocktail napkins in front of them. Her nails were decorated in blinding rhinestones and her mixed metal bangles jingled together melodically.

'Thursday night is Ladies' Night so y'all are right on time.' She handed them a menu too sticky to hold and Nia placed it on the table, wiping her hand on her jeans.

'Two whiskey sours,' Morgan ordered, without looking at it.

'A girl that knows what she likes.' Amber winked. 'Coming right up.'

'You drink whiskey?' Nia questioned. She stripped off her damp jacket, lacing it over the seat next to her. She was thinking of ordering something simple and easy to take the edge off, like a margarita or a glass of wine.

Nia glanced around, taking the place in. She hadn't been to The Red Fern in what felt like a decade. She and Sienna had snuck in once or twice in high school, just to see if they could, but she hadn't been back since.

To their right, two men sat huddled together

watching a sports game on the flatscreen behind the bar. Further toward the end, a handsy man thought he would get lucky tonight with the woman next to him, but he was too drunk to notice how she frowned every time he got close to her. A group of college girls were going shot for shot in the corner, egging each other on. None were paying Nia and Morgan the slightest bit of attention. She liked it that way.

'No, but they do in all the mob movies, right?'

Nia sighed, wishing she could rest her head on the bar, but she was afraid she might get stuck. She pulled out her hand sanitizer and spritzed where she and Morgan sat.

'We're hardened criminals, Nia. We need to start living like it!' Morgan raised her fists in the air.

'It was one night in jail, not a life sentence,' Nia responded, slapping Morgan's arms down.

'Still, that makes you the bad influence my momma warned me about.' Morgan wagged her finger at her.

Amber placed the cocktails in front of the ladies and Nia saw her hesitate before leaving them. Nia eyed her drink suspiciously while Morgan tossed out her straw and took a large gulp.

'Hmm,' Morgan commented after swallowing a third of the glass. 'Not bad.'

'Let's get down to the real business.' Nia motioned to the phone she still had stashed in her pocket. 'I found Harvey's house phone and I recorded Rosie's last message to him.'

Morgan short-circuited. 'You *took* his phone?'

'I had to! What if it comes up missing or something?'

'It *is* missing! You got it! What if they're like, tracking it or something?'

'This is Cinnamon Falls, not the FBI,' Nia deadpanned. She waved Morgan away and pulled out her cell phone, playing the video recording of Rosie's last voicemail for Morgan. Hearing it again squeezed Nia's heart.

It ended and Morgan swirled her straw around her fingers, thinking. 'She sounds scared. Like for real, terrified.'

'That's what I thought!' Nia responded. 'But why call Harvey and tell him at *that* moment? Just as we were walking out the door?'

'She sounded remorseful about something; maybe she was snooping around in Harvey's shed like you were.'

Nia leaned forward, placing her elbows on the bar. She shook her head. 'Rosie was onto something . . . something big.'

Morgan downed the last of her drink. 'Something that got her killed.'

Nia finally took a sip of her drink, letting the weight of the words, and the liquor, settle in.

'Okay, what if she found alien secrets?' Morgan had consumed two whiskey sours back-to-back and had taken to spitballing ideas.

'Morgan, please,' Nia replied. 'First it was an illegal dog fighting ring—'

'Still very possible, Nia,' Morgan interjected.

'And now alien secrets,' Nia finished.

'*Has* the CIA gotten involved? We don't know. Let's just call Jesse and find out since y'all are on speaking terms now.' Nia and Morgan fought for her cell phone.

Amber came over, pulling the friends from their absurd ideas and antics. She presented two glasses of water. She leaned over the bar, her eyes slowly roaming Nia.

'I don't mean to interrupt y'all but, I heard you talking.'

'Which part?' Morgan questioned, eyeing her back.

'I heard her call you Nia. This is going to sound crazy, but are you from The Falls?'

Referring to Cinnamon Falls as 'The Falls' was the easiest way to spot an out-of-towner. In the seconds Amber had been talking, Nia had been studying her.

'Who wants to know?' Morgan tried on her bad-cop voice for size.

'I'm Amber Delacroix. I was friends with Sienna before, well, you know.' She pushed a wet rag around on the bar that begged to be thrown in a washing machine, or incinerated. 'I'm pretty good with faces,' she explained, 'and I remember seeing yours in her pictures online.'

'Nice to meet you, I guess.' Nia didn't want to be impolite but Pink Bra Amber wasn't the first person to announce that they were friends with Sienna. After Sienna died, plenty of people claimed to be closer to Nia's best friend than she had been.

Amber cocked her head to the side. 'I'm surprised she never mentioned me. We partied together all the time back then.'

'Sienna . . . partied?' Morgan asked. 'With you?' Amber looked Morgan up and down. 'No shade,' Morgan added quickly.

'It was just her and Darius for a while. But then Darius started bringing other girls up in here and I had to let my girl know he was no good.'

Nia had never been kicked in the chest before but she imagined that it would feel similar to the pain she was feeling now; unbearable, like all of the breath was knocked out of her body. The words forming in her brain were refusing to come out of her mouth. Sienna . . . and Darius?

Thankfully, Morgan took over. 'Wait. You're saying Sienna was here with Darius Lyons? They were dating?'

Morgan's eyes latched onto Nia's. Were they still in reality? There was no way in the world Sienna would have dated Darius. She was his number one hater, especially when she found out that he was getting crowned as Cinnamon King. Sienna groaned about it for weeks, dreading the day of the Fall Festival. It didn't make any sense. But, ever since Nia had come back to Cinnamon Falls, nothing had made sense.

'Big time.' Amber rolled her neck. 'And he was cheating on her. At one point I felt like he was throwing it in her face, like who was going to be next? I told her she needed to dump his ass.'

'Sienna hated Darius.' Nia had finally caught her breath. Her mind backtracked to the day before Sienna and Darius had won Cinnamon King and Queen. Sienna was incensed that she had to share her special moment with him, and Nia had to convince her to go through with the ceremony. Sienna did her best to fake it, but the irritation was written all over her face. All of that was a lie? How could she have hidden that from her all this time?

Amber shrugged. 'Maybe that's what she told y'all, but she *loved* that boy. All I know is that it went from being the two of them to just me and Si-Si.'

Morgan sputtered out a laugh. 'I'm sorry, I can't imagine Sienna willingly letting you call her that.'

'She never told me any of this,' Nia admitted. 'When was the last time *you* saw her?'

'The day before she died. My homegirl did her hair over at my house because she was winning some kinda award, and that's when I told her what her man was up to. She said she was breaking it off that night.' Amber pulled her phone out of her back pocket and scrolled through her pictures. She flipped the phone around and there was a video of Sienna, bright-eyed with a smile that could have put the sun to shame. Her face was pressed against Amber's, both of them poking out their lips, blowing kisses to the camera. Nia wanted to listen to what Amber was saying but all she could hear was that Sienna had lied to her. Apparently, she'd been lying for a very long time.

Nia's body tingled all over, incensed in a way that cut bone-deep. She had spent all week risking her freedom to find out what had happened to Rosie. In her pursuit of the truth, she never expected to find out that her best friend — who she'd told every scathing truth to — had lied to her.

What else had she lied about? Were they ever best friends at all? And why did she have to find out from Pink Bra Amber that her best friend was actually in love with the guy she claimed to hate? She wished she could call Sienna and scream at her, and that was the worst part about it all. She'd never get to the bottom of it. She'd never get to hear Sienna's side of the story.

Her phone buzzed on the table; it was Jesse. She answered quickly, needing something to keep her grounded in reality.

'Morg said y'all are at The Red Fern?' Jesse asked, in a tense voice.

'Yeah,' Nia replied. He sounded pissed. Nia

wondered if they knew about Harvey's phone already. Maybe Cinnamon Falls PD really was the FBI.

'Come outside.' Then he hung up the phone. Nia grabbed her jacket and told Morgan and Amber that she was stepping outside. The two continued in conversation. They quickly moved on to how Morgan could get a hair appointment with Amber's homegirl.

Nia slung her hood over her head and ran to the passenger side of Jesse's blacked-out car sitting in front of the restaurant. He blasted the heat when she got in to keep the cabin warm.

'Hey,' she said, leaning over the console to give him a hug. Nia could tell something was wrong when he didn't lean toward her. He kept his eyes straight ahead. The bone in his jaw worked tirelessly. He was angry in a way that she'd never witnessed.

'Why didn't you tell me?' Jesse asked.

Nia leaned back in her seat and searched her mind. There were too many things she hadn't told him; she wouldn't know where to start. She wanted to tell him about Rosie's voicemail, but she knew he would admonish her for getting involved again, especially after he'd just gotten her out of a holding cell. It'd ruin the spark of trust they'd established. She had to keep it to herself for now.

'Tell you what?' Her insides trembled remembering that she had Briggs' phone buried in her pocket. She squeezed it to her body tighter, hoping that he couldn't see the red light flashing within.

'About Bryant. Please don't play dumb right now.'

Of all the things Nia was keeping from Jesse, Bryant never crossed her mind. She figured when the time was right, they could have the discussion about why she'd returned home. It would be a difficult conversation, one she planned to have in her own time, but small-town gossip had struck again.

How did he find out? Nia wondered. Morgan? Her mother? Would they have really gone behind her back to Jesse about Bryant? She was still reeling from finding out Sienna had had a double life. How deep did the betrayal run?

'It wasn't your business,' Nia stated.

Jesse scoffed. 'Not my business? You didn't think I deserved to know who you left me for? A married man, Nia?'

'I didn't—' Nia started. 'And how did you—'

'Half the station knows!'

The drinks hit Nia all at once. She fired back, 'I don't give a f—'

'About my feelings?' Jesse cut her off with a humorless laugh. 'Of course you don't. You left me to chase something better than this place, better than *me*, and this is what you settle for? Being the side chick?'

Nia's world was spinning too fast to keep up and she didn't want to spend another night in a holding cell for assaulting an officer. She inhaled sharply and closed her eyes. Emptying her lungs slowly, she calmed herself down.

'I didn't know he was married,' Nia explained. 'I met him at work. I thought he was single. Then I found out he wasn't.'

Jesse turned to her, but his eyes still read he was skeptical.

'I left him the second I found out.'

Jesse turned to her full on and searched her face. Silence stretched between them; only the hum of the engine and the hiss of the heat pushing through the car's vents kept them company. Every few seconds, the wipers cleared the rain from his windshield.

After a beat, his posture softened, only slightly.

'I was embarrassed, Jesse,' Nia started. 'I didn't tell you because I didn't want it to be true. I definitely didn't want you looking at me like you are right now.'

'Yeah, and how am I looking at you?' he asked.

Like you hate me, Nia wanted to say. 'I didn't come back to Cinnamon Falls to be judged, okay?'

In a quiet and measured voice, he asked, 'Then why did you come back, Nia?'

Chapter 19

Jesse

She didn't answer.

Once again, Jesse had put his heart on the line for her and she'd left him empty handed. He felt himself spiraling into a black void of madness, but he couldn't let Nia control his emotions anymore. She'd walked out of his life of her own volition six years ago, leaving him to deal with the emotional fallout. She got the clean slate and the rich boyfriend – or husband, Jesse was still fuzzy on the details – while he dove head first into a career that could have killed him just to feel anything other than the pain of abandonment and betrayal.

Nia did a number on his heart, and here he was falling all over her, waiting for her to do it again. *Don't give her the chance*, he thought, ashamed of himself. He cared deeply for Nia but there were some things he couldn't change about her. He couldn't make her choose him, no matter how hard he tried.

Jesse watched her until she safely walked back inside The Red Fern, and then he drove away. He felt like he had left his heart on the curb.

As a matter of fact, Jesse wasn't the same person she'd left, either. He was different now; especially after being the unlucky recipient of love's sting.

Truthfully, he'd been hoping that he could warn Nia about Maggie Shilling, but Raines' bomb about her ex had derailed his train of thought completely. He had to hear Nia say it for himself, and now, he wished he hadn't. The conversation wasn't worth his time, the drive to The Red Fern, or any more of his attention, especially since he had so much to figure out.

Jesse drove back toward Cinnamon Falls, sorting through the last few days. There was only one other person he trusted to help him get his head on straight.

Grace Whitfield strolled into The Griddle House two hours later. Without hesitation, or prying questions, she'd agreed to meet Jesse at the late-night diner across town. The food was questionable after breakfast hours, but the coffee was strong, and it was usually empty on a Thursday night.

Above him, an industrial light flicked uncontrollably, and the three men bunched together at the end of the bar didn't seem to care. Jesse took a seat in a worn leather booth, tucked away in a corner, and Grace settled in across from him.

She still wore her work uniform, a pair of lilac scrubs embroidered with little white daisies, and a tired smirk rested on her lips.

'Was this a professional or a friendly call?' Grace asked, taking a quick look over the menu in the metal holder.

Jesse leaned back in his seat and exhaled. 'A little bit of both,' he responded truthfully.

He needed her advice as a professional, and as his friend. Jesse stared down at his almost empty cup of herbal tea, swirling it aimlessly. It was the only thing he trusted in here.

Grace sighed, unsatisfied with that answer. 'Tell me this is about the case, and not about the woman you can't stop brooding over?'

Jesse glared at her. 'I don't brood,' he replied.

She scoffed. 'Oh yeah? Then explain why you look like you lost a fight you didn't even know you were in.'

That was exactly how Jesse felt: blindsided. Nia had dropped back into his life and let a tornado loose, ripping up everything he'd diligently planted in her absence. Just that morning, she'd claimed that she'd never stopped loving him, but she refused to give him a straight answer as to why she'd returned to Cinnamon Falls.

'It wasn't a fight,' Jesse clarified. 'It was just . . .' He didn't know how to explain what had occurred between him and Nia. As much as he wanted to confide in Grace, he knew they had a soft spot for each other, and it would be entirely inappropriate. He didn't want to ruin their friendship, especially when he was still so raw from dealing with Nia.

Grace had always been a good friend of his. When Jesse was honorably discharged from the military police, he needed a stable job that could support the drastic change in his lifestyle: caring for his parents. After being on constant high alert Jesse needed something quiet and secure. With his experience, Grace suggested the CFPD, and he'd been on the force ever since.

Jesse always thought Grace must have had a hand in making sure he got hired, but he could never prove it. Either way, he was grateful for her help.

Their friendship blossomed into a deeper, intimate connection, but the romance never curled over, even after a few dates. Still, an undercurrent of tension ran between them. As much as he was attracted to Grace's sweet personality and her kind and helpful nature, he'd never taken it further. Sharing the details of why he and Nia fought would blur the lines between them, and he had much more respect for Grace than that. They were friends and he was more than fine leaving it that way.

'It wasn't a fight,' he repeated. He didn't even sound convincing.

'Then it's a professional call.' Grace sat up straighter in the booth and waved a waitress over. She ordered a soda and a portion of French fries. 'Let's get down to business.'

'I'm sure you've heard about Maggie Shilling by now?' Jesse asked, knowing the answer to his question.

She twisted her lips. 'I've been dealing with Vernon all day. I keep telling him I can't prioritize every body that comes into my mortuary.'

'What can you tell me?' he implored.

Grace shook her head. 'Same as Rosie, blunt force trauma. This time, it was brutal.'

Jesse's stomach turned over. Ms. Maggie was a sweet woman with a gentle nature. She didn't deserve what happened to her, and neither did Rosie. He was hesitant to ask her to give more details, but she continued in a sterile manner, saying, 'The blow to the head rendered her unconscious immediately.'

'Her lips were blue.' Jesse tried to shake the memory out of his head. Maggie's face would be imprinted in his brain for years to come. 'Someone left her out there in the cold all night?'

'Possibly,' Grace said. 'It could mean a few things. She had some petechial hemorrhaging in her eyes, suggesting oxygen deprivation—'

'English, please,' Jesse asked.

'She was exposed to the elements so her body temperature would have dropped significantly. It could be cyanosis, which is if the body doesn't get enough oxygen before death, or livor mortis from the head wound.'

Her fries arrived, steaming hot and sprinkled with flaky salt. Grace smothered them in ketchup immediately. Jesse stole one on the edge of the plate, rolling the piping hot potato around in his mouth until he could swallow it without scalding his insides. Grace offered him a straw and he took a sip out of her cold drink. The combination of the hot fry and a cold, fizzy beverage scratched an itch deep in his brain.

'Good, right?' Grace smiled, popping a ketchup-soaked fry into her mouth. 'Me and my dad would come here after we sat through all the funerals when I was little. They always have the best fries.' She savored another, deep in a memory Jesse couldn't access.

'Anything else about Maggie?' Jesse asked.

Grace shook her head. 'I think they stunned her. One blow to the head and then she was out. They stuffed her in that tent bag, unconscious, and left her to die. I'm ruling it a homicide.'

Jesse hung his head. If he weren't in a diner, he would have flipped the table. Who was doing these heinous acts to the people he loved? And why? He needed to find them now.

'I keep thinking: Why Rosie?' Grace asked like she could hear Jesse's thoughts. 'Why Maggie?'

Jesse tapped his temple. 'That's what I've been trying to figure out. What did they do to deserve this?'

'What if they didn't *do* anything?' Grace asked. 'What if they were simply in the way?'

Surprised, Jesse replied, 'In whose way?'

'That's the million dollar question,' she responded. Grace pushed her fries to the end of the table and changed sides to sit next to Jesse in the booth. She grabbed a napkin from the holder and folded it open on the table. She dug around in her purse until she found a pen, then began to draw. Squiggle lines, squares, and weird shapes dotted the napkin until Jesse realized she'd been drawing a map of Cinnamon Falls.

He watched as she worked carefully. She was deep in concentration as the tip of her tongue stuck out of her mouth. When she was finished, it looked like a badly drawn treasure map with two giant Xs: one covering Rosie's Diner and another covering Harvest Square.

'I'm a visual learner.' She looked over at Jesse. 'I need to see everything all at once to make sense of it. So, let's start from the beginning.'

Grace and Jesse walked step by step through Rosie's murder; from the time they both got the call until her body arrived at the Whitfield Family Mortuary.

'When I got the call, it was just after twelve-thirty or so,' Grace revealed. She stuck her finger on a square that was labeled 'ML'.

Jesse noticed that the Whitfield Family Mortuary was on the other side of the napkin. 'What's this?' He tapped where her finger rested.

'Mayor Lyons' house,' she replied. 'He threw Darius a Welcome Home party.'

Jesse raised his eyebrow at her. 'Never pegged you for a politician.'

'Gotta show face,' she responded coolly. 'My dad was strict about maintaining relationships. Fancy drinks. Forced small talk, you know how it is.'

Jesse was happy to report that he actually didn't know how it was. 'You never mentioned it before?'

'I didn't think my whereabouts were relevant to the case, Mr. Officer,' she said, looking up at him. 'That night was crazy, anyway. Darius didn't show up until late and, oh, I almost got into an accident on the way to Rosie's.'

'He was late because he was at dinner with us— Wait, what?' Jesse asked.

Grace nodded enthusiastically. 'A little car came flying out of nowhere!' She pointed to the street that the mayor's house sat on. 'No headlights on, missed me by a hair.' She pulled her fingers apart just barely.

Something bloomed in Jesse's chest. 'Did you see who was driving?'

Grace shook her head. 'Too dark. Plus, I was racing to make it to Rosie's.'

Thoughts swirled in Jesse's mind faster than he could process.

'That mean anything to you?' Grace asked.

Jesse felt his phone vibrate with a new text message. It was from Angie. *File on your desk*, it read.

'May I?' he asked, motioning to the napkin on the table.

'Sure,' Grace responded. Jesse carefully folded the napkin and stuffed it into his pocket.

'Thank you, Grace.' Jesse spread his arms for a hug and the two embraced. He pulled her into his body, resting his chin on top of her head. Grace scooped her arms under his, her hands grazing his trap muscles. Her nails danced along the delicate skin there and Jesse squeezed her a little tighter.

'So, this is what the police do instead of stopping crime?'

Jesse froze. The sound of another person's voice ripped him from the comforting hug. He looked up to see Niles and Ms. Pearline's great-niece. He couldn't remember her name. Their hands were linked together. Niles sported an expression that looked like Jesse had some explaining to do. He glanced back and forth between Jesse and Grace, his frown deepening. Grace unfolded herself from Jesse's body and retrieved her purse.

'I should go,' Grace said sheepishly, a rose color flushing her cheeks. 'Good luck with the investigation, Officer Shaw.' She tiptoed out of the restaurant without looking back.

'Didn't realize you had a girlfriend,' Niles said, his eyes following Grace as she made her exit, before he and Shawna slid into the seat across from Jesse.

'We were discussing dead bodies, actually,' Jesse clarified. It wasn't a lie.

The two teens eyed one another. 'Is that what they call it now?' Niles asked in a knowing voice. It was only a matter of time before Nia found out, if he hadn't texted her about it already.

Jesse groaned, annoyed. 'What are y'all two even doing here? It's a school night.' He looked at his watch. It was close to eleven p.m.

'Shawna wanted pancakes,' Niles said flatly. 'What are the odds I'd find my favorite cop in here on a date.'

'It wasn't a date,' Jesse stated. 'Grace and I are friends.'

Niles flipped out his phone and showed Jesse a picture of Grace, encapsulated in his arms. Jesse's eyes were closed, and his face held a smile of natural bliss. He didn't even remember closing his eyes. It was as incriminating as it could get.

'Delete it or I'll arrest you.' Jesse was joking, but his voice was serious. He couldn't have Nia seeing that photo.

Niles rolled his eyes and made a show of deleting the photo.

'This is *so* much better than pancakes,' Niles' girlfriend commented, popping a fry into her mouth.

Before he journeyed home, Jesse stopped by the station to retrieve the file Angie left out for him. He wouldn't be able to sleep a wink knowing that the answer to all his questions could potentially be in that file.

When he arrived, the station was empty, not even Angie was manning the front desk. In the bullpen one light illuminated a desk that sat directly in front of Chief Prescott's office. The rest of the cubicles were flanked in darkness. Out of caution, Jesse clicked on his flashlight and crept toward the light.

Jesse found Bud Wade with his head in his hands. The man who looked up at Jesse wasn't his normal cheerful self. His red-rimmed eyes and flushed cheeks told Jesse that he'd been here for some time.

Without words, Jesse placed one hand on his shoulder. Wade placed a hand on top of his.

'She was a good friend of mine,' Wade said in a raspy voice. He sniffed, bringing a fist across his eyes and batted away his tears. 'And they slaughtered her like a dog. Stuffed her into some bag like old clothes! Chief isn't doing a thing about it!' Wade pounded his fist on the table. The bang reverberated around the empty office.

Jesse didn't need an explanation. Things had been rough on everyone the last few days. He felt like he'd been trapped inside a snow globe and shaken around against his will. He knew too well the emotions Wade was feeling; crushed from the inside out. He'd been feeling the same way.

'Someone needs to pay for this,' Wade murmured, choking back tears.

'We'll figure it out, Bud,' Jesse assured him. 'There's no way *I'm* going to let someone get away with this.'

'*They* are!' Bud jammed his thumb in the direction of the Chief's office over his shoulder. 'Talkin' about keeping it under wraps. I don't have nothin' against Raines and Chambers. They might've been good detectives in Atlanta, but they ain't from here . . . they don't know our people.'

'I hear you,' Jesse agreed. Wade was saying exactly what he'd been thinking since the Chief partnered him up with Chambers. Jesse lowered his voice even though he and Wade were the only two officers in the station. 'Are you thinking what I'm thinking?'

Bud Wade was silent for a moment, the officers held eye contact, silently evaluating if they could trust each other.

'Ah hell, I'm retiring anyway,' Wade grumbled. He beckoned Jesse closer to him. Jesse leaned forward and strained to hear Wade whisper, 'I don't think Briggs did it.'

Of course he didn't, Jesse wanted to say, but decided against it. There was a reason Wade was here late, alone, and as much as Jesse wanted to believe it was a random occurrence, he hadn't forgotten about the mole. Someone had gone against the brotherhood and fed Elaine Matthias information only the CFPD knew, and Jesse was willing to bet that same someone would go to great lengths to cover their tracks.

Jesse figured he could go right to Matthias and ask, but he knew the woman who taught twelfth grade journalism hadn't changed. She'd never give up her source. Jesse would have to flush them out on his own.

Jesse pretended to be shocked. 'If it wasn't Briggs, then who are you thinking?'

Wade rolled his eyes. 'Don't play that innocent role with me, rook. You know as best as I do that someone's got it out for Briggs.'

The realization washed over Jesse like a cold shower. He'd been looking at it all wrong. He'd been concentrating on Rosie and Maggie as victims, but what if they were just collateral damage? What if the real target had been Briggs all along?

'I saw that look in your eye, kid. Tell me what you're thinking,' Wade demanded, excitedly.

'I think you're the best detective we've got,' Jesse replied.

For the next hour, Jesse and Wade pored over both cases. They moved their operation from Wade's desk into the conference room so they could see everything – every piece of evidence all at once; he had to thank Grace for that tip.

Jesse tacked the map Grace made to the whiteboard, his handwritten suspect list, and the haphazard drawing of Rosie's Diner he'd made Tuesday morning. Wade retrieved Rosie and Maggie's preliminary files from the department intranet and nicked some good coffee from the Chief's office, just enough for the two of them. Jesse scrutinized the tips Angie had saved for him. The list consisted of ten tips, and most of them were the epitome of unusable.

Stanley Wheeler, who ran the gas station, said that

he saw three women lighting candles in the woods the night Rosie died. He had suspicions of a cult and wanted someone to look into it. Another read that there was a blue compact car seen flying down Cinnamon Way around eleven-thirty. It almost hit a pedestrian. Angie had put a star next to that one. He made a note to follow up on it.

'In our last meeting you mentioned the note we found.' Jesse dug through the papers scattered around and pulled out the picture Grace took of the note found next to Rosie. 'Who Will Be Next?' was scrawled in rushed handwriting.

'Mm-hmm.' Bud nodded, savoring a mouth full of coffee. He smacked his lips, satisfied after he drank the last of it. 'He really does hoard the good stuff.'

Jesse placed the note found on Maggie Shilling next to the one found by Rosie. Wade leaned over the table, his eyes scanning both papers, jumping back and forth between the two.

'You ever seen somebody copy their own handwriting this perfectly?' Wade asked.

Jesse frowned. 'What are you saying?'

Wade placed one paper over the other, holding it up to the light. He made a mad dash to his desk and fumbled around before returning to the conference room with scissors.

'I'm saying,' he said, curving the scissors around the loopy letters. He freed one word –*Who* – from the paper and layered it on top of the other. They aligned perfectly. 'They didn't write this note twice. They made a copy of it.'

Jesse looked for himself, noticing how identical each letter was.

'This was deliberate,' Jesse said in an airy voice. It felt like all the synapses in his brain were firing at once. 'Someone needed Rosie *and* Maggie out of the picture . . .'

'A cover-up?' Wade pondered.

'Of what?' Jesse asked, bewildered. 'It had to have been something terrible, something so heinous—'

Wade brought his thumb to his lips. 'Before Rosie, what's the worst thing that's ever happened here?'

Heat rose in Jesse's body, pushing out of his ears when he whispered, 'Sienna.'

Wade's eyes latched onto Jesse's and the men shared a silent and urgent understanding: they had to get out of there. They'd stumbled onto something much bigger than they'd anticipated. Jesse didn't know what it meant just yet, but it was the biggest break that he'd gotten since Tuesday morning, and it made the most sense.

Goosebumps rose on his skin. In his head he heard Chambers' voice, '*In real life, it's pretty obvious . . .*'

Quietly and quickly they packed up the conference room. Jesse downed his coffee, crumbling both their paper cups in his hand and stuffing them into his pocket. He didn't want to leave any evidence that he and Wade had been here discussing a case that had supposedly been closed.

Things were about to get tricky and he wanted to make sure he came out the other end unscathed. He had to get his hands on the folder Nia had showed him earlier in the week that she'd found in Rosie's office. He wanted to kick himself for dismissing it before.

Most importantly, he had to get to her before Niles did.

Chapter 20

Friday
Nia

Nia woke up to a pounding headache and this time it wasn't because Midnight was using her forehead for a bed. The pressure behind her eyes had a heartbeat all its own, and Nia vowed never to hang out with Morgan ever again. The girl was a terrible influence.

Yesterday, after she jetted from Jesse's car, Nia waited until she was back inside the bar to finally cry. In all her years of knowing Jesse, she'd never seen him look at her with disgust in his eyes. He'd always handled her gently, even when she was at the lowest point in her life. Yesterday, that version of Jesse wasn't in the car with her. Nia didn't know what had happened to him in the years she'd been gone, but the repercussions of her absence seemed to run deeper than she originally thought.

Nia thought he'd get over her quickly. She thought he'd move on and forget all about her. Had he been silently resenting her all these years? Did she make the biggest mistake of her life coming back home?

She couldn't think that way. Despite Rosie's death, Nia was having the most fun she'd had in a while. She reckoned she'd been healing and growing in Atlanta, but actually, she'd been avoiding reality. It was becoming clear now how much of her Atlanta life had revolved around Bryant so she didn't have to face what had happened with Sienna. All of it had been one big distraction, a curated life she'd conned herself into enjoying.

Since she met Bryant, Nia hadn't touched a doorknob or paid a bill. Anything she requested, she received. Bryant was generous just because he wanted to be. She couldn't count all the times he'd come home with roses or bought her a brand-new dress for her to wear to dinner that night.

When they were together, the extent of Jesse's romantic gestures had been buying her a heart-shaped corn dog at the Fall Fest. Bryant, on the other hand, bought her whatever her heart desired. He was a provider in every sense of the word, but he was terrible at protecting her heart when it truly mattered. She realized he'd been keeping her close on purpose. He couldn't have Nia inquiring about his life outside of her, and Nia had been too starry-eyed to realize it.

The bottom line was, he'd lied to her. And not a little lie, either. It was a world-shattering lie; something that shook her out of life's slumber.

Nia was wide awake now.

Her father peeked into her room. Midnight used Nia's face as a springboard as she jumped off the bed to greet him.

I'm going to skin that cat if I ever get the chance, she thought, as she rubbed the horizontal scratch Midnight left across her forehead.

As much as she wanted to pull the covers over her head, Nia needed to do something to keep her mind occupied. She used to hate spending her nights at the shop slinging ice cream cones to slobbery children and ungrateful customers. But tomorrow was the Fall Fest, which meant there were cinnamon rolls to prep and ice cream to churn. Her father would be up all night making enough waffle cones to support the sugar habit of a small army, and Nia knew they could use the extra help.

She'd spent enough time lurking around Cinnamon Falls for answers to Rosie's death. After Amber had dropped a bombshell that Sienna had lied to her about her relationship with Darius, Nia was all sleuthed out.

She'd hoped to find answers, but all she'd been unearthing was disappointment after disappointment. Maybe it was time to let the police do their job, Nia relented. She needed to focus on her own life now, and that started with her family.

'Dad,' Nia whispered, just before he backed out of the room. 'What time are you going to the shop today?'

Surprised, he responded, 'You got about ten minutes before I pull out of here.'

Nia threw the covers off and leapt from her bed.

It'd been three hours since Nia had last sat down. When she first got in, she was on cleaning duty. Usually, her mother diligently wiped the shop down from top to bottom after closing and before opening. Now, it was Nia's turn.

Marjorie stood suspiciously close, watching her as she used a disinfectant solution on the tables, booths, and chairs. She then went back over each fixture with a clean cloth of just water, making sure to wipe in the same motion her mother had and taking her time to make sure every nook and cranny was touched.

Once her mother was satisfied that the place was clean enough, it was on to restocking. While Marjorie sliced the fresh fruit, Nia organized and sorted the chocolate candies, then the fruity candy, and then the nuts. She moved on to the sprinkles when she heard the door's bell ding overhead.

'We're closed,' she announced without looking up. 'We'll be open in about an hour.'

'Gimme a sundae, woman,' a haggard voice demanded.

She should have known it would be Niles. 'Why are you never in school?' she asked, giving her brother a raised eyebrow. Niles shrugged. She turned to her mother. 'How come he's never in school?'

'He's a good student, what can I say?' her mother responded.

'I wasn't?' Nia asked, taken aback. She had excelled in school. She'd always gotten good grades, and she had perfect attendance. That was, up until senior year when her schedule gave her the tiniest bit of freedom. Suddenly, she understood why Niles was never in school.

'Like I said, sundae, woman,' Niles demanded playfully, drumming his fists against the glass.

'It's too early,' Nia's mother warned. 'How about a banana smoothie, honey?'

Niles smiled so wide his eyes disappeared behind his cheeks. 'Thank you, Mommy.'

Nia rolled her eyes so hard she wanted them to get stuck just so she didn't have to witness her mother treat her little brother like he was still a toddler. Marjorie disappeared to the kitchen behind the service counter. The next thing she heard was the blender.

Nia moved on to stacking the freshly made waffle cones. 'You don't even like ice cream this early. What do you want?' she asked.

Niles leaned on the counter, admiring Nia's organizing handiwork. 'Nothing, just checking in, making sure my dear sister is holding up well after a night in the slammer.'

'I was in holding for like, four hours,' Nia clarified, keeping her voice low.

'Long enough, Ted Bundy. Listen, I came in here to tell you about last night.' He lowered his voice and scooted closer. Nia did the same, practically leaning over the service counter to make sure she could hear him.

'So, I happened to be out later than usual,' Niles started.

'Oh, you just so happened to, huh?' Nia asked, incredulous. It was amazing how he could do whatever he wanted and Nia hadn't been able to take two steps out of line before her mother brought down the hammer on her. As a child, she hated how strict her mother was, but as an adult, she was grateful that her mother shielded her from the wicked ways of the world as long as she did.

He waved her away. 'Shawna wanted pancakes, so I took her to The Griddle House.'

Nia shook her head. That poor girl. The Griddle House's food was inedible after ten a.m., everyone in Cinnamon Falls knew that. Niles was going to give Shawna food poisoning.

'You were better off going to Rosie—' Nia caught herself mid-sentence and shook her head, a fresh wave of pain hitting her. It was going to take a while before she got used to Rosie not being around.

'Anyway,' Niles continued. 'We walk in and guess who we see?' His bright brown eyes danced with a secret.

'Who?' Nia asked, annoyed.

'Jesse and Grace cuddled up, real late-night, real private type of thing.' Niles turned around and pretended to kiss himself. 'Here.' He produced his phone, showing Nia a picture of Grace in Jesse's arms. She couldn't see her face, only his, and it looked like he was in a dreamland; eyes closed with a goofy grin.

Nia's hands felt numb.

'They're working a case,' she said. She didn't know if she was trying to convince Niles or herself. 'I don't care who he hangs out with.'

Niles leveled her with his eyes, giving her a knowing look. 'Right, which is why you crushed three waffle cones just now.'

Nia looked down at her hands, clenched in a fist around the waffle cones her father had spent his morning making. They were a mess of crumbles at her feet.

'Here ya go!' her mother announced, presenting Niles with his smoothie. His plain banana smoothie had somehow morphed into one with Greek yogurt and chia seeds, and a strawberry swirl for some added sweetness.

'Now this is what love looks like,' Niles said, coming around the counter and planting a kiss on his mother's cheek.

Before Nia protested, Marjorie gave her a smoothie too. 'For both my babies.'

Nia squealed, taking a long sip. Niles commented,

'That's so nice of you, Mom, to look out for the help.' He reached over to pat the top of Nia's head.

Nia glared at her brother. 'Get out!'

Niles grabbed his book bag and zipped out of the door, waving to them as he left.

On the wall next to her, the cone phone rang. It was their business line that her father had painted to look like a waffle cone. Nia hooked it under her neck and said, 'The Cinnamon Scoop, this is Nia. How can I help you?'

'Nia!' Rosie exclaimed. 'Just the person I wanted to talk to!'

Nia's breath halted in her lungs. Her heart stomped around in her chest.

'This is Rubina, Sienna's aunt,' Rubina explained.

She sounds so much like her sister, Nia thought. For that split second, Rosie wasn't dead, and this was all a cruel joke. She imagined Rosie having a laugh on a tropical island somewhere; a fruity drink in her hand, and her feet buried in warm sand, cackling at the top of her lungs at their antics.

'Oh, hi, Ms. Rubina,' Nia replied. 'Is everything okay?'

She pulled the phone away from her mouth and whispered to her mother, 'It's Rosie's sister, Sienna's aunt.'

Rubina said, 'Yes, yes, of course, dear. I was calling because, well, we are clearing out Rosslyn's house and there are some sentimental items of Sienna's that

I thought you might want. Do you want to drop by and take a look at them?'

'I'm working right now,' Nia replied, taken back. She didn't know how she felt about Rosie and Sienna's stuff being pawned off to relatives she didn't even know Rosie had before yesterday. It hadn't even been a week, and they were already cleaning out her house? 'I can see if someone can bring me by a little later.'

'We'll be here,' Rubina replied. 'Do you need the address?'

Nia knew she asked earnestly, but this was Cinnamon Falls, everyone knew where everyone lived. 'I remember the way,' Nia assured her.

'See ya soon.'

Chapter 21

Jesse

Friday morning, Shadrach, Meshach, and Abednego did their rooster thing, and after a grueling workout, Jesse beat his father to the kitchen to start breakfast. In just the few short days that Jesse hadn't been around as much, Robert had taken over breakfast duty. But by the time his father made it downstairs that morning, breakfast would be ready in the kitchen.

Before he left for the office, Jesse snagged the newspaper from Mini Charlie and carefully separated the parts he knew his parents would be interested in. Scrawling a note to them that he'd see them for dinner later, Jesse was out of the door in record time.

He'd spent most of his night trying to get the images of Maggie Shilling out of his mind. Then, when he finally moved on from that harrowing thought, his brain reminded him that he'd made a fool of himself in front of Niles, and it was only a matter of time before Nia would be ringing his line and demanding an explanation. He wanted to make sure he got ahead of it before her brother made it seem like more than an innocent hug between friends.

Jesse didn't have to scroll until he found her number in his contact list. He typed her number in from memory and called her. He was not expecting her to answer. After all, it was still early in the morning. If she did, he would have been pleasantly surprised. It rang then went to voicemail. Jesse sighed and placed his phone back in the car's cup holder, pretending not to glance down at it every few seconds to see if she'd called back.

He tried once more. It rang and went to voicemail.

Again, voicemail.

Jesse gave up and dialed the only other person he knew that could give him the answers to his questions: Morgan. She agreed to meet him at The Toasted Pecan for a cup of coffee.

Today, Morgan sported long hair with layers of purple highlights. As soon as she got close enough to hug Jesse, she pivoted and hurled her purse at his head.

'That's for making my girl cry!'

Jesse ducked too late and her purple purse collided with the side of his head. He cradled the stinging spot next to his ear. 'What?' he cried, backing away from her.

'Who do you think you are, bashing her for leaving her no-good ex?' Morgan questioned. She flopped down in a booth and Jesse followed behind her.

'She didn't tell me he was married, Morg,' Jesse explained. He slid on the other side of her and examined his fingers to see if he was bleeding.

'I should've smacked you harder,' Morgan warned. Clarissa Hargrove snickered as she dropped two steaming cups on the table. 'I got you a coffee, black, and I got hot chocolate. Also, you're paying, so give the nice lady your card.'

Jesse handed over his card to Mrs. Hargrove without hesitation and continued their conversation. 'She left me for a married dude and you're okay with that?'

'She left you, Jay, and then she met a guy who lied to her,' Morgan clarified. 'And why do you care so much? You moved on too!'

'I—'

'You've been on dates!' Morgan looked up at him with fire in her eyes. 'Haven't you?'

'Not really . . .' Jesse wanted to explain but Morgan didn't want to hear it.

'Everyone knows Grace Whitfield has been waiting for a chance with you since you got with Nia.' Morgan rolled her eyes. 'So, don't even start.'

'What am I supposed to do?' Jesse asked, frustrated. 'Just forget about the fact that she walked out on me?'

'She wanted a fresh start, Jay. It wasn't about me, or you, or anyone.' Morgan sighed. 'I shouldn't even be telling you all this . . .' She pressed her fingers to her mouth and paused. 'But she's seriously going through a tough time right now. We all are.'

Morgan listed on her fingers. 'First, she's told her man is married. She comes home and she's gotta make amends with *everyone* she pissed off, then Rosie dies, and then, for the icing on the cake, we find out Sienna lied to us. So just . . . give her some grace, no pun intended.'

Jesse had never thought about it that way. When Nia left, she didn't just leave *him*. She left her whole life behind: her family, her friends, and everything she knew. Jesse had only been looking at Nia's decision through the lens of his experience, and he didn't realize how much she'd been carrying all this time. His cheeks burned with shame.

'I might've messed up, Morg,' Jesse admitted.

She picked up her purse. 'I should smack you again,' she threatened.

'I was angry I had to find out about it through my boss *after* I put my ass on the line for her. I specifically told her not to get involved with the investigation,' Jesse explained.

'She's putting way more than that on the line for you,' Morgan mumbled. She toyed with the sugar packets on the table.

'What do you mean?'

'Every day that girl is inching closer to finding out who did this to Rosie. She's not going to stop, Jesse, no matter how much you tell her not to.'

'Please tell me y'all are not still on a wild goose chase?'

Morgan turned to scoot out of the booth. 'You need to talk to Nia, okay? I've already said too much.' She flagged over Clarissa and ordered another hot chocolate to go. 'Add it to his tab.'

'Talk to me,' Jesse implored. 'What's going on?'

'Nia's been obsessed with this, Jay. I'm scared she's getting in too deep. She snuck around in Briggs' trailer and found his phone. It's got a voicemail on it from Rosie. Some of the last words she ever spoke, and she sounded terrified.' Morgan's eyes misted with tears. 'Something is going on in this town, Jay. Something Rosie knew and I think it's got something to do with Sienna.'

Jesse had come to the same conclusion the night before with Wade. But hearing Morgan and Nia felt the same made him think that Nia could have actual evidence that would prove Briggs was an innocent man. At the very least, it could prove that Rosie was killed for retaliation; to keep her quiet. Jesse waited on tenterhooks as Morgan talked.

'The bartender at The Red Fern, Amber, said she knew Sienna, said they partied together, and that Darius was cheating on Sienna.'

'Cheating? Wait a second, Darius and Sienna were a couple?' Jesse couldn't believe his ears. Since when? What had he missed all those years? From what he remembered, Victoria had Darius on lock before he went pro. When did he and Sienna have the time?'

Morgan nodded. 'That's what we said! I couldn't even picture Sienna with Darius. She hated him! Couldn't stand to be around him for more than a second! But this Amber girl swore they were like, madly in love.'

'Madly in love, huh?' Jesse asked. He knew someone else that claimed to be madly in love and was sitting behind bars. 'How's Nia taking it?'

'She feels betrayed, of course. Sienna and I were close, but I can't compete with a friendship like theirs. I don't know how Nia was able to manage after hearing that her dead best friend was living a completely different life without her. Did we even know her at all?'

Jesse shook his head, wanting to punch himself for adding to Nia's pain. He had to apologize to her immediately. He had to make it right.

'She's hurting, Jay,' Morgan said.

As much as Jesse was concerned about Nia, his mind was buzzing with new possibilities. Darius' alibi was corroborated by the Chief and the time stamp on Will's phone. But, what if . . .

'How long did she say they were together?' Jesse asked.

Morgan shrugged. 'It couldn't have been that long. Amber said Sienna found out about Darius' double dealings the night before the Fall Fest and broke it off—'

'And then two days later . . .' The morning after the Fall Fest they found Sienna's body.

Jesse looked up at Morgan. The color had drained from her face.

She stammered, 'Do you think . . . D-did that sonofabitch kill her?'

Chapter 22

Nia

Nia had memorized the way to Sienna's house when she was in second grade. The tree-lined streets looked the exact same as they had all those years ago; except they seemed much bigger when she was younger. Marjorie pulled into the driveway and parked the car, gripping the steering wheel.

'I don't think I can bring myself to go in there, Ni-Ni,' she whispered, keeping her eyes downcast. 'I just can't believe Rosie is gone.'

Nia massaged a slow circle on her mother's back. 'I won't be long, I promise.'

As Nia walked up the sidewalk, she realized Rosie's house hadn't changed either. The one-level single family home was secluded by an A-frame canopy. Two giant ceramic pots held little white flowers that stretched toward the sun. The front door was slightly cracked so that Nia could see down the hall, and eighties rock music was blasting from someplace deep within.

'Ms. Rubina?' Nia called as she pushed open the front door.

A blast of fresh-cut florals slapped her in the face. Roses of all shapes, sizes, and colors crowded the floor. Some were in intricate vases or large ceramic holders. Other bouquets were jammed into buckets, sitting in a thin layer of water. All sported notes of loss and condolences from friends and relatives. Nia made sure to watch where she walked as she journeyed from the front door, careful not to step on any of the petals that had fallen. Under the floral scent, Nia could still smell the sweet embrace of cinnamon.

To her right, she found Rubina and Rebecca sitting on Rosie's couch, misty-eyed as they flipped through a photo album. Rupert looked on from his position at the fireplace. Half-stuffed cardboard boxes were open at their feet labeled 'STORAGE'.

Rupert noticed her first. He cleared his throat, bringing his sisters' attention to their guest. Rubina jumped up. 'Nia! Thanks so much for dropping by!'

Nia waved politely to the family. 'Got a lot going on in here, huh?' She stuffed her hands into her pockets, trying to avoid eye contact with the pictures of Sienna around the room. She was still upset about Amber's comments. What else had Sienna conveniently left out of their friendship? When, exactly, did she stop trusting Nia? And what in the world did she see in Darius Lyons?

Rubina gestured to the mess around her and placed

her hands on her ample hips. 'Just trying to get it all sorted out. Sienna's stuff is through here.'

Before Nia could protest, she was standing in Sienna's bedroom, just off from the kitchen. The soft pink walls triggered a nostalgic bubble in her chest as she remembered the pact they'd made in fourth grade: matching rooms. Nia chose a nauseating bubblegum pink that she regretted, still. On the other hand, Sienna chose a much more palatable creamy pink that had stood the test of time. It still looked feminine, but mature.

Sienna's room had been stripped: the boy band posters had been removed leaving rectangular ghosts on the wall. The photos on her corkboard holder had also disappeared, leaving only the black holes where thumbtacks had resided for decades. Nia ran her finger across one in the far-left corner. That was where her picture with Sienna lived.

Rubina presented Nia with a sealed cardboard box. Inside, the contents rattled around, and Nia wondered what could be in it.

'I know you and Sienna were thick as thieves. We found some stuff in her room that we thought you might want.'

Nia hesitated. 'Are you sure? I mean, this is your family . . . I—'

Rubina cut her off. 'She was your family too. I can see it in your eyes how much you miss her.' The bubble in Nia's chest got a little bigger. 'If having any of this brings you peace, please, take it.'

Nia looked up at Rubina and noticed again how much she resembled her younger sister. They had the same stern yet loving eyes that looked like she could see every thought in Nia's head. Her hair was even styled the same, in a shoulder-length bob; though Rubina's didn't have the badass streak of gray in the front. Rubina shook the box at her.

'Thank you,' Nia managed to say. 'She meant a lot to me.'

Nia realized this was all she had left of Sienna and Rosie, a box of things. They were just memories now, only living on in her heart. The bubble in her chest exploded and before she knew what was happening, Nia was sobbing. Rubina pulled her in for a hug and they stayed like that for a long while, together.

Chapter 23

Jesse

Jesse floored his car through downtown's tight streets. He used his badge to get through Fall Fest blockades in preparation for the inevitable celebration.

Mayor Lyons had been clear that nothing, not even a freak act of nature, would prevent the festival from happening. Jesse wondered if the mayor would cancel it if his own son was accused of murder. He hooked a right onto Main Street and found an open spot across the street from The Cinnamon Scoop.

Jesse had spent the morning completing his rounds in record time, including firing off a quick text to Wade: *Found something. We need to meet.*

It was now midday and Nia still hadn't called him back. Jesse needed to speak to her. If Morgan was right, Nia was holding onto evidence that could clear Briggs' name. It could also launch an investigation into one of the most powerful families in Cinnamon Falls. With Wade's expertise, they could bring a case so damning against Darius Lyons that the Chief would have to take it into consideration. But the Chief wouldn't listen to Jesse alone.

Meeting with Wade last night, then Morgan this morning, had put a battery in Jesse's back. He had to do what was right.

Jesse walked into The Cinnamon Scoop to find Nia's father, Walter Bennett, behind the counter; a clipboard in his hand and a tower of waffle cones beside him.

'Officer Shaw.' Mr. Bennett leaned over the service counter and offered his hand. Jesse shook it and took an open stool at the counter. 'What can I do for you, young man?'

'I'd like to speak with Nia if that's possible, sir.'

He chuckled. 'I figured that. She's out right now running an errand with my wife.'

Jesse deflated. He needed to speak with Nia now.

'You know what's funny? I couldn't pay you to look this way the last six years, and now, here you are.'

Jesse's cheeks burned. Despite what he and Nia shared, Mr. Bennett had always been like a second father to him. He had spent so much time at their house that he'd got to know the Bennetts' inner workings, and Walter set a fine example of what it took to be a husband, a father, and a businessman. After his own father, Jesse considered himself privileged to have more examples of strong and stable men.

'It's been rough,' Jesse admitted.

Mr. Bennett nodded. He poured dark soda in a glass and plopped two scoops of vanilla ice cream over the top. He plunged a straw within the oozing mess and slid it toward Jesse. Root beer floats had been his favorite since he was a kid.

'I watched you grow up same as my Ni-Ni. I consider you one of mine. Take my advice about Nia and just give her some time. She's trying to piece her life back together.'

Jesse took a sip. Instantly the tension he'd been holding released itself.

'That's Ma-Clara's classic vanilla.' Mr. Bennett smiled knowingly. 'One spoonful of that could cure anything.'

'How much do I need to eat for stress?' Jesse joked.

'I've eaten two tubs in the last two days, so you tell me.' The men shared a brief laugh.

Just then, the bell chimed over the door and Jesse expected to see Nia and Mrs. Bennett. Instead, William Reed walked in, finishing a conversation on his cell phone. He leaned over the counter and dapped Mr. Bennett.

'Can I get a vanilla Shirley Temple for the little one?' he requested.

Jesse noticed Will's blacked-out coupe parked on the corner. Angel was probably in the passenger seat counting the seconds until her daddy returned with her sweet treat. Jesse joined him at the counter to wait for his drink.

'Coming right up,' Mr. Bennett answered.

'Fall Fest tomorrow?' Will asked, pointing to the leaning tower of waffle cones in the window.

Mr. Bennett nodded, wiping his hands on a towel and slinging it over his shoulder. 'You know it,' he said. 'The mayor is having this thing come hell or high water and I don't want to be caught unprepared.'

'Smart man,' Will replied. 'The way things have been going, you gotta be ready for anything.'

'I hate to say it . . .' Mr. Bennett started. 'I don't know if this is an appropriate thing to say, but uh . . . I don't think Harvey Briggs killed anybody.'

Jesse raised an eyebrow at the man. 'You're not the only one.'

Mr. Bennett scooted closer to them. 'They expect us to believe that the richest man in Cinnamon Falls snapped and killed two women? It just doesn't sit right with me.'

Jesse nearly spit his soda out. Will chimed in, 'Harvey Briggs is the richest man in Cinnamon Falls?'

Mr. Bennett nodded his head emphatically. 'At one point selling classic cars was a booming business.'

'What changed?' Jesse asked. From the looks of Harvey's lot now, the money had long since run out.

'He stopped cold turkey right after Nia's friend went over the Falls. I went up to Briggs' spot and asked about a seventies Barracuda. My uncle drove one and I thought he had the coolest car, plus it was time to give that ol' station wagon a rest. I had a little stashed away and Briggs told me he stopped sellin' cars flat out, just like that.' Mr. Bennett snapped his fingers and produced Will's order.

Will frowned and took a sip out of his daughter's drink. 'Can't be true. The mayor's been busy collecting cars. He told me at the party he's been gettin' them through Harvey Briggs for years. He must've thought you didn't have the coin, Mr. B,' Will joked.

Mr. Bennett pointed at Will with a slick smile. 'He must not know who he dealin' wit'.' The two slapped hands and Jesse felt so light on his feet he could have been blown over with a feather.

After saying his goodbyes, Mr. Bennett promised that he would deliver the message to Nia that Jesse was looking for her. Jesse hoped he would because it was looking like the only person who could prove Briggs' innocence was Nia.

Chapter 24

Nia

It'd been six years since Nia had sat down for dinner with her family. She had to physically remove Midnight's booster seat from her designated chair at the kitchen table. She hoped she didn't wake up dead tomorrow.

'Y'all gave the cat my seat?' Nia asked.

'She lives here!' Niles replied, a mischievous smile playing at his lips. 'We couldn't leave the chair empty all this time.'

Her father took a seat from the dining room and brought it into the kitchen, securing Midnight's booster seat. Midnight hopped onto the cushion and he pushed the chair up to the circular glass table. Satisfied, Midnight snuggled down into the seat, curling herself in a ball. Nia could have sworn she saw a smirk aimed in her direction.

Nia felt her phone vibrate in her pocket. It was Morgan. Ever since they'd found out about Sienna's lies, they'd been clinging closer to each other, dissecting each instance of their friendship to determine if what Amber said held weight. Neither she nor Morgan could decide if what Amber had told them was true. All they knew was what Sienna had said to them all those years ago and Nia wanted so badly to believe the friend she'd had since they were in first grade. But her nagging gut was telling her that Pink Bra Amber might have been closer to Sienna than Nia had ever been.

'No phones at the table,' her father warned, around a mouthful of her mother's juicy baked chicken. 'This is family time.'

'What if it's Jesse, honey?' Marjorie said, eyes tight with worry. 'He might know something more about Rosie?'

Walter relented with a wave of his hand, allowing Nia to answer the phone. The family watched intensely.

'Hey, Morg,' Nia replied. The table deflated and returned to their plates.

'Have you seen the news?' Morgan asked.

Nia jumped up. 'What happened?' She dashed out of the kitchen toward the living room. She frantically dug around in her couch cushions to find the remote.

'It's Maggie!' Morgan cried. 'They found her at Harvest Square!'

Niles came in and found the remote first and turned the TV to the news station. The family crowded into the living room; her father refused to leave his dinner plate, scurrying into the room while shoveling rice into his mouth.

Elaine Matthias was live at Harvest Square. In the background, dozens of uniformed officers were scattered around, rolling out neon yellow tape, forcing the festival crew to remain outside of the boundaries.

'If you're just tuning in with us, it's another sad day in Cinnamon Falls. Maggie Shilling, the Director of Hospitality, and the driving force behind the Fall Fest, has just been found deceased.' Elaine stepped out of frame, and returned a few seconds later with a crumpled tissue in her hand. She lifted her cat eye glasses and wiped her tears. She took a deep breath and continued. 'Authorities have not made an official statement, but one must wonder if this is the work of a serial killer right here in our midst . . .'

'A serial killer, for real?' Niles asked to no one in particular.

Marjorie cried, 'I can't take another minute of this!'

On the screen, Elaine muttered, '. . . What has become of our beloved Cinnamon Falls?'

After dinner, Nia found herself sprawled across her bed, watching her ceiling fan blades play a sad game of tag.

Her father had locked all of the doors and forbade

Nia and Niles to leave after dark. He dared anyone to test his steel resolve. Nia had never seen him this serious about anything.

Deep down, she was shaken to her core. The place she loved so much as a child was turning into something she didn't recognize. Who was doing this? Who was picking the Cinnamon Falls community apart? Who, Nia wondered, *would* be next?

The thought made her sit up in bed. The box of Sienna's things had been staring at her since she brought it home. Maybe, she thought, she might find the answers to the questions that had been running rampant through her mind since Amber blew up her world.

She found some scissors in her desk and ran them down the center of the cardboard box. The flaps freed themselves, opening to reveal the contents inside.

The first thing Nia saw was her own face. She pulled out two handfuls of Polaroids: all the pictures from the corkboard on Sienna's wall. There were people from high school she hadn't seen in years, and she even found a few embarrassing photos of herself and Jesse together. Morgan was scattered among the crew, decked out in purple as usual. Nia admired her commitment to the color.

There were also friendship bracelets and a corsage from junior prom. Nia vividly remembered the black dress Sienna wore. She'd fought with Rosie about wearing red lipstick because her mother thought she'd look too grown up. Looking back, Nia could see Rosie's point, but Sienna looked stunning in the photo of that night, like one of those vintage pin-ups.

Nia also found a journal, secured by a flimsy lock. A collage of magazine cutouts littered the front and back cover from when physical media was still a thing. Sienna had cut and pasted a bunch of letters of various fonts on the front that looked like a ransom note. It read, 'If You're Reading This Mind Your Business'.

She flipped the book over, running her fingers across the written pages she couldn't access, torn between curiosity and guilt. Would Sienna have wanted her to read it? She would be invading her best friend's privacy; reading all her intimate thoughts and feelings about herself and the world around her. If Nia was dead, would she want Sienna to read her diary?

Nia gripped the book in her hands. All the answers about her best friend's private life lived in these pages. Had Rosie read it? The lock didn't look tampered with. Nia knew it would only take one turn of a bobby pin and she might have all the answers she'd been looking for.

She dug around in her hair for a pin and retrieved one from the bun she'd styled earlier that day. She took the end in her teeth and was ready to unlock Sienna's secrets when her phone rattled on the nightstand beside her.

Nia reached over to it, expecting it to be Jesse. He'd called a few times but she didn't have the energy to hear what he had to say. She had her finger primed for the decline button when she realized it was Bryant. At the last second, she decided to answer it. She'd left too many things undone in her life. It was time that she faced the music so that she could move on, truly.

'Hey,' she said.

Bryant was silent on the other end. 'Nia?' he asked at last. She hadn't heard his voice in almost a week. All the voicemails he'd left were deleted instantly. 'Are you there?'

'Yeah,' she responded. 'I'm here.'

'God, I've been trying to reach you,' he cried. He sounded worried and desperate.

'I know,' Nia said. That was the whole point of ignoring someone, not being able to reach them.

'Please, Cookie, just let me explain,' he begged.

Nia had always hated the nickname he'd given her. When she first introduced herself at Gildman & Sons, he thought she said her name was Nilla like the wafer cookie and started calling her Cookie around the office as a joke. After they grew serious, it became a term of endearment for him. She wondered what he called his wife.

'Explain that you have a whole wife?' She was regretting answering the phone now. He should have started by groveling, not whatever this was.

He sighed. He sounded like he was in the car. Nia glanced at the time on her phone, it was nearly eight p.m. Shouldn't a man with a wife be headed home? If she were still in Atlanta, she'd be rounding out dinner, washing dishes, while Bryant got ready for the following day. Where could he possibly be? She shook the thought out of her mind. He was no longer her concern.

'It wasn't like that, Cook. It's complicated.'

'Oh, complicated,' Nia responded sarcastically. 'That must be a new way of saying, "I lied to you and I'm a terrible person".'

'I made a mistake,' he admitted. 'But I never lied about my feelings for you, Cookie.'

Fire erupted in Nia's belly. 'Don't,' she warned, feeling heat rise all over her body. She was getting angry again; that tangible, ferocious rage she'd felt after his wife left her open-mouthed on her own front porch.

She was emotionally raw; from Rosie to Sienna, Jesse and now Maggie, Nia was slowly losing her resolve.

'Just tell me where you are, please,' Bryant begged. 'I need to see you, face to face. We need to talk about this.'

Nia's fingers tightened around the phone. 'I don't want to see you,' she said through gritted teeth. 'You owe me nothing.'

'Cookie, please,' he pleaded.

Nia had options. She could give in, hear him out, let him explain. She could even try to forgive him if her heart was ready for that. She could finally close this chapter for good and move on. She took a deep breath. Bryant was not the answer.

'Bryant, I can't.'

Before she could second guess herself, she hung up. Stomping across the room, she threw open her bedroom window. The moon hung low in the sky, a cloud of fog covered the streets. In her hand, her phone vibrated again. It was Bryant calling back. Now that she'd answered, he probably figured it was only a matter of time before she answered again.

With all the strength inside her, Nia launched her phone at the moon. She didn't care where it landed. After she heard it smack the front lawn, she closed the window.

Chapter 25

Jesse

Jesse returned to work that evening to submit his patrol log and bumped into Mrs. Guy, who wanted to report that someone had overturned her trash cans in the alley behind her store. She refused to let Jesse leave until he took pictures of the damage, which were a few minor scratches to the sides of the cans. Despite his annoyance, Jesse did his due diligence and included it in his findings.

Chambers and Raines had gone for the day already, Angie reported, and would be back in time for Maggie Shilling's memorial service that evening. She also hadn't seen Wade very much, but Jesse knew that he wouldn't miss Maggie's service or his shift on night patrol. He was anxious to tell Wade about what he'd discovered about Darius and Sienna, and Harvey's business dealings. They needed to plan their moves to bring it to the Chief. It was risky, but it would be worth it if it meant getting an innocent man out of jail. It also meant he was one step closer to finding Rosie's real killer.

'How did the tips turn out?' Angie asked, her voice just above a whisper. 'I know a bunch of them were kind of silly. Did they help you at all?'

'Actually, yeah.' Jesse was glad she'd reminded him. He unfolded the tip list from his pocket and laid it out flat on his desk. He pointed to the starred tip about the blue car. 'Can you tell me how many people own blue compact cars in Cinnamon Falls?'

'Sure.' Angie shrugged. 'It will be a huge list, though, Shaw,' she warned.

He spread his arms wide, gesturing to his empty cubicle. 'I got all night.'

She hesitated to step away. She leaned in close and whispered, 'Does Chief know you're doing any of this?' She looked up at the Chief's closed office door, worried.

Jesse hung his head. He knew she knew the answer to her question. 'Can we keep this between me and you?'

Angie bit her bottom lip, her eyes darting between Jesse and the Chief's office. 'I need this job, Jesse.'

'I understand,' he responded. Angie had three small children at home. He didn't want her getting her hands dirty more than they already had been. She'd done him a solid by calling him to get Nia out of holding. He didn't want to compromise her anymore. 'Show me how to do it, then.'

Angie leaned over his shoulder while he pulled up the precinct's intranet. Angie showed him a complicated system of searching and filtering to find registration information for all 141 blue compact vehicles in Cinnamon Falls.

Jesse filtered out any non-native Cinnamon Falls residents. If Grace's memory served her correctly, the car was navigating the streets without headlights. Only people who were familiar with the tight, cobblestone downtown streets would be able to do that.

That brought the list down to fifty-seven people. Lastly, he filtered out anyone over the age of sixty. Twelve-thirty is too late and too dark for most seniors to be out galivanting, especially without headlights. There was no way Evelyn and Robert would be out past five p.m. during the dark fall and winter months. That brought the list down to twenty-two people; that was much more doable. Jesse printed the list of names and addresses and got to work.

He needed to find if any of the twenty-two people on the list had any connection to Darius Lyons. It was a long shot, but it made the most sense to him. Both Grace and Will had mentioned that Darius was late to his Welcome Home party. What if he was late because he took someone's blue car, drove to Rosie's, and then drove back home in time enough to be seen and create an alibi?

What about Maggie? he asked himself.

Maggie must have seen Darius. Jesse recalled the

spooked look on her face at Rosie's candlelight vigil. Was she holding back? Did she know who killed Rosie? Since she and Rosie were meeting late Monday night, Maggie could have seen Darius return to the diner. He could have killed her to keep her silent. He shook his head. There were too many details missing, and Jesse's main priority was to account for that gap in time between when he saw Darius leave Rosie's and the next day.

Jesse checked the only resource he had left: social media. He typed in each person's name, carefully clicking through their friends list, searching for any connection to Darius, or any evidence that they'd made an appearance at his Welcome Home party, all to no avail. He reached person number fourteen, Tammy Nathan.

He double and triple checked the name, remembering how Harold Bones had praised Victoria's mother's looks a few days ago. Jesse remembered Victoria saying that all of her friends and family were at Mayor Lyons' to celebrate Darius returning home. Could it be possible that Darius took her car to kill Rosie and returned to the party in time to take pictures and shake hands?

Jesse couldn't tell if he'd stumbled onto another lead or another dead end, but he was willing to take a chance on either. He hated that Darius had got his potential mother-in-law caught up in his crimes, but Tammy Nathan was officially a person of interest.

Chapter 26

Nia

Nia's home was eerily silent that night. No deep bass of her father's snores on the living room couch while a too-loud action movie ran away on TV with Midnight curled on his chest. There were no muffled murmurs of her mother's hum while she straightened up the house before bed. She didn't hear Midnight's paws walking the creaky wooden floors, slipping from room to room, on her usual nighttime patrol. It was the kind of silence that wrapped around her, making her hyper-aware of her own breathing and restless thoughts.

Growing up, she'd loved the night's chorus: the occasional gust of wind rattling the trees, a distant hoot of owls, or the rumble of a car engine traveling through her neighborhood toward another destination. She was surprised how quickly she'd gotten used to the quiet nights again. After years of living in Atlanta, she would sleep with sponge ear plugs and a white noise machine so she could block out the constant hum of the city's nightlife: car horns and traffic, emergency sirens, or the obnoxious screams of drunken college kids. Bryant would laugh at her as she stuffed plugs into her ears.

'You can't tune out the world forever,' he said. 'You'll have to learn to live with it.'

Except, he'd been part of the noise too. Here, she could finally hear herself think.

Sighing, Nia grabbed the remote and turned on the TV for some background noise. A rerun of Elaine Matthias' news segment flickered on the screen, covering Maggie Shilling's memorial ceremony. The footage showed a thin crowd at Town Hall.

Under normal circumstances, Maggie's homegoing would have been packed with friends and family, stories shared over potluck dishes, and lots of laughter mixed with tears. Knowing that there was a potential serial killer running around had kept most of the town at home. Cinnamon Falls was buttoned up tight tonight. Nia had bigger things to focus on now, including figuring out what she was going to do with her own life.

Without her phone, Nia could concentrate without distraction and work on all the things she'd been avoiding. She wrote two letters: one to Bryant explaining that she was done. She didn't want to listen to any of his excuses or make any space for him in her life. The other, she wrote to Gildman & Sons; a resignation letter. She hadn't expected it to feel so satisfying to write. The moment she sealed the envelope, she knew she was never going back.

There was only one more item on her list to make peace with: Sienna's belongings. Scraps of a life that had been cut short. Nia's gaze drifted toward the box at the edge of her bed.

Nia ran her fingers across the box's lid. Photos, jewelry, everything they once shared, things that, at one point, meant everything. The journal stood out among it all, whispering to her.

Without second guessing, Nia pulled apart another bobby pin from her hair. She slid it inside the small lock. With a slight flick of the wrist, she felt a soft click and the lock unlatched with ease. Somehow, the journal felt heavier in her hands. She traced her fingers on the edges of the ink-stained paper, knowing what was inside would change everything. Nia flipped to the last entry in the diary – the day Sienna found out Darius had cheated on her, and the night before she died.

Nia's hands tightened around the journal. She held her breath while she read:

Today, everything changed. Amber told me she saw Darius at the bar again last night with another girl. Another. Like the first time didn't matter. Like the promises he made to me were just air. Like I didn't matter.

I've been lying to everyone. To Nia. To

Morgan. Even to myself. They're going to hate me when they find out about us.

They all said he was no good. A player. A smooth talker with muscles and just enough charm to make you feel special before he moved on to the next. They thought he was dumb, shallow, a walking cliché in a football jersey. I laughed it off, pretended they were right but I wanted them to be wrong. Deep down, I knew they weren't.

I knew when he started pulling away, when his text replies got shorter, when he suddenly had 'practice' at weird hours. I didn't say anything to my girls because I didn't want to hear 'I told you so.' I didn't want to admit that the boy I had crushed on secretly since freshman year — the boy I thought I had finally won — was never really mine to begin with.

God, how stupid am I?

I gave everything to him. I defended him, lied for him, covered up all the red flags and called them love. And for what? So he could toss me aside like all the others?

Shelly. Victoria. Denise. Amber said there were more — maybe two, maybe five, who even knows anymore. All of them smiled to my face while sneaking behind my back. I feel sick just thinking about it.

This morning, I saw him walking up to me with that stupid grin, like nothing was wrong, like I didn't know. I couldn't even look him in the eye. I turned and walked the other way before I did something I'd regret.

Instead, I wrote him a note, stuffed it in his locker and walked off without looking back: Who Will Be Next?

I hope he reads it over and over, wondering if I'm going to tell someone, if I'm going to blow it all up. I hope he panics the way I've cried. I hope he feels even a fraction of the betrayal he handed me so easily.

I'm done. It's over. I wasted so much time on him when I should've been listening to the people who actually love me. After tomorrow, I'm done with him. Done pretending. Done lying. I'm done breaking my own heart.

Nia had tears in her eyes as she finished reading. Sienna was devastated at Darius' betrayal. If Nia had known Sienna was going through all of this, she would have taken Darius out herself.

On the TV, Elaine Matthias droned on. She talked about the possibility of a serial killer in Cinnamon Falls and what that could mean for the residents. Then, it flashed to a photo of a piece of paper. In hasty handwriting, were the words 'Who Will Be Next?'

Nia's breath caught in her throat. She paused the TV and glanced down at Sienna's diary.

'No,' she heard herself say.

With shaky hands she placed the journal next to the television, her eyes darting back and forth between Sienna's journal and the killer's note. Her heart galloped around in her chest when she realized the handwriting was more than similar – it was identical.

Sienna wrote that note.

But, Sienna isn't alive, her brain reminded her.

How could a ghost's note show up at Rosie's crime scene six years later?

Nia leapt off her bed, wishing she hadn't thrown her cell phone out of the window.

Niles' bedroom was almost pitch black save for the three mounted computer monitors that cast a blue haze over the rest of the room. His room thankfully didn't smell like eggs anymore, but her little brother was still unnecessarily junky. Snack bags, empty water bottles, and used tissues littered the ground. Laundry in various stages of cleanliness were tossed in corners of the room, while his unmade bed was occupied with strewn papers and open textbooks.

Her brother was stationed at his computer desk. His cell phone was propped up on a video call with someone, while he played a game on screen that had a lot of shooting and blood. Nia slapped his headphones off his ears when he didn't answer her urgent knocks. She reached over and muted his video call.

'Tell me you have offline access to the County Records system?'

Niles sighed, glancing down at his muted phone. 'Ni-Ni, can you *please* take a break from committing crimes? I'm really starting to worry about you—'

Nia grabbed his mouse, found an open browser, and typed in a replay of tonight's newscast. She fast-forwarded until she found the part where Elaine Matthias showed the note found at both crime scenes. Nia held Sienna's diary up to the screen.

'Okay, well, that's creepy,' Niles admitted with a nonchalant shrug.

Nia rolled her eyes. 'Can you get into the records office or not?' she demanded.

'Of course I *can*, but that doesn't mean I will. All this stuff is tracked. As soon as I enter my username and password all my clicks are being monitored. They'll know everything I clicked on before I even go into work tomorrow afternoon.'

'So use someone else's,' Nia pointed out. 'You said yourself that people forget their passwords all the time. Log in using their credentials and then change all their passwords on Monday.'

Niles narrowed his eyes at her. 'Is there rehab for criminals? You need it.'

Niles logged into the County Records website. 'Pull

up Sienna's autopsy report,' Nia instructed, her voice much sharper than she intended.

Niles hesitated and shifted in his chair. His fingers drummed anxiously against the desk while he waited for the screen to load.

'Wait, you don't think that Sienna wrote that note, do you?' Niles asked. He looked at her with a sadness in his dark eyes that made her throat tighten. 'I know the last few days have been hard, but Sienna's gone, Ni-Ni. She's—'

Nia groaned, pressing the heels of her palms into her eyes. She knew her brother was just trying to protect her, but she wasn't chasing ghosts here. This was real. She was chasing the truth. She only had one more missing piece and then she could take it all to Jesse. He couldn't deny the evidence she had this time.

She swallowed down her frustration and replied with a tight-lipped smile, 'I know that, okay? This isn't about me not accepting her death. I just need to know what *really* happened to her.'

She paced in the small space behind his chair and the sea of dirty clothes, her heartbeat racing. She was close, she could feel it. 'If I can prove that Darius found Sienna's note, that meant he'd known Sienna was going to break up with him the day before they were crowned at the Fall Festival.'

'So what's the big deal?' Niles asked, running a hand over his waves. 'They fake it for that stupid drive down Main Street and then they go their separate ways.'

Nia stilled; a cold, sick feeling twisted in her gut. 'Except, Sienna didn't go her own way. She died that night.'

Niles' face paled as the words sank in.

'What if . . . she didn't jump off Barkwood that night. What if . . .' Nia couldn't bring herself to say it.

Niles blinked, realization dawning in his expression. '. . . Darius pushed her?'

Nia nodded, her throat too tight to speak.

Niles spun back toward his computer and his fingers flew across the keyboard. The click of the keys filled the silence as he typed and scrolled through the database. The screen flickered as documents loaded. A few more keystrokes until there was one final click.

'Got it,' Niles announced.

Sienna's death records. Niles clicked on the first attachment, her autopsy report.

'"Cause of death . . . suicide by drowning,"' Niles read aloud. His eyes darted across the screen as he read. He pointed to the bottom of the document. 'Signed by Chief Vernon Prescott.'

Nia's stomach plummeted. Her heart hammered harder in her chest as she dashed out of Niles' bedroom. She knew she'd seen another version of Sienna's autopsy report in Rosie's folder. She'd kept it. She grabbed the plastic bag of paperwork from under her bed and rummaged through the bag, her fingers fumbling through the pages. They scattered across the floor, but she barely noticed. Her pulse roared in her ears. Finally, she found it; Rosie's copy. She clutched the paper to her chest and ran back to Niles' room, practically slamming the page on his desk with trembling hands.

Nia's eyes scanned two versions of the same document: one from the county database and one Rosie kept hidden. She read aloud, voice unsteady, '"Cause of death, Inconclusive. Injuries consistent with drowning."' Her breath caught in her throat as she traced the signature at the bottom of the page. 'Signed by Genesis Whitfield.'

Niles sat up straighter. He looked between the two reports and then back at Nia. 'Someone deleted this one,' he whispered.

Darkness pressed in around them. Only their ragged breathing and the hum of Niles' computer filled the silence.

Nia's hands curled into fists. 'When Chief Prescott signed this, he had no idea it wasn't the original.'

Niles spoke with a voice barely above a whisper. 'And guess whose dad he works for?'

Nia's stomach twisted into knots. The realization hit her like a freight train. 'Darius Lyons.'

Chapter 27

Saturday
Jesse

Jesse had just drifted off to sleep when his phone rang, vibrating angrily against his nightstand. He groaned, rubbing his hands over his face. He blindly reached for his phone, nearly knocking over the lamp, and pulled it to his ear.

'Shaw,' he answered gruffly, already fumbling out of the bed. It was the third time this week, and he was growing used to losing sleep.

Wade's voice was sharp and serious. 'I'm on Main Street doing my patrol. You better get down here to The Cinnamon Scoop. It's a wreck.'

Jesse froze mid-motion. 'What?'

'You heard me right.' Wade sighed. 'The front window's smashed in. The place has been torn apart, Shaw. You need to get down here, asap.'

Jesse was already on his feet, yanking jeans over his hips and pulling a sweatshirt over his head. He grabbed his weapon and badge off his dresser before hurling himself down the stairs toward the garage.

He brought the cell phone back to his ear. 'Is anyone hurt?'

Jesse stuffed his feet into a pair of sneakers by the front door, grabbed his jacket and keys. He was out the door within minutes.

'Nah, looks like the place was empty. But something feels off.'

Jesse reversed out of his garage and spun into the street. He slammed his car into drive, flooring the accelerator. His roaring engine cut through the silence of his neighborhood as he sped away. 'I'll be there in ten minutes,' he said, and hung up the phone.

From the moment Jesse turned off the highway and onto Main Street, he could see the damage to The Cinnamon Scoop. Glass glittered like ice on the pavement, reflecting the glow of the police cruisers parked outside the ice cream shop. The front window was completely shattered like someone had thrown a sizeable object through it. The door hung open at an unnatural angle, like someone had kicked it in.

Wade stood by the door's entrance, his arms crossed, jaw tight, while Chambers and Raines stood by, red-faced. Jesse stepped out of the car and took in the devastation. His heart squeezed in his chest. The Bennetts were going to be crushed. Everything they'd worked for, for generations, had been destroyed in one night. The Cinnamon Scoop was the cornerstone business of Cinnamon Falls. How could anyone have stooped this low?

Jesse approached the scene open-mouthed in disbelief. Wade, Raines and Chambers didn't stop their bickering as he got closer.

'Get out of the way, Wade,' Raines demanded. 'I'm the officer in charge!'

'I'm not moving until I see Shaw,' Wade replied, his chin jutting toward the sky.

'I really don't want to have to arrest your old ass,' Chambers warned.

Wade squared his shoulders, leveling his gaze on Chambers. 'I'd like to see you try.' The only thing Chambers had above Wade was height. Even though Bud Wade was nearing sixty-five, he still had the muscular frame built by the discipline of the military. Chambers had the reach, but Bud had the strength, and that was all that mattered. Jesse had his money on Wade.

'I'm here,' Jesse called. He wedged himself between Wade and Chambers.

Wade brought his attention to Jesse and his murderous gaze softened. He placed his hand on Jesse's shoulder. 'It's bad, brother,' he warned.

Jesse nodded, steeling himself. Wade stepped out of his way and let him inside. The once-cozy shop was unrecognizable. Tables and chairs were overturned, some completely broken in half like they'd been launched across the room. The leather stools at the service counter had been slashed, tufts of foam spilled out of the seats. Angry sledgehammer-sized holes dotted the quartz countertops, breaking it into a thousand tiny pieces. Behind the counter, the register's drawer had been ripped open. Dozens of tubs of melted ice cream pooled on the floor. The waffle cones Jesse remembered being stacked up in the far corner just a few hours ago had been tossed and broken on the ground. The distinct smell of spiced vanilla, caramel, and cinnamon lingered in the air.

Jesse spun on his heel to see Wade, Chambers, and Raines directly behind him at the door, taking in the damage.

'Told ya, it's bad,' Wade exhaled.

'We need to call the Chief,' Raines said.

Jesse swore under his breath, taking one more hesitant step forward. He turned in a slow circle, taking in all the violence of the destruction. This wasn't some punk kids breaking in for fun and stealing a few things. This was calculated. Personal. Someone was sending a message to Nia's family. Jesse shook his head. He'd warned her about getting involved.

'Forced entry?' Chambers asked.

'They broke the glass and the front door was kicked in, man,' Jesse scoffed.

'No alarms, though,' Raines added. On the wall next to her, an alarm system's panel was glowing green. All was well according to that. 'They weren't worried about getting caught.'

'No one was on Main Street tonight,' Jesse pointed out. 'No one would have seen them anyway.'

'Everyone was at Town Hall for Maggie's ceremony,' Wade agreed.

'Not everyone,' Chambers mumbled.

Jesse shook his head. 'The serial killer business made tons of people stay inside. Maggie's service was scarce.'

Chambers flipped out his phone.

'Wait, who are you calling?' Jesse asked.

'Dispatch! We need to call it in.' Chambers spun around and put the phone to his ear, tiptoeing back outside of the shop.

'Someone's got it out for your girl,' Raines said and followed Chambers outside.

With a heavy heart, Jesse called Mr. Bennett. The phone rang twice before Walter picked up. The phone rustled while Jesse waited for the man to get his bearings.

'Jesse, everything alright, son?' Mr. Bennett sounded alert for a man who had just been shaken from his sleep.

Jesse heard Mrs. Bennett in the background. 'Is Nia okay?' she whispered.

Jesse hesitated, glancing around at the wreckage. He didn't know where to begin. How could he tell this family that everything they loved had been destroyed?

'Mr. Bennett, I . . . I need you to come down to the shop.'

There was a pause and more rustling on the other end. Then, Walter's voice replied, tight with controlled panic, 'What happened?'

Jesse squeezed the bridge of his nose. 'Sir, it's been vandalized.'

Walter took a sharp breath. 'I'm on the way.'

Exactly ten minutes later, Jesse watched the familiar Bennett sedan arrive. His stomach twisted while he waited on the curb. The car jerked to a stop, barely making it past the police cruisers before the doors burst open all at once. All five Bennetts spilled out onto the sidewalk, Midnight included. Niles clutched her in his arms and covered her eyes when they approached, taking in the wreckage. For a moment, no one moved; the scene before them was hard to take in.

Marjorie gasped; a sound so raw and emotional it cut through Jesse's chest. Then, came the wailing. She clutched Nia like she was drowning, and her daughter was the only thing keeping her upright.

'Oh my God,' she sobbed, her voice cracking under the weight of devastation. 'Not our shop!' Marjorie's legs buckled and Nia caught her before she collapsed completely.

Nia's own face was streaked with tears; her body shaking while she held onto her mother. Her eyes remained locked on the ruins. Her dreams, her childhood, their family history . . . it was all gone. Jesse stopped himself from pulling her into his arms.

Walter Bennett, ever stoic and solid, stood motionless beside his family. He didn't shed a tear, but Jesse could see his rage in the fists clenched tightly by his side. His knuckles went white and his gaze darkened, his sharp eyes scanning the wreckage with precision. When he finally spoke, his voice was even but filled with steel.

'Tell me everything,' he demanded to the officers standing around.

Wade gave him a solemn nod and explained, 'I was doing my night patrol down Main Street when I saw it.' Mr. Bennett's jaw tightened. 'The alarm didn't sound, sir. We would have come immediately had it reported to the station. This isn't petty vandalism. They went out of their way to destroy things.'

Jesse whispered, 'This wasn't random, sir, this was intentional.'

'What did we do to deserve this?' Marjorie asked between sobs.

Walter exhaled slowly, his nostrils flaring. He turned to his wife, daughter, and son, clinging onto each other. His murderous expression softened for just a moment when he wrapped his arms around them.

'We'll fix it,' he said firmly. 'They won't take this from us.'

Marjorie nodded weakly, pushing her face in her

husband's neck. She unleashed another sob that could have snatched Jesse's heart out of his chest.

Nia lifted her chin, her expression hardened beneath the tears. Jesse knew that look. It wasn't just grief, or heartbreak, or rage, it was determination. Whoever had done this thought it would break the Bennetts, but they had another thing coming.

The wee hours of Saturday dragged on. Raines and Chambers allowed Walter and Marjorie to walk the parlor to ensure nothing was missing in case they were dealing with a robbery. After Walter's meticulous inventory and physically restraining Marjorie from cleaning up, Jesse convinced the family to head home after their horrific early morning.

Jesse had waited all day yesterday to talk to Nia. They had much unfinished business that could wait for another time, but Nia swore she couldn't wait another minute to talk to him. Jesse promised to bring her home straightaway. Midnight's yellow eyes watched him closely from the rear window as the family sedan pulled off.

'This is my fault,' Nia whispered. She banged her fists on the dashboard of Jesse's car, frenzied. She'd gone from a tearful mess to a murderous rage in a matter of seconds. He couldn't judge her; if his family's legacy had been vandalized, no one could stop him from seeking justice, and not the kind found in a court of law.

'There's no way you could have predicted this, Nia,' Jesse responded, trying to keep his voice even. It was killing him seeing her cry. The rage was building up in him so intensely, he could feel steam coming from his ears.

Nia whipped around. 'You said yourself that this was intentional, right?'

'We think so,' Jesse said. 'We found out they cut the power, that's why we didn't get the alarm. No power meant no coolers. The ice cream was going to melt anyway. Why throw it around the floor? Slashing the seats, damaging the counters. It all feels very personal.'

'Someone is trying to stop me, Jesse.' Nia plucked at her fingers nervously. She tucked her trembling hands under her thighs. Then, her thighs began to shake. Nia glanced over her shoulder at the empty street.

'I found out how Sienna really died tonight.'

Dazed, Jesse asked her to repeat herself. 'You did what?'

'I'm pretty sure Darius Lyons pushed her off Barkwood, Jay. Niles and I found the autopsy report. Someone must have found out that I was getting close to this. It's the same people who killed Rosie . . . and Maggie . . .' Nia's eyes were wild with fury and Jesse could barely keep up with her story. 'I took

Briggs' phone and there was a message on it,' she stuttered.

Her brain was moving faster than the words could come together. 'Rosie's last words. The last words she ever said to the both of us.' Nia spun around to Jesse, her eyes big as the moon. He'd never seen her so animated before. 'In Sienna's diary was the note! The note the killer left!'

'Wait, Nia, back up!' Jesse could barely comprehend anything Nia was saying. All of it was jumbled together, coming out all at once. 'You actually *stole* Briggs' phone? Morgan said you found—'

'You can have it back, okay?' she cried. 'It's all right here.' She pulled out a shattered cell phone that looked like a tractor had run over it. She retrieved another white cordless phone. She shoved them in Jesse's hands.

For the first time since Jesse left the military, he was scared. He was shaken to his core watching Nia unravel like this. She was talking in gibberish circles and he couldn't make out anything she was saying. He placed both his hands on her shoulders, turning her body toward his. He hooked one finger under her chin, bringing her attention to his face. He watched as her eyes slowly connected with his. Somewhere in there was the woman he loved.

'Breathe with me,' he said.

Nia copied him as he took one deep breath in for four seconds, held it for four, and breathed out for four seconds. They did it again until the version of Nia he knew returned.

'Start from the beginning,' Jesse said. He noted the time on the dash. It was well after three in the morning, but he could wait for Nia forever.

Jesse made sure Nia's seat belt was secure as he sped toward Old Man Milton's farm. His headlights cut through the heavy fog hovering over the streets. Nia told him everything, and finally he had the full picture. It was more than obvious that Darius had killed Sienna that night, and Mayor Lyons had covered it up.

He wanted to shout to Wade that they'd been right. Raines, Chambers, and Prescott were too busy being yes-men to see what was right in front of their faces. But, if he was going to prove it, he had to put Briggs' phone back. When the police collected the evidence from his house, Jesse would play Rosie's voicemail for the team. That would prompt them to start the investigation over, and hopefully, Briggs would go free.

Jesse made sure to park his car across the street from Harvey's Used Cars. He then wrapped the phone in a towel after scrubbing it of Nia's fingerprints. If someone was up there waiting for him, he wanted to be prepared. He fished around for the axe he kept in the back of his car.

'What will you need that for?' Nia asked.

'Stay in the car,' he ordered.

He hopped the fence, trudging up the dirt road until he reached Harvey Briggs' trailer.

According to Nia, Harvey's back door was open when she'd visited, so he hoped he wouldn't have to break in. Harvey's truck was right where Nia said it would be and the door to his bedroom slid open without a hitch. As Jesse suspected, the place had been rummaged through and trashed just like The Cinnamon Scoop had been. He crouched down and tossed the phone under the bed where Nia said she'd found it.

When he turned to leave, he noticed the shed Nia warned him about. It wasn't anything remarkable; it looked like an outbuilding that hoarders used when they had too much stuff and not enough space. He'd missed it before when he came with Chambers just a few days ago.

Jesse pulled out his flashlight and trampled over the overgrown brush until he reached the front of the shed. He felt his pulse speed up as he saw that the door was bolted shut by a rusty padlock. He had just the thing for that. With one swing of his axe the lock came loose, tumbling down and disappearing into the tangle of leaves at his feet.

The door creaked open, and he jumped back and tightened his grip on the axe, preparing himself for whatever might be inside.

A green 1970 Mercury Cougar two-door coupe convertible sat before him. It would have been in pristine condition had it not been for the front bumper. The front of the classic beauty was smashed in like it had been in a head-on collision. The bumper was scratched; the paint job ground down to show the metal underneath. A spiderweb of cracks exploded from the center of the demolished windshield.

Behind him, leaves crunched. Jesse whirled around, weapon at the ready, to find Nia wide-eyed. Her hand was clasped over her mouth in shock.

'This is the car,' she said breathily. Her trembling hands reached out to touch the hood and Jesse pulled her back.

'Don't,' he warned. 'Whose car?'

Nia could barely talk when she replied, 'S-Sienna's.'

Nia gestured for Jesse's phone. He pulled it out and she searched Sienna's name in his internet browser. The article about her death from *The Cinnamon Chronicle* appeared first. The first picture linked in the article showed a smiling Sienna right after being crowned Cinnamon Queen, waving to the crowd. Darius Lyons sat beside her, doing the same; smiles crowding both of their faces.

They were sitting on top of a vehicle.

It was the exact one they were staring at, except the front wasn't smashed in, and Sienna was still very much alive.

Chapter 28

Nia

The morning of the Fall Festival should have been a joyous one for the Bennett family. Normally, they would wake up before the sun, in that pre-dawn haze of the morning, and head to Harvest Square. As the very first business in Cinnamon Falls, The Cinnamon Scoop always had a prime location at the festival, directly in the middle of the square. At the height of the festival, lines would snake through the crowd for a cone of Ma-Clara's signature cinnamon swirl ice cream.

Nia's morning should have been filled with the earthy scent of freshly ground cinnamon, the hum of the espresso machine churning out their much-needed caffeine fix, and the laughter of her family as they prepared for a long and fulfilling day ahead.

Instead, The Cinnamon Scoop sat in ruins. Nia stood on the sidewalk, her hands braced on her hips, looking at the boarded window, her heart aching at the sight. Ancestral agony plagued her. The sorrow of her grandmother and the disappointment of her great-grandmother weighed on her shoulders.

The normally vibrant shop, alive with history and tradition, was nothing more than a crime scene now, covered in plywood and police tape. The quirky and inviting googly-eyed Cinnamon Scoop mascot, hand painted by her father twenty years ago on the shop's windows, was shattered in the street. She and her father spent the morning sweeping the glass from the sidewalk, ensuring the festival goers wouldn't hurt themselves.

Nia traced her fingers over the bricks, remembering how proud her grandmother was to pass it down to her father. She remembered how her father beamed with pride when he was handed his personal ice cream scoop. The same one Ma-Clara had used when she first ran the shop.

And now?

Her family wouldn't be part of the Fall Festival for the first time since the town's inception. Nia was too sad to be angry anymore. She'd been stewing all night. Her mother was too distraught to get out of bed, and her father hadn't slept a wink, up pacing the floor, waiting by the phone for the call that he could return to the shop.

When Raines called and gave them the all-clear that morning, Nia begged her father to let her join him. Wordlessly, he agreed. Sylvester James graciously opened his general store early so her father could grab some plywood, and together, they boarded the window.

Inside, Nia and her father got started on the spilled ice cream first. Her hands clenched the mop until her palms hurt. Whoever had done this had taken more than just their livelihood; they'd stolen their legacy.

And Nia knew exactly who was behind it.

She played the distressed daughter role all morning, working tirelessly alongside her father, cursing whoever did this, and crying together when the severity of the devastation hit them all over again.

Meanwhile, the Fall Festival was in full swing, transforming Cinnamon Falls into something enchanted and magical. Main Street was unrecognizable with canopies of amber and gold leaves overhead until they reached Harvest Square.

Booths lined the sidewalks, brimming with local vendors selling fresh apple cider, cinnamon sugar doughnuts, pumpkin-shaped candles, and hand-knit scarves.

Occasionally, people knocked. They peered inside, pressing hopeful faces against the door, asking, 'Are you open?' One child in a Cinnamon King T-shirt clutched a crumpled dollar bill, his lip trembling when Nia gently said no.

Word spread quickly. Someone left a paper cup on the doorstep labeled 'Scoop Strong'. By noon, it was full of cash. Neighbors, festival goers, even tourists who'd heard about the break-in stopped by, not just to drop off donations, but to offer hugs, baked goods, or just to say, 'We're so sorry. We miss you. You'll be back.'

Walter stood silently behind the counter, staring absentmindedly like he could see through the boarded window at the swirling joy just beyond. Nia held the tip jar in her hands, overwhelmed by the warmth of a town that had lost so much, but still chose to show up, to care, to hope.

The Fall Festival went on: joyous, colorful, and magical, and as the day inched closer to the Cinnamon King and Queen ceremony, Nia plotted, waiting for the perfect opportunity. All the pieces had fallen together for her. All that there was left to do was execute.

Once the floor had been mopped, and the broken furniture had been removed, Nia felt better. The countertops and barstools were still ruined, but at least the floor wasn't sticky anymore. Her father closed the shop, refusing to look toward Harvest Square where the Fall Fest was still in full swing. It would go on until night pressed in.

'Want to grab one of those juice smoothies? Or one of those corndogs you like?' Nia tried to reach her father. He'd been dull behind the eyes all morning, no small talk could pull him out of his thoughts.

He shook his head. 'I'll wait here 'til you get back,' he offered, and slid inside the car.

A squeal sliced through the air as children ran

through the crowded streets, faces painted like pumpkins, ghosts, and whatever superhero was trending. They dashed between games and hay bale mazes, and the scent of roasted and kettle corn lingered in the air like a comforting blanket. A jazz band played on the Town Hall steps, their saxophones and trumpets adding to the charm that wrapped around Cinnamon Falls like a hug. The energy in the air was electric.

Nia couldn't care less about any of it. She and Jesse had promised that they would go together to confront Darius, but after seeing the look on her father's face, she knew she couldn't wait any longer.

She zeroed in on the parade procession lining up on Cinnamon Way. She didn't have any rehearsed lines, only her steely determination to keep her company as she stormed through Main Street toward her destination. When she reached the intersection, she spotted a line of classic cars sat parked, one behind the other, down the street.

Excited seniors and their even more excited families crowded Cinnamon Way, cameras at the ready. Nia shoved her way through the crowd, ignoring the murmurs and gasps of surprise as she marched toward the float, undeterred.

The newly crowned Cinnamon King and Queen were positioned at the back, waiting for the procession to begin. Nia recognized Lil' Charlie, Charlie Kent's son, but wasn't familiar with the new Cinnamon Queen. The brown-eyed beauty looked down at her from atop a convertible. She pushed her long curls out of her face. The golden Cinnamon Queen crown sparkled in the late afternoon sun.

'You lookin' for someone, Ms. Nia?' she asked with concern in her eyes.

'I— how did you know my name?' Nia questioned, caught off guard.

'Everybody knows the Bennetts, plus you look just like Niles.' Her smile lit up her face, but only briefly. 'He talks about you all the time. I'm sorry about The Cinnamon Scoop.'

Nia had to remember to be nicer to her brother. Maybe on the 29th of February, she considered.

'You looking for Mr. Lyons?' The Cinnamon Queen pointed over her shoulder toward the school house behind her. 'Last I saw him he was in the gym.'

Nia started to walk away when Lil' Charlie leaned over to her. 'Can you tell him to hurry up? My ass is hurtin' up here, man,' he complained. 'We been waitin' on him forever. Unc already had his moment. It's time for ours.'

'Stop cursing before I tell your daddy,' Nia scolded. Lil' Charlie clammed up at the mention of his father and took a quick glance around, making sure he wasn't around.

Nia sprinted toward the school and ran around the side of the building toward the gym's back entrance. The door was propped open with a deflated basketball and Nia crouched down to peek inside.

The gymnasium was as she remembered it: twin golden bleachers stacked to the ceiling and navy blue brick painted walls with a meticulous hand-painted mural of a howling timber wolf, outlined in gold. Except, in the six years she'd been gone, the timber wolf she'd known and loved had been edited to include none other than Darius Lyons; a side profile shot of him in his Cinnamon Falls uniform, clutching a football in his hands. His high school jersey had been encased in a frame above the door with his signature painted underneath.

Her eyes settled on Darius, standing in the center of the floor. The Cinnamon King crown rested snugly on his head while he spread his arms wide, a king's scepter in one hand. It was the perfect shot; the mural behind him, his jersey above his head. He was immortalized. The King of Cinnamon Falls.

Even the best kings got stabbed in the back. Ask Julius Caesar.

The sight of him made her blood boil. Nia couldn't wait to slap the smug smile off his face. She pulled the door open and stepped inside. Victoria had her back to the door, dutifully snapping pictures of her man on a cell phone.

'We on the way out now,' Darius called absentmindedly when he heard the door slam.

He saw Nia over Victoria's shoulder at the last second.

Nia wanted to say something that would strike

fear in his cowardly heart, but her words tumbled out quicker than she intended.

'You killed Sienna.'

In retrospect, she should have probably rehearsed some lines. The words struck the walls of the empty gym, reverberating, creating an echo chamber around the three of them.

Victoria whipped around. Darius froze and the cocky smile melted from his face.

'I don't even know what you're talking about,' he scoffed. He adjusted his suit jacket like it was suddenly too small for him.

'Let me refresh your memory,' Nia replied. She had no plan of attack, no forward thinking or prepared speech. She was armed with the undeniable truth and that was all she needed.

'Sienna broke up with you right before the ceremony, didn't she?' Nia's body was shaking with rage when she pointed at Darius. She wished her finger were a knife. 'She knew about your cheating, and all your lies, and left your sorry ass!' she spat.

Panic crowded Darius' eyes as he glanced at Victoria. 'Oh, she didn't know about Sienna,' Nia said airily.

She turned her attention to Victoria. 'They were together up until the Fall Festival.' Victoria gave Darius a look that could have wounded if she had a weapon.

'You couldn't take her leaving you, could you?'

Nia crept toward him, just as Darius took a timid step backward.

'Listen, it wasn't like that!' he cried, dropping the scepter. 'It was an accident, okay? I didn't kill her, I loved her! I—'

Before he could say another word, a loud crack echoed in the gym. Nia heard herself scream. Instinctively, she crouched down and covered her head. She looked up to see Darius staggering forward, slack-jawed. Then, his eyes rolled backward. A snake of blood slithered down the center of his face before he landed on the hardwood floor with a sickening thud.

Victoria stepped around Darius' body, his scepter in hand, with her chin lifted in the air. She almost looked bored with the whole ordeal, like somehow, her day had been ruined. Nia's knees were trembling, her pulse pounded in her ears, and her heart thrashed against her ribcage, but her mind had never been clearer.

'*You* killed Sienna.' The realization snatched her breath away.

Victoria shrugged, examining the bloody scepter in her hand. She wiped it on Darius' suit jacket.

'She was going to ruin everything,' Victoria said plainly. 'That crown . . . this future . . . was mine.' She beat her chest with her fist. '*I* was the one who loved him. She took my moment from me once and I vowed to never let it happen again.' Her fingers tightened around the scepter, and she took a step toward Nia.

Nia was incredulous. 'You killed her over a crown?'

'I made a sacrifice for my future!' Victoria snapped, her scream echoing so loud Nia had to clap her hands over her ears. 'He would have done anything to get back in her good graces, and I couldn't have that. Sienna did me a favor by letting him go and I needed to make sure she never came back.'

Victoria flashed her diamond engagement ring. Nia's world tilted, freefalling into madness. The weight of Victoria's words crushed Nia's chest. Her knees had finally given out and she braced her fall with her hands meeting the cool floor.

'Rosie?' Nia managed to ask.

Victoria shook her scepter at Nia. 'That old bitch wouldn't stop talking about her stupid daughter, so I had to make sure she stayed quiet . . . permanently. She put up a hell of a fight, I must say.' Victoria raised her gown, revealing splotches of black-blue bruises all over her legs like she'd been dragged. Nia was willing to bet that there were more under her makeup. 'All this because I made her daughter roadkill,' she tisked.

Nia felt like she'd been kicked in the stomach. She doubled over and heaved, her brain whirring. How could Victoria know about Rosie's suspicions . . . after all these years?

Rosie was right. Sienna hadn't killed herself. Darius

hadn't pushed her. She was murdered; run over in the street and left for dead like an animal. Rosie knew there was more to Sienna's death and had died because of it.

The pieces of the puzzle fell together in Nia's head like raindrops after a drought. 'Maggie must have seen you leaving Rosie's that night,' Nia muttered.

Victoria tilted her head. 'I warned her not to say anything. But I just couldn't trust that she wouldn't keep her mouth shut. This *is* Cinnamon Falls, after all.'

'Rosie kept the original autopsy report, you know,' Nia said. 'You won't get away with this.'

Victoria smirked. 'You're so funny, Nia. You really think you know everything, don't you?'

'I know you're not walkin' out of here a free woman,' Nia argued.

'I've killed three people in this town. How do you think that is?'

Nia couldn't answer.

'What's one more?' On the floor, Darius groaned; his body squirmed as he tried to regain his strength.

'Two more!' She kicked Darius in the stomach. He let out a sickening *oomf* absorbing the blow, and he didn't move again.

'I wrapped my whole life around this sorry sack of shit, and this is the fuckin' thanks I get?' Victoria roared to an invisible audience. 'After all I sacrificed for him! All his damn daddy kept talkin' about was how I ruined his future. What about *my* future, huh? What about *me*? Everything was about this fuckin' idiot! *I* kept that family together. I was the one who suggested dumping Sienna's body at The Falls. If it wasn't for me, he'd be a washed up has-been, hooking up with skeezy teenagers, and reliving the glory days for the rest of his life. I built this house and I'll be damned if you think you're going to burn it all down.'

Nia barely had time to brace herself before Victoria lunged toward her. The scepter sliced through the air, aiming straight for her head. She dove just in time as the golden rod whistled past her ear. It collided with her shoulder and a shockwave of pain radiated through her body. Nia smacked the floor, her heart pounding, and pushed away from Victoria, her shoulder screaming in agony. Victoria raised the scepter again, eyes burning with unhinged determination.

'You should've stayed out of this, Nia,' Victoria said, as she took the scepter in both hands.

Nia steadied herself. She only had seconds before Victoria swung again.

This was it. Either she fought or she died.

And Nia had never been one to go down quietly.

Chapter 29

Jesse

Lil' Charlie looked like he'd swallowed a bee's stinger when Jesse ran up to him. Despite his attitude, Jesse was impressed with how well he cleaned up. The young man sported a tailored black suit with cufflinks so shiny they were in competition with the diamonds in his ears. His locs were pulled away from his face in a braided style that rested on his shoulders. He flipped around the golden watch on his wrist. He and the young lady beside him had bored expressions that read they were tired of waiting.

Cinnamon Way was backed up with impatient parents, students, and families eager to watch the seniors make their tour down Main Street. Even more were in the crowd to get a glimpse of their hometown hero, Darius Lyons.

Not if Jesse got to him first.

'What's the holdup?' Jesse asked the teenagers.

'Unc, I can't cuss or Ms. Bennett gon' tell my dad,'

he mumbled, pointing his chin to his father who was just steps away. He was deep in conversation with Mrs. Guy and hadn't looked their way.

'I give you permission,' Jesse whispered. 'Tell me what's going on.'

'We waitin' on Mr. Lyons,' the Cinnamon Queen reported.

Lil' Charlie pointed toward the school. 'He's been in the gym forever. I thought Ms. Bennett would've got him out here by now.'

Jesse's blood ran cold. Before he knew what he was doing he had taken off, his boots pounding the pavement as he sprinted toward the high school's gym. A crowd was spilling out of the school's front door.

'Tell his ass to hurry up!' Lil' Charlie yelled after him.

The sounds of the festival surrounding him had dulled into background noise, his focus razor-sharp. He took the steps leading up the gym two by two and slowed once he reached the back door. It had been propped open with a deflated basketball. He kicked it aside and slung the door open, which slammed against the wall behind it with a bang.

Jesse's eyes locked onto Nia first, lying on the ground, cradling an arm with her face twisted in pain, struggling to get up. Victoria stood over her, gripping the golden scepter like a weapon.

He didn't think, only reacted. He charged forward

with a burst of speed and dipped his shoulder low, tackling Victoria before she could land a fatal blow. She screamed as the two of them went crashing to the hardwood floor, the scepter clattering out of her grasp.

Using all his weight, Jesse pinned her down. He managed to turn her over, his knee digging into her back, as he yanked her arms behind her. Jesse was surprised how strong she was as she bucked and kicked under his pressure.

'You're done here,' Jesse growled as he slapped handcuffs on her wrists.

She thrashed beneath him, her voice venomous. 'You idiot! You have no idea what you've done!'

Jesse ignored her and turned his focus toward Nia. She was shaking, still on the ground, her eyes wide with shock. They darted from Jesse to Victoria and back and forth. He wanted to go to her and cradle her in his arms. But he heard rushed footsteps echoing in the hallway. He looked toward the double-door entrance. Mayor Lyons burst into the gym.

He stopped short at the scene before him: Darius unconscious on the ground, Victoria pinned under Jesse, and Nia in tears.

His face twisted in frustration. 'What in the hell is happening?'

Jesse stood, snatching Victoria up from the floor in one move. He kept a firm grip on her cuffs.

'Tell him to get off me!' she screamed.

Mayor Lyons crossed the room to his son, dropping down to his knees beside him. 'Can you hear me, son? Someone get me an ambulance!'

The double doors crashed open once more and Grace Whitfield dashed inside, her eyes wide, taking in the scene. She hiked up her long lavender gown and dropped down next to Darius.

'He's not breathing,' she said urgently. She started chest compressions, counting under her breath.

'Darius!' Victoria screamed and thrashed around, but Jesse wasn't letting go. 'Get me out of these cuffs! Let me help him!'

Chief Prescott was the next person through the doors. 'We've got a street full of people waiting. What is going on in here?' he boomed, taking in the scene before him. Jesse had never been happier to see another person in uniform.

'Victoria was going to kill Nia, sir,' Jesse reported, gesturing between the two women on the ground.

Nia's voice was hoarse, but strong. 'She killed Rosie and Maggie!'

'You have no proof!' Victoria scoffed.

'Get me an ambulance!' Grace screamed amidst the arguing. 'Or he's going to die! He's got a weak pulse, please!'

The Chief pulled his shoulder radio to his mouth and called for an emergency vehicle.

Nia pulled herself up from the floor, determination blazing through her tear-streaked face. 'Rosie had the original autopsy report, the one that proves Sienna was murdered!' She fixed her gaze on the mayor.

Jesse nodded in agreement. 'We found the car at Briggs' place. Sienna didn't kill herself, sir. I can prove it.'

Everyone had gone silent, chests heaving, their eyes darting back and forth. Then, slowly, Mayor Lyons' expression shifted. It went from feigned concern, to calculated indifference. He pushed off Darius' body and stood, smoothing out his suit.

That was when Jesse knew that it wasn't just Victoria.

It went higher. Much, much higher.

'Well,' Chief Prescott sighed and unholstered his gun, racking a bullet into the chamber, 'that's unfortunate, Shaw.'

Jesse's blood ran cold. Victoria wrenched away from his grip. The mayor reached inside his suit jacket and pulled out his own weapon, cocking it with an eerie calmness. He aimed it between Jesse's eyes.

'I knew you'd make a fine detective, Shaw,' Prescott said, his voice frigid. 'I had high hopes for you, son. All you had to do was let Briggs go to county. He was a two-time felon. He would have never gotten out.'

Nia crawled toward Jesse and he instinctively stood as a barrier between her and the weapons.

'All of this, for Darius?' Grace piped up, her voice tiny with fear.

The mayor spread his arms wide. 'Do you know how much money *my son* has brought to Cinnamon

Falls? The tourism, the press. This place was dead before my son came along!'

Beside Jesse, Nia mumbled, 'Meeting with A. L.' She pointed to the mayor, accusation deep-set in her eyes. 'Rosie found out Sienna was murdered and she took it to you! She thought you'd help!'

'That crazy woman wanted to send my only son to jail. It was laughable!'

'So, what now? You kill us all?' Jesse responded.

Prescott shook his head. 'I tried to stop you. I took you off the case, and you still wouldn't quit. You made me trash your little girlfriend's shop last night after we found her snooping around on the county database.'

Nia unleashed a sob.

'And yet you're still here,' Prescott added. The Chief gave Jesse a look that almost seemed apologetic. 'You didn't give me much of a choice, son.'

Jesse's pulse hammered. He was outnumbered and outgunned.

But he had a plan.

He glanced down at his watch, hoping the risk he was taking wouldn't end up in bloodshed.

'That's my fault. Rookie's mistake,' he said with a smirk.

For a second, nothing happened. Then the back door of the gym exploded open.

Wade and Chambers stepped inside, guns raised.

'Cinnamon Falls Police!' Chambers yelled.

'Drop your weapons!' Wade demanded.

The mayor's eyes went wide before he turned and bolted for the exit. Jesse didn't hesitate and took off straight after him. He burst through the gym's double doors into a long hallway, where throngs of people were waiting for the festival to begin. The mayor shoved through the crowd, knocking people aside, desperate to escape. Jesse was tight on his heels, pushing harder, as people leapt out of his way. Mayor Lyons turned, shooting wildly over his shoulder. Jesse ducked as bullets whizzed past his ears, and pursued him relentlessly.

The mayor made it to the school's front steps and it was only a matter of time before he got swallowed up by the larger crowd in the streets. He dashed down the steps and made a sharp turn onto Cinnamon Way. Then, Raines stepped out from behind Lil' Charlie's car, her gun drawn.

'Going somewhere?'

The mayor skidded to a stop and Jesse slammed into him from behind, tackling him to the pavement. The crowd erupted in gasps with horrified expressions. Jesse hauled the mayor up by his suit jacket and shoved him into Raines' arms.

'Get him out of here,' Jesse growled.

'Unc!' Lil' Charlie shrieked, jumping up and down in the back of the car. 'You still got it!'

When Jesse made it back inside the gymnasium his eyes searched for Nia. She looked up at him from her spot on the floor and time halted. He didn't hear the chaos of the scene or the thoughts in his own head. All he concentrated on was her.

She stood up and ran toward him and he didn't stop himself from meeting her halfway. She launched herself into his arms and he caught her with ease, holding her close. Her hands curled into his sweatshirt, gripping him like she was afraid that he'd disappear.

'You're okay,' she whispered. 'I heard the shots and I thought . . . I thought—'

He cupped her face, tilting her chin up. 'I got you,' he promised.

Before he could second guess himself, he kissed her. Not soft and slow like he imagined their first kiss to be. It was desperate, consuming, a promise sealed within. Nia melted against him, his hand fisted in her hair, pulling her impossibly closer. When they finally pulled apart, dizzy with passion, Jesse rested his forehead against hers.

'Remember when you promised to stay out of it?' Jesse asked, a smile playing on his lips.

'I don't recall,' Nia responded with a sarcastic curl of her lips.

Jesse felt like he'd float away when she kissed him again.

Chapter 30

Jesse

'Shaw, I owe ya one!'

Back at the station, Chambers raised a glass of whiskey to Jesse, his voice loud and full of reluctant admiration. One by one, the other officers did the same, lifting their glasses in a rare moment of unity.

They had raided the Chief's office stash: the good stuff, the kind he used to drink when he thought he was untouchable. Now, with the Prescott name disgraced, the bottle had found a better purpose: a toast to justice finally being served.

Satisfied, Jesse leaned back in his chair, his own glass dangling between his fingers. 'You owe me three,' he corrected, throwing the shot back along with the rest of them. 'One for Victoria, one for Mayor Lyons, and one for Chief Prescott.'

'And one for Harvey Briggs,' Raines added, setting her glass down with a sharp clink.

Jesse exhaled, shaking his head. 'So, four! You owe me four.'

'Whose side are you on?' Chambers groaned at Raines, who just shrugged with a rare chuckle. It was the first time he'd ever seen the woman smile.

Raines crossed her arms. 'I gotta admit, I thought you were batshit,' she said bluntly. 'I didn't want to believe that we overlooked so much.'

'Wasn't just me. It was Wade who helped me see the bigger picture.'

All eyes turned to Bud Wade, who was sitting off to the side, clutching the empty whiskey bottle like it was a prized trophy.

Jesse tilted his head. 'You were the mole, weren't you? You leaked that info to Elaine Matthias.'

Wade's cheeks flushed. Raines shot out of her chair, eyes narrowing. 'You what?'

Wade lifted his hands in surrender, swiping at his flushed face. 'I had to. Elaine was the only person I could trust to get the truth out there. Cap was so focused on Briggs, he was ignoring everything else.'

Chambers laughed sharply. 'I should lock you up right now, Wade.'

Wade just shrugged. 'And miss the party? Not a chance.'

Jesse shook his head, a half-smile tugging at his lips.

'It was the rookie who found the car,' Wade pointed out. 'Still had the dent in it from where she hit Sienna.

And when we searched Lyons' house, we found copies of the note Sienna wrote to Darius in Victoria's luggage, along with the murder weapon, Rosie's cast iron skillet.'

Chambers scoffed. 'The girl was obsessed.'

Wade leaned forward. 'So how did you figure out it was Victoria?'

Jesse took a deep breath. 'I didn't see her coming. I was focused on Darius once Morgan told me that he and Sienna were some secret couple.'

'That must have been how Rosie put it together too,' Wade commented.

Jesse nodded. 'Then Grace Whitfield told me she almost got hit by a small car leaving the mayor's house the night of Darius' party. Angie got that tip about a blue car on Main Street around the time Rosie died. A quick search led me to Tammy Nathan, Victoria's mother. Now, Victoria told me at Cinnamon Grove that all her family and friends came to Darius' party that night. I'm figuring she took her mother's car while the party was in full swing, drove to the diner, killed Rosie, and was back before anyone even noticed.'

Chambers shook his head, disbelief evident in his tone. 'All of this over Darius Lyons. Man's not even that good.'

Raines exhaled. 'Money, status, power, it does that to people. In a small town like this? I can't imagine how far back the Lyons' dirty dealings go.'

Jesse nodded, his mind churning through the web of corruption they had just begun to untangle.

'Chief Prescott—' Jesse started.

'Vernon,' Raines corrected, her voice firm.

Jesse tilted his head, accepting the shift. 'Vernon was the chief for twenty years. Lots of things have probably slipped through the cracks. How long do you think he'll get?'

Raines took a slow sip of her drink. 'That's up to the District Attorney. Seeing the forged documents and comparing them to the ones Rosie had was the nail in the coffin for Prescott.'

Chambers frowned. 'How'd your girl even find those?'

Jesse exhaled deeply, rubbing his jaw. 'Grace had the original. She must have given Rosie a copy. When she found the shed on Briggs' property, got inside, and saw the car, that's when she put it all together. She'd gone to the mayor for help but sealed her own fate.'

Silence fell over the group as he continued.

Wade let out a low whistle. 'She must've been terrified.'

Jesse nodded. 'That's why she left Briggs that voice-mail. She was deeply in love with him and felt guilty for snooping, but knew she couldn't ignore what she found. That's why Victoria killed her. She knew Rosie wasn't going to stay quiet the minute she saw Darius' face again.'

Chambers shook his head. 'Hell of a way to go.'

Jesse's jaw tightened, the weight of the past week settling into his chest. Rosie had fought for the truth until the very end. And now, because of her, justice had finally been served.

Angie stepped between the group, clearing her throat.

'Jesse, you've got someone waiting for you.'

The entire station turned, their gazes following Jesse's as he looked toward the lobby. There stood Nia, her hands tucked into the sleeves of her sweater, rocking on her heels as she gave a small, nervous wave. Jesse immediately pushed to his feet, his heart jumping into his throat.

'Gotta go, boys.'

He shook hands with Wade and Raines, giving Chambers a nod before turning toward Nia.

'Yo, rook!'

Jesse groaned, stopping mid-stride. He turned to face Chambers, already bracing himself.

'Listen—' Jesse started.

'Nah, you listen.' Chambers cut him off, his voice serious for the first time since Jesse had met him. 'I want to apologize, man.'

Jesse blinked, surprised. Chambers scrubbed the back of his neck, looking uncomfortable, like the words didn't come easy. 'I misjudged you. I heard you were some tough military dude trying to play cop in a small town and figured—'

'That I was an idiot?' Jesse finished, raising an eyebrow.

Chambers huffed out a laugh, shaking his head. 'Not in those exact words.'

Jesse just crossed his arms, waiting.

Chambers sighed. 'I left Atlanta PD thinking this place would be safe, quiet, a break from the chaos. A homicide detective in a town with no homicides? Sounded like a dream.'

Jesse didn't laugh.

'I'm sorry for doubting you.' Chambers exhaled sharply. 'You put together a damn near foolproof plan to take down an entire corrupt department. It's not up to me, but I think you'd make a hell of a detective. I'm honored to serve alongside you, partner.' Chambers stuck his hand out for a handshake, a truce among the brothers in blue.

Jesse stared at him for a long moment. He wanted to let his pride get in the way, to brush it off, to remind Chambers of all the ways he'd underestimated him. But Chambers had extended an olive branch, and Jesse wasn't the kind of man to hold grudges.

'It's all good,' Jesse finally said, reaching out to shake his hand.

Chambers smirked. 'Cool, cool.' Then, he nudged him toward the lobby. 'Now go get your girl, man.'

Jesse didn't need to be told twice. He was done looking back. It was time to move forward.

The station buzzed with a rare kind of electricity,

equal parts relief and disbelief. Officers gathered in small clusters, talking animatedly about the arrests, the press coverage, the evidence that was still being logged. Phones rang. Papers shuffled. A coffee pot hissed in the background.

But Jesse couldn't hear any of it. Not really. He only saw her. Nia waited patiently, arms wrapped around herself. She looked tired but radiant and when their eyes met, Jesse's heart stumbled in his chest.

He crossed the station with slow, deliberate steps, not caring about the curious glances or hushed whispers from the other officers. Jesse didn't stop until he was standing right in front of her. Nia blinked up at him, her lips parted, like she had a thousand things to say and didn't know where to begin.

'You did it,' she whispered, her voice shaky with emotion. 'You actually did it.'

He reached out and tucked a loose curl behind her ear. '*We* did it. I never could've gotten here without you.' His thumb lingered against her cheek. 'You never stopped digging. You never gave up on Sienna. Or Rosie. Or this town.'

Nia breathed out and took a step closer. 'And you never gave up on me.'

He smiled softly, and the weight of the last six years, the heartbreak, the confusion, the fear, it all melted away in that moment.

Without thinking, Jesse leaned in and kissed her. Warm and steady, full of everything they hadn't said, everything they couldn't before. The kiss unfolded slowly, like it had been waiting patiently all along.

Someone in the bullpen whistled. A smattering of applause broke out, and someone's voice carried from behind them: 'Finally!'

Nia laughed into the kiss and pulled away, her cheeks flushed. Jesse kept his forehead pressed to hers.

'You hungry?' he asked, brushing her arms with his fingertips.

She nodded. 'Starving.'

'Come back to my place,' he said, his voice low. 'I'll cook.'

Nia raised a brow. 'Since when do you cook?'

'I'll have you know I make a mean grilled cheese.'

She smiled. 'That sounds perfect.'

As they walked out of the station, fingers intertwined, the cool evening air greeted them like an old friend. For the first time in a long time, it felt like home.

Chapter 31

Sunday
Nia

Nia decided in her sleep that when she woke up, she was going to press charges against Old Man Milton and his roosters. They were loud, insistent, and completely unnecessary. She groaned and buried her face in the pillow beneath her as Shadrach, Meshach, and Abednego bid Cinnamon Falls a good morning.

The air was cool and crisp, and the scent of pine and fresh-cut grass wafted in from an open window. The sheets beneath her were silky soft, the mattress firmer than she normally liked it, but comfortable. But it was the scent that gave her pause.

The familiar scent of warm cedarwood and a hint of earthy cinnamon.

Her eyes snapped open.

Jesse.

She was in his bed.

She turned over expecting to feel his solid frame

beside her. She found the spot next to her empty, the sheets already cooled.

Snatches of sunlight filtered in through the curtains. Her gaze darted around the dimly lit bedroom. It was meticulously neat, not even a worn pair of jeans slung over an armchair. His gun, badge, and cell phone rested, one next to the other, on his nightstand. It buzzed with an incoming call from Chambers.

Memories from the night before flooded back to her.

The chaos, the screaming, the unraveling . . .

The moment she collapsed in Jesse's arms, unable to let go.

The kiss . . . the kiss . . . the kiss . . .

It was the sweet juicy cherry on top of a cool cone of cinnamon swirl ice cream.

Heat flushed her face and she let out a girlish giggle. Jesse wasn't kidding, he could actually cook. The grilled cheese sandwich he made could have been sold in gourmet shops across the country. Fluffy soft bread sandwiched piles of gouda, mozzarella, and aged cheddar cheese while the salty crunch of thick sliced bacon rocked her world. They shared the sandwich in the dim light of the kitchen, careful not to laugh too loud so they didn't wake his parents. They felt like they were in high school again, before life got complicated. Before growing up pulled them in different directions. It felt like they had somehow found their way back to that simpler time.

Nia sat up and stretched, her muscles throbbing.

Her shoulder was still achingly sore from yesterday, reminding her that the adrenaline had long since worn off.

Victoria's crazed expression as she'd stood over Nia flashed in her mind's eye. Nia pushed the thought away.

It's over, she told herself. Nothing could hurt her anymore.

She'd watched Victoria get walked away in handcuffs. Chief Prescott and Mayor Lyons were both thrown into the back of a car and whisked away. She didn't know what kind of future awaited them, or how deep the corruption ran between the two of them. All she knew was that she could finally rest.

Nia pushed aside the covers and padded barefoot toward the French doors that led to the balcony. She parted the curtains and was met with the most beautiful sunrise she'd ever seen over Barkwood Bridge. She stepped outside, wanting a closer look at the sky that was streaked in shades of coral and gold, like brushstrokes across a canvas.

The cinnamon trees shimmered with morning dew, their branches reaching toward the sun as it peeked above the hills. Light spilled across the bridge in ribbons, casting a soft glow over water beneath it. The morning mist curled around the supports of the weathered wooden beams like ghostly fingers. It'd been years since she'd stepped foot there, and looking at it now made her chest tighten.

It was the last place that Sienna was seen alive. The place where Cinnamon Falls claimed another life. She had avoided it for so long, but standing on Jesse's balcony, she felt Barkwood call to her. She wanted to go. She wanted to stand on that bridge and not feel fear. She wanted to breathe again.

Can I really do it? Nia thought to herself.

She barely heard the door open behind her before feeling Jesse's warm embrace. He wrapped his arms around her waist. His beard tickled the sensitive skin on her neck and it made her knees wobble. She clutched onto the balcony railing to steady herself.

'You're up early.' Jesse's voice was gravelly with sleep. She leaned into his embrace, letting him be her anchor.

'How far can you shoot?' Nia asked.

Jesse drew back. 'Why?'

'You really have to do something about those roosters,' Nia replied.

Jesse chuckled, pressing a kiss to her temple. 'I'll be sure to file a noise complaint.'

They stood there, together, encapsulated in their own thoughts, admiring the golden beauty of a sunrise over Cinnamon Falls.

'You want to go?' Jesse asked after a long bout of silence.

Nia's fingers tightened around his strong biceps. 'I do,' she admitted.

'But?'

She swallowed hard. 'I don't know . . . if I can do it alone.'

Jesse turned her around so that she was facing him and Nia couldn't decide if the sunrise over her hometown was the most beautiful thing she'd ever seen, or if it was staring into the eyes of a man who loved her intensely. 'Then we'll go together when you're ready.'

The sincerity in his gaze made her chest ache. Jesse had always been there, even when she left; even when she didn't know how to ask him to stay.

She nodded. 'Okay.'

The smell of sizzling sausages and fresh coffee curled through the air, and Nia inhaled the welcoming scents as she descended the stairs into Jesse's kitchen. He stood at the stove, flipping pancakes with effortless ease, an apron tied loosely over his pajamas. The golden-brown pancakes sizzled as he stacked them high, the scent of cinnamon and vanilla filling the cozy space.

At the small breakfast nook, his parents sat in their designated spots, bickering over a crossword puzzle, their voices blending with the gentle hum of the radio playing old Motown classics. It felt achingly familiar and surreal at the same time.

Nia had spent so much time with them growing up. Jesse's mother pushing extra food onto her plate, his father pretending he wasn't listening to their teenage conversations while reading the newspaper. They had witnessed everything: her and Jesse's innocent friendship, their first kiss, their late-night studying turning into whispered dreams of the future. And later, they had witnessed the split. The breakup. The silence. The years apart.

Nia hesitated in the doorway, her heart stammering, unsure of how she would be received. She had spent so much time avoiding home, avoiding these moments, that she didn't realize how empty her life had been without them. But now, standing here again, in the glow of a sunlit kitchen, it felt right.

'Morning, sweetheart,' Ms. Evelyn greeted, her voice warm, steady, unwavering.

Her gray hair framed her face in soft, bouncy layers, and her kind eyes sparkled with something unreadable. A knowing. She was dressed in a chunky, cable-knit sweater, the kind of comfortable, mom-style comfort that made Nia all too aware that she was standing in Jesse's clothes. Ms. Evelyn probably noticed but said nothing. Instead, she simply waved her in.

'Come in and have some breakfast, baby. You look like you could use a real meal.'

The invitation was so effortless, so natural, as if no time had passed at all. She stepped inside, tentatively at first, her fingers curling at the hem of Jesse's borrowed shirt. Jesse turned around from the stove, a grin tugging at the corner of his mouth.

'Morning, trouble.'

The deep rasp of his voice sent a ripple of something warm and familiar down her spine. But before she could respond, Mr. Robert lowered his newspaper, peering at her over his glasses. His face was unreadable at first, but then he said, 'Jesse finally did something right, bringing you back here.'

Nia let out a soft, startled laugh, the tension in her shoulders melting away.

'Dad,' Jesse groaned, shaking his head as he plated the pancakes. 'Behave.'

But Ms. Evelyn only smirked, nudging her husband. 'Robert, leave them be.'

Nia slid into the seat across from Ms. Evelyn. Jesse set a steaming cup of coffee in front of her, the rich aroma wrapping around her like an old memory. She held the mug with both hands, inhaling deeply, letting the warmth seep into her fingertips. Jesse slid into the seat beside her, his thigh brushing against hers, sending a pulse of awareness up her spine.

'So,' Ms. Evelyn started, stirring her tea, her knowing eyes locked on Nia's. 'How long are you staying this time?'

The question was gentle, but weighted, laced with something unspoken, something fragile. The room fell quiet, save for the soft swish of newspaper pages flipping. Nia looked around: at Mr. Robert pretending not to listen but very clearly listening, at Ms. Evelyn, patient and unreadable but somehow expectant, at

Jesse, who had stopped eating, watching her closely, waiting. And suddenly, she knew the answer.

She wasn't just visiting. She wasn't just stopping through before running away again. She had spent years convincing herself that Cinnamon Falls wasn't home anymore. But sitting there, wrapped in warmth, familiarity, and love, she knew that maybe . . . it was time to stop running.

Nia took a slow sip of her coffee, letting the truth settle on her tongue.

Then, she looked up at Ms. Evelyn and smiled.

'For however long you'll have me.'

After breakfast, Nia waited outside for Jesse to finish getting ready for work. She'd watched her fill of the morning news where Elaine Matthias tore into Mayor Lyons and Chief Prescott like a lioness dismantling her prey.

The headline flashed across the screen:

CORRUPTION IN CINNAMON FALLS:
MAYOR AND POLICE CHIEF ARRESTED
IN MURDER COVER-UP

Elaine had been relentless, detailing every misstep, every lie, every abuse of power. Nia knew her hometown would never be the same again. She had also caught the update on Darius. Elaine reported that he was stable but still under close surveillance, and expected to make a full recovery. He was going to be fine, but his football career was over for the season. Still, she had to hear his side of the story. What happened that night with Sienna?

Nia took a seat on Jesse's front steps letting the radiance of the sun settle against her skin. Things felt different in this part of town, lighter. So light that she knew she had to let go of the things that were holding her back. She'd written Bryant a letter earlier in the week, too preoccupied to put it in the mail. But, now, there was nothing standing in her way.

Her gaze fell to her hands, where she clutched her phone, or at least what was left of it. Jesse had kept it from the other night and managed to get it to hold a charge. The screen was shattered beyond repair but she could still see her background photo. It was of her and Bryant from months ago, smiling, arms wrapped around each other at some swanky rooftop bar in Atlanta she couldn't remember.

Nia studied the photo. Who was that girl? The woman in the photo was a stranger. She was polished, her makeup pristine, and her hair curled to perfection. She was wearing a fitted blazer, holding a glass of champagne, smiling at a man she thought she would spend forever with. The truth was, she didn't recognize herself. So much had changed since she took that picture. That version of Nia was gone.

Before she could talk herself out of it, she dialed his number.

Bryant answered on the first ring. 'Nia?' His voice was breathless like he'd been waiting on her call.

She closed her eyes, exhaling softly. 'Hey, Bryant.'

'Thank God, I've been worried sick about you, Cookie. Where are you? Let me come get you, please.' His voice was urgent, pleading.

She opened her eyes, staring out at the quaint town she vowed never to return to. The quiet hum of the morning. The warmth of a loving home.

'I'm home,' she said, letting the words settle deep in her bones. The final screw in her back unwound.

A beat of silence danced between them.

Bryant answered hesitantly, 'You're . . . in Atlanta? Where? Are you coming back home?'

Nia shook her head even though she knew he couldn't see her. 'No, I'm not.'

'Come on, Nia. Let's talk, face to face.'

She exhaled sharply. 'We are talking, right now,' she said, her voice firm. 'And this will be the last time.'

Bryant let out a humorless laugh. 'So, you're done, then? Done with Gildman & Sons, done with me, done with everything you worked hard for? Throwing your life away for . . . for what?'

Nia's grip tightened on her phone. Once upon a time those words would have scared her. But now, the things she'd worked for didn't feel like anything she'd built. They felt like things she'd been buried under.

'For me,' she said proudly. 'I'm throwing that life away for me.'

'Nia!' he pleaded.

She didn't flinch, didn't waver. For the first time she wasn't scared of losing him because she'd found everything she'd been looking for: herself. 'And tell Mr. Gildman I quit!'

Behind her, she could hear Jesse's footsteps padding down the stairs. She stood and with all the force in her body slammed her phone to the ground. She watched it shatter in a million pieces. Glass and plastic splintered across the concrete steps.

And it felt good. Real good.

Jesse peeked his head out of the front door. His eyes trailed from the shattered phone to her face. Nia appreciated the fact that he didn't comment.

'Raines said Darius is awake. Want to take a ride before I drop you at your parents?'

'Absolutely,' Nia responded.

The steady *beep-beep-beep* of the heart monitor and a low volume TV were the only sounds in Darius Lyons' hospital room when Nia and Jesse stepped inside. The dimmed fluorescent lights cast a sickly glow over his bruised face; his once-polished athlete's body was now a mess of wires and IV drips. A fresh bandage was wrapped around his head.

Darius shifted slightly, wincing as he turned his head toward them. His eyes looked hollow, the weight of years of deception pressing down on him.

'Figured they'd let you come back,' he muttered, his voice hoarse but clear. Darius gestured to the officers stationed outside his hospital room. Raines had informed the patrolmen that Jesse and Nia were coming, and authorized their visit before Darius was transported elsewhere.

Nia crossed her arms. 'Not sure what you think we're here for, but if you're waiting for sympathy, you're out of luck.'

Darius chuckled bitterly, then winced, sucking in a sharp breath. 'Nah,' he rasped, 'I know what I deserve. But I also know why you're here.'

Nia stepped closer. 'Then start talking.'

Darius exhaled deeply, his fingers clenching and unclenching against the thin hospital sheet. Nia steeled herself inside.

'I don't know what Victoria told you, but I loved Sienna. To be real, I didn't even care about winning Cinnamon King that much, but my father . . . he was obsessed. He wanted me to be this huge football star, someone who would make the Lyons name bigger than it already was. The crown was just another step toward that; another thing he could brag about to his rich buddies.'

Darius scoffed, shaking his head. 'I found her note in my locker and it had me shook. I begged her to stay with me. But, the night of the Fall Fest, Sienna broke my heart. She told me she was done. She knew about Victoria, about all the other girls . . .' His jaw tensed, and for the first time, guilt flickered across his features.

'I was furious. Not just because I loved her, but because I couldn't lose her. I was so damn caught up in the image, in my father's expectations, that I let my pride get in the way. I yelled at her. I told her she was ruining everything, that she was making a mistake leaving me. She just . . . looked at me. I'll never forget it. It was like she was looking straight through me . . . like she was disgusted with me.'

His voice broke slightly, but he swallowed the sob down. 'She got out of the car, slammed the door and told me to go to hell. I should have stopped her. I should have gotten out and begged her to get back in. But I was angry. I was so damn mad that I just drove away and left her there.'

The room felt smaller, the weight of his words pressing down on them all. If police officers weren't outside the door, Nia would have snatched every cord from his body and watched him suffer. She tamped down the raging thoughts in her head.

'I'd gotten too fucked up that night at The Red Fern, drinking Sienna away. Victoria told me she'd drive home and I passed out,' he continued after a beat. 'She must have seen Sienna walking on the road.

She told me later that she didn't even think, she just . . . reacted and hit her.'

Nia's breath hitched, her fingers digging into her arms. Jesse's jaw locked, his hands clenched into tight fists. Darius let out a slow, shuddering breath.

'By the time I woke up, it was too late. Victoria was freaking out, saying she didn't mean to do it. That she'd panicked. I didn't know what to do so I called my father.'

Jesse shook his head. 'And that's when Mayor Lyons got Chief Prescott involved.'

Darius nodded, his Adam's apple bobbing as he swallowed hard. 'He told me he'd take care of everything. That no one would ever find out. And the next thing I knew Sienna was found at the bottom of the Falls.'

Nia felt sick. Her stomach churned, and she had to brace herself against the hospital chair to keep from collapsing. Darius looked up at her, his eyes pleading.

'I swear to God, Nia. I never wanted her to die. I was a coward. I let them clean up my mess, and I never questioned it. Not once. But I didn't kill her.'

Nia's throat felt tight, her emotions tangled between grief, anger, and disbelief.

'You didn't have to,' she whispered. 'You let it happen.'

Darius didn't argue. Because he knew she was right. Jesse ran a hand over his face, shaking his head again.

'And the car? How'd it end up in Briggs' shed?'

Darius' expression darkened. 'My father said he handled it. He told me not to ask questions. That Chief Prescott had gotten rid of it. He said it was taken care of so I believed him.'

Jesse shook his head. 'Guess Harvey Briggs had other plans.'

At that moment, the hospital TV flickered, drawing their attention. Elaine Matthias appeared on screen, standing in front of Harvey's property, the shed now surrounded by police tape. The subtitles on the TV read:

> Authorities have uncovered what they believe to be the car that struck Sienna Rose six years ago, hidden on Harvey Briggs' property. Sources say the car was never dismantled as previously believed and remained intact all these years. The vehicle was processed for DNA, revealing a positive blood match to the victim. This discovery raises new questions about the official ruling of Sienna Rose's death, questions that will undoubtedly shake Cinnamon Falls to its core.

Darius breathed raggedly, his gaze locked onto the screen. 'Victoria has always been a little crazy, but I never thought she'd take it this far,' he muttered. 'I never meant for any of this to happen.'

Silence stretched between them. The weight of years

of buried secrets now exposed for the entire town to see. Darius had lost everything. His father was going to prison. His football career was over. His name ruined. And the worst part? He'd deserved every bit of it.

He turned back to Nia, his expression haunted, his face darkened.

The memory struck Nia like a lightning bolt. 'It was you I saw at Rosie's memorial,' Nia said.

He hung his head. 'I can't undo what happened.' His voice was barely above a whisper. 'I wish I could. But I can't.'

Nia's lips trembled, her anger warring with the memories of the boy Darius used to be. A broken man lay before her now, drowning in the wreckage of his own choices.

Jesse's hand found the small of her back, grounding her. Nia wanted to say more, but karma was having her way with him now. There was nothing left for Nia to do.

She said simply, 'Good luck, Darius. You're going to need it.'

Chapter 32

Jesse

Jesse pulled into the long, winding dirt driveway that led to Harvey Briggs' trailer, for what he hoped would be the last time. He passed the rusted metal gate, half-open, leaning on its hinges. The property stretched back into thick woods, tucked away as if its owner had been trying to keep the world at arm's length.

Jesse killed the engine of his patrol car and sat for a moment, gripping the steering wheel. It had been a long week. Scratch that. The longest damn week of his life. And yet, there was still one last thing he needed to do.

He wasn't sure what to expect from Harvey now that he was a free man. Jesse had fought like hell to prove his innocence, but innocence wasn't the same as being guilt-free.

Harvey Briggs had been officially cleared of Rosie and Maggie's murders, but the man had taken one hell of a beating – physically, mentally, and legally.

Jesse hadn't been able to shake the thought that if things had gone a little differently, Harvey might still be rotting in a jail cell for crimes he didn't commit.

Nia placed her hand on his, giving him the strength he needed to climb out of the car and walk toward the front porch. The gravel crunched under his boots as he walked, eyeing the run-down trailer before him. A single porch light flickered, barely illuminating the sagging wooden steps. The house, much like its owner, had seen better days.

The sounds of the forest floated around him: crickets chirping, the rustle of leaves in the wind, the distant sound of a woodpecker hammering away. He knocked once. Then again, harder. A moment later, the door creaked open.

Harvey Briggs stood in the dim light of the entryway, clutching a frosted beer bottle and looking about ten years older than the last time Jesse had seen him. His face was tired, lined with years of hard living and harder choices, his salt-and-pepper beard unkempt, eyes sunken with exhaustion.

For a long second, no one spoke.

Then Harvey huffed, leaning against the doorframe. ''Bout time you two came by.'

Jesse shoved his hands into his pockets and glanced over at Nia, who stuck close to him. 'You got a minute?'

Harvey snorted. 'If I say no, you gonna leave?'

Jesse smirked. 'Not a chance.'

Harvey grumbled something under his breath but stepped aside, letting them enter. The aftermath of the police raid was everywhere: overturned furniture, shattered glass, papers scattered like fallen leaves. The house smelled damp like it had rained inside the place. There was also the undercurrent of dust, old motor oil, and regret.

Nia silenced a gasp behind her hands and Jesse took in his surroundings, what was once a home. Harvey's kitchen had been demolished. The wooden frame that kept up his cabinets had been knocked away; his sink lay on its side in the floor, and the carpet, just from where Jesse stood, looked like it was soaked through.

They inched forward just slightly, careful not to walk over the remnants of a broken picture frame. The glass had spider-webbed across the floor, the image beneath it barely visible: a younger Harvey, arm slung around a woman who looked vaguely familiar. Maybe his mother. Maybe a sister. Either way, it didn't matter now.

Jesse was stunned into silence. Briggs had just been cleared of a heinous crime and came home to nothing. Harvey sat in the wreckage of his home, his elbows braced on his knees, hands folded like a man who had seen too much in one lifetime. The bags under his eyes were darker than before, his already lean frame looking even more hollow in the dim light of the single lamp that still worked. Jesse took in the destruction around them. Cabinets yanked open, couch cushions slashed, overturned shelves with books and files spilling across the floor.

'They did a number on this place,' Jesse muttered.

Harvey let out a bitter chuckle. 'Yeah. No shit.' He took a long swig of beer.

Jesse grabbed a fallen chair. He set it upright, motioning for Nia to sit. Harvey hesitated for a second before lowering himself onto the couch with a groan. Jesse pulled another chair up across from him.

'I suppose you came here to hear my side of things,' Briggs muttered, his voice lower now, more weighted.

'We want to know everything,' Nia responded.

Jesse leaned forward, meeting eyes with the man. 'The truth.'

Harvey's jaw ticked, but he didn't argue. Instead, he leaned back and released a sigh that sounded like it had been building for years. He ran a hand over his unkempt beard. For a long time, Jesse thought he wouldn't answer.

Then, with a deep sigh, Harvey said, 'She was the best damn thing that ever happened to me.' His voice was low, raw with something Jesse couldn't quite place, grief, regret, or maybe both.

Jesse didn't interrupt.

'I loved that woman,' Harvey admitted, eyes fixed on the floor. 'More than I ever let on. But Rosie? She didn't trust easy. She kept her walls up, even with me. I never meant to fall in love with her. I found myself visitin' her diner over and over. That woman can throw down in the kitchen.'

Jesse and Nia nodded, agreeing, reminiscing on all the meals they devoured at her counter.

'I finally built up the courage to ask her to dinner. She brought me these little white flowers from her garden for me. Me. I ain't never had a woman do that for me.' Harvey's cheeks reddened like he was reliving a sweet memory. 'Before I knew it, I'd fallen for her and I knew if I told her about my past, it'd ruin everything.'

The pair stayed quiet, letting him speak. Beside him, Nia wiped her tears with a tissue from her pocket.

'There's a million things I should have told her,' Harvey admitted. 'Like why I settled in Cinnamon Falls and why I hid that damn car for Vernon all those years ago.'

Jesse leaned forward. 'Tell me what happened, Briggs.'

Harvey chuckled dryly. 'You really don't let things go, do you?'

Jesse smirked. 'Occupational hazard.'

Harvey rubbed a hand down his face, exhaling loudly.

'Rosie was a real nature girl. She used to walk my property sometimes, just poking around. Said she liked the quiet out here. One day, she stumbled on the shed out back. She asked about it, said she'd never seen me go in there. I brushed it off, told her it was for storage. But Rosie wasn't stupid. She didn't believe for one minute that Sienna had killed herself, and she definitely didn't believe that the shed was just for storage. After she talked to that coroner, she started to doubt everything, even me.'

He took a deep breath. 'And one night, I caught her trying to break in.'

Jesse felt his pulse rise.

Harvey's hands clenched around the beer bottle. 'I lost my temper, man. I grabbed her. Shook her. Hard. It was the worst thing I'd ever done. I couldn't live with myself.'

Jesse's jaw tightened. 'So that's how she got the bruises.'

Harvey nodded, his eyes hollow. His voice dropped to a whisper. 'I hated myself for it.' He stared at the beer in his hands like the bottom of the glass bottle held all the answers he was looking for. 'I left that night. Couldn't stand to look at myself. Drove straight out of town, figured if she hated me, at least she was safe.'

Jesse's stomach coiled tight. 'And when you came back, she was dead.'

Harvey nodded slowly, his expression crumbling for the first time. 'She was the only person who ever made me feel like I was worth a damn. And I threw it away.'

Jesse swallowed down the frustration rising in his

chest. He let the silence stretch between them before finally asking, 'Why didn't you get rid of the car?'

Harvey leaned back, his eyes dark with something Jesse couldn't place. He let out a long breath, rubbing his hands together.

'I wish I had. If I thought for one second that car had anything to do with Sienna's death, I would have driven it to the courts myself! I didn't know what it was for but I didn't trust Prescott for one second. He threatened me to get rid of the car. Dangled my record over my head if I didn't. I always knew that bastard would throw me under the bus whenever it suited him,' Harvey said, his voice bitter. 'But that car was my only ace in the hole, just in case I needed the leverage.'

Jesse narrowed his eyes. 'Leverage for what?'

Harvey scoffed. 'For survival, kid. Cinnamon Falls don't take kindly to two-time felons and people who know too much.' Harvey glanced up, his eyes sharp despite his exhaustion. 'I told Rosie to stay out of it. These people will kill to protect their secrets.'

Nia shook her head. 'You should've come forward years ago.'

Harvey gave her a knowing look. 'You and I both know this town don't run on honesty. You think that would've saved me? You think anyone would have *listened* to me? The old junkman? They killed my Rosie. They woulda killed me too, left me to rot if it hadn't been for you two.'

Jesse hated that Harvey was right. He hated that Rosie had caught the wrong end of the deal. Jesse studied him. The man looked broken down, but there was something else there too. Relief. Like a weight had finally been lifted, but it'd cost him everything.

'Wade told me you were, uh, the one who kept pushin' to prove I was innocent,' Harvey said after a moment. 'Said you two never stopped diggin'.'

Nia knocked tears away with her fist. Jesse said, 'I loved Rosie like my own mother and I needed to find the truth.'

Harvey studied them for a long second. Then, without a word, he pushed himself to his feet and motioned for the pair to follow.

'C'mon,' he muttered. 'I want to show you something.'

Jesse and Nia hesitated before standing, stepping over broken furniture and shattered glass. The carpet squelched with water as they tracked through the house until they reached the sliding glass door off his bedroom. They exited out of the door, and down the steps to Harvey's truck.

'Hop in,' he said, motioning to Jesse as he climbed in the driver's seat. Nia hung back, opting to stay inside until they returned.

Jesse hesitated, his hand hovering over his service weapon just in case he needed it.

'If I'm not back in ten minutes, take my car,' Jesse told Nia, handing her his keys.

She nodded, her eyes still misty with tears. 'I'll be right here.'

Jesse relented and folded himself into Harvey's truck and the two journeyed through his property: past the tree line of Old Man Milton's farm. About half a mile away from his trailer, Harvey maneuvered his vehicle into a small section of trees that had been cleared; Jesse turned before getting out. He couldn't see the road or Harvey's trailer anymore.

In front of them, a steel garage sat in complete contrast to the rest of the property: pristine and untouched by destruction. Harvey hopped out and Jesse followed his motions, his boots crunching against the leaves and fallen twigs as they approached the garage tucked away behind the trees.

Harvey punched in a code on a glowing number pad. The door unlatched and Harvey pushed up the sliding door. A cool wind greeted Jesse, carrying with it the scent of old leather, motor oil, and nostalgia. Harvey flipped on the lights, revealing a collection of six classic cars lined up like museum pieces. Jesse's breath caught in his throat. He'd never seen anything like it.

At the front of the lineup was a cherry-red 1965 Ford Mustang, its polished chrome grille gleaming like it had just rolled off the showroom floor. Next to it sat a jet-black 1957 Chevrolet Bel Air, its signature tailfins jutting proudly, whitewall tires pristine beneath the curve of its body. A few feet away, a deep emerald 1969 Pontiac GTO Judge looked like it was built to race the wind; low-slung and muscular, with its bold orange decals intact.

A sky-blue 1964 Cadillac DeVille convertible rested with its top down, white leather seats glowing under the overhead light like ivory. Beside it, a midnight-purple 1970 Dodge Challenger stood tall and defiant, its aggressive stance demanding attention. But the one that stopped Jesse cold was at the far end, a 1987 Chevy Caprice, its midnight-black candy paint so rich and glossy it looked like you could fall into it. Chrome trim sparkled like diamonds against the dark body, and its square frame gave off a quiet confidence, like it had nothing to prove. Each car had its own unique life, tucked away like secrets Harvey had been waiting years to share.

Jesse let out a low whistle. 'Damn.'

Harvey smirked, crossing his arms over his massive chest. 'A man's gotta have his vices.'

Jesse ran his fingers over the hood of the cherry-red Mustang, shaking his head. 'And here I thought you were just an old junkman.'

Harvey chuckled. 'You saved my ass, Shaw. And I don't forget when someone does right by me.'

Jesse raised a brow. 'What are you saying?'

Harvey pulled a black case off a shelf. He unzipped it, revealing an assortment of keys and held it out to Jesse. 'Pick one.'

Jesse blinked. 'You serious?'

'Dead serious. Consider it a debt repaid.'

Jesse glanced at the cars, then his gaze landed on the Chevy Caprice in the corner. Sleek. Timeless. Powerful. And built like a damn tank.

He smiled slowly. 'That one.'

Harvey chuckled, nodding. 'Knew you had good taste.'

Seven days ago, the last person on Jesse's mind was Nia Bennett. Six years had passed without her, stretching into what felt like a lifetime of unfulfilled purpose. He had lived on autopilot: work, home, home, then work, a rinse-and-repeat cycle that offered predictability but no real satisfaction. He had convinced himself that this was enough. That the rigid structure of his life was necessary, a safety net to keep him steady, unshaken, unaffected.

But then Nia stormed back into his world. In just a few days, she had dismantled everything he thought he knew. Jesse didn't realize just how tightly wound he had been until she cut the cords. Suddenly, he felt awake again. The dull weight in his chest was replaced by something dangerous, something electric.

Hope. Possibility.

The town was winding down from one of the most chaotic weeks in its history. But for Jesse, his world had never felt clearer.

Nia sat beside him, quiet but fully present, her

fingers laced together in her lap. She wasn't looking out the window, lost in thought like she had been all week. She was looking at him. Not just glancing, and sneaking peeks, but really seeing him.

Jesse turned onto the familiar back road leading toward Barkwood Bridge. She knew where they were going, and she hadn't protested. That told Jesse everything he needed to know.

Jesse let the hum of the tires on the gravel road fill the silence between them. The Caprice roared through stretches of untouched forest, the wild cinnamon trees lining the path like silent spectators. It reminded him of Rosie. Of Sienna. Of Maggie. Of all the moments that had shaped them into who they were now.

The autumn leaves twirled in the breeze, their deep oranges and reds blending in with the setting sun above them. Jesse stole a glance at Nia, watching as her expression shifted with the scenery. Her shoulders weren't as tense. Her hands weren't clenched. There was something softer in her now, something open.

Nia exhaled, breaking the silence. 'I used to love this drive, before everything happened.'

Jesse kept one hand steady on the wheel. 'And now?'

She hesitated, her fingers trailing along the hem of her sweater. 'I don't know.'

Jesse reached over and squeezed her knee, his thumb grazing slow circles over the fabric of her jeans, grounding her. 'You will.'

Her gaze flickered to him, her expression soft and searching. For the first time since they'd reunited, Nia looked comfortable; she didn't look like she wanted to run. She looked like she wanted to stay.

The Caprice rumbled to a stop near the clearing before the bridge. The moment Jesse killed the engine, the air thickened, weighty with unspoken words and the ghosts of the past. Nia inhaled deeply, pressing her palms against her thighs, like she was bracing for something bigger than herself.

Jesse turned to her, taking in every detail: the way the setting sun cast a glow on her face, the way her lips parted slightly, the way her breath hitched like she was on the edge of a decision. He had spent years convincing himself that they had been nothing more than young and reckless, blinded by nostalgia and a false sense of forever. But looking at her now, he knew that was a lie. He had never stopped loving her. And maybe, just maybe, she had never stopped loving him either.

'Ready?' His voice was gentle, steady. She nodded slowly. But when she reached for the handle, Jesse stopped her. 'I'll be right there with you. I promise.'

Nia turned back to him, her worried expression softening into something tender. 'I know.' A slow smile tugged at her lips, small, but real.

In that moment, Jesse realized something. He didn't just want this moment with her.

He wanted every moment. For the first time since she came back, he wasn't afraid of what that meant.

Barkwood Bridge stretched over the Falls; a rushing monster of water that could swallow any burdens laid before it. The last time Nia was here, she was a teenager, standing on this very bridge, trying to understand how she'd lost her best friend. Jesse had been an anxious adolescent who only wanted to make things better for her.

Now, she stood as a woman, one who had fought to uncover the truth, despite the pain she'd endured to find it. She gripped the wooden railing, staring down at the rushing waters below.

'I don't know what to say,' she admitted.

Jesse stood a step behind her, giving her the space she needed. 'Say whatever is in your heart,' he advised. 'When I come up here, I like to imagine that whatever I tell the water is me letting it go. The water does the rest.'

Nia took a deep breath. 'Sienna, I miss you, every damn day.' Tears slipped down her cheeks, but she didn't wipe them away. 'I spent years being angry at you for giving up, for leaving me here. But you didn't give up, did you?'

The Falls rushed beneath their feet and Jesse heard the weight of every word she spoke.

'They took you from us! And they almost got away with it too.' Her knuckles whitened as she twisted her hands along the wooden railing. 'But we know the truth now. I swear to you, Sienna, I won't let them take anything else from me.' She took a deep breath and continued. 'Your mom never stopped fighting for you. Thank you, Rosie, for showing me what love really looks like.'

Jesse nodded solemnly. He knew in his heart of hearts that every moment he'd experienced in the last week had led them to this moment right here, together.

Nia and Jesse walked the short distance back to the parking lot. The sky had started to shift, streaks of pink and purple painting the horizon. Jesse watched Nia, the way she breathed easier now, the way her shoulders didn't carry the weight of an unsolved mystery. He knew that this was his moment.

'Stay,' he offered.

He'd been thinking about when the best time would be to ask Nia about her future. He thought that he'd give her time to settle down, but he didn't know if he'd have another minute with her, let alone a day, or another experience. He couldn't leave it up to chance that she'd stay in Cinnamon Falls, and he couldn't let her walk out of his life again without putting up a fight.

She blinked up at him. 'What?'

Jesse stepped closer to her, tucking a runaway curl behind her ear. 'Stay in Cinnamon Falls. With me.'

Her breath faltered. Her eyes met the ground. 'Jesse . . .'

'I know you didn't plan on this,' he continued, despite his voice being full of emotion. 'Maybe you thought coming back here would be temporary until things blew over, but we both know that's not true anymore.'

He tilted her chin up. 'You belong here, Nia.'

Her lips parted, her eyes searching his. 'With you?' she asked.

Jesse chuckled. 'Yeah, if that's what you want.'

Her gaze flicked down to his mouth and back up to meet his eyes. Before he could say another word to convince her, she kissed him.

This kiss was different. Not the adrenaline-fueled embrace they'd shared before. This was slow, filled with the weight of their history, of memories, full of every unspoken word they ever left unsaid between them. Jesse wrapped his arms around her waist, deepening the kiss. Nia sighed into him, her fingers bracing the back of his neck, grounding herself in the moment.

When they finally pulled apart, Jesse asked, 'Does this mean you're staying?'

'Yes,' she answered truthfully. 'I'm staying.'

Jesse closed his eyes, exhaling deeply. 'Good,' he said aloud. He couldn't imagine another day without Nia in it.

From their vantage point, they could see the twinkling lights that lined Main Street. Cinnamon Falls wasn't perfect. But Jesse vowed to protect it. He squeezed Nia's fingers as they walked back toward the car.

'What now?' he asked.

Nia glanced up at him, her smile playful. 'Well, I

did promise to help my dad rebuild The Cinnamon Scoop.'

Jesse smirked. 'I can run you down there. But, first . . .' He turned, pulling her against him one more time. 'One more kiss,' he teased.

She laughed, tilting her head up toward him. 'Make it count, Shaw.'

And under the Cinnamon Falls twilight, he did just that.

Epilogue

One Year Later
Nia

Shawna Daniels pulled the bus to a smooth stop outside Rosie's Diner. She gave Nia a satisfied smile before she opened the doors for her to exit.

'Five minutes,' she reminded her.

Nia nodded in response. She knew the drill. If she wasn't back in five minutes exactly, Shawna was pulling off to the next stop. She never actually left Nia, even if Eddie did take more than five minutes to make her order, which was unlikely.

Nia got up early to commute to Lawson & Lawson, her new position in Asheville as a research assistant. She discovered that Shawna wasn't a bad driver, she was simply a morning person. Nia never had another experience like she had on her first day back in Cinnamon Falls, and all the bones in her body were grateful for that.

The aroma of freshly brewed coffee and warm

cinnamon buns greeted her as she stepped into Rosie's. The place still felt like hers even after the renovations: the same cozy booths and checkered floor, and the hum of conversations from the locals catching up on either a late dinner, or an early breakfast.

Eddie Rutherford had stepped up to run Rosie's Diner after she passed. He kept all of her original recipes, including her signature apple cider, but added his own twist. Now the menu included a blueberry lemon scone, a cinnamon crunch latte, and a new breakfast burger that had the entire town obsessed.

Nia approached the counter, watching as Eddie charmed the morning crowd, balancing three plates in one hand while conversing with a group of men in overalls who looked like they'd been working long hours overnight.

'Mornin', Nia, the usual?' he asked, stepping around the service counter.

Nia nodded. 'And please tell Sam I'll take an extra cinnamon bun to go.'

Eddie grinned. 'Always the extra cinnamon bun. You're getting predictable, Bennett.'

A few minutes later, Eddie returned with a cinnamon crunch latte with extra whipped cream and sprinkles and two deliciously warm cinnamon buns. Nia placed a few bills on the counter and told Eddie to keep the change. He added it to the shared tip jar.

'Have a good day!' she called, before hopping back on the bus to head toward Asheville. Nia handed one of her cinnamon buns to Shawna, a thank you for waiting.

'You're the reason my hips are spreading,' Shawna joked.

Nia settled in for the ride, ready to enjoy the scenery of the lush trees zooming past her window. The early autumn sun cast a warm glow over the town, the golden hues reflecting off the leaves like tiny flickers of fire. When she passed The Cinnamon Scoop, before they got on the highway, she couldn't help but smile.

The once-damaged shop now stood tall and proud, its fresh cream-colored exterior gleaming in the sunlight. Newly painted trim in a soft cinnamon brown framed the windows, making the cozy shop look even more inviting. The iconic sign above the entrance, which had been sliced to pieces, now shone bright and brand new, the golden lettering reading:

THE CINNAMON SCOOP – A BENNETT FAMILY
TRADITION

Out front, a sprawling patio had been added, complete with wrought-iron tables and twinkling string lights that would illuminate the space in the evenings. Hanging flower baskets overflowed with rich autumn blooms, bringing vibrant color to the shop's entrance.

Through the large display windows, Nia could see the updated interior: a blend of nostalgia and modern charm. The counters had been refurnished, the old stools replaced with sleek but classic diner-style seating. A new chalkboard menu hung above the register, hand-lettered with their bestselling flavors and a few exciting new additions.

But most importantly, the heart of The Cinnamon Scoop remained the same, and Nia knew that no matter how many upgrades they made, this place would always feel like home.

A warm sense of pride swelled in her chest. All the hard work, the late nights, the stress of rebuilding after the break-in had been worth it, and tonight after work, she would be standing in that shop, surrounded by friends, family, and half the town, celebrating the grand reopening.

As they pulled onto the highway, Nia took one last glance at the shop through the bus's back window, her heart full.

Alexis Chambers, Director of Hospitality, worked diligently, honoring Maggie Shilling's lifelong tradition of decorating Main Street the week before the Fall Festival. She'd done an amazing job keeping the broken heart of Cinnamon Falls pumping after intense tragic losses. She balanced on a ladder while workers fed her strings of orange and red chrysanthemums to hang above the doors.

A year ago, Nia had been lost, unsure if she even wanted to be here. Now, she couldn't imagine being anywhere else.

The air outside The Cinnamon Scoop buzzed with excitement as the town gathered in the cool evening. String lights twinkled above the sidewalk, illuminating the faces of people chatting in anticipation, bundled in scarves and light jackets. The line stretched down the block, winding around the corner, the sweet scent of vanilla, cinnamon, and caramel drifting into the crisp air.

A large ribbon had been strung across the shop's entrance, a giant pair of scissors resting in Nia's hands. She glanced at her parents, standing proudly beside her, then at Niles and Midnight, cradled in his arms of course; Morgan, Jesse, and the rest of her friends cheered from the sidelines.

'Cinnamon Falls!' Nia said, projecting her voice over the excited murmurs. The once-ridiculous cinnamon bun hat, which meant much more now, slipped down over her eyes. Niles stepped up to readjust it on her head. 'Thank you all for being here tonight. This place means everything to my family, and we're so excited to officially welcome you all back to the new and improved Cinnamon Scoop!'

With a satisfying snip the ribbon fell to the ground, and the crowd erupted into cheers and applause. The moment Nia pushed open the doors, people rushed inside, eager to experience the shop's long-awaited return.

The interior gleamed with its fresh renovations: a new glass display case showcasing homemade waffle cones, fresh toppings, and an expanded selection of ice cream flavors.

The classic tiled floors had been polished to perfection, and the counter was now sleek and modern but still had its small-town charm. Ma-Clara was somewhere, beaming.

Nia moved behind the counter, throwing on her apron, while her father manned the cash register, laughing with customers as he rang up orders.

'This place looks amazing, Nia,' Bud Wade said as he stepped up to the counter, a satisfied grin on his face. 'Cinnamon Falls wouldn't be the same without it.'

'We couldn't let a little break-in take us out,' Nia said proudly, scooping a generous helping of cinnamon swirl into a waffle cone.

'Damn right!' Chambers added, nudging Jesse. 'And your boy here had a big part in making sure justice was served.'

Jesse smiled shyly, his cheeks reddening. 'Just doing my job.'

Raines stepped forward, crossing her arms. 'Speaking of jobs, Jesse, I think it's time we told her.'

Nia raised an eyebrow. 'Told me what?'

Raines smirked. 'Jesse made detective.'

Nia gasped, turning to Jesse with wide eyes. 'Wait, seriously?'

He nodded, rubbing the back of his neck. 'Yeah, I got the official word this morning. Chambers is my new partner, and Raines, after serving as interim for a year—'

'Is your new Chief of Police,' Raines finished, lifting her chin with pride.

The shop erupted into cheers, and Nia threw her arms around Jesse's neck, hugging him tight.

'You deserve this,' she whispered. 'I'm so proud of you.'

'I couldn't have done it without you, babe,' he murmured, kissing the top of her head.

Morgan wiped a fake tear from her eye. 'I love when my friends glow up.'

The line of customers finally slowed, giving Nia a moment to breathe. She wiped her hands on a towel and Jesse leaned against the counter, looking far too smug for his own good.

'What?' she asked, narrowing her eyes.

'Come outside with me,' he said instead, reaching for her hand.

Nia blinked. 'Now? We're still open.'

'You've been going non-stop all day,' he replied. 'Five minutes won't hurt. Come on.'

He pulled her gently through the front door of The Cinnamon Scoop. The fall air was crisp but not cold, and the soft glow of string lights lit up the exterior. Jesse pulled out a seat for her.

Nia crossed her arms, suspicious. 'What's this about?'

'Nothing,' he said, but his smirk gave him away. In the short year they'd spent together, Nia had picked up on his tells, the twist in his lips, and the twinkle in his eye. He was up to something, but she couldn't figure out what.

Her answer came when her father appeared in the doorway with a sundae in hand.

'Special delivery,' Walter said with a wink and handed the bowl to Jesse. 'Your favorite.'

Jesse took it with a grin and passed her the sundae; a perfectly scooped bowl of cinnamon swirl, drizzled with caramel and a single bright juicy cherry on top.

Nia raised a brow. 'You're buttering me up for something.'

'Just take a bite,' Jesse implored, practically glowing under the lights.

Through the window, she saw Niles with Midnight perched on his shoulder, their faces pressed to the glass. She watched closely and Nia wondered, just for a second, if there was cyanide in it.

Something in the way Jesse was watching her made her stomach flutter. Nia dipped her spoon in, scooping up the ice cream with practised precision. The familiar flavor melted on her tongue, cool and sweet, but something solid bumped against her teeth.

'What the hell?' she mumbled, fishing whatever was in her mouth out with her fingers.

Her breath caught.

A ring.

A sparkling, diamond engagement ring glinted in the light from the shop window. Her eyes snapped to Jesse, who was no longer standing over her.

He was on one knee.

'Nia Bennett,' he said softly, his voice trembling just enough to make her heart ache. 'You've always been it for me. Since we were kids, since you left, and especially now that you've come home. Will you marry me?'

The world narrowed to just him. The boy who used to toss pebbles at her bedroom window. The man who chased truth when no one else would. The man who, despite all the chaos of the past year, made her feel safe and seen. Nia's heart pounded in her chest. Tears welled in her eyes.

'Yes,' she choked out. 'Yes!'

He slipped the ring onto her finger, and Nia surged forward to kiss him, wrapping her arms around his neck as the lights blinked softly above them. Laughter and music from inside The Cinnamon Scoop filtered out as their families watched from the windows: Marjorie, Walter, Niles, and even Morgan with her hands cupped around her mouth, cheering like they'd just won the town raffle. They came pouring outside, whooping and clapping as Jesse and Nia stood, still tangled together.

Nia's father held up a phone. 'He did it, Evelyn!' He spun the phone around to show Jesse's parents on a video call, their faces crammed in the screen, smiling widely and waving. Nia had finally convinced Jesse that his parents were grown enough to go on vacation for their anniversary. He'd been worried sick for two weeks.

'Our boy's getting married,' Robert beamed.

Marjorie stood next to Walter, waving to Jesse's parents. 'We'll celebrate when you two love birds get back!'

'That was really smooth,' Morgan commented, finishing off Nia's forgotten ice cream. 'Like, I'm actually impressed, Jay.' She asked, 'How do you feel, Nia? Because I, for one, am already stressed.'

Nia exhaled slowly. She thought about Jesse. She thought about Sienna and Rosie, Maggie too, about Cinnamon Falls, and about every single choice that had led her here. Then, she smiled, content.

'Like I'm exactly where I'm supposed to be.'

Acknowledgments

Hi Mommy! *waves*

To my parents and family, thank you for your unwavering support. Your faith in me carried me through all the tough times and pushed me past all the self doubt. You all continue to show up for me, pour into me, and cheer me on. I am so grateful to be part of you. Granny, thank you for not killing me for writing on your new car with that rock. I still stump everyone in two truths and a lie. And now look, my writing has finally paid off! Thank you Momma for sending me and Ree to Granny's house down the country for the summer. It gave me the inspo I needed to create this world.

To my close friends, you all's encouragement and love carried me through, honey! Thank you for celebrating with me every step of the way. You all remind me that joy is best when it is shared. This is a win for us all! To my library colleagues, thank you all for the best inspiration! The stories and experiences

ACKNOWLEDGMENTS

we've shared are quite literally unbelievable. I am so incredibly honored to work beside you all every day. The work we do is so, so important and often thankless, but it never goes unnoticed.

If you're reading this, support your local library! (Or else!)

To Charlotte and the entire Simon & Schuster UK team, thank you for this incredible opportunity to bring Cinnamon Falls to life! Your blind trust in me and my ability is truly humbling. Thank you to every person in every single department across the pond who supported this book from start to finish. Thank you to my lawyer for all of your advice and answering all of my early morning emails without complaint. To the OG Necole Ryse readers, thank you for all the comments, messages, and DMs! Your opinions and feedback mean the most to me. Thank you for holding me down since 2013! The girl is trad published, can you believe it? Check me out!

None of this would have been possible without Crime Writers of Color. To all crime writers who look like me, keep writing! Your story deserves to be shared!

And finally, to you, the reader, thank you for turning the page and taking a chance on this story. Hit me up and let me know what you think! (Unless you didn't like it.)

xo,
Necole

About the Author

R. L. KILLMORE is the pseudonym for the author Necole Ryse. Necole has been writing since she was four years old, when she triumphantly wrote her ABCs on the hood of her grandmother's brand-new Volvo. When she's not writing, she's weeping into a stack of unfinished manuscripts, abandoning exercise regimens, scolding innocent children in libraries, or listening to other people's conversations.